How much of your private life
would you expose for fame?

ALL ACCESS

Omar Tyree

The *New York Times*
Bestselling Author of *Flyy Girl*
For The Love of Money, Just Say No!
Leslie and *Diary of a Groupie*

When veteran Atlanta broadcast news anchor Judy Pierce joins a celebrity gossip website, she lands a major interview with volatile superstar Shawn Blake. The embattled entertainer then invites her into a reckless and unfiltered world that changes her life and career for the worse.

Reported of having gang affiliations, domestic violence disputes, multiple child support cases and murder charges—all of which never stick in court—Blake is viewed by some as Hollywood's next Denzel Washington. But is this up-and-coming and troubled actor all that he's rumored to be—a real badass—or is it only an act?

Seeking confirmation, Judy gets involved in his all access invitations, and the fallout of rumors and social media attacks begin to unravel her family and job security. With a six-figure income, a dedicated husband, a solid reputation and two children in grade school, Judy has far too much to lose.

Already in too deep, she finds herself in the middle of Shawn's volatile world of crime, desperate associations and public slander. Wishing she had never met the man, Judy scrambles to regain her sanity, while protecting her family... and her life.

A Novel

Omar Tyree

ISBN: 978-0-9710397-4-2
Library of Congress Catalog Number: 2015910010

Edited By: Maxine Thompson
Copyedited By: Shavonda K. Simmons
Proofread By: Cheryl Ross
Typeset By: Nicola C. Mitchell
Galley Corrections By: Dabinique N. Magwood

First Printing

Manufactured in the United States

Distributed By Ingram Book Group Inc.,
Afrikan World Book Distributors
& www.OmarTyree.com

Also By Omar Tyree

The Traveler; Welcome to Dubai
Pecking Order
The Last Street Novel
What They Want
Boss Lady
Diary of a Groupie
Leslie
Just Say No!
For the Love of Money
Sweet St. Louis
Single Mom
A Do Right Man
Flyy Girl

The Urban Griot Series

Cold Blooded
One Crazy Night
Capital City
College Boy

Anthologies

Dirty Old Men
Dark Thirst
Not in My Family
The Game
Proverbs of the People
Tough Love; The Life and Death of Tupac Shakur
Testimony

Young Adult Books
Sneaker Kings

Children's Books
12 Brown Boys

Business Books
*The Equation; Applying the 4 Indisputable Components
of Business Success*

Autobiographies
Mayor for Life: The Incredible Story of Marion Barry Jr.

Original Ebooks
Psychadelic
The Traveler: No Turning Back
Insanity
Corrupted

Poetry Books
Poetry: For the Love of Black Women

ACKNOWLEDGMENTS

The following list of family, friends, business associates and supportive readers believed enough in the vision, professional skills, determination and brand execution of Omar Tyree to help launch **OTI**—Omar Tyree Incorporated—where I will continue to master the art of writing, publishing, speaking, marketing and selling quality and thoughtful books and other intellectual content for the worldwide community:

Devin "Egypt" Robinson, Aubrey Watkins, Keenan F. Norris, Ramon Jacobs & The Jacobs Brothers, Miasha Coleman, Twanja Windley, Mario Martelli Clark, Sean Ingram, Mr. Wayne A Brewer, Steve McAlpin, Frank A. Jones Jr., Arthur Wylie, Dale Godboldo, Rovella Williams, Colin Gibson, Tina Branch, Jocelyn Justice, Brittani Williams, Edward L. Blunt, Chris Campbell, Jeff Nance, J. Ivy & Tarrey Torae, Corey "Latif" Williams, Tamika Stewart, Melissa Martin, Brian & Byron Bailey, Jared Holloway, Dabinique N. Magwood, Barbara Morning, Pamela Hawkins,

Fallon Guess, Grace McKissick, Craig Sutters, Tressa Epps, Randy Crumpton, Kevin Powell, Shavonda Simmons, Christopher King, Dr. D.L. Teamor, Shatrece Buchanan, Frederick Williams, Janella I. Betances, Diane Wallace Booker, Samuel E. Ford, Villard Delva, Marcella Nixon, Patrick O. Peterson, Seandra Atkinson, Jarvis Holliday, Raoul Davis, Annika Murray, Denise Jones, Belle Bromfield, Eboni Chili Pepa, C. Wallace Booker, Sheri D. Neely, Elbee Bussey, David Gold, Arkeah S. Jacobs, LaTasha Jackson, Malik Davis, Sonya Jenkins, Taneeka E. Wagner, Jamie Jones, Chequita Capanna, Nileyah Mary Rose, Joanne Johnson, Shanisha Ray, Dana Rettig, Regina Renee Bulliner, Nicole Reddick, Emmanuel Ohonme, Kimberley Brooks, Kellie Dutton, Dawn Roberts, and last but not least; The McLaurin Family, The Briggs Family, The Simmons Family, The Tyree Family, The Alston Family, The Randall Family, The Crawford Family, The Rideout Family, The Brown Family, The Henderson Family, The Robinson Family, The Gibson Family, The Johnson Family, The Neal Family, The Sherman Family, The Myers Family, The Cyphers Family, The Boykin Family, The Lutu Family, The Forbes Family, The Adams Family, The Cole Family, The Stewart Family, Powell, Werts, Thomas, Hilton, Carvello, Reed, Mitchell, DeBose, Cooper, The Charlotte Sports Families of Hill, Nance, Wiley, Kelson, Ganey, Campbell, Montgomery, Plaskett, Walker, Aaron and Smitty, who have kept us going with your bonds of friendship, and everyone else who buys this Omar Tyree book and others, I thank you ALL in advance.

Sincerely,

Omar Tyree

ALL

ACCESS

1... THE INVITATION

Judy Pierce parked her black Mercedes sedan in an open spot in front of a local bar on the west side of Atlanta, determined to take a chance on something different. The veteran broadcast anchor in her mid-thirties had a two o'clock meeting in the seedy, refurbished corridor that did most of its business at night. And on this breezy afternoon in October, she felt a bit nervous about what to expect.

She flipped down the vanity mirror to check her face, hair, and outfit. Satisfied with her sultry smooth skin, minimal makeup, and professionally styled hair, she flipped the mirror back up and grabbed her large black leather bag from the passenger seat.

She pulled out a bottle of perfume from the bag and contemplated using it. She held the small, fancy bottle up in her right hand and paused. "Nah."

After tossing the perfume back into her bag, she checked the time on the dashboard. It was 1:53. Judy swung her feet out of the car in a pair of colorful Reebok running shoes, took them off, and quickly changed into her black heels. She stood tall and confident in the street, wearing a dark-blue skirt suit.

"Okay, let's do this," she said to herself. And she rumbled toward the entrance of the bar.

Inside the empty bar, a team of opportunistic videographers, Chase and Walter, set up their cameras and adjusted the lighting.

Walter, the taller and heavier of the two, with shoulder-length dreads, a full beard, and a mustache, grinned as he placed two mahogany chairs in the middle of the room, facing each other.

"Man, this is *crazy*. We've only been in Atlanta for a few months, and we land something like this already."

Chase grinned with the hairless face of a teenager and fought to keep his composure. He wore a red Washington Nationals baseball cap as he adjusted his camera for the third time on a tripod.

"That's what we came down here to do—make moves. I got tired of the same scenes in DC. Either we're gonna do this, or we're not. So, if this is where it's at now, then Atlanta's where we need to be."

"No doubt," Walter agreed.

Judy walked in behind them. "I see you guys are on your job."

Chase turned and smiled at her. "Definitely."

Judy placed her bag on a table. "So, you actually think he's gonna show up?"

Walter looked at Chase and allowed his partner to do the talking. He was the mastermind behind the celebrity website idea anyway.

"That's what he said. Especially once we told him *you* were involved," Chase answered.

Judy gave him a curious look. "What is that supposed to mean? He's only doing this because of me?"

"That's what it sounded like to me. He wanted to see if you would do it."

Judy tightened her brow and grunted, "Hmmph."

At three minutes after two, the telephone rang behind the bar.

The manager picked it up on the second ring. "The Shot Bar."

"Hey, man, is she there yet?"

The buff manager peered across the high counter in Judy's direction. "Yup, she's here." In his tight black muscle shirt and bulging biceps, he looked more like a bouncer than a barkeep.

"Aw'ight, I'll be right in."

Outside The Shot Bar, another black Mercedes—a four-door jeep with dark-tinted windows—pulled up and parked across the street.

Shawn Blake, an eight-year veteran of Black Hollywood, checked his grill inside the mirror. He was ebony brown with a sharp, low haircut, a trimmed mustache, and steely dark eyes. He topped off his look with a chocolate leather biking jacket.

A first impression meant everything, so Shawn liked to tease with a hint of danger. It never failed to keep women guessing about him . . . and imagining things.

He stepped out of his vehicle wearing ostrich boots and blue jeans, and strolled casually toward the bar as if he had forever to arrive. He walked through the door at nine minutes after the hour and nodded to the manager. "Thanks, D."

"No problem."

Judy faced the star attraction and beamed with pleasure. So did Chase and Walter.

"You weren't even playing," she commented.

"Time is money, right?" Shawn responded. "Why would I play with it?"

Judy nodded. "Why *would* you?"

Shawn approached her and squeezed her hands in his for a warm greeting. "Nice to meet you. I saw you on cable news a few times."

"Oh, really?"

He grinned, mischievously. "Yeah." He looked around at the

chairs, lights, and cameras. "Which chair is mine?"

"The one on the right," Chase answered, pointing. "And thanks for doing this, man. We *love* your work."

Shawn held up a black power fist and took his seat. "I appreciate it."

Judy sat down beside him with her notepad, ready to go.

Walter approached Shawn with a miniature clip-on microphone. "You can clip this near the top of your jacket."

Shawn did and looked right into Judy's brown eyes. "So, what do you want to know?" he teased.

They hadn't even started recording yet.

"The people want to know a lot. But how much are you willing to tell?" Judy challenged him.

Shawn licked his lips and grinned. "It depends on what you're trying to ask me."

"All right, we're ready," Chase signaled from behind the cameras.

Judy tossed her notepad on the floor and went right into it. "Greetings, ladies and gents, this is Judy Pierce of *Hotlanta Celebrity News*, where you get it first and you get it real. So we're about to bring you the *heat* from Shawn 'Hollywood' Blake, the infamous heart stealer, live and in person. And we're very honored to have him."

With one take and no errors, Shawn was impressed with Judy's delivery. However, he didn't like being called an "infamous heart stealer." Nor did he like the "Hollywood" moniker she had planted on him. However, she did it all so smoothly that he found himself caught up in her rapture.

"Yeah, I'm here," he grumbled.

"So, tell us, Shawn, you're pretty raw with your co-stars on camera. Are you that hard on a woman in your real life?"

"Sometimes things happen in the heat of the moment, you know."

"What, like making babies?" Judy asked.

Shawn winced, thinking about his two situations. "Those kinds of mistakes happen sometimes too. But it's not like I have four or five situations out here."

"But when you read a script from a movie, you know what's coming, right? Can't you forecast some of the things that happen in your real life?"

"Can you forecast the news?" he countered.

"We can with the weather."

"Well, life is more than just the weather, man. I get all kinds of stuff that happens that I have nothing to do with. That seems like every day of my life."

"Well, it seems to me that you put *yourself* in those situations. Why don't you just stay home for a spell and take a break from it all?"

Shawn exhaled. He began to fidget in his chair and look anxious. Her questions were quickly getting under his skin. She even got the bar manager's attention. He looked over the counter in alarm. *Is this girl crazy, talking to him like that?*

Chase and Walter remained wide-eyed and nervous. They also thought Judy was tipping the scale. But as long as Shawn answered her, things were good. In fact, they considered the interview groundbreaking. It was more than they had imagined it would be.

Shawn said, "So, what am I supposed to do, hide myself in the house and stop living my life?"

"To a certain degree, that's the price of fame, ain't it?" Judy said. "I can't do everything that I like to do either. So I can only imagine what it's like for you. You have to be even more disciplined."

Shawn thought about it and nodded. "I see what you're saying."

Judy looked surprised. "You mean, no one's ever told you that before? You have that many 'yes' people around you? Sometimes you just need to change the company you keep."

Shawn looked away and sighed. It sounded like a parental lecture.

Uh oh! Chase thought, eying his camera screen. *He's about to go off in here.*

On cue, Shawn unclipped the microphone from his jacket and stood abruptly.

Please don't hit her! Walter panicked. He didn't know what to expect from the volatile actor. He just didn't want to be in the middle of it.

"If you really want to know about my life, you need to be there," Shawn stated. "So I want to invite you to a few things to hang out with me."

Before Judy could respond, Shawn dug into his jacket and pulled out a business card.

"What are you doing?" she questioned. She expected him to finish the interview.

"I'm giving you a private number."

"For what?"

"So you can call me."

Judy looked confused and miffed. "Oh, this is some bullshit," she snapped. "I thought you *agreed* to do this."

Shawn laughed it off and dropped his card to the floor on top of her notepad. He was stunned by her audacity and realness, but he figured he had said enough. So he headed back toward the front door.

"I did agree to it," he told her, "but we're gonna do it *my* way." He looked back to the manager on his way out. "Aw'ight, D. Thanks."

"No problem."

As he walked out, Judy looked into the camera and shrugged. "Well, there you have it. And you saw it *first*, right here, on *Hotlanta Celebrity News*." She grinned and said, "The heat got too hot."

Walter smiled and shook his head. "She's crazy, man," he mumbled to his partner. But he liked it.

Judy stood from her chair and unclipped her microphone. "I hope you didn't think I was going to *baby* that man."

"No, but we didn't think you would go that *hard* on him," Chase said, chuckling.

Judy set the ground rules. "Look, what you get from me on

16

cable news in the morning is totally different from what I plan to do out here. And if you want me to do these celebrity interviews online, then I'm coming with the *real*," she warned. "These people get too much of that babying nonsense already. That's why he acts the way he does now. No one ever calls him out on his nonsense."

Walter continued to grin. "But then they won't want to do interviews with you."

Judy thought about that. "If the views are there, we'll get a lot more interviews than you think. It's all about the numbers."

Chase said, "I hope you're right."

Walter looked down at the business card on her notepad. "Are you gonna take him up on his offer?"

Judy cringed. "What, to hang out with him and his cronies? Hell no, I'm not doing that. I'm not some young video chick. I have a husband and family at home. So, we're gonna edit this thing down and get what we can get out of it. Three or four minutes of hard questions and answers are all we need for a blog interview anyway, and we'll keep it moving. Otherwise, I may as well just stick to what I do at the cable station."

Chase's heart skipped a beat. "Aw'ight," he quickly agreed. "We'll get what we can get out of it. And this'll make you relevant outside of just the local Atlanta cable news. People can watch you on this all over the world."

Chase was at Judy's mercy. He was glad she had agreed to do *anything* with them. An interview with Shawn Blake from Judy Pierce was a major scoop, so every chance he got, he made sure to butter up the pot with why it was so advantageous for her to do it.

Judy drove back to her northwest Atlanta suburb of Alpharetta to pick up her two sons from school before rush hour.

"Good afternoon, Mrs. Pierce. Great job on the morning news," said Ms. Hamilton through the driver side window. "It looks like a lot of fun."

Ms. Hamilton was a young, rosy-cheeked third-grade teacher

who helped monitor the car line after school. She held fantasies of her own of being a popular newscaster if she could stand the pressures of critique.

Assuming as much, Judy returned her smile. "Some days are better than others."

"Oh, yeah, that goes for all of us."

With their normal exuberance, Marlon Jr. and Taylor bounced into the backseat of their mom's Mercedes from the pick-up line. In fourth and first grade, both of Judy's boys were rough and tumble as they wrestled their way into the car.

She looked back and yelled, "Cut it out and buckle your seatbelts. Every day it's the same thing with you two. And Marlon, you're getting too *old* for this."

"But *he* started it," her oldest barked.

"Marlon, he's six years old. You're nine. *Act* like it."

Ms. Hamilton grinned as she closed the car door behind them. "Those are kids for ya'."

Judy sighed and grinned. "All right, we'll see you tomorrow."

She pulled out into the road behind a line of cars and headed for home.

"What are we having for dinner?" Taylor asked.

Judy took a breath and exhaled. "I have to look at what's left to cook. Mommy's been running around so much lately that I haven't had a chance to grocery shop. And you both can be a little too picky with food sometimes."

"Not when you order pizza," Marlon hinted.

"Well, you're not getting pizza tonight."

"Awww, mannn," Taylor whined.

"You can't eat pizza every night, Taylor. That's only for the weekends," Judy responded.

Taylor paused. "I wish it was the weekend."

Marlon chuckled.

"Marlon, don't you provoke him. I will have *both* of you eating cheese broccoli for the rest of this week. Do you hear me?"

"Noooo," Taylor wailed.

"Try me, and see what happens," Judy teased. "You both have

18

to learn how to eat more healthy food and *like it*."

"We would like it if it tasted good," Marlon countered.

"Marlon, everything does not have to have *ketchup* or sugar in it. Okay? Now I'm done talking about this. I don't want to hear another word from either one of you. You're going to eat whatever I cook."

There was silence and long faces in the back of the car as Judy finished their short drive home in peace.

That evening, Marlon Sr., in his champagne Range Rover, had a peaceful drive home from work as well. Clean shaven, well built, and dressed in a brown UPS uniform, he looked down at a new text message on his cell phone and grinned. Then his wife called.

"Yeah, I'm right around the corner," Marlon answered.

"Stop and pick up a pizza for the boys. I thought I had more fish in the freezer, but I don't."

Marlon grimaced. "So, why don't you tell me to pick up more fish?"

"Because I don't feel like cooking it now. It would have been thawed out and in the oven already if I had more at home."

"All right, but it's gonna look like you're caving in to the boys on a weekday, because I *know* that's what they wanted. They always want pizza."

"Yeah, I know, but I don't feel like fighting with them tonight. So just grab a few pizzas on the way home."

"How did your big website interview go today?" Marlon asked.

"I'll tell you about it later."

Marlon hung up and eyed another humorous text message. He chuckled and sent out a return text as he swerved on the Alpharetta road.

"Shit, girl, you gon' make me crash out here," he joked to himself.

When Marlon arrived at their gated, five-bedroom home, hidden in the woods, he punched in the security code and waited for the heavy black metal gate to slide open to the right. He then parked in front of the garage beside his wife's black Mercedes. He climbed out of his vehicle, tall and lean. With two hot Papa John's pizzas in his arms, he felt like an October Santa Claus.

"Ho, ho, ho," Marlon boomed as he walked into the foyer.

"Daddy brought piz-zaaaa!" Taylor yelled. He rushed to his father's legs as Marlon walked into the house and turned left toward the opened-space kitchen.

"I heard that's what the Pierce boys wanted for being good in school today," he hinted.

Marlon Jr. grinned and kept his silence at the kitchen table as he did homework. He wasn't as excited as his brother, and he had good reason not to be. He knew at any moment his mother would drop the bad news about his day.

"Yeah, well, *Junior* didn't have a good day at school. Look at his test score in math," Judy commented on cue.

Marlon Sr. placed the two boxes of pizza on the stove counter and walked back to the kitchen table, where he looked down at a large red "D" that was marked on his eldest son's math exam. He picked the test up to examine it further.

"Marlon, we went *over* this already, man. You have to show your *work* on these problems."

"But I got the right *answer* on most of them," his son pleaded.

Judy said, "And you still got a *D*, Marlon. You know why? Because you didn't do what you were told to do. You don't get to make the rules in school. You're there to *learn* them."

Her husband sighed and shook his head. "You're still racing to be the first one finished, aren't you?" he asked his son. It was obvious. Marlon Sr. nodded and said, "All right, no outside playing for you this weekend. And no video games either. So you'll have plenty of time to read a book and practice showing your work in math."

Marlon Jr. frowned and dropped his head at the table without comment.

Judy shook her head and kissed her husband on the lips. He was a rock-solid husband and father.

"So, what else is new?" Marlon asked her.

She smiled. "I'll tell you about it later."

In the privacy of their bedroom that evening, Judy was finally ready to tell her husband about her day. And she spared none of the details.

Marlon cringed in bed. "You said all of that?" He looked debonair, wearing the black silk pajamas that his wife had bought him.

"I most certainly did. I wasn't giving that man a pass. He needs to answer for himself."

She climbed into bed beside him, wearing a beige silk chemise with no bra or panties. They had been a comfortable couple for a dozen years and married for ten, after first meeting at a communications conference in Baltimore. Marlon had never been intimidated by Judy's professional drive for success, and she loved his calm and steady demeanor.

"So what did he say?" Marlon asked.

"He started to answer most of it, but then he shut it down and ended the interview."

"Yeah, I bet he would. He wasn't expecting you to sock it to him like that. He was probably thinking it was gonna be friendly."

"Yeah, that's what they *all* think. Everybody's supposed to be so nice to them. So they're shocked when you're not."

Marlon thought about it. "What if someone was mean to you like that?"

Judy frowned. "Are you kidding me? I get nasty comments every day on my hair, my outfits, my makeup, my delivery, and even some of the news that I have nothing to do with. You just have to have tough skin and deal with it. It's the price of being in the public eye. But I don't give people anything *extra* to comment on in my *private* life. That part is on him.

"By the way, you look good in those silk pajamas," she teased. "When did you get those?"

Marlon chuckled. "Ahh, I think some woman who likes me bought them for my birthday," he joked.

"Some woman who *likes* you? You better put a *name* on her."

Marlon laughed and leaned in to kiss his wife. "Thanks, honey."

She smirked and said, "So anyway . . . he tried to leave me his business card to hang out with him, talking about, 'If you really want to know about my life, then you need to be there.' "

That got Marlon's attention. "He said that? And what did you say?"

"I told him that was some bullshit."

Marlon laughed again, knowing his wife well. "Yeah, these folks have no idea how bold you are off the air."

"They have no idea how hard I've *worked* to get there either," Judy added. "All they know is my smiling and joking face on the news. So I need an opportunity like this to put some more *teeth* in my career, and for more people to know me nationally."

Marlon shrugged. "Well, maybe you should do it then."

Judy eyed him, confused. "Do what?"

"You know, see what this guy's life is really like. You're a professional; you know how to handle yourself."

"Are you *serious*? I'm not following this man around. If he wants to do an interview, then just do it."

"Yeah, but he's giving you *more* than an interview. This is like an all-access pass," Marlon quipped. "How many people do you think he invites to do that—especially media people?"

He had a point. Judy paused to consider it. "Yeah, but *why* would he want to do that? I mean, I know what *I* can get out of this interview . . . some extra work of celebrity news scoops. But what does *he* get out of me following him around? You know? So I don't trust him."

"You don't have to trust him, just trust yourself," Marlon

countered. "You'll have your camera guys right there with you, right?"

"Wait a minute, you are *serious*," Judy cracked.

"This is why you agreed to do these celebrity interviews in the first place, right—to spread your wings? You even went to bat with your bosses about it. So, why back out now?"

He was really tempting her, but Judy didn't take the bait. She shook it off and said, "I have to think about it. In the meantime, let me watch my new show."

She grabbed the remote and changed the station to ABC's *How to Get Away with Murder*. Then she leaned into her husband's shoulder and relaxed to watch it.

At six in the morning, Judy presented the early news on WATL Cable with her co-hosts—a dark-haired Michael Westford and a blond Wendy Livingston.

"Wake up, Atlanta. It's Friday and time to get ready for the weekend. I'm Judy Pierce, and this is the *Atlanta Morning News*."

The three of them presented the local reports on crime, politics, business, traffic, construction, community events, and other announcements while filling in the gaps with light-hearted humor. Judy was proud to be the lone black woman and lead anchor on the show. She introduced the weatherman, the local sportscasters, and during the break, told her co-hosts about her opportunity to shadow the infamous Shawn Blake.

Michael and Wendy looked thrilled.

"So, are you gonna do it?" Wendy asked first, with a cup of coffee in hand.

"You *have* to," Michael added. "This is the kind of opportunity that you want."

Judy paused, realizing the obvious competition between them. Michael and Wendy would both want her lead anchor position if she ever decided to move on to something else, which was not yet the case.

"I'm still thinking about it," she said.

"What did your husband say?" Wendy asked.

Before Judy could answer, Brenda Avant, a regal African-American executive producer, slid into the room and seized her attention. "Can I see you in my office?" she asked and walked back out.

Brenda had sucked the air out of the room. No one spoke another word as Judy walked out and headed down the short hallway toward her office.

Here we go, she thought to herself as she followed the much older woman.

Once inside her office, Brenda took a seat in the comfortable black leather chair behind her desk and waited for Judy to join her.

"Close the door and have a seat," she stated as soon as Judy walked in.

Judy did as she was told and took a seat in front of Brenda's desk.

"What's this about you offering interviews to Bob without me knowing about it?"

Brenda was straight to the point as usual. Dressed and styled immaculately, she had worked her way up the ladder at several news stations for the past forty years, and she did not like being disrespected or taken lightly. So Judy was careful with her every word.

"With all due respect, you already told me you had *no* interest in celebrity interviews."

"So you took it upon yourself to go over my head?"

Judy felt hot and uncomfortable in her chair. "I mean, I just asked him—"

"No, you did *more* than just ask, you cut a *deal* with him," Brenda snapped.

Judy was speechless.

While forming the tips of her fingers into an arrow across her desk, Brenda continued. "Let me remind you that *I'm* the one who hired you here, and *I'm* the one who fought for your promotions. So don't catch *amnesia* with your aspirations."

As Judy swallowed her pride and exhaled in silence, Brenda poured it on her.

"I've been around this business long enough to know what happens to *most* of the people who think they have these great ideas. And when they don't produce, you're out that door and there's nothing I can do to help you. So keep your *eyes* and *mind* on longevity," she advised. "Do not get sidetracked by these little . . . *jump offs*. Because that's what they are, exciting little *booty calls*."

Judy grinned and looked away, forcing herself not to laugh at Brenda's attempt to relate to the youth.

"You laugh at this old woman if you want, but this here is a *marriage*," Brenda said, pointing to her diamond ring. It was the perfect size and shape for her finger. "That's what *lasts*; but you go right ahead and do it your own way like you know something. And I'll be right here when you're done."

Brenda leaned back in her chair with confidence. She asked Judy, "And where will you be?"

At a low-key condo in northeast Atlanta, Shawn Blake sat up in an oversized bed with a burnt-orange satin quilt and pillows, wearing nothing but his smooth ebony skin. Two sleeping beauties shared his bed to the left. They were naked and oblivious to the cable news channel that Shawn watched on the large flat-screen TV across the room.

He studied Judy carefully on the screen, feeling that he knew more about her now that he had met her. So he grinned and shook his head at all of her corny television news jokes, knowing it was far from her real personality.

"Hmmph," he grunted. "Everybody's acting."

At a low-key condo in northeast Atlanta, Shawn Blake sat up in

Back at the cable news station, once the morning news

concluded at 10 a.m., Robert "Bob" Truesdale asked to have a few words with Judy in his office. Minutes later, she sat down in a much larger office than Brenda's, with a perfect window view of Interstate 285. Judy had some interesting information to share with her boss. She told him all about Shawn Blake's invitation to follow him for his "real" life story.

Bob listened to it all patiently and nodded. "That's wonderful."

An attractive and wealthy man in his sixties with a full head of silver hair, Bob didn't have to wield the fear of God that Brenda used. Everyone already knew his power. As the owner of the station, he could fire you with a smile and go on with his day. Judy kept that in mind as she spoke to him.

"Yeah, but I don't want to jeopardize everything that I've built here at the station," she commented. Brenda's words of a career marriage were still fresh on her mind.

"Why would you think that?" Bob asked her casually. His calm demeanor was the opposite of Brenda's, and that made Judy skeptical.

"If these celebrity website interviews are not as successful as we all *hope* they'll be, I don't want that to have a negative impact on what I'm already known for," Judy answered.

Bob understood her fears and continued to nod. "In that case, maybe it's better to do a big perspective piece once or twice a month instead of doing a bunch of smaller interviews. You know what I mean? That way they're presented as something special."

The man was so casual in his power that it felt unreal.

Judy nodded and agreed with him. "Yeah, that makes a lot of sense."

"And if you have a chance to follow this guy around for a few weeks and present a great story, that would put you head over heels over every other reporter, and you'd have some of the folks in Hollywood envious," he joked.

Judy realized she was quickly losing her argument against doing the celebrity interviews. Bob seemed to be all in.

"Would we be able use the professional editing tools that we have here at the station?" she quizzed him.

Bob shrugged. "Why not? But I would make sure your reports differ from anything else that they do. You may want to call your pieces, 'Judy Pierce Presents,' and exclude them from marketing anything with your name on it otherwise. Legally, we could demand that from them anyway."

Judy interpreted his words and understood the slippery slope that Brenda had warned her about. Bob would allow her to create her own stories with the outside camera crew and website, but if anything was presented wrong or backfired, he was already hinting at an "us" against "them" scapegoating.

Judy sighed and attempted to back out of the arrangement. "Yeah, but at the end of the day, this may all be a reach. A lot of these new ideas start off well, but then they can just fizzle out. Then you stop and ask yourself, 'What the heck was I doing?' "

She even laughed it off, to try to come across as if she took herself lightly, but the boss didn't go for it.

"Judy, we all have our doubts about trying new things. But you were quite confident when you came to me about this a few weeks ago. And it took me a while to accept the idea myself. But now I agree with you. Like you said, it's another way of stretching our audience."

Before Judy could get out another word, Bob's office phone began to buzz. He needed to get back to work, but Judy's day at the office was over.

He leaned forward in his chair with new urgency. "Judy, you may only have one chance to do something like this before someone else grabs it—someone who's much less talented than you are. So go ahead and do it. You're still young and you only live once. And enjoy your weekend."

Judy walked off the elevator with her bags and headed into the parking garage toward her car like a zombie. All she could think about was the mess she had gotten herself into. She climbed inside the car in her Reeboks and didn't move.

"Shit," she fumed. "I'm not that damn young to be hanging out with this nonsense. I have a *family* at home."

Suddenly, every word that Brenda Avant spoke that morning sounded like the gospel.

"That damn woman," Judy mumbled. *But she's right,* she told herself. She couldn't get Brenda's warning off of her mind. "But now, if I don't do it, I'll look like a coward . . . Shit!"

Judy considered herself braver than most. Her audacity was what got her the job in the first place. *You can't think about longevity until you're in a stronger position,* she reasoned.

Okay . . . I didn't move here to Atlanta to become a coward. That's why I brought this deal up to Bob in the first place. So it is what it is.

She popped open her glove compartment, where she had stuffed Shawn Blake's business card. She had refused to even carry it inside her bag. As she drove, she flirted with tossing it out of her window. But she didn't, because she realized it was an unusual opportunity—for better or for worse. So she stared down at his 810 area code and felt conflicted by the new challenge. Then she forced herself to call him.

2... MICHIGAN BOYS

"So, what made you change your mind?" Marlon asked his wife that evening. They were back inside the kitchen after he had arrived home from work.

Judy was too frustrated to explain. She just wanted to get the interviewing over with.

"I brought it up to my boss a few weeks ago, and now he believes in it. So if I choose not to do it, how will I look *now*?"

"Like a woman who changed her mind," Marlon answered. "You don't have to prove anything to him. This is not your job. This is extra."

"Yeah, but I started this whole thing, Marlon, so . . . I have to finish it. That's what we teach our children, right?" She turned to face him near the refrigerator.

Marlon sighed. He no longer liked the idea. In fact, he had only been pulling her leg about it the night before, but Judy was quick to remind him of his previous endorsement.

"I thought you said to go ahead and do it. What did you tell me last night?"

"That was last night. I didn't think you would actually do it."

"Well, why even talk about it like that? What happened to me trusting myself? That's what you said, right?"

Marlon was silent in a no-win situation. He could try and put his foot down like a Neanderthal, but that would look hypocritical after the support he pledged to his wife the night before.

"You don't really have to do this, Judy," he advised instead. "Like you said, if he's not gonna do a regular interview, then screw it."

Judy grimaced. "I don't believe you. After all that you said last night, you're changing your mind now?"

Marlon grinned, knowing that he was wrong. "I just don't trust the company that this guy keeps. I read up about him online today, and he hangs out with a bunch of guys from Michigan."

"Yeah, that's where he's from," Judy confirmed. She pulled out a two-liter bottle of Coke from the refrigerator and poured herself a tall glass.

Marlon looked concerned. "I don't mean to stereotype, but those guys from Michigan aren't really down here for regular jobs—if you know what I mean."

"Exactly! That's why I wasn't jumping up and down to do this. I feel like a damn undercover cop already."

"Then don't do it then."

Judy figured Shawn wouldn't allow anything to happen to her while taping. That would incriminate him, and the man still had a career to protect.

"I doubt they're going to act crazy while I'm around him," she blurted.

Marlon poured his own glass of Coke. He took a sip to wet his throat and argued, "You don't know that. This guy could be that crazy. He *is* from Flint, Michigan, right?"

Judy looked at her husband sideways. He was only making it worse.

"Now, here we go. And where are we from, Marlon? What're the stereotypes about Indianapolis? I'm slow, and don't know nothing, and don't know how to dress? I ain't been nowhere and don't know how to act around money?" she asked him, breaking down her English purposefully.

"And what about *you* from Maryland?" she continued. "You're just a big *crab*-eating country boy, trying to act like you're from

30

DC or Baltimore when you're not? What's your stereotype? I mean, just *stop it*."

"You can make jokes if you want, but Michigan is Michigan. They're not down here to work like the average citizen. They have bad *history* here. And *recent* history too."

"Yeah, and so do racist white men from the surrounding areas of Georgia, but they don't stop me from doing what *I* need to do."

"And you're not hanging out with them either."

When their son Taylor galloped into the kitchen in earshot of their argument, Judy said, "That's enough," and drank her Coke in silence.

Taylor looked around and asked his father, "Daddy, you eat crabs in the country?"

Marlon and Judy looked at each other, while sharing their glasses of Coke, and laughed.

"I was only teasing your father, baby," Judy explained to her son.

"No, we *did* eat crabs in the country. I'm not ashamed of that. It was Maryland," Marlon admitted. "Everybody ate crabs there unless you were allergic."

Saturday evening, Judy searched through her walk-in closet of mostly professional outfits and shoes, trying to decide on her dress code for the evening. She remained anxious about joining Shawn Blake at the first event she was invited to—an album release party downtown— but she was determined to go through with it.

"This is nothing but meeting new people," she told herself.

Chase and Walter called to follow up with her as she continued to push and pull through her deep closet of clothes and boxes.

"We want to get there by seven thirty so we can deal with all the lighting and sound issues," Chase told her over his cell phone.

"Okay, I'm getting dressed now," Judy lied. She still hadn't picked out what she would wear yet. Her outfits were all too professional or dressy for a young and casual outing.

Hell, I need to buy some new, hip clothes, she admitted to herself.

Meanwhile, Marlon Sr. forced himself not to bother with worrying about his wife. He watched a children's movie in the family den with their two sons instead. He was determined to not let his wife's outing bother him. However, Judy tossed the event back into his face anyway.

She hustled into the den and announced, "All right, I'm leaving out. I'll call you on my way back in. Come on, babies, give Mommy a hug and a kiss."

In a black hip-hugging dress with gold-accented heels, Judy looked and smelled better than Marlon hoped she would.

"Where you going, Mommy?" Taylor asked.

"To a media event," Marlon Sr. answered gruffly from his spot on the sofa. He didn't plan on moving to hug or kiss her either.

Judy took in her husband's sour demeanor and blew it off. *He'll get over it.*

She stared at his face and lips but declined to kiss him like she wanted to. He looked too moody for that. "All right, so . . . I'll call you. Okay?"

She nearly pleaded for his recognition, but Marlon didn't say another word. So Judy shook her head and went on about her business.

"So damn *petty*," she mumbled up the hallway toward the front door. "Whatever."

At 8:02, Judy arrived at the parking lot on North Peachtree Street, where Chase and Walter were anxiously waiting outside with their equipment.

As soon as she parked and climbed out of her car, she asked them, "Is anyone here yet?" She felt guilty about her tardiness, but the parking lot was fairly empty.

"They won't let us in yet," Chase informed her.

Judy frowned as they headed toward the front door. "Why not?"

"I don't know if he told them we were coming or not," Walter added.

Judy shook her head, expecting the worst. "Here we go with the nonsense."

They approached the front door of the restaurant with their camera equipment and met resistance from a mountain of a man in all black, who blocked them from entry.

"Who are you?" He extended his giant brown hand in front of them. He looked six foot five and three hundred pounds.

"I'm Judy Pierce. We were invited out by Shawn Blake to cover the album release party tonight."

The giant man shook his head, denying it. "I don't know anything about that."

"What if we call him and he tells you himself?" Judy questioned.

The big man studied her for a second. "You got his number?"

Judy pulled out his business card from her purse and dialed the number, even though it was already saved in her phone. She did it just to show the man up.

"Hey, Shawn, this is Judy. We're at the door with our camera equipment, but this *huge* man won't let us in. Do you need to talk to him?"

"Is his name Alex?" Shawn asked her over the line.

"Is your name Alex?" Judy relayed to the giant.

"Yeah."

She immediately handed him her cell phone. "Shawn wants to speak to you."

"Hello," the giant man answered gruffly. He listened to Shawn's familiar voice and began to smile. And his smile transformed him into a giant teddy bear.

"Well, what's good, man? When you showing up tonight?" He listened again and nodded, while Judy, Chase, and Walter continued to wait there at the door. "Yeah, but Benny C. already got a camera crew. And you know how he is with stuff like this, man. You shoulda let him know about it earlier."

Judy eyed him down and awaited the verdict as Alex handed her phone back.

"So, are we good?" she pressed him.

Alex pointed to her phone. "Talk to Shawn."

"Hello? Is he going to let us in or what?" she huffed through her phone.

"I'm on my way down there now. I'll work it out."

"So you just want us to stand here at the door?" Judy snapped. She couldn't believe it. She was incensed at his unprofessionalism and tardiness.

Walter turned away and chuckled. He couldn't believe it either—how incredibly real Judy Pierce was away from the cable news station. She had gone from vanilla ice cream to hot sauce.

"You can go in, you just can't take the cameras with you," Shawn explained calmly.

Judy grimaced. "Well, that defeats the whole purpose of us being here."

"Aw'ight, I'll be there in a minute."

"Wait a minute. Hello? . . . Hello?" With no answer, Judy looked vacantly at Chase, Walter, and Alex. "Okay, this is some bullshit. I'm ready to go home."

"You gotta be more patient," Chase said. "This is not the cable station. We're on their time now."

"No, he needs to respect *our* time," she argued.

"But he said he's on his way, right? So we just need to wait for him," Chase responded civilly.

Judy took a deep breath to calm her nerves. "All right."

By the time Shawn Blake pulled up in his black Mercedes, people had begun to arrive at the album release party in waves, and most of them were young, hot women in their twenties. Judy had been observing their contemporary dress as she waited.

Some of these outfits are not bad, she admitted. She was pleasantly surprised.

Walter grinned, watching it all himself. "This is classic colored people's time. They may as well have said eight thirty instead of eight."

"Then they would have shown up at nine," Judy quipped.

"I just wish we could have filmed it all," said Chase.

They focused on Shawn Blake, who climbed out of his vehicle with three bullish passengers.

Here we go, Judy thought. *Now I get to meet his whole Michigan crew.*

However, Shawn's friends paid her no mind as they approached the front door of the establishment with an abundance of swagger.

"What up though, Alex? You out here chillin'?"

"What's good, fam'? I was waitin' on y'all."

There were smiles, hugs, handshakes and male camaraderie between them.

Shawn approached to address Judy, Chase, and Walter alone, with no introductions to his crew. He pulled them aside and said, "This is a little complicated. We already have a camera crew set up for tonight, and I don't wanna show up my man Toot by having y'all here with cameras just on me. This is my man's night for his new album."

"So, why even invite us here then?" Judy questioned.

"You can still enjoy yourself and see how I'm living. You just can't use the cameras tonight."

Judy looked at Chase and Walter. "This is crazy." She felt ridiculous even being there.

Chase shrugged and said, "Aw'ight. We'll just check it out then."

"So, you still want to stay?" Judy asked to make sure.

Walter spoke for both of them. "Yeah, it's cool. We're already here now." In fact, he couldn't wait to go in, cameras or no cameras. Walter had eyed some of the prettiest women in his *life* walking in.

"Yeah, y'all my special guests tonight," Shawn said. "So just come on in and enjoy yourself."

Outside of the tastefully dressed women, there was nothing special about the album release party that Judy hadn't seen in a thousand rap and R&B music videos. Everything was overdone. The expensive wines, jewelry, designer clothes, flirtations, and VIP pecking orders were all over the room. As a special guest of Shawn Blake, Judy found herself right smack in the middle of the chatter, and the music wasn't loud enough to drown it out.

"Who is she? Is that his new woman?"

Judy smiled and ignored the comment. But that didn't mean she didn't think about it.

These little damn girls are acting up in here already, she mused. *You can't even stand next to a man these days without the bullshit.*

Shawn ignored the chatter himself as he pulled Judy through the crowd. "All right, you already met my man Big Al at the door. Let me introduce you to the rest of them."

"They're all from Michigan?" she quizzed him.

Shawn stopped and grinned. "Flint, Michigan. What you know about that?" He spoke it like a man who was proud of his home. Judy could read the shine of pride in his eyes.

"I heard it's a pretty rough place," she told him.

"Naw, don't believe everything you hear. We got a bunch of hardworking citizens in Flint."

"I bet you do."

"Hey, Little L., this is Judy Pierce from Atlanta cable morning news," Shawn introduced her. "This is my man Larry."

Introverted and short, Larry nodded and flashed a couple of gold-capped teeth. He was dressed in all white as if it was a white party, from a white Kangol cap down to his white-on-white Air Jordans.

"Nice to meet you," he mumbled. He seemed to like long legs, as the two women standing beside him were both tall and wearing long-leg-revealing skirts.

"Are you a rapper too?" Judy asked him. She couldn't figure

out his age. Larry looked anywhere from twenty-five to thirty-five, with an easy maturity about him. Shawn was thirty-one himself.

Larry smiled and answered casually. "Naw, Toot's the rapper."

"So, what do you do?"

Instead of answering her, Larry looked at Shawn. "Is she in here reporting too?"

The two young ladies smirked at his clever response. Judy was barking up the wrong tree.

Shawn joked and said, "She don't know any better."

"Well, you better teach her," Larry told him.

Shawn whisked Judy away without further comment.

"What was that all about?" she asked.

Shawn smiled it off. "You're just *bold*, man. You'll ask a person anything."

"We're trained to be bold in the media. That's my job."

"Well, you need to tone that down and just relax in here. You see your two cameramen are having a good time," Shawn hinted. Chase and Walter had struck up a conversation with a few women across the room.

Judy looked in their direction and grinned, knowing better. "They're talking movies and acting. They're probably offering those girls a couple of roles."

"That's how they got you?" Shawn cracked.

"Actually, I asked *them* to do this. I checked out their work online and liked their quality. And they're very professional too."

Shawn nodded. "I can see that. You wouldn't have it any other way, right?"

Judy grinned. "You already know."

"Aw'ight, well let me introduce you to Devon and J.J."

"Walker?" she joked instinctively.

"Naw, James John Pendleton," Shawn answered as they moved toward two more of his friends. They were taking selfies near the bar. Devon was penny brown with a full beard of groomed facial hair, while J.J. was a lighter brown with a goatee and elaborate tattoos that covered part of his neck.

"Hey, fam', this is ahh . . . Judy Pierce from Atlanta cable morning news," Shawn stumbled.

"You forgot who I am already?" Judy joked.

"Yeah, it be like that sometimes," Devon responded, chuckling. "Shawn knows too many women."

"Yeah, you get around too many beautiful women and their names all start to blend together," J.J. added.

"That just means they weren't special enough," Judy countered.

J.J. grinned. "Is that right?" His eyes were watery and bloodshot as if he had been doing a lot of drinking and smoking. So Judy studied him with skepticism.

Is his ass high in here or what? she wondered.

"I've seen you on the cable news a few times," Devon said. "So, you try'na get a close-up on my man now, huh?" Devon looked more presentable and friendly.

"Not like that," Judy told him. "This is all *business*."

"Yeah, it always starts off that way," J.J. blurted.

Judy eyed him sternly. "And it will *remain* that way too."

"Yeah, she's about her shit, man," Shawn spoke up to alleviate the tension.

Devon nodded, believing him. "It's all good. So, she try'na do a story on you?"

"We working on something," Shawn answered. It was obvious he hadn't spoken to his friends about what they were doing yet. Judy made note to ask him about that later.

"Uh oh, here comes the man of the hour," J.J. announced, looking back into the crowd. The music became louder as the crowd grew excited.

Judy looked back herself to see what was going on.

"That's Toot and Benny with the camera crew," Shawn told her. Walking in with them were six stout women in tall heels with colorful, studded leashes around their necks.

Judy was mortified. "Is all of that necessary? Those women are not *animals*."

Shawn looked embarrassed by it himself, sinking his face into his hands.

"That's what Toot wanted," J.J. commented.

"Anything to keep the people talking, right?" Devon added.

"That shit work too," J.J. argued. "He gotta keep competing with these Atlanta rappers."

"So just make better *music* then," Judy advised. She was ashamed to even witness it. "And these girls have *no* self-respect, wearing some shit like that."

"They probably just some girls they hired from the strip clubs," J.J. offered and grinned. It was amusing to him. He wasn't offended at all.

Judy had heard enough from J.J. already. She turned to give the tattoo-neck brother a piece of her mind, but Shawn quickly pulled her away before she got the chance.

"Let's go. You want to meet these guys?" he asked her, referring to Toot and Benny.

Judy eyed him with a warning. "If you really want me to." She didn't plan on holding her tongue with anymore of his friends. She found their actions distasteful.

Shawn thought about it and was immediately intrigued. He was curious to see what Judy would say to them. So he shrugged and said, "Let's see."

The young man named Toot wore blood-red leather pants, a blood-red shirt, and a matching red baseball cap that spelled "TOOT" across the front in white caps. On his feet were a pair of classic red and black Jordans. He topped off the look with a gold medallion, a gaudy gold bracelet, and an expensive gold watch. He was in his early twenties—the youngest of the bunch—and all that Judy cared about was reprimanding him for his disrespectful presentation of black women for obvious shock value.

However, Toot grabbed a microphone and began to perform songs from his new album before Shawn and Judy could reach him.

"Aw'ight, let me introduce you to Benny C. instead," Shawn said, rerouting them through the crowded room.

"Is he the one who paid for all of this?" Judy asked. She had overheard Alex speaking about Benny C. in authoritative terms earlier.

"Yeah," Shawn confirmed. "He started a record label. He wants to start producing movies next."

"Starring you?" she asked.

"Naw, not all of them. We got a lot of people we're connected to now."

When they arrived at Benny's elevated table in the VIP section, the clean-shaven man was the cool and calm opposite of Toot. In his mid-thirties, Benny C. was dressed in boring black and brown, and there was no crowd around his table. He didn't need it. Everything about him spoke of casual power. In fact, he reminded Judy of Bob Truesdale at the cable station.

"Hey, Benny, this is umm—"

"Judy Pierce from the Atlanta cable station morning news," she spoke up, cutting Shawn off.

Benny looked up from his cell phone and responded with charm. "Aw'ight, a real news lady. Well, what's good? Are you objective?"

"Are you?" she asked him back.

The man paused. She had caught him off guard. "Naw," he answered with a grin. "I just call it how I see it."

Judy wasted no time, going right in on him. "And how do you see these women you walked in here with tonight?"

Benny looked out at the stout women on leashes and answered the question calmly. "I look at it as any other model show. Look at Victoria's Secret; they come out in panties and bras, wearing wings. At least our girls got clothes on."

Shawn chuckled. "For real, right?"

"Would you let your wife, girlfriend, daughter, mother, or sister walk in here like that?"

Benny shook his head immediately. "Hell no. But if that's what you gotta do to make your money, I can't knock you for it."

"But you don't mind *paying* for it, so you're in here taking advantage of these women."

Instead of being offended or defensive, Benny chuckled. "Damn, where'd you find her?" he joked.

Before Shawn could answer, Judy said, "Where did he find *you*?"

"In the neighborhood. We came up together. It's all love."

"Is it really? Or is it all just *cash*?" she quipped.

Shawn looked at Benny. Benny continued to smile—he was easy under pressure. He nodded and said, "I like her. She keep it all one hundred. You know exactly where you stand with her."

"That's how it *should* be," Judy barked.

Two beautiful women approached to join Benny at his table. He said, "All right, well—"

"Judy."

"Yeah, well, we're all in here to enjoy ourselves tonight. So if you don't mind, we can finish up your interview at another date and time."

"Yeah, I just wanted her to meet you," Shawn told him.

"She's lovely. And I'm pleased to meet you. I look forward to talking to you again."

When they walked away, Judy told Shawn, "Your friend is very phony."

"So are you, on the news every morning," Shawn fired back. "We're all out here acting."

He couldn't wait to tell her that. He had held it in his back pocket like an ace of diamonds.

Judy smiled and countered, "That's my job. But what's *his* excuse?"

"Maybe it's his job too. Sometimes we gotta work hard to keep the peace. And Benny's a lot better at doing that than I am," Shawn hinted.

When Judy thought about it, Shawn had not been bad that night. In fact, he had been the perfect host. So she complimented him.

"Yeah, I haven't seen you do anything crazy tonight. You've been a perfect gentleman."

"Because I'm walking you around," he admitted with a chuckle. "And like I told you, this night is for my man Toot. It's not about me tonight."

Judy looked at the young performer as he continued to entertain the crowd while a hired camera crew recorded it all. "I see," she mumbled, unimpressed.

"I'll be right back," Shawn said. "Let me run to the restroom for a minute."

Judy nodded. "Okay."

She took their break as an opportunity to reconnect with Chase and Walter in the crowd.

"So, what do you guys think so far?"

"They got some hot-ass camera equipment," Chase commented enviously.

Judy smiled and shook her head. "Is that *really* all you think about?"

"They got some fine women in here too," Walter added.

"Well, I see what you guys think about," Judy said. "You're so *easy.*"

"How's it been so far hanging out with Shawn?" Chase asked her.

She shrugged. "He was just introducing me to his friends for the most part. It's nothing really to report about."

"And were you giving them a hard time?" asked Walter.

Judy smirked. "Of course."

As the three of them continued to catch up, the whole Michigan crew, including Toot and Shawn, gathered at Benny C.'s VIP table to take pictures and speak to the camera. Alex, Devon, J.J., and Little L. were all in tow.

"This is where it all started, right here, baby! We got Flint, Michigan, in the house, taking over the ATL. It's the Michigan Boys, all day and all night," Toot announced, buffered by yells from the crowd. Obviously, they had a supportive Michigan fanbase.

Judy watched it all and figured their night had not gone badly—once she'd gotten past the disappointment of not being

42

able to tape anything. But just when she was ready to announce it as a good night, a turbulent situation popped up out of nowhere.

"We need to talk," a woman demanded of Shawn near their table. She wasn't quite thirty, but she was clearly older than most of the other young women in the room. Dressed in blue jeans and flats, she was obviously not there to impress anyone either.

Judy stopped and watched her from a distance.

"Not here," Shawn stood and told the woman tersely. He looked around as if searching for someone to bail him out.

"No, we need to talk *now*."

Judy watched from the distance as Shawn's pleasant brown face turned into the pained grill of a demon. "Girl, if you don't get the *fuck* out of here . . ."

Before their argument could escalate into something physical, Alex stepped out in front of the disgruntled woman and pointed toward the door. "I didn't see you come in here, but you weren't invited, so it's time to leave."

"Don't you put your hands on me," she barked.

"Don't make me *have to*," Alex warned her.

Wisely, the woman turned and made her way back to the door. Alex followed her out, while keeping a safe distance.

Judy felt an urge to follow them both to see what would happen next. Instead, she watched Shawn have a tension-filled conversation with Benny at their table, while she tried her best to read their lips.

"I told you, man, she's fucking *crazy*," Shawn complained.

"Calm down, bro', we'll get to her. Just calm the fuck down."

Shawn retook his seat, allowing Judy a chance to witness Benny's calming influence on him. *I see,* she thought.

Once the enraged actor made eye contact with her across the room, he stood back up and headed in her direction.

"Did you see that shit?" he asked Judy.

"Yeah, I saw it."

"Well, that's what I mean. I'm in here having a good time, minding my own business, and she wants to bring that nonsense in my face."

"Is that one of your children's mothers?"

"Yeah. And don't think I haven't been paying her, because I *have*. She just wants to keep fucking with my life now. She wants me to be as miserable as she is."

Well, why even get involved with her? Judy thought. She kept that question to herself. She already knew the answer. Relationships were complicated, especially with so much available eye candy in the room. Shawn could have had twenty different women that night. However, once he got what he wanted from them, he had no idea how much they wanted from *him*.

"That's why it's better to be married," she mumbled to him, thinking about her husband and kids at home.

"Yeah, if you can find the right person," Shawn debated.

Judy shook it off. "You just have to commit to someone who believes in the same things that you do."

"And how easy is that for me to do now?" he questioned. He had a point. He was a good-looking and single superstar. "These women will lie out of their minds in here."

"This is the wrong place for you to look," Judy advised him.

"Anyway, we're about to head out to this after-party in a minute. You try'na go?"

Judy looked at the time. It was already past eleven. "Oh, hell no. If three hours can fly past like that, imagine how late I would get home from an after-party. But I thank you for inviting me out tonight. It's been umm . . . interesting."

"Well, thanks for coming. This was a pretty quiet one."

"I was just thinking about that, before *that* happened."

"That's just how random it is too. I don't even know how she got in here."

"Alex left the door to take pictures with you all," Judy reminded him.

"Yeah, but they still got regular security at the door."

"But do they know who she is?"

"They could see that she wasn't *dressed* for it. They should have stopped her on dress code alone."

Judy sighed. "I'm ready to head back home to my family. I'll see you around."

"All right, I'll call you up for the next one. Drive safe."

Judy turned and found Chase and Walter. "So, are you guys going to this after-party?"

"What after-party?" Walter asked.

Judy paused. "Oh, so . . . nobody told you then?"

"Yeah, they told *you*," Chase teased. "But it's plenty of parties in Atlanta on a Saturday night. Are you going?"

"Hell no, I'm not going. I'm going straight home to my husband. My work day is *over*, and it's been over since yesterday."

Judy arrived at home after midnight with one thing on her mind. She peeped in on her two boys, who were sound asleep in their rooms, before she entered her own bedroom.

There, she found Marlon asleep as well.

Perfect! she thought as she closed and locked their door. She slipped off her panties while keeping on her black dress.

"I thought you said you were gonna call me on your way in," Marlon boomed through the darkness and startled her.

"Shit, I thought you were asleep. I wanted to surprise you."

He rolled over in bed to face her. "Surprise me with what?"

Judy pulled down the sheets and climbed on top of him. "I'm a little horny."

"From what?"

"A couple of drinks and thinking about you."

She tugged his boxers down to handle his manhood. Marlon didn't bother to stop her.

"So, how did everything go tonight?" he asked as his wife straddled him.

Judy shrugged. "The same young people running around. If you've been to one party,

you've been to them all. It's just a big old fuck factory. And I just wanted to come back home and be with my husband."

Marlon grinned under her weight. "Is that right?"

"You see I locked the door, don't you?" Before he spoke another word, Judy went down and wet him up with her tongue to make sure he was excited.

"Oh, shit," Marlon groaned, squeezing his eyes shut.

Once his manhood stood at full attention, Judy climbed back on top of him and slid him inside.

"Mmmmm," she moaned, arching her back as she pushed down onto him. "Don't you ever worry about me forsaking you," she said.

Marlon grabbed her hips and pushed her down deeper. "Are you sure?"

"Yesss, Marlon, *yesss*," Judy squealed. She pushed her hands into his chest to steady herself. "But take it slow," she told him. "Take it slow . . . take it . . . *slooow*."

"Hello? What's going on?" Judy complained over her cell phone. Her coworker Wendy Livingston had called her at 6 a.m. this Sunday morning as if it were a workday. Judy had been sleeping like an angel before her phone buzzed.

"Oh, my *God*, you're *okay*!" Wendy shouted. "I'm watching the weekend morning news *right now*, and they said that *Shawn Blake* was in a shootout last night that left a man shot and *killed* outside of a nightclub."

"What?" Judy sat up in bed and searched for her remote to turn on the TV. She caught the tail end of the report, which featured bystander interviews at the scene of the crime.

"They were beefing about something out in the parking lot, and then gunshots started going off. People were running everywhere," a young man stated at the scene.

"Are you're *kidding me*?" Judy asked rhetorically. "It's a good thing I didn't go."

"But you were around him earlier, right?"

"Yeah, at the release party."

"Well, how was it? Was he acting out there too?"

"No. I mean, there was one incident, but . . . it was just all of his friends there for the most part."

"Well, I'm glad that you're okay," Wendy said. "And I guess you won't want to hang out with this guy anymore. He's the real deal."

That thought stuck on Judy's mind as she hung up. She didn't consider Shawn to be a real deal badass at all. Then again, she had only been around him for three hours in a controlled environment. Even there he had nearly flown off the handle. So she remained curious about him.

"What's wrong?" Marlon grumbled from his pillow. Her coworker's early phone call and the TV had disturbed him from his sleep.

"I'll tell you about it when you wake up," Judy promised.

It looks like I'll need to hang out with this man again to find out who he really is and why he keeps getting himself into trouble like this, she thought.

3... HARD DECISIONS

Later that morning, Judy was forced to talk. Everyone wanted to know about her evening out with Shawn, starting with her husband. So they took a quiet seat alone in the living room, while their boys read books in the den.

"Just imagine if you would have gone to this after-party with him. You could have been caught up right in the middle of the gunshots."

Judy considered that for a moment. "We don't even know what happened yet, Marlon."

"There you go with your reporting. What more is there to know? You already know this guy gets into trouble every other week. He has a *problem*. Case closed."

Judy kept it all in perspective. "The idea here is to find out *why*. That's the job of a good journalist. Reporting is one thing, but investigating is another."

"Well, you're not an investigative reporter. You're a news anchor."

Judy held her tongue, hesitant to speak on her ideas.

Marlon read the silence and asked her, "Okay, so that's what you're trying to do now?"

"I mean, it didn't start off that way, but—"

"No," Marlon blasted, cutting Judy off. "You don't need to be involved in that. You're not even getting *paid* for this."

Judy frowned. "You don't know that. This could definitely pay dividends for us down the line."

"Yeah, but we don't *need it*. We're doing just fine. Have you looked around at how we're living lately?"

Judy sighed as her cell phone continued to buzz on the sofa. She ignored it and asked, "What's so wrong with wanting to spread your wings a bit? I thought you were behind me on this."

"Yeah, before it changed to you following this man around. And his films have only been average, if you ask me. He's no Denzel Washington; he's just a new kid on the block."

Judy shook her head and grinned. "You are being so hypocritical right now. So, all of that *talk* you were doing the other night about supporting me and *trusting* myself was all just a game to patronize me? Is that it? And you didn't think that I would really do it?"

"You don't *need* to," Marlon insisted. "I figured you would see the light."

Judy had heard enough. She stood up to leave the room. "You're being full of it right now, and it's *petty*. If you don't believe in it then don't even say it. Why play around with me?"

She left Marlon Sr. sitting there by himself in the den, fuming, while she began to answer her calls up the hallway.

"Hey, girl, I saw you calling me. What's going on?"

"You already *know* what I want to know. I couldn't even *think* straight this morning. So spill the beans, girl. What happened?"

It was Alexandria, the young makeup artist from the cable station, who Judy had become close friends with.

"If you're talking about this after-party thing, I wasn't even there. I only went to the album release party from eight to eleven," Judy informed her. "All of that after midnight stuff is past my bedtime. And the girls were all your age in there. So maybe you should do this instead of me."

"I wish I *could*. But I'm still just a young nobody. All he would want to do with me is get in my pants."

"Girl, you're crazy," Judy said and laughed. "I still have to find out what happened at this after-party thing myself. I'm waiting to call him now."

"Well do it then," Alexandria pressed her. "What are you waiting on? It's after eleven o'clock. He should be up by now."

Judy nodded as she approached the sliding glass doors to her backyard patio and walked out into the October breeze. They owned nearly an acre of well-manicured land with a stretch of healthy green grass, beautiful tall trees, and wetlands. She took a seat on a cushioned patio chair and relaxed in her black and grey workout clothes.

Marlon's right, we do have it good, she mused. *But still, what's so wrong with challenging yourself to do more?*

"So, are you gonna call him or what?" Alexandria pressed, breaking Judy from her daydream.

"Yeah, I'll call him eventually. He's not going anywhere. Calm down."

"All right, well, let me know what happens when you do."

"Don't worry, I'll share it all in my big news feature on him," she teased.

"What? Girl, that may take *weeks.*"

"Exactly. Your generation doesn't have any *patience.* Everything is right now. So wait and suffer."

"All right, be like that. But I wouldn't do that to *you.*"

"Yeah, but I wouldn't press you about it either. That's the difference between being experienced and still learning."

Alexandria paused. "Okay, you got me there. You are the one with the experience."

And Brenda has twice as much experience as me, Judy thought to herself. *But she may be a little too damned old now.*

"Before I let you go, what do you think about Brenda Avant?" she asked the younger woman. Alexandria had just hit her mid-twenties.

"Oh, now she's a straight up *O.G.* I don't even like being around her. I get nervous when she even walks in the room."

"An O.G.?" Judy questioned.

"Oh, come on, Judy—an original *gangster.* You know, *old school.*"

"I know what the term means; I just haven't heard a *woman* being called that."

"Yeah, you can call anyone an O.G. now if they have that *swag.* And she definitely has it. You'll be an O.G. too one day. You got swagger. That's why I look up to you."

Judy smiled, bemused. "I don't know if I should accept that as a compliment or what."

"Oh, it's a compliment, believe me. There're not a lot of people to look up to these days. They'll say one thing and do the next. But you do your job and keep it real, while holding down your family at the same time. And you gotta respect that."

Judy continued to smile. "Thank you. I appreciate it."

"And you deserve everything you get."

When Judy hung up, she felt inspired. *Isn't that nice?* she thought. Alexandria had given her the energy she needed to call Shawn and get her interrogation over with. So she leaned back in her patio chair and dialed him promptly.

"Hello."

"This is Judy Pierce, Shawn."

"I know who it is."

"So, you have my number locked in already?"

"Yup."

There was a pregnant pause before she continued. "I guess you already know what I'm calling to ask you about."

"I didn't have anything to do with it."

"You were just in the wrong place at the wrong time, right?" she asked him sarcastically.

"That's about it."

"Come on, Shawn. How many times are you gonna claim that nonsense? That's like people in court claiming they don't recall significant details."

"Look, man, all I know is that people see me and immediately attach my name to shit. So, if I'm even there when something goes down, then 'Shawn Blake did it.' This is getting real tiring, man."

"Then stop being out there then. It's that simple."

"Yeah, I wish you could have come out last night so you can see how simple it's not. Because it's *not* that simple."

"So, you're telling me that if you went home to bed last night instead of going out to this after-party, your name and image would still be in the news this morning?"

"Yup. They would have been following whoever I went to bed with."

He sounded overdramatic and cynical. Judy declined to comment on it. Instead she asked him, "Why did you even decide to do this interview with me? No one put a gun to your head." It was the moment of truth.

Shawn paused and contemplated his answer. "I need someone I can trust to tell my whole story . . . in case I don't make it."

Now he sounded depressed and ready to die.

"And you just up and chose *me*? You don't know me enough to trust me like that."

"True. But I got a good feeling about you. You tell the truth and you're not *afraid* to tell it. But a lot of people can be bought. That's the fucked up thing about America right now. You think you're cool with somebody and they're out trying to make a buck off you."

"You mean like your friend, *Benny*?"

"At least I know him. He's a snake that I can get my hands around. But I don't really know all these other snakes."

"Surround yourself with more *angels* then," Judy advised. "Give yourself a chance to stay out of trouble for a change."

"That's what I'm trying to do with you," he countered.

Before she responded, Judy looked back into the house to see if Marlon was around. The conversation was leaning toward being personal, and it would be uncomfortable for her husband to take.

"First of all, I'm no angel. And you're a little too old for the big sister mentor thing. Just do what you're supposed to do. Don't you have a new movie to work on or something? How do producers, directors, and your agents feel about this crap you get involved in?"

"They deal with it. Obviously it hasn't stopped me from making new movies, right? I'm set to co-star in this Vegas film called *Love Gamble*. We start filming after New Year's. It's about this college girl who gets involved with two hustlers to pay her tuition. I'm supposed to play the slimy one," he added with a chuckle.

Judy thought about what her husband had said concerning Shawn's acting not being up to par.

"Is it a good script? I didn't really like that last *Two Way Street* movie," she admitted. "It came across like a cheap television special."

Shawn laughed harder. "See that? That's what I mean. A lot of women said they liked that movie. But I didn't really like it either. So I'm with you."

"Why did you do it then?"

"To keep my name out there. I mean, everybody talks that 'next Denzel Washington' shit, but he had to do a lot of corny movies to find the right ones too."

"Not as many as *you* have," Judy countered bluntly.

"Look, you wanna write my next fucking movie? Let's meet up for coffee and talk about it," he challenged her.

"That's not what I do."

"Well, let's meet up and talk about it anyway."

Judy looked behind her again as if she felt guilty of flirting. "I don't want to be shot at," she quipped. "I have a husband and family to look after."

"Yeah, that's boring. That's why you wanna do more. Why did you want to interview me?"

He caught her off guard with that. "Because you said yes," she answered. "I just wanted to see if you were serious."

"But you still want to interview celebrities. If not, then keep doing your morning news show on cable, laughing at corny-ass jokes. 'It's gonna be a scorcher of a day outside. Ha, ha, ha,' " he mocked her.

Judy couldn't help but laugh. "Whatever. I don't have to make up a bunch of *excuses* about my life though."

"Yeah, 'cause ain't shit going on with it. You know you wanna hang out with me, man."

He was getting a little too cocky, so Judy set him straight. "Let me tell you something; I have a normal life over here, okay? A *good* life. I don't have to do any of this extra shit. So you can find yourself another little *flunky* to follow you around. I'm not that girl."

Judy waited for him to say something foul so she could abruptly end their conversation, but he didn't. Instead, he told her, "I can respect that. I don't want a flunky. I want a woman who can hold her own. Because when the bullshit hits the fan, you gotta be strong enough to deal with it. And a *flunky* won't be. You feel me? So I need *you*."

Marlon popped into view right in the nick of time. Judy spotted her husband through the glass door and said, "All right, well, I have to go now."

Marlon joined her outside on the patio as if he had overheard something. "What was that about?"

"You know what it's about. Everybody's calling me up to ask the same questions."

Marlon took a seat in his casual weekend clothes, and Judy's cell phone started to ring immediately. She looked down and read

Michael Westford's number, her male co-host.

She looked at her husband and asked, "You want me to take this call?"

Marlon looked away toward their backyard and exhaled. "Do what you're gonna do, Judy. You always do anyway."

Okay, do I massage his ego? she thought. *Or does he just need to grow the hell up?*

Judy decided to enjoy her husband and family while ignoring her cell phone for the rest of the day. She fixed a big family picnic lunch of hot dogs, hamburgers, and beans, and played out in the backyard with her sons. Then she cooked barbecue chicken and mashed potatoes for dinner before the family watched a comedy movie in the den. And after she put her boys to bed, she still had energy left to satisfy her husband. But there was no ignoring the many questions that would arise at work that Monday morning about Shawn. Alexandria was the first in line, waiting bright and early for answers inside the powder room.

"What happened to you yesterday? I tried to call you three times."

Judy sat in the high chair to have her makeup applied for the cameras. "Obviously I wasn't answering. I just wanted to enjoy my family in peace for a minute. I mean, it *was* my weekend off, right?"

Alexandria smiled back with perfect white teeth and a radiance that never failed to light up the room. "I can't be mad at you for that. You have those two beautiful babies and an awesome husband to please. I can't wait to have my little family one day."

Judy eyed her and barked, "Well, get started on it. You're young, pretty, fun, intelligent, career-oriented. Surely there're plenty of guys who would love to have you. You're *gorgeous*. So what are you waiting on?"

Alexandria laughed as she applied Judy's makeup. "Thank you.

But, girl, you can't just up and grab anybody. These young guys are crazy out here these days. I think you grew up in a better generation than mine."

"Are you calling me *old* now?" Judy complained.

"No, but you and your husband *are* from an older generation. You understand what's really important out here. That's why I admire you so much."

Wendy Livingston rushed into the room, running late, and ended their lovefest.

"You know the Shawn Blake story is up on the *ACM* site this morning," she commented.

Judy's eyebrows rose. "What? Aren't they based in California? It's still the middle of the night over there."

"*American Celebrity Media* has news sources everywhere now," Wendy informed her as she replaced Judy in the makeup chair.

"The *National Urban Report* will be next. They're based right here in Atlanta," Alexandria added.

"You need to get the scoop on this, Judy. You have his personal number, right?" Wendy pressed her.

"You definitely do," Michael Westford interjected as he walked into the room. He held a cup of coffee in his right hand and a folded newspaper in his left.

Judy felt outnumbered. All eyes were on her. "I did talk to him, and he said he wasn't involved in it."

Michael shrugged. "Of course he's gonna say that."

"Well, what else do you expect him to tell me?"

"Then hang out with him and see what's going on for yourself," Wendy suggested. "That's what he offered you to do, right?"

"Yeah, and get caught up in the middle of it?" Judy said.

"That's true," Alexandria agreed.

"I can tell you this," Michael jumped in, "Bob isn't going to like you missing out on a story that you're this close to."

"That's true," Alexandria cosigned as she finished up with Wendy.

Judy felt trapped. "You know what, guys? This is more about my *safety* than a *scoop*. I could hang out with this man and anything could happen."

"Yeah, you could become a star," Michael countered sarcastically.

Judy eyed him with apprehension. *He must be anticipating me leaving. I don't trust him at all.*

Nevertheless, he was right about their boss wanting an exclusive. That much was certain. Judy thought about that herself.

Minutes later, she even found herself having to rehash reports of the shooting on their morning news:

"A man was shot and killed early Sunday morning after a skirmish in the parking lot of a southwest Atlanta nightclub. Several witnesses allege that popular actor Shawn Blake may have been at the root of the incident," Judy read from the teleprompter.

The report aired several interviews from witnesses who all placed Shawn Blake at the scene of the crime. Judy immediately felt guilty about it. She even wondered if Shawn was watching her that morning.

Okay, this is crazy, she mused. *I need to find out the truth.*

As the cable station moved on to other Monday morning stories, Judy's mind remained on Shawn's predicament. Was he really guilty of involvement in the weekend shooting, or were television-hungry bystanders namedropping to get on TV?

"So, do you think he did it?" Wendy asked her during a break.

Judy was stunned. "Did what?"

"You know, ordered a hit?" Wendy was even grinning when she asked.

"*Soprano* style," Michael added, jokingly.

It was all lighthearted and fun as usual. But Judy was no longer laughing.

"That's not funny, guys," she complained. "Someone *died* Saturday night."

Her serious tone killed the jovial mood on the set.

Maybe I really should find out what's going on with this man to stop people from assuming the worst about him, she thought. *Then again . . . I don't want to get shot at either.*

During the longer break in their broadcast, Judy sought Brenda Avant out in her office for more advice.

"Yes?" Brenda asked from behind her desk. She was a guarded and tactful woman who kept herself busy with constant research to produce and improve the news.

"I wanted to ask you a question about objectivity," Judy said.

Brenda studied Judy as she quietly took a seat in front of her desk. "What do you want to know?"

"I'm just wondering if everyone gets a fair chance to present their story."

Brenda frowned. "Of course they don't. This is not the business of *equality*; this is the business of *ratings*. Now are you asking me this because of your actor friend and the murder that happened early Sunday morning?"

Judy was hesitant to admit it. "I mean, there's always two sides to every story, right?"

"Actually, there's *more* than two sides, but no one cares anymore about the *truth*. They only want the side of the story that they believe."

Brenda was so hardcore that Judy couldn't find any weaknesses to break through the cracks. "I just think this man is getting a bad rap," she blurted.

The veteran producer stared at her. "Let me tell you something. Every time I wanted to believe—with all of my heart—that someone was innocent, there were always more details that complicated things."

"That's exactly what I mean. This case is not cut-and-dry either," Judy argued.

Brenda held up her right hand to stop her. "Are you here to seek my blessing for these celebrity features that you intend to do with Bob? Because if you are, you're wasting your time. You're not going to get it."

"What's so wrong with giving people a vehicle to express their side of the story?" Judy pleaded. "I just feel like so many celebrities and public figures are being victimized by everyone now. And we're not being objective with them at all. We're *attacking* them."

"And how long have you felt this way? For two *weeks?*" Brenda pressed her. "Baby, please. You have your own life and a family to worry about. Leave this other stuff alone."

Brenda pointed to the computer screen on her desk. "I walk in this office every morning and read the most ridiculous things ever. Nothing surprises me with these people anymore. Young women smash each other over the head with champagne bottles. They make sex tapes of themselves and sell them for profit. Young men have five babies with five women and don't marry any of them. Then they get probation and community service and don't even show up in court."

Judy was speechless as Brenda continued.

"I grew up in an era where we marched in the streets for serious community issues that benefited us *all* as a *people*, and we didn't get months and years of probation when they arrested us. They sent us to *jail*. But now you want me to give you my blessing for these egotistical babies who want to complain about objectivity. *Please.*

"They need to stop giving these *vultures* so much of their personal lives and do something more for the community," Brenda snapped. "And I don't mean for national charities either. I mean to do something specifically for black people—African-Americans.

Hmmph," she grunted. "These people don't need any more cameras to tell their stories, they need *counseling*. Now I'm done. I have work to do."

She waved her hand toward the door for Judy to make her exit.

Judy sighed and stood up to leave. She made it to the door and said, "The media's not interested in their community work. It's all about the *ratings*, right? So people have been trained to only pay attention to the bad news now."

"Well, if you want to make a change, you retrain them to love the *good* news," said Brenda.

Judy stepped out of her office, determined to find balance in the media. "I guess I'm on my own to try and see how this works out," she mumbled. She knew her boss, Bob Truesdale, would still be receptive to it. But her husband was another story.

Marlon's just going to have to deal with it. She had made up her mind to cover Shawn Blake's story.

That Monday morning at eleven o'clock, Shawn Blake looked down at Judy's number coming in on his cell phone as he lay in his bed alone. "Now you want to call me up after you dog me out on the news," he grumbled. He thought about not answering her call, but he couldn't help himself. "Hello."

"First of all, I want to apologize for this morning's broadcast," Judy began. "I don't know if you noticed it or not, but I wasn't so happy-go-lucky this morning. If you even watched it."

"Yeah, I watched it. I watched all these damn people y'all found to drop my name in shit just because they saw me out there."

"Well, if you already know that's going to happen—Anyway . . ." Judy cut off her rant. "I wanted us to meet up somewhere quiet for lunch and talk about how we're going to do this."

A slight smile stretched across Shawn's face. "You can meet

me at the same bar on the west end."

"About what time, twelve thirty?"

Shawn looked over at his clock on the mahogany nightstand.
"Yeah, we can do that. You're not bringing your camera guys,
are you?"

"Not just to talk about it, no. We need to figure this all out
first."

"Aw'ight, I'll see you there then." He hung up the phone and
nodded, feeling satisfied. "Somebody needs to know all of the shit
I go through." He stood up to start getting himself ready when his
cell phone rang again.

He looked over and read Big Al's number. "Hey, Alex. What's
going on?"

"Are you all right, bro'? You need anything?" Alex asked him.

Shawn paused as he walked into his private bathroom. "I'm
good. It's not bothering me. It is what it is, Al. I'm used to it now."

"Are you sure, man? You know how you go into your little
quiet moods when you start thinking a lot."

"I'm good, man, I got this. I'm an actor. I just need to meditate
on these things every once in a while, that's all. I can use some of
this stuff in my roles."

"Are you good to show up in court tomorrow?" Alex asked.
"You know I'm going there with you, right? You can't be missing
no more court dates, bro'. Fulton County trying to give you time."

"They've been trying to give me time *forever*, for anything
they can find on me. But you know that ain't gon' happen. So I'll
see you tomorrow then."

"What are you doing for the rest of the day?" Alex asked.

Shawn looked into his wall-to-wall bathroom mirrors and
grinned. His firm muscles and smooth brown skin were perfect for
up-close cameras and seduction scenes.

"Licking my wounds," he teased.

Alex laughed hard. "Oh, yeah? Well, tell her I said hi."

"You already know," Shawn joked.

When Shawn arrived at The Shot Bar to meet up with Judy, she had already ordered a salad and a Coke at her table and was going to work on it with her fork.

Shawn smiled. "You didn't want to wait for me before you ordered?"

Judy shrugged and continued eating her salad. "It doesn't make a difference to me. You're paying for it either way." She peeked at her wristwatch. "And it looks like you have a habit of being late. I come from an industry where we're trained to be *punctual*."

Shawn eyed her, intrigued. "So, do I even get three strikes with you or what?"

Judy frowned. "Three strikes to do what? You've had enough strikes already, haven't you?"

The bar manager was forced to look her over again. *This broad is crazy!* he thought, remembering their last encounter. *She's always busting his balls.*

"All right, I've got some rules of my own," Shawn said. "Number one: no cameras or recording devices, and that includes your cell phone. I want you to memorize my story."

"And how would I authenticate that? As far as people know, I could be making it up."

"Naw, they trust you. You got a spotless reputation. The white folks love you too. That's important to have in America. White money runs deep."

"I guess you would know, you're still acting," she quipped.

Shawn grinned. "And you're still broadcasting. Did they say it was okay back at the office?"

Judy paused and took a breath. "You know what would be wonderful? If everyone did what they were supposed to do, we would never have any problems in life."

Shawn stared at her. "You wouldn't have a *job* if everyone did what they were supposed to do. What would you cover on the news then, a bunch of church stories? Firemen rescuing cats out of trees? Come on, you know better than that."

She nodded. "I do know better. In fact, that's my first question for *you*. If you allow yourself to be used and abused and discarded before you have a chance to wake up and smell the coffee, then what's your next act: shooting independent films with your friend Benny? What will you do when that deep money dries up?"

Shawn nodded back at her. "That's why I'm trying to get you to tell my story now. Like tomorrow, I got another court case. Can you come down to that?"

"It's at one o'clock at Fulton County for an assault and battery charge?" Judy asked.

Shawn grinned. "I see you did your homework."

"Of course. Finding a court case on you is like finding chocolate bunnies on Easter. *Easy*. You have a long track record."

Shawn stood up to leave again, miffed by her candid comments. "Aw'ight, so we start tomorrow then. I'll see you in court. Big Al will get you in. And this is for your food."

He left a fifty dollar bill on the table.

"Thank you," she told him on his way out.

"No problem. And keep the change for the next one."

4... SHAWN'S WORLD

The man named Little L. from Shawn Blake's group of Michigan friends climbed out of the low-sitting passenger seat of a burnt-orange Lamborghini and walked alone into a plush Atlanta recording studio. Wearing all black in a long leather overcoat, he strolled through the reception area and past security without being searched. They had been waiting for him.

Thick bass and percussion music played in the background of an engineering booth on the right side of the hallway, while a tall pretty-boy singer recorded sweet melodies over it.

L., short for Larry, listened to the infectious groove and nodded as a crew of young men welcomed him into a private meeting room down the hall to the left.

"What's up, player?" they greeted him cautiously.

Larry barely acknowledged them with a nod. He walked into the room and sat down in a comfortable black leather chair in front of a long wooden conference table. He then pulled out a large manila envelope from his overcoat. He sat the envelope down on the conference table and spoke only to the oldest man in the room, who sat at the opposite end of the table.

"What's good, old timer? We all agree on this?"

Larry's dark-brown face was emotionless; the older man

cracked a meager smile. With a clean-shaven face and a touch of gray hair around his temples, he looked down at the envelope and asked Larry, "How much you bring us?"

Larry opened the envelope and started counting hundred dollar bills that he stacked into ten individual piles on the table.

The older man watched him. He was not moved. "Surely you guys value Shawn's freedom more than ten thousand dollars. I know you can do better than that."

Larry sat back in his chair and grinned. "This looks like a nice spot you got here, man. I know you wanna keep it open. And we open for partnerships. But you gotta play ball first."

"For us to play ball, you need to put up more than that," the older man commented.

Larry kept his cool. "I was sent here with money and a message. If we keep it all about the money, then it's cool. But if we get greedy on some personal shit, then other things can happen."

Larry left his words at that as the younger men around the room began to fidget. There were four of them in their twenties, and none worried Larry at all. He was still a few years from thirty himself.

In his late forties, the old timer nodded and responded calmly. "We all heard about what happened over this weekend."

"Of course you did. It's all over the news. That's what happens when people get out of line," Larry told him. He held out his dark hands and said, "But me, I'd rather do business like this, 'cause I've been on that other side, and it damn sure ain't as sexy. Coming up in The Factory gave us a steady serving of the bullshit. So my gangsta's all one hundred like these Benjamins on the table."

Before any of the young Southern guys could respond with the wrong words or body language, the older man spoke quickly to keep the peace. "So, what do you want him to say?"

Larry shrugged. "It don't really matter, as long as he don't say the *wrong* thing. So he can say he was misquoted, or he don't really remember the details. I mean, whatever. That's up to y'all to figure out. Just make it work and we can stay in business."

"Why not just drop the charges then?" one of the younger men suggested.

Larry thought about that for a moment. "Dropping the charges don't get you no attention. But if you go to court with it, you get to work the national media. So what y'all need to do is let it all go down like we planned, then you can start talking about his album and we all get money together."

The old timer grinned and agreed with it. "Go get Ricky," he told one of his youngsters.

Moments later, the pretty-boy singer walked into the room with them.

Larry looked into the man's handsome brown face and told him the plan. "You can dis my man Shawn and Toot all you want after tomorrow's court case, just don't say the wrong thing while you up in there."

The pretty-boy singer looked at the older man for guidance.

"We'll come up with something," the old timer told him. "This is all to benefit your career. So Shawn Blake gets off tomorrow."

The young singer didn't argue. He looked down at the money on the table and shrugged.

"All right then." They walked him back out of the room to finish his recording.

Larry stood up from his chair and cracked his first smile. "Nice doing business with you, Gene. That's the way we stay smarter now. It's all about that numbers game. So let us know what you come up with, and we'll go from there."

The old timer grinned and showed him back out.

"Tell Benny I said hi," he told L. outside the building.

"You already know," Larry responded. He strolled over to the burnt-orange Lamborghini that was still parked at the front entrance and climbed back in on the passenger side.

Devon looked at him from behind the wheel. "Everything good?"

Larry closed the door back behind him. "Of course it is."

And the elaborate sports car pulled off into the street.

Back inside the studio meeting room, one of the younger guys remained furious. "Why you let them buy you off and punk us like that, Gene?" he barked at the old timer. "I wanted to throw that money back in his fucking *face*. Ten thousand dollars ain't *shit*, man! And all that trash he was talking about Flint, Michigan, ain't shit either. Fuck that Factory shit!"

The angry young man pulled out a black Glock pistol and barked, "I'm from Bankhead, boy, we don't play that. I'm one hundred in here too."

The older man shook his head, took a seat, and exhaled. Young and angry men never understood anything. "Keith, if you're not being bought off these days, then you're not really *in* business," he said. "And it's not the small money that's important; it's the *relationships* that count. Those guys have a lot more money than what you think."

"Yeah, and they just played us *cheap*. He probably had more money in his jacket," Keith commented. He was long, gangly, and fierce, with tall, wild hair that fit his personality.

Gene grilled him. "So, what would you have us do? Rob the man for a few thousand dollars? Then what? You really think he just walked in here by himself for no reason? *Everything* is a message, son. So I advise you to learn how to play *chess, poker, Scrabble* and any other game that takes some real *thinking*. But this is not *checkers*, where you just gon' jump over people and expect to be *crowned.*

"You'll all end up *broke* and *dead* with nobody to blame out here but yourself," he barked. "Now get your ass out of here and go do something constructive. And put the damn gun away."

Keith eyed him and slowly put away his piece. "Aw'ight, let me bump into shawdy on the street again."

As he began to walk out of the room, Gene told him, "I don't want any bullshit from you, Keith. You hear me? Business talks, bullshit walks. How many times I need to tell you that?"

"Yeah, I hear you," the young fiery man grumbled.

"You *hear me*, but are you *listening*?"

"I'm *listening*," he snapped. "I know what business is. And I know they need to come with more of it too, if they wanna keep their little golden goose safe. 'Cause I know the man they shot this weekend. I know his *people*. And they don't *care* about the money."

"And that's why he's dead," Gene countered. "That's exactly what I'm telling you. They're *broke* and *dead*, because they don't understand *business*. You don't beef with guys who have more money than you. You *partner* with them."

Keith frowned and walked out without another word. Gene exhaled at the table as the other young guys followed behind him.

"I need to start doing gospel music," Gene mumbled.

That same night, Benny C. and the guys enjoyed themselves at their weekly Monday Night Football party at The Shot Bar. Nearly two hundred people were there, except for Shawn.

"So Gene agreed to everything?" Benny asked Larry. He cuddled a drink in his hand in a short, clear glass, while Larry chewed on a toothpick.

"He had to. What else was he gon' say?" Larry answered and grinned. "He know they got a new album to put out. So like you said, he needs *partners* and not enemies."

Benny nodded and took a sip of his drink. He was elegant and casually dressed as usual. As he took his smartphone out from his sports jacket, he said, "The blog sites been blowing up all day, so we should have a great turnout at court tomorrow."

"And our boy gets off like Teflon again," L. predicted.

Benny looked around at the lively crowd and said, "Where is Shawn now? Is he here yet?"

Before Larry could answer, an exotic young woman slid up beside Benny.

"Hey, Benny, how are you doing? It's nice to finally meet you again."

Benny held up his drink to temper her excitement. "Hey, gorgeous, one minute. I'll get right to you." He turned back to L. for his answer.

"Big Al said he's chilling at the house again," Larry told him.

Benny looked concerned. "With that reporter woman, Judy Pierce?"

"Oh, I don't know about all that."

"I heard she was here with him earlier," Benny said.

"Yeah, you hear a lot of shit that I don't hear. That's why you 'da boss," Larry joked.

Benny chuckled and turned back to the exotic woman who waited patiently at his side. "Now, where were we again?" he asked her.

She smiled with double dimples and caramel skin as smooth as warm lotion. Her thick black hair was just as smooth and cut at the shoulders. She wore a burgundy one-piece velour dress that hugged every curve imaginable.

"I was just saying that it was great to finally meet you again," she repeated.

"And you're excited to meet *me* and not Shawn? Are you *sure*?" Benny quizzed her.

She chuckled. "Everyone's not excited to meet actors. Some of us like normal businessmen."

"Well, that excludes me. I'm not normal."

"I don't mean normal like in *average*," she explained. "I mean *normal* by not being in the spotlight. You kinda fill in the edges around the room. I've watched you do it."

Benny smiled seductively. "Yeah, you're right about that. I do fill in the edges," he teased.

The woman chuckled and leaned into him softly. "You're bad."

"And I gather you like that about me. So don't leave here without me seeing you again."

"I won't. And my name is Sekoya."

"Gomez?" he asked.

She looked stunned. "Yes, you remember me?"

Benny faked confusion. "The name just came to mind for some

reason. Maybe I asked about you or something."

Sekoya was tickled. "Now I'm really impressed. So I'll definitely see you later."

"As you should," he told her.

She stroked his arm knowingly. "Yup."

Benny watched her walk away and knew what he would be into that night. He felt like a director, preparing the next scene in a movie. He then hunted down Alex in the room.

"Hey, Al, so Shawn's chilling at the house tonight? He's not coming out?"

Alex nodded. "You didn't call him?"

"Naw, you know, I don't like bothering him all the time. You gotta give the man his space. He's been under a lot of heat lately."

Alex started to comment but decided to keep the peace instead. "Yeah, he's just trying to max out tonight."

"With that reporter from the cable station?"

Alex shook it off. "I don't know about all that."

"Has he talked to you about her?"

"Outside of the release party, naw."

Benny nodded, unsatisfied with the lack of information. "All right, I'll ask him about her."

Speaking of the release party, Toot, J.J., and Devon were enjoying a loud time near the bar as they argued about wagers.

"I'll put a *thousand* dollars on Green Bay to whip Detroit's *ass* next time," J.J. challenged Toot.

"Make it *five* thousand if you that confident. We get Megatron back next week," Toot barked.

"He ain't even the best receiver on the team no more. Golden Tate y'all best receiver now."

Devon said, "I can't believe you still root for Green Bay instead of Detroit. You not from Wisconsin, bro'."

"Yeah, but Green Bay been making me money over the years. Detroit been *losing* my money," J.J. countered.

Noticing the level of commotion they were causing with their volume, Benny headed over to pull J.J. aside. "You not high on that shit tonight are you?"

J.J. looked hurt and offended. "Naw, man, I'm good. How come you don't ask nobody else that shit?"

"You're the only one getting high all the time."

"Come on, B, look at all the shit Shawn gets into. You don't bother him like that."

Benny eyed the tattoos on his friend's neck disgustedly. "Shawn makes us all *money* too," he said. "But you keep getting us into *bullshit*, and I'm tired of wiping your ass. So I'm ready to let you shit on yourself next time and see how you like that. That shit that happened this weekend was all because of you."

His tattooed friend looked away in silence, feeling guilty.

"Yeah, I thought so," Benny snapped. "Now calm your ass down in here and act like you got some sense."

Miles away from the football party, on the opposite side of Atlanta, Shawn engaged in a more private affair at his open-spaced condo in the northeast. His place had been professionally styled to his liking, with rich, dark colors, expensive paintings, and artwork. He sat at his candle-lit dinner table and stared gently into the deep-brown eyes of an ebony-brown beauty.

She said, "I can't *believe* I'm actually sitting here with you. And you can *cook*."

Two hot meals were served with lemon-pepper chicken breast, potatoes, and asparagus tips on fancy plates, just like at a restaurant. Shawn included two tall wine glasses and, at her request, a sweet bottle of Moscato.

"I taught myself to dabble a bit," he responded. "I learned to cook my first few years out of college." He chuckled. "I got tired of fast food meals and paying tips at restaurants."

Her eyes sparkled across the table like black diamonds as the candlelight danced in front of her. The Atlanta skyline twinkled beside them through the large glass window to her left.

"Waitresses have to eat too, you know," she commented, then took a bite of potatoes.

"Would you rather be here or at a restaurant?" Shawn quizzed.

She looked around at the spoils of his wealth and took in the comfort of their privacy. It was very peaceful there.

"Is that even a real question? Of *course*, I like it better here."

He took a bite of his chicken and shrugged. "Some women just want to be seen. It feeds their egos, especially if they're dressed for it."

His special guest wore an enticing cream-colored dress with a split up the front and matching heels. Gold adornments around her neck, wrists, and ankle accented her outfit perfectly. She was worthy of being seen. So she smiled and admitted to it.

"That's true, but not all the time. Sometimes we just dress for ourselves."

Shawn grinned. "That's what you say. But a split like that makes people look."

She laughed. "And they *should*. But we only respond to who we want."

"So I'm assuming you want me tonight," he said on cue.

She took a bite of chicken. "Maybe. But I also have to respect myself. You have a reputation."

"You knew that before you came over here."

"And I wanted to investigate whether it was true."

"You can't believe everything you hear. You know that, right?"

"Yeah, but sometimes the things you hear *are* true."

Shawn took a sip of Moscato to calm down. "What do you believe now?"

"Well, you have *manners*. And you can definitely cook. But we're just getting to know each other." She took a sip of wine.

Shawn gulped down his wine and told her boldly, "Not tonight we're not. You said you wanted to experience something *different*. Isn't that what you told me?"

She looked confused. "This *is* different. I've never been in a stranger's house before on a first date."

"Oh, so now I'm a *stranger*?"

"Basically. I don't know you *personally*; I just know your *work*."

Shawn sat back in his tall dinner chair and studied her. She was not moved to change her strong stance at all. He could read her steadiness.

"Well, this is awkward. I got too much on my mind right now to entertain a *stranger* tonight. I got a lot going on tomorrow. Now I have to call a few women I know to come over and keep me company after you leave."

She stared at him and barked, "You did *not* just say that." She set her fork down on the table as if she had instantly lost her appetite. "I guess your whole celebrity attitude is showing up now. After just ten minutes? You must be *crazy*."

Shawn nodded. "I am crazy. That's what it takes to be in this business. If you want something normal, you go back to that tomorrow. But if you're here with me tonight, you already know what it is."

Her mouth dropped open in shock. "You don't even give a woman an *hour* before you come off like that? You just throw it all out on the table. We didn't even finish our food yet."

"Shit, if I'm not a *'stranger'* then we got all night. But if you wanna play that little girl role, like you don't know what time it is, then we're ending this charade after dinner, 'cause I can't *afford* no more confusions. I'm ready to start making women sign contracts. I'm tired of that back and forth, he say, she say shit. Either you're down with me or you're not."

The woman was stunned. She gathered herself at the table and shouted, "Well, you have *problems*, mister. And I'm not gonna be a part of that. So you can give your damn homemade dinner to whoever else you got coming over here. I'm *leaving*."

She grabbed her small purse from the floor and stood up from the table. Shawn stood up with her and was eager to show her the way out.

She strutted toward the door in her loud heels and mumbled to herself, "I have never been through some shit like this in my *life*. You won't *ever* have to worry about seeing me again."

"Yeah, now I'll just read the bullshit that you'll say about me

74

in a blog or on social media," he responded, following her out.

She turned to face him furiously. "Then why treat me like this, if you know that's gonna happen?"

"I'm not telling you to go and put this out there. That's what you'll decide to do. You'll get your little fifteen minutes and then try to stretch it into an hour. I have nothing to do with that. That's *your* decision."

She studied his reserve and countered, "And you'll go through all of that just because you can't get what you want? You'll put your whole reputation and career on the line for *this*," she said, pointing at her firm body in her tailored dress. "Is it really that serious?"

"When you need it, yeah . . . it is. That's why I don't play these games." He waited there to show her out the door.

She slammed her purse down on the floor, defiantly. "All right, if that's all you want. Fuck it." She kicked off her heels and began to strip out of her clothes right there at the doorway until she stood butt naked in front him. "Now what?"

Shawn took a look at her beautiful naked brown body and burst out laughing, embarrassed. "Shit, you got me. I wasn't expecting that."

She laughed along with him. "Yeah, I wanted to flip the script on your ass. In real life, I would have walked out. But was that good acting?"

She continued to stand there naked as Shawn continued to chuckle.

"Yeah, that's good acting. That'll get you a role in a heartbeat."

"But I would never really take my clothes off," she told him. "I just did it because I know *you*. But that's messed up though, for a woman to act like it's all one hundred and then try to get all *moral* at the end. If she won't go to the house of a regular man on a first date, then don't go to the house of a celebrity either. That's when you know she's hypocritical."

"Exactly," Shawn agreed.

"I am gonna break you off, though," she said. "We already know each other like that. So you can forget about calling them other chicks. I just gotta eat this food first. That shit was *good*."

Shawn couldn't keep himself from laughing. He needed the amusement.

His lady friend began to redress. "You've come a long way from our days at Michigan State. I remember you used to love fixing chili with instant rice. Then you'd put too much hot sauce in it and had my eyes watering."

"That only happened *once*, Kenya," he reflected. "But yeah, you came a long way too. You didn't have a body like that when I knew you."

Kenya frowned. "Yeah, I'm a grown-ass woman now with three kids."

"Well, you're still in shape for having three kids."

Shawn followed her back to the dinner table while she carried her shoes and purse. "I worked my ass off in the gym to do it too," she bragged.

"So, what happened to your marriage?" he asked.

Kenya eyed him across the table as they sat back down.

"What happened to *your* marriage?"

Shawn shook his head. "I've never been married."

"Well, my husband started acting like he's never been married either. So I said, 'If that's what you wanna do, then let's go ahead and call it quits so we can raise these kids in peace, and I can do my own thing too.' And just like he was tired of me, I was tired of his ass too. So we get along a lot better now after the divorce. There's no more pressure on us to be perfect."

Shawn nodded. "I wish my life could be that simple. I got involved with two of the craziest women ever. And you wouldn't think that when you first meet them."

Kenya started back on her food. "It's the fame and money that turns them out like that. You know how many football and basketball players we went to school with who are mixed up in that same shit? These girls start counting up that money and act crazy. And some of these guys get money and forget who they are."

Shawn eyed her and felt guilty. "It's hard being the same man when everybody treats you differently though. It's real easy to start believing the hype. You get dragged into it."

Kenya nodded. "You could've at least made a new circle of friends, Shawn. That whole *loyalty to your home* thing can get crazy. We both know how the 8-1-0 can be. It's a little too real sometimes."

"That's exactly how my life is right now, too real. It seems like the whole world is in a movie that I can't stop. I wake up each morning and find that I'm still on the set."

"Like *Groundhog Day*?"

"Yup. Exactly."

She bit into a tip of asparagus. "So, what are you gonna do about it?"

Shawn sat up straight in his chair and thought long and hard. He wasn't even hungry anymore. The food had gotten cold.

"I don't know, man. I'm just trying to make sense of it the best way I can. So, I umm . . . invited this news reporter out to see what I go through on an everyday basis, just to give her an inside perspective, you know?"

Kenya heard that and cringed. "A *news* reporter? With all the blog sites and social media shit that you're already hated on? Why would you want to do that? I already gotta keep defending you as my friend and Spartan alumnus every time your name pops up. Now you want to trust somebody in the *media*? All they're trying to do is make money off of you, Shawn," she pleaded. "Them people don't care about nothing but selling a damn *story*. They will hunt you down, ruin your life, laugh about it on TV, and move on to the next one. I can't *stand* them damn people. They don't want to be around me."

Shawn imagined that. "Yeah, they'd have you arrested right beside me."

"I know they would. And they would catch a beat-down beforehand too."

"And you'd be all over the news, trying to explain yourself. But the camera speaks louder than words," he warned her. "That's the world we live in now. They would YouTube you to death."

Kenya paused and shook her head. "Damn. Well, I'm glad I'm just a regular citizen on my way back home to Lansing. But you gotta go to court down here tomorrow."

Shawn looked into empty space and mumbled, "Yeah, it's right back to the damn circus. That's why I wanted a media person to see it from my side of the table. And I *trust* this girl. She's *real* like we are. That's why I like her."

Kenya sat in silence and allowed him to meditate for a minute. "Okay. Can you heat this food up in the microwave for me?" she asked through the silence.

Shawn laughed, loving their friendship. He grabbed her plate of food and stood from the table. "I got it. I was starting to think you liked it cold."

She laughed. "No I don't. I don't like a cold bed either," she hinted.

Shawn smiled and loved it all. It was the realness of life when you knew and trusted somebody.

5... PURE CRAZINESS

Judy showed up at the Fulton County Court building in downtown Atlanta on that Tuesday afternoon. She joined a crowd of local and national media hounds and gawkers who were expected, including reporters from *American Celebrity Media*, the *National Urban Report*, the local networks, and a reporter and camera crew from her own WATL Cable.

"Hey, Judy, are you here to cover the Shawn Blake proceedings?" a group of eager coworkers asked her on sight. As a morning news anchor, Judy was higher up in the station's pecking order.

"I'm only here to watch and listen. So treat me like a regular citizen," she answered and grinned. "I'll see you guys on the way out."

Only she wasn't a regular citizen; she was Shawn Blake's special guest. Alex, his massive friend and protector, waited for her call near the courtroom doors. As soon as she hit a rough spot in the crowd, Judy texted him to let him know that she needed his assistance to get in.

—*I'm coming out now*—he texted back.

"Aren't you Judy Pierce from WATL Cable?" a young woman in her early twenties questioned. She wore clumpy, brown-framed glasses, and had made it to the front of the crowd in hopes of getting into the courtroom herself.

Judy eyed the radiant light-brown woman and cringed at her loud and seemingly random outfit. She wore every color possible from lime green, red, orange, baby blue, brown, off-white, and purple in various pieces, including a neck scarf.

What in the world is this girl wearing? Judy wondered. *Is she taking style tips from Nicki Minaj or what?*

Her outfit was blinding to the senses and apparently put together to draw attention, which had worked. Even her pinned-up light-brown hair featured streaks of electric blue.

"Ahhh, yes," Judy confirmed hesitantly, admitting she was the cable anchorwoman.

"Oh, wow. Whose side are you on?" the young woman asked her.

"Whose *side* am I on?"

"Yeah, Shawn Blake's or Ricky Slim's?"

"Ricky Slim?" Judy questioned.

"Oh, so you must be on Shawn's side then. You didn't know Ricardo had an R&B mix tape out as Ricky Slim?"

"He does? Well, how convenient," Judy responded nonchalantly. She didn't feel like talking, she just wanted to get inside the courtroom.

"Yeah, it's a hip-hop and R&B fusion record," the chatty young woman informed. "It's really cool too. So this now becomes his breakout party. He's following the script like a real *pro*. You get into a serious beef with a real star, and then launch your own career while the news is still sizzling hot."

Judy spotted Alex pushing his way through the crowd. She was happy to see him.

Thank God! she thought as he reached out to grab her hand.

"Hey, my name is YellowGirl1, okay?" the young woman shouted.

Judy shook her head and was happy to get away from her. As she entered the courtroom behind Alex, she said, "These kids are getting obnoxious."

"Yeah," he grunted as he forced their way through the crowd.

By then, it was 1:48 p.m., and Shawn had been sitting up front quietly with his lawyer in a navy-blue suit. He had made it into court early to avoid the chaos.

"You have a seat up here," Alex told Judy, leading her closer to the front.

As she turned to the left to take her seat on the second row bench, she noticed the same unruly woman from the album release party sitting one row behind her. A professionally dressed black woman sat beside her in a pants suit, appearing to be her lawyer.

Toward the far end of the second row sat another woman with a young child in her lap. She sat beside a professionally dressed white man, who appeared to be *her* lawyer.

Judy observed it all for her personal research. *Okay, this is going to be a trip,* she thought. *It looks like both of his baby mommas are here, and one of them actually brought his daughter to court.*

The prosecution, including Ricardo "Ricky Slim" Morgan and his group of supporters, all sat on the right side of the room. They appeared to be younger and less professionally dressed than Shawn's group. The young victim was absent a suit, preferring to wear blue jeans, a light-blue button-up shirt, and Nikes.

I guess he's going for the young and innocent look, as if he doesn't know any better, Judy mused.

The jury was seated on the far right, toward the front corner. They were a mix of young and old, black and white, male and female.

Judy looked in their direction and took note of everything. In her opinion, everyone inside the room was suspect. They were all humans with flaws and imperfect stories of their own.

"Daddy," the child to her left mumbled in Shawn's direction up front. The cute little girl looked five or six, with long dangling legs in sheer stockings under a yellow church dress and shiny black shoes.

"Shush!" her mother cautioned her. She was a pretty woman and obviously desperate to make a point by having her daughter there. But was it helpful or a distraction to Shawn? He forced himself to remain focused and not look back at her.

The angry mother behind Judy reacted to it as well. "She shouldn't have even brought her here."

Her attorney quickly raised her hand to stop her from bickering again.

Oh, my God, if they start that up in here . . . Judy imagined.

But they didn't get a chance to.

"All rise," the bailiff announced as a black woman judge walked into the courtroom and headed to her high chair, front and center. "Fulton County Court Judge Davida Howard presiding. Please remove your hats."

Several young men, mainly on the prosecution's side to the right, removed their baseball caps and winter hats.

"You may be seated," Judge Howard spoke. As soon as everyone sat down, the judge held up the case paperwork in her right hand and looked directly at Shawn.

Didn't I just hear this young man's name in the news over the weekend? she thought but was not allowed to acknowledge in front of the jury. *He couldn't stay off the streets for another few days before his day in court?*

With a reporter's intuition, Judy read the judge's eyes on Shawn immediately, and she assumed that she recognized him.

How can anyone be objective in these kinds of cases? Judy wondered. Nevertheless, public court proceedings were the American norm.

As the jury members looked on from the far right, Shawn kept his poise on the advice of his attorneys.

Judge Howard remained serious and hardened as she introduced the case. "All right, case number two thousand one hundred and eighty-four, Ricardo Morgan and the State of Georgia versus Shawn Blake. Defense, how do you plead?" she asked Shawn's attorney.

"Not guilty, Your Honor," said the defense.

The judge looked to the assistant district attorney on the prosecution's side.

"Are you calling Mr. Morgan to the stand?"

"Ah, yes we are, Your Honor."

The judge nodded to the young victim. "You may take the stand."

Ricardo stood and walked over to the wooden box and chair in front of the judge, where he continued to stand before the jury.

"Raise your right hand," the bailiff commanded. "Do you solemnly swear to tell the truth, the whole truth, and nothing but the truth, so help you God?"

"Yes."

The ADA stood and proceeded to ask his line of questions. "So you say that this man, Mr. Shawn Blake to my left, struck you in the head with a close-handed fist or a hard object?"

Ricardo looked straight ahead at his attorney and answered, "Yes. If it wasn't his fist, it was definitely something hard."

"Like the butt of a gun?" the attorney hinted.

"Objection, Your Honor. He's insinuating undocumented objects for the jury," Shawn's defense attorney complained.

Judge Howard nodded. "Objection sustained. There's no record of a gun in this incident."

"But you *were* struck in the head by something hard that knocked you forward and off of your feet?" the prosecuting attorney continued.

"Yes."

"And you'd had a prior run-in with this man over a parking spot that evening. Is that right?"

"Yeah, he was in the parking lot with his guys, like five minutes before it happened."

The attorney eyed him and frowned. "So, he was with other men?"

"Yeah, he's always with other guys," Ricardo answered.

"Objection, Your Honor. That's more speculation," said the defense.

Judge Howard exhaled and agreed. "Objection sustained. Unless you're around Mr. Blake on an everyday basis, your speculation about his friends is not valid evidence in this courtroom."

"Well, he was with people that night," Ricardo argued.

The prosecuting attorney cringed and seemed unfamiliar with the new testimony. He said, "But it was *definitely* Shawn Blake who struck you?"

Ricardo peeked in Shawn's direction and paused. "I mean, it was *one* of them who hit me."

Assuming a moment of fear and intimidation in his client, the attorney attempted another approach. "You were not threatened recently by Shawn Blake or his friends, were you?"

"Objection, Your Honor!" the defense shouted.

The prosecuting attorney lost his poise. "Your Honor, this man's group of friends and his violent lifestyle has impacted my client in such a way that it has become difficult for him to honestly testify against him in court."

"Objection!"

"Objection sustained. Counsel, your comments are misleading and have no merit in this courtroom," Judge Howard scorned the prosecutor.

"Yo, I'm not afraid of him," Ricardo spoke up. "I'm just saying, I don't know which one of them hit me."

Judy grinned and couldn't believe her ears. *Did he just say that? Oh my God!*

"He's just trying to get paid," someone commented out loud. "Ain't nobody hit him. He tripped over his own feet."

"Order in the court!" Judge Howard demanded.

The prosecuting attorney became desperate. He said, "Your Honor, this man has had a documented history of violence that follows him, including a recent *shooting* and murder this past weekend. Now who's to say that it won't happen again to *my client*?"

"Objection!" the defense repeated.

"That's not happening to me," Ricardo stated. "I don't care how many Detroit friends he got. He's just an *actor*."

Shawn looked back at Judy and shook his head. That triggered a reaction from the angry mother sitting in the row behind her.

"So, who are you, his new woman?" she grumbled in Judy's direction.

Judy turned and faced her instinctively. "I'm a professional news anchor and a reporter."

The spurned woman stared her down. "And? You're still a *woman*," she barked.

Again, her lawyer tried to calm her. "Rhonda, please. No."

"Okay," she snapped.

Judy turned away and thought, *Yeah, this girl is definitely crazy.*

In fact, the entire courtroom had spun into disarray, so the judge called both attorneys to her bench to consult with her. "Are you okay with your witness?" she asked the prosecution.

"No, I am not," the attorney answered. "My client has obviously changed his story under duress, and it has *everything* to do with the history of intimidation of the accused. This man was just involved in a *murder* this weekend. How could my client not be influenced by that?"

The defense argued, "Your Honor, this is the type of unfortunate innuendo, speculation, and false accusations that my client has been forced to live with just because he happens to be a popular public figure. These various individuals are obviously taking advantage of that for their own private and public gain. So, if Mr. Morgan cannot identify my client as the man who *supposedly* hit him with whatever *object*, then what do we really have here?"

A waste of my time and the public's money, the judge answered without voicing it. She shook her head. *These cases are a mockery and an embarrassment to the pursuit of justice.* She looked back to the prosecution. "Do you need a few minutes with your witness?"

The ADA looked to the defense and imagined the field day they would have in court with an obviously compromised witness. "Yes, I need to have a few minutes with him," the prosecution replied.

The ADA approached Ricardo on the stand and asked him quietly, "Why did you change your story? You didn't speak about him having friends there before."

Ricardo scowled as if he was offended by the question. "Come on, man, that's obvious. Guys like him always have bodyguards and stuff with them. You see that big guy he walked in here with, right?"

Understanding that he was fighting a losing battle, the attorney took a breath and exhaled. "You do realize that you're throwing your case out the window, right?"

"No, I'm not," Ricardo argued.

"Yes, you are," the attorney barked. "I would strongly advise us to take a recess and think this over. You don't want to allow the defense to cross-examine you with this new story of yours."

Ricardo shrugged. "I'm not afraid of them. Bring it on."

"It's not a matter of being *afraid*; it's a matter of being *smart*."

Over the attorney's right shoulder, Ricardo could see that a few of his supporters were getting restless. They knew what the plans were and still didn't like them.

"That's enough for me, man," Keith mumbled as he stood from his seat to leave. Another young man decided to leave with him, while Gene, the wise, old music producer, remained calmly seated.

Judy continued to watch everything from the left side of the room as the prosecuting attorney tossed up his hands in frustration and turned to the defense.

"Okay, he's your witness."

Shawn stood from his chair and smiled from ear to ear, happy to have dodged another bullet in court. He shook his attorney's hand and turned to receive his young daughter, who jumped into his arms from her mother.

"Dad-deeee!"

Shawn held her up high and kissed her, oblivious to all of the commotion that was going on around him. He was happy to be an exonerated man again.

"Oh, it won't go down like that on our day in court," Rhonda announced. "You can count on that."

Shawn overheard her and looked back at Judy, knowingly.

So, he jumps out of the frying pan and right back into a fire, she mused as she prepared to leave. *Now he has to face the media on his way out.*

Fortunately, the angry mother headed up the aisle toward the exit before them.

"Hi, I'm Kenya, a good friend of Shawn's from Michigan State," a well-dressed black woman introduced herself to Judy in the aisle. She extended her hand with a pleasant smile.

Judy nodded and shook her hand. "Pleased to meet you. I'm Judy Pierce."

"He told me. You have a big job to do. He's gotten a real bad rap these past few years, and he's not even like that," Kenya commented as they headed toward the exit together.

Judy accepted her opinion without comment.

"I like how you handled Rhonda too," Kenya added. "That girl doesn't make any sense."

Judy smiled and kept her cool as camera crews and reporters awaited Shawn Blake and Ricardo Morgan to exit the courtroom and answer their barrage of questions. But most of the questions directed at Shawn were about the events of the weekend.

"What do you have to say about the shooting that occurred late Saturday night?"

"Is it true that you have a group of friends who would take out anyone who threatens you or your acting career?"

"Are you really untouchable, Shawn?"

Shawn ignored it all while carrying his daughter out behind Alex.

However, Ricardo "Ricky Slim" Morgan was ready to answer any line of questions the media had for him.

"I'm just trying to put it all behind me now, man. I got better things to do with my own career. I'm still working on my first album."

YellowGirl1 popped up beside him in her colorful outfit and smartphone to record everything. "What do you plan to call your first album, *Dodging Bullets*?" she joked.

The professional journalists eyed her with reprimand, but she had managed to get a chuckle out of Ricardo, along with his undivided attention.

"Naw, I won't call it that. But that could be a good song idea."

"Cool. Could I write it with you? My name is YellowGirl1."

The singer looked at her and said, "Yo, I've heard of you. You got a blog site, right?"

She smiled broadly and squealed, "Yeah, that's *meee*, the one and only."

Gene frowned at her nuisance and nudged her out of the way. He wanted his young singer to answer more questions from the *official* media.

"Well, excuse *you*," YellowGirl1 barked at him.

While the local and national media clamored for their stories, the Fulton County Police had their own line of questions to ask Shawn Blake, and they wanted their questions answered down at the station. Two detectives, one male and the other female, approached him with a half-dozen officers in tow right as the actor reached the sidewalk outside the court building.

"Shawn Blake, we have a warrant for your arrest for the conspiracy and murder of Mr. Charles Wilson on early Sunday morning."

Once again, Shawn looked back at Judy. She stood nearby with his attorney, Alex, his daughter's mother, and Kenya.

Shawn was still carrying his daughter before he handed her back to her mother.

"So, you guys waited all this weekend to show up right after my court case?" he commented to the arresting officers. "That's classic harassment."

"We figured we wouldn't have to chase you down this way," the baldheaded black male detective quipped. His partner was a young dark-haired white woman.

"*Noooo*, Daddy," Shawn's daughter wailed. She reached out to grab him as her mother pulled her away.

"I'll see you later on, okay?" Shawn promised his daughter. "Daddy'll be back."

Judy was appalled. She looked to his attorney and asked them, "Can they do that?"

The lead attorney let out a sigh of exhaustion. "Evidently, they wanted to make a scene like everyone else."

The television cameras and reporters rushed to capture fresh images of Shawn Blake being placed in handcuffs and led into the squad car. As the officers helped Shawn duck his head into the backseat, Kenya eyed Judy on the sidewalk.

"Are you getting all of this? This is what he has to go through now."

Shawn's daughter continued to cry hysterically while struggling to free herself from her mother. "Dad-deeee! Dad-deeee!"

Judy shook her head in disgust as she watched it all unfold. *Yeah, this is crazy,* she told herself. *I know his lawyers will get him back out, but damn! Talk about toying with a man's mind and family. It doesn't get any worse than this. He gets off in court only to be arrested again right out in front of the building with his daughter there. How will this affect her?*

Minutes later, Shawn sat calmly at a table in an interrogation room.

"You know you have nothing on me, man," he told the bald detective who sat opposite him.

"Not as much as we want. Not yet," the detective admitted. "I just wanted us to introduce ourselves to you today. My name is Detective David Todd, and this is my partner, Laura Weinberger. We want you to know that from here on out, we'll be on your case twenty-four-seven. So don't get too comfortable and don't make any mistakes."

Shawn looked up at the dark-haired detective standing near the door. She stared back at him as if inviting his comments. Shawn didn't give her any. Instead, he told the bald detective, "Nice to meet you. Can I go now?"

Like clockwork, his attorney was already working to bail him out, so the detectives didn't bother to retain him any longer.

"I think we accomplished what we wanted today," the detective commented.

Shawn stood up behind him as they headed back toward the door. He eyed Detective Weinberger again and couldn't help himself. "I guess you don't talk much."

"I speak when I need to. You have a problem with that?" she snapped.

Shawn assessed her tough-girl demeanor and looked back at Detective Todd. He shook his head and answered, "Nope," before he walked out of the door to find his lawyer waiting for him.

As Shawn walked away with his attorney, the detectives shared a private moment.

"So, what now? We wait for him to make his mistakes?" Detective Weinberger questioned.

"Exactly. You didn't mind me putting you on the spot like that, did you?"

She shrugged. "It's part of the job. I know what you're doing. If he has a history of intimidating people, we want to see if he'll try it with us."

"With that in mind, maybe you should've been a little softer with him," Detective Todd advised her. "You could have at least *smiled*."

Detective Weinberger grinned. "I assume he gets enough of that already."

"But not from a pretty detective."

"Watch it," she warned him playfully.

Shawn walked out of the downtown Atlanta precinct as a free man again and sniffed the October air. "This has been a long day, man. But I'm glad it's over," he told his attorney.

However, his lawyer was not pleased. "What do you plan to do with your life and career, Shawn? Do you even care about all of this?"

"Of course, I care. What kind of question is that?"

"It doesn't seem like it. All you have to do is make yourself a note to stay away from this stuff. Just practice being *boring* for a while. Let your movies be your adventures."

Shawn shrugged. "I *am* boring."

"Only in your *own mind*, Shawn, but not to the rest of us," his attorney said. "Not to the people who hang around you."

On cue, Alex pulled up to the curb behind the wheel of Shawn's black Mercedes and popped open the passenger door.

Before he climbed in, Shawn watched his attorney walk in the opposite direction. He continued to think about his words of advice.

"What's wrong, man?" Alex asked him.

"Outside of me being arrested again? Nothing." He climbed into the passenger seat and closed the door as his friend drove off.

6... MEDIA RELATIONS

Shawn arrived back at his condo and walked in to find Benny waiting on his living room sofa.

"Shit, man. You gotta let me know when you're coming through," Shawn complained.

Benny looked up from his smartphone and smiled. "This case just hit the jackpot, man. Social media is going *wild* with this one. You got about eight stories going on."

"Eight stories on what?"

"One of them was asking whether you should have had your daughter in court."

"I didn't ask for her to be there. Her mother did that on her own."

"Yeah, but she was still there, so they're blogging about it."

"Saying what?"

"That you shouldn't have had her there."

Shawn shook his head and sat down beside Benny. "I'm glad you're amused by that shit, man, but nobody fucks with *your* life."

Benny looked at him and frowned. "Would you stop your damn whining? Look at how you're living. These broke-ass people don't live like you. That's why they want to read about you. This shit is the new drug," he explained, holding up his cell phone. "They check these sites every hour of the day for news."

Shawn looked at Benny reading his phone and chuckled. "It looks like you addicted to it too, bro'. You check them sites every day yourself."

Benny smiled before he turned serious. "I'm addicted to this money. That's all one hundred. You entertain the people, and they buy it. That's all we're doing. We're selling entertainment to the people."

"But we can do that with the movies I'm in, man, not with my real life."

"Your real life *is* the movie now," Benny countered. "They actually *care* about the shit you do. You know how important that is? That's money in the bank. You can't make money when people don't care. Like Toot's album. Ain't nobody buying that shit," he admitted. "That's a tax write-off for us. I just did it to give him something to do.

"In this day and age, people care more about the *person* than the product, because it's too much product out there now," Benny continued. "You got people giving away shit for free every day now. So they only care about who it's coming *from*."

Shawn sat in silence and let it all sink in before saying, "The cops got two detectives following me around now. So watch yourself on your way out."

"You know who they are?"

"Yeah, they arrested me today. Detectives Todd and Weinberger."

"Weinberger?"

"Yeah, she's a white woman cop. Her partner Todd is a baldheaded brother." Shawn eyed his ambitious friend and added, "But don't try them, bro'. They're waiting for us to make a move. It's like they expect it."

Benny nodded. "All right. You need to lay low for a minute now anyway. But what's up with this reporter woman?"

Shawn played ignorant. "Who?"

"You know who I'm talking about, man. Judy Pierce."

"Oh, she's just um . . . trying to do an inside interview on me."

"For what?"

"To get my real story," Shawn answered frankly.

"You sure you want to do that, man? I mean, your life is a little more complicated than she's used to. I've seen her little news shows or whatever. And it's a bunch of little silly shit."

Shawn shook it off. "Naw, bro', she's real. That silly shit is just what she does for TV. In real life she gets it." He smiled and added, "You saw how she got into it with you at the release party, right? That's how she does everybody."

"You actually expect her to look out for you?" Benny questioned.

Shawn paused and nodded slowly. "Yeah . . . I do."

Benny took a deep breath and stood up to leave. He looked around at Shawn's wealth inside the condo and felt good. "I feel like we've come a long way from The Factory in Flint, man. Now we making *safe* money. So don't ever worry about anybody putting you away in jail. That shit ain't gon' happen. You too important. We'll fuck around and put a whole Atlanta *block* in the grave first. You feel me?"

As he walked toward the door, Shawn stood up to show him out. Benny turned and gave his partner a pound before leaving. "Don't let none of this weak shit out here come between us, man. From where we come from, it's us against the world, fam'. I got you. Always."

Shawn nodded and hugged him. "That's all one hundred."

Once Benny left, Shawn felt he had some serious thinking to do about their friendship. He stood there and reflected on Judy and his attorney's concern about his career.

He asked himself, "So, what happens to me when the people no longer care?"

The media attention surrounding Shawn's court case was so intense, that nearly everyone in the Atlanta metropolitan area had seen it, and they all assumed that Judy was part of the local news teams covering it. Why else would she be standing right in the thick of the crowd?

"I guess you have a rough one on your hands this time," Ms. Hamilton commented at the car line. Judy had arrived to pick up her sons from school as usual.

"Excuse me?" she asked the young, impressionable teacher before driving off. Her two boys were already in the backseat.

"The Shawn Blake court hearings on television," Ms. Hamilton mentioned.

"Oh, I'm not covering that. I was just there."

"Well, they had you all over the news with it."

Judy looked puzzled. "What do you mean?"

Her confusion baffled the teacher as well. "All of the camera shots had you right in the middle of it. Especially when they arrested him on the sidewalk. You didn't know?"

Judy thought back to the scene. Then it hit her. She raised her hands to her face and gushed, "Oh, my God! Yes, that was all unexpected. It came out of nowhere. They had me on camera with that?"

"Yeah, you were right there, reacting to it."

"God, I wasn't even thinking about that. He had his daughter with him, and I was too busy wrapped up in his family moment."

"It looked as if you were *shocked*."

"I *was*. The man had just gotten off in court and then they arrested him again."

"They arrested who, Mom?" Junior asked.

"Yeah," Taylor instigated.

"This is grown folks' business," Judy told her sons. "Anyway . . . I guess I'll see it all on the news when I get home tonight."

"You sure will," Ms. Hamilton said. "All right, I'll see you guys tomorrow."

Judy drove off thinking about what the teacher had said. *God, I wonder how many people saw that. Was I on the national news too? Maybe I need to call my mother in Indy and see if she saw it.*

In the midst of her thoughts, Judy's cell phone buzzed,

revealing a collection of missed texts and messages. Judy had been listening to music on her drive home instead of monitoring her phone during the day.

"Wow, a lot of people were trying to reach me, and I was sitting here listening to Beyoncé," she mumbled to herself with a chuckle.

"You're not listening to Beyoncé now," Junior responded.

"Because I have my two *babies* in the car and Beyoncé has adult content on her albums."

"I'm not a *baby*, Mom," Junior protested. "I hear Beyoncé songs at school. Kids have them on their iPods."

"Who, the *older* kids?" Judy asked him.

"Mom, I'm in *fourth* grade now. There's only one higher grade there."

Judy panicked. "Oh, *God*, that means you're *graduating* next year."

"Duhhh," Junior responded.

"Hey, I don't like that," Judy snapped. "You watch your mouth."

Who does he think he's talking to? she mused. *I'm not some little white television mom. I will smack his damn lips off for that nonsense.*

Once she made it home and got her kids settled in with their homework, Judy wanted to prepare a meal while returning some of her messages and phone calls. Then she would watch the local and national news. Her first call was to Alexandria. She put her on speakerphone.

"Girl, you were all *over* the news today," the makeup artist told her.

"So I've heard. I haven't even seen it yet," Judy responded nonchalantly. She chopped beef, carrots, potatoes, and added smaller vegetables and seasoning for a homemade pot of stew.

"It looked like you were a part of Shawn's *team*, to be honest with you."

"I was. I wanted to be able to see things from *his* perspective and not from a media angle. I guess I succeeded, because I wasn't even thinking about the cameras," she admitted. "A teacher brought it to my attention at my sons' school today."

"So, you've really decided to hang out with him then?"

Judy paused. She hadn't told her husband yet. "Shit," she mumbled.

"What? You messed up your dinner already?" Alexandria assumed.

"I'm not that bad at cooking. I'm just getting started with it. I just forgot that I didn't tell Marlon about this yet."

Alexandria paused. "Oh. Well, it's still media work. He should be able to understand, especially after this. Shawn Blake's life is a *riot*. Who better to follow right now?"

"Yeah, but that's the part that Marlon doesn't like. If Shawn were a choir boy, my hubby wouldn't be as concerned about it."

"Who wants to cover a choir boy? That wouldn't get any ratings, unless you called it the *Naughty Choir Boys Club*, with craziness on the show."

"I know, right?" Judy agreed and laughed. "These networks are coming up with slimy TV shows for everything. I have to agree with Brenda on that. More than *half* of these reality shows are completely wild."

"That's what the people want. So, you either give in to it, or get passed over."

"Ain't that a damn shame? People have no morals anymore."

"I mean, it is what it is," Alexandria threw in. "Sodom and Gomorrah."

"Anyway, let me finish cooking this food so I can at least fill up Marlon's belly when I tell him," Judy quipped.

"Unless he *knows* already. I mean, it *was* all over the news. You think they don't have televisions where he works?"

Judy knew Alexandria was probably right. "I'm sure they do, somewhere. But, you know, I'll deal with it when he gets home."

"All right, well, I'll see you in your chair tomorrow morning."

Judy hung up and thought again about calling her mother, but decided against it. "Let me deal with Marlon first, and I'll call Mom later on tonight," she told herself over the stove.

Marlon was on his way home and was *steamed*. He had seen the news reports of Shawn's court case and didn't like that his wife hadn't told him she would be there. He held in his anger with plans of letting her have it at home.

He walked into the door after six. The house smelled delicious, filled with the aroma of fresh hot food.

"Hey, Daddy. Mom's dinner is ready," Junior told him.

Taylor jumped on his father's leg for a fun ride into the kitchen, but Marlon pushed him off. "Not today, Taylor. Dad's not in the mood."

Judy overheard him and knew what his tone meant. *He saw me on the news already. Oh, well. We'll just have to deal with it then.*

"Hey, honey," she greeted him at the kitchen.

"Mm-hmm," Marlon grunted. "So, how was your day today? Anything interesting happen?"

Judy eyed him and paused. "You're talking about the Shawn Blake court case, right?"

"How come you didn't tell me you were going?"

"Marlon, you're already having a hard time with this, so what would have happened if I had told you in advance?"

"I wouldn't have been *blindsided* by it at work. You *knew* you were wrong. That's why you didn't say anything."

"Wrong about *what*, Marlon, doing a *job*?"

"That's my point; this is not your *job*. You don't need to do this."

"It's not about me *needing* to do it, Marlon; it's something that I *want* to do," she admitted.

Judy's comment caught Marlon off guard. "Oh, so now you're all into it like *that*, regardless of how I feel?"

Judy was cautious with her words. "Marlon, it's a *job*, and I plan to be very professional, as usual. Now what is the *problem?* Would this be as big of an issue if Shawn were a woman?"

Marlon was careful with his own words. "Like I said, you always find ways to do what you want to do." He walked away and mumbled, "Then flash it right in my damn face on the news."

Judy looked at her kids, both sitting at the kitchen table. She didn't want an argument with her husband in front of them, but she responded from instinct. "Marlon, I wasn't thinking about the cameras . . . I was just *there.*"

He turned to face her incredulously. "You weren't thinking about the *cameras?* Well, what the hell did you think was gonna be there? You work for a cable station, don't you? You're gonna tell me you didn't know they were *there?*"

"I wasn't on duty for this, Marlon. I wasn't reporting."

"Well, what the hell were you there for?"

Judy looked at her sons again and decided to keep her poise. "Please don't raise your voice at me, Marlon. You're overreacting."

Marlon stared at her from the middle of the room. Then he shook his head and walked away toward the bedroom. He had lost his appetite.

"Daddy doesn't want you to do a job with Shawn?" Taylor asked his mother.

Marlon Jr. looked at his brother and knew better. Judy was too frustrated to reprimand him. "I guess not," she commented.

In a flash, Junior turned around from the table to stare his mother down. He held up his open palms for an explanation. "Mom? You tell *him* stuff and not *me?*"

Judy held up her right hand and warned him, "Don't start with me, now. Eat your food."

Although Judy was willing to make up with her husband, Marlon avoided her for the rest of the evening. He didn't want to make up. He wanted her to leave Shawn Blake alone. *Period!* But the more Judy thought about it, the more it bothered her that her husband was so insecure. So she tracked him down in the den to have a word while he watched the NBA preseason games on the sofa.

She stood in the doorway in her nightclothes. "You are really acting *childish* about this, Marlon."

"So are you," he told her calmly. "All you have to do is not do it. I don't want to hear nothing else."

Judy cringed. The kids were in bed, so she had no more *reason* to be poised. "You don't want to *hear* nothing else? Is that what you said?"

Marlon stared at her. "You want me to say it again?"

"Please do."

Marlon hesitated a second. He said, "I know how you are, Judy. You're gonna do it anyway. You're *already* doing it."

While he spoke, his cell phone lit up from the sofa. He had a new text message.

"Who is that?" Judy asked. The question jumped out of her mouth without thinking. She usually didn't ask him about his phone calls and texts, but it was well after ten o'clock on a weeknight.

Marlon looked up from his phone and answered, "Shawn Blake. He's checking in to see how I'm doing tonight."

Judy was not amused. "You're acting like a real *asshole*," she snapped and walked back out. "I should have grabbed his fucking phone," she mumbled to herself up the hall. But she couldn't leave this time. Marlon was getting under her skin. She wanted a full-blown argument with him to blow off the steam, but he wasn't giving her one. So she marched back into the room to start it.

"Let me see what he said then?" she demanded, reaching for her husband's phone.

"Now you know good and well I'm not the damn kids," Marlon said.

"If you don't trust me to be professional with what I'm doing, then I don't trust you either."

"I'm not the one hanging out with movie stars."

"Because your *job* doesn't call for it. If I started tripping about you knocking on the doors of lonely housewives all day in your truck, how would *you* feel?"

"I'm not on the truck like that anymore. I only had to do that for the first few months before I became a supervisor."

"You still had to do it when they needed you to. But you're tripping about me hanging out with him, so let me see what he said."

"You know I was joking, right?"

"Well, I'm *not*. Now give me the phone."

"No!" There was no playfulness in his tone.

Judy stared at him sharply. "That's exactly how I feel."

Satisfied with pushing her husband back on his heels, she left the room again, feeling victorious. Only now, she wondered who had been texting him.

Is he fucking cheating on me? she asked herself as she walked back to the bedroom. *Shit. Now I'm wondering if I should have even pressed him about that.*

The next morning as Judy sat in Alexandria's chair getting her makeup done, Marlon's mysterious text message was still on her mind. She told her work friend all about the episode.

"So, how would you feel if your man wouldn't give you his phone?" she asked Alexandria.

Alexandria paused, cautiously. "I don't have a steady man like that, so I wouldn't even want to see his phone. I wouldn't want my feelings getting hurt."

"Well, I'm saying if you *did* have a man."

Alexandria shook it off. "We're in *totally* different generations. I don't want a man looking at my cell phone either."

"Look, I'm not that much older than you. If you don't have anything to hide, then what's the problem?"

Alexandria continued to balk. "You're talking to the wrong person. I'm not even going there."

"What about you, Wendy? Would you look at your man's cell phone?" Judy asked her coworker as soon as she walked in. Wendy was in her early thirties, still unmarried with no children.

She cringed. "For what?"

"That's what *I'm* saying," Alexandria interjected.

"Because you had a *reason* to," Judy pressed.

Wendy thought it over. "Well, if I have to stoop to looking at a man's phone because of trust issues, then he's definitely not the one for me. I wouldn't want to *confirm* anything that way either. It just seems . . . I don't know, petty. I would rather he just tell me."

Alexandria looked at Judy to see how she would respond.

"Well, neither of you have been *married* either," she barked.

Wendy shrugged. "I've been with the same boyfriend for three years, and I never even think about checking his phone. Wait a minute. You're talking about *your husband*? What's going on with *that*?"

Judy realized that she had gotten too deep into the conversation. "Actually, I was only discussing the issue theoretically with Alexandria, because she seems so dead set against it."

Wendy said, "I agree with her. Once you start checking cell phones, next you'll be hiring a private investigator. I have better things to do than getting involved in all of that."

Judy shook her head. "You're way overdramatic."

"No I'm not. Phones are very private these days. That's why they have all kinds of access codes on them now. Anyway, the real question is: How was your day in *court* yesterday with Shawn Blake?" Wendy perked up when she asked the question.

As she finished Judy's makeup, Alexandria remained silent for a change and let the two news professionals talk.

"It was *crazy*. Everything about it was crazy. The victim took the stand and started talking about Shawn being with a bunch of guys and not knowing which one hit him. Once he said that, it was over. And Shawn had *both* of his baby mommas in court. One even brought his daughter."

"I saw that on the news," Wendy mentioned.

"So by the time they arrested him again, I had seen just about everything."

"Just imagine how much *more* you'll see once you're around him," Wendy hinted as she took the chair.

"We'll see," Judy responded.

Before Judy left the station that morning, Bob Truesdale wanted to see her in his office again for an update. As usual, he sat calmly and relaxed behind his large desk with his great view of the highway behind him.

"So, how are you feeling about your ah, project? I heard you had quite the eventful day yesterday."

Judy chuckled to lighten the mood. "Yeah, it was something all right. But I'm moving forward with it. I plan to catch up with Shawn today. Yesterday was just too hectic, and I had to run back home to scoop up my boys from school."

Bob nodded, listening to her patiently. "And your husband is okay with it?"

The question stunned her, but Judy kept her cool with a smile. "It's funny that you ask that, because we just kind of worked it out last night. I guess any husband would be a little concerned about his wife covering such a difficult man."

"I thought about that myself. So I wanted to ask you again if you were okay with this."

Judy paused, recognizing an exit to climb her way out—*if* she wanted to take it. But she had fought too hard to create this opportunity to back down from it.

"At this point, I'm ready to go for it. And it looks like his case is getting hotter by the minute. He's going to have more days in court to come, so his story is not going anywhere."

"It's definitely not," Bob agreed. "If you were ever going to shadow a celebrity from a newsworthy perspective, Shawn Blake is unquestionably a *hit*. You just have to remember to keep your head when you're around him."

"You think he would be a bad influence on me?"

Bob opened up and chuckled. "Celebrities have been known to become bad influences on a lot of us. Trust me, I speak from experience."

"What, you've had a few run-ins with celebrities?"

"Are you kidding me? Once you get into a business that uses cameras, you're gonna run into quite a few charismatic people with big ideas. I've heard pitches a hundred times about the awesomeness of new films in a myriad of ways. Let's just say that I've *learned* from it. I've learned a *lot* actually. And I know how persuasive they can be."

"I can only imagine. I guess it's my turn to learn."

"We'll see," Bob commented.

Judy laughed, but she didn't like the staleness of her boss's response. She'd expected him to say more, to give her some advice. So she forced herself to ask, "Are there any pointers you would like to add?"

"Yeah, stay on your side of the street," Bob joked. "And remember that you're a reporter at *all* times."

Judy smiled. *That's much better,* she thought. "Thank you."

On her way out of the building, she had to pass by Brenda Avant's office to gather her things. As she reached the senior producer's door, she wondered if she should drop in and ask to talk.

Judy peeked in the open door and made eye contact with Brenda, but Brenda looked away and returned to the work on her desk. Judy got the message and moved on.

"She's not giving me her blessing," she mumbled as she continued down the hallway.

Inside her office, Brenda Avant stopped from her work a moment to exhale. She looked up toward her office door and thought about Judy again before shaking her head. Then she went right back to work.

7... GETTING TO KNOW YOU

Judy sat across from Shawn at their same table in The Shot Bar.

"So, this is obviously where you like to meet?"

"Yeah, this is my place. I feel comfortable here. People don't bother me."

Judy looked around and said, "No one's ever here during the day."

"That's exactly why I like it. It's peaceful for me."

Judy nodded. She understood—the man needed peace. "So, what was your life like growing up in Michigan?" she asked. "Tell me about it."

"It was cold," he joked and laughed. "A lot colder than it is down here."

"Well, I know that. It was cold in Indianapolis where I grew up. So I can imagine what it was like in Michigan. But what was it like for *you*?"

Shawn began to fidget. He was uncomfortable with the topic. "Flint is out of the way of Detroit. It's not Ann Arbor. It's not East Lansing. There are no big-time colleges there. All we got is car factory jobs. That's what the whole town is about. It's like we're just working people. That's why we're so strong together. But when the work is no longer there for you, poverty and crime are what you have left," he explained. "But I tried to be a good kid."

"You *tried* to be a good kid?"

"As good as I *could* be. I never did any time in prison. I went to MSU in East Lansing. I got a degree in theater. I started doing a few commercials. Then my film career took off."

Judy stared at him and said, "I can get all of that from your resumé. I want to know who you are at your *core*."

Shawn smiled it off. "The more I do films, the more I try to figure that out."

"Okay, that's bullshit," Judy said. "If you want me to help tell your story, then you need to open up to me. This is not a magazine piece where you can get away with that artistic shit. You gotta keep it real with me."

Shawn leaned back and laughed again. "Who are *you* at your core?" he challenged her. "You do a lot of fake shit on TV too."

"I do, but I know who I am. I have *not* lost myself."

"Well, who are you?"

"I'm an ambitious overachiever from Indiana. I do what I need to do to get where I need to be. So don't let the pretty face fool you. When Steve Harvey put out that book and movie, *Act Like a Lady, Think Like a Man*, he was talking about *me*. My mom always said I should have been a boy."

The bartender overheard her from behind the counter and chuckled. "You can say that again," he mumbled to himself.

"I got into a lot of fights coming up in Indianapolis too," Judy continued. "Girls thought I was all on that pretty shit, and I wasn't going for it. So a lot of them found out the hard way and got punched in the mouth. I even beat a girl's ass in college at Ball State."

Shawn was intrigued. "For what?"

"You know, the usual man shit. This girl talked to a football player who liked me, but I wasn't giving him any play. I don't want to stereotype all football players, but he was one of those rude, disrespectful guys who would talk to girls any old kind of way and treat them bad. He didn't talk to *me* that way, but I already knew how he was, so I wasn't going there," she explained.

"So anyway, this girl approaches me in the cafeteria to make a damn *scene*. And she says, 'Um, excuse me, are you fucking with my man?' And she's saying this while I'm standing in the *line*, not at a private table or anything. So all of these people were around us, looking at me, right? And I'm thinking, *This girl's about to get her ass kicked.* Because she really didn't know me like that.

"You know how you go away to college and these new people really don't know you like they *think* they do?" she asked Shawn.

He nodded and said, "Exactly."

"So, the whole time she's talking, I'm already sizing her ass up. She was thicker than me with her two girlfriends on the side. But they were the kind of girls who I *knew* weren't gonna fight. They were both the lying, instigator types. 'I didn't say that,' " she mocked with a girly voice.

"So I told the girl like Aaliyah, 'Look, your man is feeling me, but I'm not feeling him. So you need to go check your *man*. I've never touched him, and I don't like him. Okay?'

"You know, I kept it real with her because that's how I am," she went on. "Everyone on campus already knew that he was trying to holler at me, so there was no hiding from it. But I was very firm with this girl to let her know that I'm not that type, so don't bring that shit to me."

Shawn listened to her as if she were explaining a scene in his next movie. Even the bartender was listening.

Judy said, "And do you know this girl pointed in my face and said, '*Bitch*, I know you fucked him!' And she's *lucky* I put my food tray down when she stepped to me, because I would have beat her ass *with the tray*."

Shawn burst out laughing again.

Judy pierced her eyes like her husband's last name and kept the story going. "When she said that, I hit her with a right cross to her face. Bang! And a lot of girls like to put their heads down and just wail at you blindly, so I measured her head with my left hand out and hit her in the face again. Bang! And when she started swinging all wild with her head down, I leaned back and hit her with both hands, like Floyd Mayweather Jr. Bang! Bang! Bang! Bang!"

She became animated at the table, demonstrating with her balled fists. Shawn and the bartender were both loving it.

"The girl didn't even *touch me*," Judy boasted. "When everyone saw that, they were like, 'Damn, she fight like a *boy*!' Even the guys respected me after that. So when I started asking people to help me with things, they were like, 'Shit, give that girl what she needs,' you know?"

Shawn was beside himself in amusement.

"So that's who I am, a born *fighter*," Judy said. "I came down here to Atlanta twelve years ago to get a piece of this peach cobbler pie that everybody kept bragging about. Now I have two beautiful sons and a humble, good husband. I do my job, and I love my family. That's who I really am . . . at my *core*."

Shawn was blown away. He eyed Judy across the table with her strength, truthfulness, and determination. He was immensely satisfied. "That's why I like you," he told her. "I *need* somebody like that."

"You're gonna have to open up and trust me then, Shawn. That's what we're here for, right? Tell me who you are."

Shawn raised his hands to his face and folded them. He nodded to her before he spoke, accepting her trust. "When my father lost his job and left my mom, she didn't take it too well. She spent like the next five years of her life trying to find herself."

As he spoke, he began to rub his hands together uneasily.

"She tried to find it in drugs, other men, the streets, and that shit was embarrassing, man. You gotta go to school every day and kids are talking about how they saw your mom on the streets doing whatever. And it wasn't even a *joke*."

He searched Judy's eyes with real hurt in his voice. "You feel me?"

Judy accepted his pain and nodded back. "I feel you. That's real."

Suddenly, Shawn looked toward the door and stopped. He glanced over Judy's left shoulder as someone walked in behind her.

"Hey, what's up, man?" a familiar voiced addressed him.

Judy turned to see who it was. "Oh, hi, Chase, Walter. How are you guys doing? I've been meaning to call you back."

Chase nodded slowly and didn't look too pleased to see her. "What're y'all up to?" he asked. The moment was awkward.

Shawn read the tension and spoke up. "We're talking, man, just getting to know each other. I told her we don't need cameras for a while. I need to feel comfortable first."

Chase looked at Shawn, then back to Judy. "Okay, but . . . we at least wanted to know what was going on with you. I mean, we saw you were down at the court case and everything."

"Yeah, it's just been really hectic the past few days, that's all," Judy said. "Everything was happening fast. But we would have eventually caught back up, you know?"

She attempted to keep the mood light, but Chase had more on his mind.

"Well, you know, we um . . . got a couple new people to interview, so—"

Judy cut to the point and held up her index finger to Shawn. "Excuse me one minute." She stood up from her chair and walked Chase toward the door. That left Walter with Shawn.

"So ah . . . how does it feel to be a free man after your court case?" Walter asked him.

Shawn shook his head and grinned. "I was never going anywhere."

Parked up the street from The Shot Bar, Detectives Todd and Weinberger sat inside an unmarked sedan, watching everyone who walked in and out of the establishment.

"If this is where he likes to hang out, it's easy to track him here," Weinberger said from behind the wheel.

Todd looked forward in silence, as if he were already bored with everything that was going on.

"You think we might want to set up a wiretap with cameras inside?" Weinberger suggested.

Todd shrugged. "Eventually. But we want to make sure he's meeting folks here that may lead to something. We don't want to waste a budget on anything fruitless. So far, these folks look harmless."

"What about at night?" Weinberger hinted.

Her older partner nodded. "That's more likely when we'll be onto something. But we'll need to see it first."

Weinberger sighed, disagreeing with the wait-and-see process. "It's kind of screwed up that a budget stops us from doing what we need to do."

"Yeah, well, welcome to America. We need to okay the money first before we do anything now. We can't *afford* to waste it."

He continued to watch the door as the news anchor walked out, followed by a younger man.

"Mrs. Judy Pierce," the detective mumbled. "So, you think she's doing a story on him?"

"Yeah, she's dressed like she came straight from work. Look at her," Weinberger said.

"That don't mean a thing. Some women get off from having affairs while dressed in their work clothes."

"You really think she would meet him somewhere as open as this if they were fooling around?" Weinberger asked. "I mean, come on. People know her in Atlanta."

"I wouldn't put anything past *anyone* these days," said Todd.

"Then she's going to have a conversation with someone right in front of the place? Yeah, that makes *a lot* of sense," Weinberger cracked.

Todd looked back at her and grinned. "When you get some more seasoning on the job, you'll understand why I'm so cynical."

Judy stopped on the sidewalk outside the bar. She turned and told Chase, "I know what we originally agreed to do, but he changed how he wanted to do it. So, I could either agree to what he wanted or nothing."

Chase shook his head and waved it off. "I'm past that now. What I'm saying is this: We have other celebrities now who want to do interviews with you, especially after they saw you all over the news when Shawn got arrested."

Judy sighed distastefully. "After all these years reporting the morning news, I get caught on camera at *one* court case and it's like people *just* discovered me. That's unbelievable."

Chase grinned. "That's the power of celebrity news. You can do it all now. Hang out with Shawn to get his story, get other celebrity interviews, and still do your morning show."

Judy became curious. "Who do you have lined up?"

Chase ran off the names of several reality TV stars that lived in the Atlanta area, but Judy was not at all interested. She remained poised when she responded to him.

"Yeah, they're not really on Shawn's level as far as real *talent* is concerned. Shawn still has some fine-tuning to do himself, but he's way out in front of them."

"I mean, I know they're reality stars and all, but people still follow them, *millions* of people across the country," Chase pitched.

Judy thought about her boss and Brenda Avant back at the cable station.

There's no way in hell I'm interviewing a bunch of reality TV stars. I'm sorry, she told herself. *I don't even watch that stuff.*

She said, "Chase, no offense, but . . . Shawn Blake is a *big* story. These reality show people though . . ." She stopped to figure out how to put it.

Chase jumped in before she had a chance to finish her thought. "Don't sleep. Reality show stars have taken over TV now."

"But is that a good thing or a bad thing?"

Judy could hear Brenda's hard words of advice and feel her eyes beaming down on her. *These people don't need any more cameras to tell their stories, they need counseling.* Reflecting on Brenda's keen observations, Judy decided she was not going to be talked into doing it.

She told Chase, "I'll tell you what. I can introduce you to a couple of up-and-coming reporters who would *love* to do that, and I'll just focus on the big stuff."

Chase grinned and chuckled at her attempt to back down. "They want *you*, Judy, not some up-and-coming reporter," he said.

Judy frowned. "Why?"

"Because they know you're a professional. After they saw you out there with Shawn, they know that you *care* too. The cameras don't lie."

"Yeah, because he was being *arrested* in front of his *daughter*, over a bunch of *hearsay*. I just reacted naturally. I reacted like *any* mother would."

"And the people *loved it*," Chase said.

Judy hesitated. She was in a quagmire. So she told him the hard truth. "Look, my boss is not going to allow me to interview a bunch of reality TV show people. That's not gonna happen. So, our next best option is to audition a few girls who could do the job just as well or *better*—pretty girls with a lot of personality. And I know just the type."

Chase exhaled. He felt defeated. "All right, but what if they're not any good?"

"Then we find some who are. But my focus is on Shawn right now."

Chase calmed down and nodded. "Has he told you a lot?"

Judy smirked. "I was just about to get something *good* when you walked in the door. Then he stopped talking like he did the first time we had him."

"Well, at least he's ready to open up to you now."

"*Slowly*," Judy complained. "Let me get back in here, and we'll link up soon to audition some girls."

By the time they walked back in, Shawn was having a drink at the bar as he talked to Walter. "Y'all work everything out?" he asked, concerned.

Chase nodded. "Yeah, we got it." He reached out his hand for respect. "Thanks for trusting us, man."

"No problem."

Chase looked at Walter and said, "Let's roll. Let them get back to what they were doing."

Walter looked at his drink on the counter and felt conflicted. "Aw'ight, fuck it." He tossed the drink to the back of his throat and stood up straight from his stool.

"You're not driving are you?" Shawn asked.

Walter looked at him and frowned. "I'm good after one drink. I'm from DC. We not rookies."

Shawn chuckled and said, "My man," and gave him a pound.

"So, where were we?" Judy asked, alone with Shawn again.

"And thanks for getting me out of that. That was really awkward. I know he thought I was dodging him."

Shawn grinned and said, "I could tell. It was all over his face as soon as he walked in. You didn't even tell them you were working with me?"

"I really didn't have a chance to. Everything is happening fast, just like I told Chase. I was still having a problem trying to decide if I would even do it."

"You hungry?" he asked her out of the blue.

Before she answered, Judy thought about the time. They were running out of it. "How long is it gonna take? I still have to pick up my sons from school today."

Shawn shrugged. "You got plenty of time for that. It's not even two o'clock yet."

"Yeah, but I don't want you to eat before you finish talking to me."

"To tell you the truth, man, once they walked in, it kind of broke my groove a little. But we can get back into it eventually."

"Today?"

Shawn chuckled. "Probably not today. I mean, I'm hungry now."

"Shit," Judy piped. "How are you gonna be an actor when you keep putting off the performance?"

"I gotta study my script first," he countered. "But we'll get there. That's all one hundred. So stop trying to make a sprint out of a marathon."

Judy relaxed on the stool and took a deep breath. "All right."

Back at home with her husband and kids, Judy continued to feel guilty about her decision. Marlon still didn't like her putting in the extra hours to cover a volatile actor, but he figured her excursion would soon be over. Meanwhile, he continued to spend his evenings alone inside the den, watching television.

Frustrated by the separation, Judy strutted into the room again in her nightclothes. "Marlon, how long are you gonna do this?"

He looked up from the sofa and stared at her without a word. His answer was obvious.

"Are you really asking me that?"

"Yes, I am."

He looked back at the television. "I don't know why," he mumbled. "I'm not that complicated."

"So, you're gonna stay in here every night until I stop interviewing him?"

Marlon refused to respond. Judy sat down beside him anyway.

"Well, he finally started to tell me his life story today, so it shouldn't be long now. But he started off with the same old *ghetto* narrative we've heard a million times before. His father loses his job, leaves his mom and family, and then his mom turns to the streets while destroying the peace of mind of her son."

That got Marlon's attention. "What did you expect? You're not gonna get anything *groundbreaking* from this man. It's the same old story for a lot of them. Just look at all these rappers and athletes. 'My daddy left us and I had to become a man.' That *is* the black narrative."

"Not for everyone," Judy argued.

"Of course not for everyone; but they don't care about households like this one. There's not enough drama involved. The husband gets mad because the wife wants to take on an extra assignment at work? They can't sell that. That's *petty*, right? Who cares about that? It's not deep, dark, and bloody enough."

Judy didn't dispute it. Instead, she asked him, "So, what's the black woman's narrative?"

Marlon didn't hesitate. "He beat me, he cheated on me. I never knew my real father so I was looking for a daddy in all the wrong places. I started ho'ing, stripping, and gold-digging and had four kids out of wedlock . . . until I got saved and found Jesus. Now I just want to show the world, you know, how much I've changed and what I'm still struggling through with my four baby daddies, on my new reality TV show."

Judy smiled and stared at him. Marlon had left her speechless. "Did you write that down or read it from somewhere?" she asked.

"I don't need to write it or read it. It's on TV and in the news every day. It's to the point now where you can memorize it. And they're all getting *paid* for it too."

"Not all of them," Judy argued. "But . . ." She couldn't find the words to express what she felt at the moment. "Are we really that bad now?"

"It's gotten even worse since we elected the first black president," Marlon said. "We got all happy to have a black man and woman in the White House, and the Republicans went and took all the money and jobs away. Now I end up working at UPS with a bachelor's degree."

"You said UPS was *consistent*. And you work at the *headquarters* as a *supervisor* now. Not at some regular UPS building."

"It *is* consistent. That's why I'm happy to be there. People will always need to ship and receive packages, no matter what the economy is like. But now you got family members shipping food and clothes and whatnot. That's how bad it is. It's *real* out here."

Judy wasn't expecting that kind of conversation at the moment, but her husband had her thinking. "So . . . if all that is the black narrative, then what's the white narrative?"

Marlon rolled it off his mind again. "Cancer, Alzheimer's, autistic children, alcoholism . . . charity events, stocks and bonds, technology, and global enterprise. They're on something totally different from us. *You* should know that, you work on a cable news show. Just think about all the stories involving white people versus black. Their stories are always about human progress and trying to live longer. We just get the same shit over and over again: crime and entertainment. Now they got *you* covering Shawn Blake. Think about it."

Judy stood up. "Okay, you're starting to piss me off now. They didn't *tell me* to cover Shawn Blake. It was *my* decision. And white people have crime and entertainment stories too. *More* than we do."

"And they *own* the networks to tell it however they want to tell it too."

Judy stared at him *hard*, as if she wanted to hit him.

Marlon stared back. "Why are you mad at me, because it's the *truth*? I may work at UPS, but you didn't marry a damn *dummy*. I have a college degree too. And despite what America may *think*, we *do* receive an education at black schools."

"I didn't say that you didn't," Judy snapped.

"Well, I'm just reminding you. Bowie State."

"Whatever," she told him and walked out. "You need to just bring your ass to *bed*," she shouted from the hallway.

Marlon grinned and chuckled. "I'll come to bed when I'm ready."

Before she forgot, Judy called Alexandria. She got her voicemail. "Hey, girl, this is Judy. I wanted to talk to you about an opportunity to umm—"

Alexandria called her back while she was still leaving the message, so Judy switched over to her second line.

"I guess whatever it is, it couldn't wait until the morning, huh?" Alexandria quipped.

Judy paused. "I don't know if you want everyone at the job to know about it. You know how they can get."

"I sure do. So, what's up?"

"Okay, I talked to my two camera guys from DC today that I told you about, and they want you to audition for them to interview people."

"Girl, *stop*! You're *serious*?"

"Yeah, I'm serious. But I have to warn you. They have a bunch of reality TV show people lined up to interview. I told them I couldn't do that, but it would be good for you to cut your teeth on the easy ratings."

"Oh, so you're giving me the dirty work, huh?"

She had caught Judy off guard. "I mean—"

"I'm only kidding, Judy. I know that would be a step back for you, but it's a step *up* for me. I just don't know if I could deal with their attitudes."

"Sure you can. Just remember that most of them are media whores. Any news is good news for them. They don't care. Just be your crazy self."

"So you *do* think I'm crazy?"

"Of course, you are. We're *all* crazy."

"Well, I'm glad you're finally admitting that. I knew it all the time," Alexandria cracked with a laugh. "Okay. So, when do they want to do it?"

"I'll talk to them about it and let you know."

"All right, do that."

8... LOOSE ENDS

Benny sat across from J.J. inside of a makeshift recording studio while Toot worked on a remix of his song inside a small recording booth. The studio looked undone, with unpainted walls and unstained wood, as if they were still working on it. They were.

Benny looked at The Factory Studio as a break-even investment. He planned to package recording time to dozens of wannabe musicians and artists in the Atlanta region.

"So, how are we gonna fix this?" Benny asked his friend. He wasn't paying attention to the music. At the moment, he was only concerned about James John Pendleton and his recklessness.

J.J. shrugged with an unstableness that revealed his habits. "I can do it, man. I can clean up, bro'." He could have been a bright and handsome man if it wasn't for the entanglement of drugs that dulled his skin, clouded his vision, and crippled his decision-making. But his addictions had taken over.

Benny eyed him and put his hands together in a prayer. "I'm not even talking about that right now. I'm talking about this murder charge they're trying to pin on *Shawn*. *You* pulled that trigger."

Devon and Larry stood against the walls in the small private room and listened in with no comment. Benny was speaking with something important on his mind.

James looked around at all of them, as if pleading his case. "It was just a reaction thing, man. I said it was my fault already."

"We all know it was your fault. But that don't change the situation we're in," Benny explained. "They got cops following Shawn's every move because of you. We can't have that. It's too tense for him now. You know how Shawn can get. He got a temper and a new movie coming up that he gotta prepare for. So we need to take that heat off of him."

James frowned and said, "Ain't nobody gon' talk. Right, L.? It's the code of the streets."

Larry remained speechless.

Benny shook his head and said, "It ain't gon' work like that this time. Fulton County want something on this one *bad*. The lawyers told me they're talking conspiracy shit, like Shawn told somebody to do it. And now that he got detectives following him, they gon' look for any loose ends they can find to pin something on him. Which is *you*. So you gotta give yourself up. I already thought about it."

J.J. looked around the room again with wide eyes, as if a shockwave had struck him.

"Naw, I can't do no more jail time, man. I ain't goin' back in there."

Benny opened his palms and said, "You gon' *have* to. There ain't no other way."

"Yeah, it is, just nobody *talk*, man, like usual. Right, Devon?"

James was looking for anyone in the room to agree with him.

Devon sighed and shook his head. "You need some kind of drug intervention program, man," he said. "Maybe you can get cleaned up this time."

James jumped out of his chair and yelled, "You don't get cleaned up in jail. You get a lot of *bullshit* in there. You ain't never been to jail before, Devon."

"That's 'cause he knows how to control himself," Larry spoke up.

James looked down at Benny, who was still sitting calmly in his chair. "Well, if Shawn can control *himself*, he won't have no problems. They don't have nothing on him, right, but a bunch of people talking shit. So tell him to keep his cool instead of treating him like a *kid* all the time.

"You let him get away with anything," J.J. continued. "You don't tell *Shawn* to go to jail. You pay his way to keep him out."

"First of all, sit your ass back down," Benny shot back. "I'm talking to you."

J.J. eyed him cautiously and looked over at Larry, who hinted toward the gun inside his long leather coat. James sat back down quietly in his chair.

Benny told him, "You gotta stop being so jealous of our boy, man. Shawn been taking care of us for *years* now—even you."

J.J. frowned and barked, "No, he hasn't. We been taking care of *him*, every time he gets in some trouble. He ain't even made that much money off them movies."

Benny nodded and kept his poise. Then he leaned back and hurled an open right hand, smacking James violently across his face and out of his chair.

"Damn!" Larry responded.

Before James could defend himself from the floor, Benny was all over him, smacking him left and right as the grown man scrambled in vain to escape the beat-down.

Through the booth's glass window, Toot saw what was going on and stopped recording to watch. Devon hated to witness it, but there was nothing he could do. His boy had been fucking up and needed the reprimand.

When the fury of sudden violence ended, Benny stood over his fallen friend like a conqueror. "Now sit your ass back in that chair."

James gathered himself from the floor and sat back in his chair with visible welts on his face and tears in his eyes. Benny sat back down in the chair in front of him.

"If you wanna act like a *bitch*, I'ma treat you like a *bitch*," he barked. "And I've *been* to jail. But I know how to *control* myself now. All this petty bullshit you keep talking about Shawn gotta stop, bro'. You ain't *him*, okay? Deal with it!

"We've been getting all kinds of money off of Shawn," Benny explained. "You don't understand how this new shit work, do you? Well, let me tell it to you. You get one guy in the house that get money, who the people love, and you blow him the fuck *up*! Then we *all* get to eat! What part of that shit don't you understand?

"Shawn Blake is the fucking *man*!" he shouted at him. "That's all you need to *know*. We don't have time for that crabs-in-a-barrel shit. If you wanna hate on somebody, make sure they're from somewhere else—Miami, New York, Atlanta—I don't give a fuck. But you don't hate on *Shawn*. We all from *The Factory*, the 8-1-0. The fuck is wrong with you?

"Now I'ma tell you again," Benny concluded. "You gon' turn yourself in out of *love* and you *not* gonna run your mouth while you're in there. And we'll take care of your kids and their mothers. That's all one hundred. But there comes a time in life when we all have to be responsible for the decisions we make. Your time is *now*."

Benny sat back in his chair and tossed up his hands. "If you act like you don't wanna do it, then you gon' force me to play a game of chess. And you damn sure ain't the king and queen. You at the *front* of the board."

In the silence, all eyes were on James John Pendleton. He looked up at his friend Devon, who dropped his eyes to the floor. There was no way out.

Larry told him, "Look, man, if they don't get somebody, they're coming after *all* of us. They're after Shawn *first*, because they know that's where the money is. We can't have that shit."

Benny had no more to say. He only watched and listened.

J.J. finally nodded and mumbled, "Aw'ight. That's what I gotta do then."

Benny reached out to him for a handshake and looked into his bloodshot eyes. "It's what's good. We'll make that happen."

In the southeast Atlanta suburb of Decatur, another congregation of black men gathered in the living room of a barren apartment. Keith and a few members of Ricky Slim's production team met up with some angry men about the recent murder outside the Atlanta nightclub.

"So, you say you know who did it? 'Cause I was about to bust that boy Blake. He ain't untouchable out here," said the ringleader, a thick-bodied hard rock. The man was well in his thirties with rough, grizzled facial hair.

"Yeah," Keith confirmed. "I'm waiting on the word to catch up to him now."

"Tonight?"

"You ready to do him right now?"

The grizzled man scowled at him. "Am I ready to *do him*?" He walked over to a latched closet door and pulled out a massive black shotgun. "That was my li'l *cousin* they kilt out there, dawg. Of *course* I'm ready to do him. This ain't no damn *game*. My spirit won't let me *sleep* at night over this shit. It's like he been talking to me. 'Get these motherfuckers,' you know?"

Keith's followers looked on with anxiety, but he kept his poise. He said, "That boy Blake ain't have nothing to do with it. His people told me the police are trying to frame him. So after everything go down, just make sure you say that."

The grizzled man looked on and thought about it. "They're trying to protect him *like that*?"

Keith nodded. "They want his name out of it. That's the only reason they're giving the shooter up. They don't want the police fucking with Shawn."

The grizzled man nodded, still thinking about it. "So, he really is untouchable then. But if he worth money *like that*, then what we get out of making his problem go away? You see how we living in *here*, right? We ain't living like *him*, I know *that*."

Keith said, "You know they got the money. They wanna see if it go down first."

"Oh, don't worry about that. You give us the motherfucker that kilt my li'l cousin, and it's a *wrap*."

On cue, Keith's cell phone rang. He looked down at the

number and said, "Hold up," while stepping out of the room to talk in private. "Hello . . ." He listened for confirmation before he responded. "Aw'ight, consider it done." Then he returned. "That was them. I know where he at now."

As Keith and his guys drove away in a black Yukon jeep with oversized black rims, they were finally able to breathe again.

"Man, that dude was *crazy*. You see that big-ass shotgun he pulled out?" his partner commented from the passenger seat.

Keith chuckled from behind the wheel. "I told y'all he was."

"You also said he didn't care about the money," another passenger said from the back.

"Yeah, he damn sure asked you for the money," said the partner up front.

Keith exhaled in silence. He mumbled, "Yeah . . . everybody want money now. We all need the shit. So after they do the job, they get paid, just like we got paid."

"What if he gets killed or arrested?" said the third passenger, sitting behind Keith.

Keith shrugged. "He don't get no money then."

"Naw, if he gets arrested, he might want to talk in jail with no money, dawg," said the second passenger from the back.

"Who gon' believe a criminal?" Keith questioned. "If he was really about that money, he woulda got it upfront like we did. So as long as everybody keep their mouth shut, we'll just see what happens. Anybody in here got something to talk about?"

"Naw, player, we know what it is."

"We don't have nothing more to say about it then. Let him do what he do."

Back in Atlanta, Devon drove J.J. to his apartment on the southeast side, not far from Decatur. He looked over from his Cadillac Escalade steering wheel and asked his friend, "Are you all right, man?"

James didn't answer him right away. He was daydreaming, looking out the passenger-side window.

"You all right?" Devon repeated.

J.J. looked at him and snapped, "Naw, I ain't aw'ight, man. My whole damn *face* is still stinging."

"Well, you brought that on yourself, man. I keep telling you about talking that shit about Shawn. I don't know why you keep doing that," Devon barked at him.

"Because I'm talented *too*, man. And I look better than Shawn. Y'all all know that. But now Benny putting out an album for *Toot*? When do I get to do something?" James complained. "I feel like I'm wasting my life away down here, man. I'm ready to go back up to Flint or something. I ain't try'na go to jail down here because of him."

"Because of *who*? You're the one who pulled the trigger. Don't blame that shit on Shawn. Nobody told you to flip out like that. You need to get yourself together, man. Don't try to run back home either. Just face your medicine like a *man*. Call it an act of self-defense, like we talked about."

James frowned. "I got a criminal record already, bro'," he said. "They not gon' let me off on that self-defense shit. I don't even have a permit for a gun."

Devon listened to his friend and shook his head as they pulled up to the curb in front of his building. "All you had to do was keep your love for The Factory, man, but you keep hatin' on Shawn on some old petty shit and acting foolish. You brought this all on yourself, bro'."

James scowled. "That ain't even his real last name," he said.

"Come on, man, he been using that name since *college*. You gon' bring that up now too?"

"I'm just saying, if we can do all that for *him*, how come we can't do some things for *me*?"

Devon stared at him as he parked the truck. "I can't even believe what's coming out of your mouth right now, man. Are you

127

that *weak*? For real?"

"It ain't about being *weak*. I'm just keeping it one hundred. Everybody wanna feel important for *something*," J.J. explained. "I'm just tired of being a side man, that's all. We all out here rooting for Shawn like cheerleaders with skirts on. And Benny the main one."

Devon continued to shake his head in pity. "That's the problem with black people now, J. Everybody wanna step out of their position. So, if you want me to say it, I'ma say it."

"Say what?"

Devon stared at his friend and told him, "You a *coulda been*, J. We all know you handsome, but you *wasted* it. You coulda been a model, a *pimp*, or *something*. But you never had the focus to be no damn actor or rapper. That shit takes *focus*. Shawn got it. You don't. So deal with it, bro'. Too many black people trying to be what they not."

James argued, "You don't know what I coulda been, man. I coulda been a handsome doctor or something. Why a pretty black man always gotta be a pimp?"

"Aw'ight, well, you coulda been a sweet-talking preacher then," Devon joked.

James mumbled, "Man, let me get the hell out of here and go to bed. You fuckin' wit' me now. You don't know what I coulda been. I could still be a preacher if I want. All you gotta do is *believe* in me. Y'all don't believe in me, man, that's the problem."

As J.J. opened the door to climb out, Devon told him, "You gotta believe in *yourself* first, J. And get off that *juice*."

"Whatever, man. I'll see you tomorrow."

James closed the door and walked up the sidewalk. Devon started the truck back up and pulled off into the street. Through his rearview mirror, he could see his friend already lighting up a joint outside of his building.

Devon shook his head and mumbled, "This boy just won't learn," as he turned left at the corner and disappeared up the street.

The grizzled man from Decatur sat in the passenger seat of a rusty old sedan that was parked up the street from where Devon had dropped off his friend. There was a driver up front and another passenger in the back, all carrying loaded guns.

"Yo, that's him right there, Dave," the driver commented to the ringleader. They all watched as the tattooed man smoked a joint outside of a five-story apartment building about thirty yards in front of them.

"Aw, this too easy," Dave stated, stroking his grizzled beard with his free right hand. He cradled his shotgun in his left. "Hey, Che, I want you to jog across the street and call out his name when I raise my fist, aw'ight? Then I'ma run up and bust him one time in the chest. And he gon' bleed like a pig. So let's go."

Che climbed out the back and quickly crossed the street to move into position.

Dave told his driver, "All right, Marcus, as soon as I give Che the signal, I want you to start the engine and pull into the street. Then I'ma bust him in the chest and we out of here."

Marcus nodded from behind the wheel. "Aw'ight."

Dave quietly climbed out of the passenger seat with his shotgun held low and to the left. He walked five yards ahead, without being noticed, before he raised his fist up to Che across the street.

"Hey J.J., what's up, man? What's been up with you?" Che called out.

J.J. looked across the street and froze, trying to identify who was calling him.

"Do I know you?" he asked while searching for objects in the man's hands.

By the time he saw the second man running up from his left, it was too late.

BOOM!

Dave shot him one time in the chest at pointblank range and blew him off his feet as the sedan pulled out of its parking spot. Dave ran and jumped in the passenger seat as Che climbed into the back. The job was done in minutes.

Hearing the big bang of the shotgun, followed by the churning wheels of a car, several tenants looked out their windows. They spotted the bloody victim on the sidewalk, wheezing his last breaths as he stared up at the moon and stars through the chill of the night.

"Oh, my *God*! Call the police!"

9... EXPLANATIONS

Judy read the early morning news reports that came across her desk and froze. "James John Pendleton? Why does that name sound so—"

Oh, my God! she stopped and thought with wide eyes. *That's Shawn's friend J.J. from the album release party. I wonder if this has something to do with the shooting?*

She was not naïve enough to believe that his killing was random. But she declined to speculate out loud in front of her co-anchors, particularly since they didn't know she knew the man.

"Yeah, they say his whole chest was caved in," Wendy commented.

"That's what generally happens when you get shot with a sawed-off," Michael added.

"How do you know all of this?" Judy asked them.

Wendy shrugged. "I mean, they never let us deliver it all, but you know the medical reports were more detailed than this. And after a while, you just *know*."

They are so insensitive sometimes, Judy thought. *Am I that way too? God, I hope not.*

Michael noticed her concern and frowned. "Judy, what's been getting into you lately? You can't ever take this stuff too seriously.

You'll depress yourself. You have to treat the news like a doctor does new patients. Come on, you know that already. We report on people who die every day."

Wendy awaited her response. All that Judy could think about was the idea of white news versus black news that her husband had mentioned. Like Marlon said, far too much of black news was negative.

Okay, I can't get into the race thing this morning, Judy thought. *I have a job to do.*

She nodded quickly and said, "You're right. My bad." However, she was glad that Wendy was assigned to read the shooting report that morning instead of her.

"A man was shot and killed in front of a southeast Atlanta apartment building late last night. Several tenants, who heard the fatal gunshot outside their windows, said it sounded like a drive-by.

The station cut from Wendy to interview footage. "Yeah, you could hear the gunshot and car tires speed up the street," an eyewitness stated at the scene. "When I looked out my window, I could tell the guy was in bad shape. He was lying flat on his back out on the sidewalk."

Wendy continued to report, "The twenty-eight year old man has been identified as James John Pendleton, better known as J.J."

Judy followed the teleprompter anxiously awaiting a link to Shawn Blake and the nightclub shooting. That link was never made.

I'll ask Shawn about it myself as soon as I'm off the air today, she decided. First she stopped by Brenda Avant's office to check in with the veteran producer.

"Are you satisfied yet?" Brenda asked her pointedly.

Judy looked perturbed as she sat down in front of her desk. "What do you mean?"

"Have you found what you've been looking for?"

"Not yet, but I'm still working on it."

"And what exactly are you working *on?*" Brenda challenged her.

"A more introspective piece on Shawn Blake," Judy answered. "I'm trying to dig deeper to understand the news that surrounds him, particularly with Shawn as a *black man*," she emphasized for effect.

Brenda nodded. "You think that makes a difference?" she asked.

"I figured it *should*," Judy stated.

"Since when? Since when has it made a difference to *you*?"

"I mean, I've always thought about it. I just haven't talked about it much," Judy answered. "We have an objective job to do that includes *everyone*. But now I have an opportunity to do something extra, and I can't understand why I don't have your *support*.

"I'm not planning on doing anything unprofessionally. I have great *plans* for this piece," she argued. "I mean, you're the one who keeps talking about what you had to go through to earn respect for black people thirty and forty years ago, yet you chew me out about what I plan to do *now*."

Brenda paused and looked toward her open door. She wasn't expecting Judy to bring up the race issue today. She asked her, "Well, how deep do you intend to go with this? Thirty minutes? An hour?"

Judy hadn't thought about the details yet. How much time would she need to edit an introspective piece on Shawn? "Once I get everything I need, I'm sure I can tighten it up a lot more than that," she answered.

"You think you can get it down to six to eight minutes?" Brenda quizzed her.

Judy wavered. "Maybe twelve to sixteen."

"How many *hours* do you plan to put in for that?"

"Does it matter?" she snapped. "As long as I get the *story*, right? You're acting as if I don't know what I'm doing. I may not have been a news professional as long as you have, but I have put in a few years doing this. Give me a little bit of *respect*."

Brenda kept her poise and simply stared at Judy. Realizing her angry tone, Judy exhaled and calmed her nerves to apologize.

"I'm sorry. I'm just um . . . a little frustrated," she admitted.

Brenda nodded and breathed deeply herself. "We *all* are frustrated with the news," she said. "Truth is, none of us know what we're doing anymore. We just seem to be feeding a nation full of insatiable children now, children have a ruthless addiction to sour candy. I don't see how your report on Shawn Blake will amount to anything different than that."

She tossed up her hands and said, "But I don't know. Maybe you can prove me wrong."

Judy nodded back, determined. "Maybe I will."

Shawn discussed the news about their friend J.J. with Alex, who came to visit him bright and early that morning at his condo.

"You know who allowed this to happen to him, right?" Alex hinted.

Shawn sat at his dining room table in deep thought as Alex towered beside him. Loose script pages were spread out on the table in front of them.

"I was up all night studying this script for my director's meeting today. I didn't even get up to watch the news this morning until you called me," Shawn mumbled. He was exhausted, still trying to process everything.

"You doing what you need to do. I ain't mad at you," Alex told him. "I just wanted to let you know that J.'s murder wasn't an accident. Did Benny say anything to you about him before it happened last night?"

Shawn shook it off. "Not at all. We just talked about me and my career."

Alex pulled a chair out and took a seat across from him. "You know with J. out of the way like this, it clears your name from that nightclub shooting, right?"

"You're saying it was planned? Nobody pointed him out on anything," Shawn commented.

"Not yet, but we'll soon see. Watch." Alex placed his massive hands on Shawn's paperwork and added, "Just like this movie script, *everything* is planned now. Benny's more of a director than the guys you're meeting up with today. All he talks about is manipulating shit now. You notice how much he's on his cell phone? He's all about these blogs, Twitter, and all that other social media shit. Instagram."

Shawn smiled and chuckled. "Yeah, he said umm . . . my real *life* is the movie now."

Alex's face lit up with surprise. "See that? I'm telling you, man. He doing something *extra*, bro'. Benny don't have no fuckin' *hobbies*. Even the women he deals with are pawns."

Shawn shrugged. "Yeah, but he don't have no control over the media."

"Why not? If he can control what people say in your court cases, why can't he control the media?" Alex suggested.

"Come on, Al, nobody controls the media. They do what they want to do," Shawn argued.

"Not when they need *money*," his friend countered. "Think about it. They got more of these unprofessional news sites popping up every day now. They all need money to operate, right? So who's to say you can't work both sides? You pay them some money to get started, then give them articles to follow."

Shawn continued to shake it off. "You startin' to sound like these hip-hop kids, running around out here talking about the Illuminati."

Alex stared him down. "Are you saying it don't *exist*?"

"Yeah, but they're not involved in all the petty shit that these *kids* think they are. We read all about that stuff in college."

"We did too. But it's *all* connected now, man," Alex insisted. "Who would have thought that Facebook would become a billion-dollar company? I remember when that shit first started. All of a sudden, people I had never talked to before wanted to be my *'friends'* and shit. The next thing you know, this nerd-ass white boy is a billionaire.

"You think Benny don't know that?" Alex continued. "He talk

about *you* like that all the time now. And he won't let nothing happen to you. J.J. was expendable, especially with his drug issues, hot temper, and attitude."

"I got a hot temper too," Shawn responded. "We *all* got tempers. It's what growing up in the 'hood does to you."

"Yeah, but your temper creates *numbers*. That's what all this new technology is about, if you think about it—the matrix of numbers. Who controls them and who don't?"

Shawn smiled. "It sounds like you've been up all night thinking about this."

"I'm just saying, man. Look, we come from The Factory of Flint, Michigan, right? Now what happened to our city when our employment numbers went down? Every fucking thing disappeared. So when President Obama first stepped into office, what did he do? He saved the auto industry, the banks, and housing. Numbers, numbers, and *more* numbers. And the country didn't have a *choice* no matter *who* the president was."

Shawn raised his index fingers to his temples. "Yo, it's a little too early in the morning for all this, man. You making my head hurt." He stood up and said, "I need some orange juice and Tylenol now. You want something to drink?"

"Yeah, give me some water."

Shawn frowned, heading into the kitchen. "Water? That's all you want?"

Alex rubbed his big belly under a lightweight Adidas jacket. "I'm trying to lose some of these extra pounds on me, bro'."

"By drinking *water*?"

"Every li'l bit counts."

Shawn grabbed a couple of glasses and opened his refrigerator for the orange juice and water. Then he popped two Tylenols from his medicine cabinet. As soon as he brought the glasses over to the table, his cell phone rang from his pocket. He placed the drinks on the table and looked at his phone.

"Ah, it's Judy calling me."

Alex took a sip from his glass. "Yo, are you serious about her?"

"Naw, it's strictly business, man. She's good people."

His friend nodded. "Cool. I like her. She don't seem like the okey-doke."

"Naw, she's not," Shawn confirmed. Then he answered her call. "Hello."

"What more can you tell me about your friend, J.J., this morning?" Judy asked him.

Shawn paused. "Well, good morning to you too."

"I'm sorry. Good morning. It's been a long one already for both of us, I'm sure."

"I'm really just now getting up, myself. I was up all night studying this script. So I'm just now getting the news."

"You didn't watch us this morning?"

"Not until after y'all already covered it. By the time I turned my TV on, y'all were talking about the protests in Ferguson."

"Yeah, they're gonna have a trial for the police officer who shot Michael Brown coming up. It's gonna be another mess, like the Trayvon Martin case in Florida. And we still have to keep fighting in this country to tell our stories, like what I want to do with yours. What time can we link up today?" she pressed him.

Shawn looked at Alex and cringed. "Umm . . . I don't know if today is gonna be a good day. I gotta see how everyone in my team is dealing with this first. Then I have a director's meeting to prepare for."

"I understand. I apologize for being so forward this morning. I'm just eager to do a good job, that's all."

Shawn thought of another idea on the fly. "How would you umm . . . feel about interviewing my daughter's mother, Annette? She has a pretty good understanding of me."

Judy paused. "You would trust her to do that?"

Even Alex looked up in alarm from the table.

Shawn said, "You still have to validate it all through me, right? Annette could at least give you more of an understanding of where I'm coming from. That way you're still building your information on me."

"And you're sure she would agree to do that?"

"Yeah, she already asked about you from the courtroom."

"Everybody's asking about that," Judy mentioned.

"Well, let me give you her number and let her know that you'll be calling."

When Shawn hung up, Alex asked him, "Did you just do that? You gave her Annette's number to do an interview?"

Shawn shrugged. "Annette still worships me, man. And this way I get to find out what she's really thinking. Because Judy *will* tell me."

Alex nodded and grinned. "You wouldn't give her *Rhonda's* number to talk to though, right?"

"Naw, Rhonda won't even go there. They were ready to get into it in court."

"Well, what did Benny say about this reporter being around you?"

Shawn sipped his orange juice. "He's curious about it, but he didn't really say anything negative. If he's all into the media like *you* say he is, then I guess he likes it."

"I don't know about him liking *her*. She don't seem like the negotiating type."

"She negotiated with *me*."

"Yeah, you're the man she wants to deal with. She won't want to deal with Benny like that," Alex assumed. "She already has money from her regular job, right? Benny likes to deal with people in *need*."

"You got that right," Shawn admitted. "We'll see what comes out of it when we all get together tonight."

Outside Shawn's condo, not far away from where Alex had parked his black Lincoln Navigator, Detectives Todd and Weinberger sat again in their unmarked car.

"So, they all have different models of black SUVs?" Weinberger commented to her partner.

In the passenger seat, Detective Todd shuffled through a file of the entire Michigan crew—Shawn, Alex, Benny, Larry, Toot, Devon, and James John Pendleton.

"Yeah, they have a lot more affiliates to check into, but these are the main seven," Todd informed her. "Minus one, now."

"And you're saying that he's gonna be fingered as the shooter?" Weinberger questioned.

Todd stared at her, knowingly. "I keep telling you, nothing in this business surprises me anymore. I like to come up with the most obvious explanations and stick to them until I'm proven wrong. According to their records, J.J. was the most likely candidate for them to sacrifice. He's the one guy in their gang who *doesn't* drive anything. His license was revoked after numerous speeding tickets and a DUI. He also served three years in prison in Michigan for drug possession, conspiracy to distribute, and assault with an illegal firearm."

Weinberger nodded. "And what about this guy?" she asked as Alex returned to his truck, parked right out in front of them.

Detective Todd looked and shrugged. "He's pretty clean. A high school football star who played some college ball for the Michigan Wolverines in Ann Arbor. They probably have him around for his size and loyalty. You know, the big lovable bodyguard type."

Weinberger grinned. "You just place them all in a neat little cookie cutter, huh? But if *I* were to do that, as a Georgia white girl, I'd be called a stereotyping racist," she said.

Todd continued to stare at her. "In this business, stereotypes are a part of the job. Every time I tried to give someone the benefit of the doubt, whether white, black, Hispanic, or Asian, I got bit in the ass for it. So I learned not to do that anymore. But I'm glad you're still young enough to keep the faith. It serves to balance me out a bit.

"Anyway," he continued, "this guy Bernard Chavis is the obvious ringleader. At thirty-four, he's the oldest of the bunch, and he did a total of five years hard time in prison for a number of drug and weapons charges, including a bid for strong-armed robbery.

But he hasn't been in trouble for years now."

Weinberger shrugged. "Maybe he's wised up."

Todd frowned. "He's wised up, all right. That's the part I *don't* like. *Supposedly*, he's been making his money off of property, entertainment events, and other investments now. But where did he get *that* money from?"

"Maybe Shawn cut him a few checks. Isn't that what loyalty forces you to do?" Weinberger suggested.

Todd thought about that. "Of course. But it also works the other way around. If the boys in the 'hood know that a guy is about to fall into some money, they have a tendency to look out for him—especially with the older guys. This guy Benny gives me that vibe. We just gotta wait for him to make a mistake for us to prove it."

Judy made the call to Annette late that morning, hoping that Shawn had already briefed her. She even hung around the downtown area to make herself available for a possible meeting.

"Hello."

"Yes, this is Judy Pierce, calling for Annette."

"Oh, hi, this is Annette. Shawn told me you would call."

"Did I catch you at a good time?"

"It's perfect, actually. I was just about to do lunch."

"Oh yeah, where? I'm downtown now."

"Okay, I'm in the Midtown area on Peachtree. You can meet me at The Greek Cafe in . . . I don't know, ten, fifteen, twenty minutes?"

"Let's say fifteen," Judy told her. "I'll have to park."

"I know, right? But okay, I'll see you there."

Judy met up with Annette at the popular Greek restaurant near Georgia Tech University in Midtown, and they found a convenient table in the back corner of the room, where they could talk in peace. The eager newswoman wasted no time getting into the beef of their conversation over a loaded Greek salad and a Coke.

"I must admit, I was shocked to see you bring your young daughter into court like that. Did you not know it was going to be an all-out *circus*?"

Annette sighed. She was dressed professionally in a dark-blue business pantsuit. It was far from the church girl look she had worn into the courthouse.

"I try to do anything I can to help keep him out of jail," she answered. "My methods may seem extreme sometimes, but I know exactly what I'm doing."

Judy eyed her style of dress and her calm demeanor and actually believed her. Annette looked like a regal sister on a *Black Enterprise* magazine cover.

"Were you surprised by the verdict?"

"Not anymore. People are always accusing celebrities of things these days. That's just part of the territory of having fame and money. So you may as well keep your lawyers on speed dial. Then this young guy, 'Ricky Slim,' turned right around and started promoting his new album off of this, while Shawn gets arrested again. Ain't that a damn *trip*?"

Her calm logic and casual tone threw Judy off. She was expecting a wildly emotional mother who was out of touch with reality. Instead, she found the opposite: a woman who seemed to know how everything moved around her.

"So . . . what do you do exactly?" Judy asked her curiously.

"Real estate. I have my license and everything. I was told years ago that housing is the only real money that black business people understand. So, if you don't have some new reality TV show, a nine-to-five job, or a marriage to someone who's stable, then make sure you always own some houses."

Judy was speechless. She wasn't expecting that kind of wisdom from her.

"Ahh . . . so what about Rhonda? What is *her* problem?" she asked, bringing up the other mother. She wanted to create *some* kind of drama. So far, Annette's interview was proving to be anticlimactic.

"You'll have to ask *her* that question," Annette answered. "She's still stuck on her *love jones*, I guess. When I first got involved with Shawn, I was the balance-out girl. He would talk to me about everything. Over time, I just realized that we weren't going anywhere because he was so damn *selfish*. He was not really a bad man, but everything was about *him*. In a way, I can see *why* now. He has to think that way to be successful. But that's why he won't marry anybody. A lot of these guys are selfish like that now."

"What about the rumors of his domestic violence issues?"

Judy was certain she would get a rise out of that.

Annette paused to finish eating her bite of grilled chicken. She asked, "Did you see that video of Janay Rice being punched out in the elevator?"

"Far too many times for comfort," the veteran newswoman answered.

"Exactly. That's why women only bring up that kind of stuff when they absolutely *need* to, or when they're trying to get something out of it. Otherwise, why would you want the whole world to know that you got your ass kicked? So that's always a difficult issue to talk about. I'm not even involved with him like that now."

"But did he do it or not?" Judy pressed her.

"Has your man ever kicked your ass?" Annette asked her back.

Judy cringed. "Hell no. My husband knows better than that."

"Well, let's just leave it at that then. They *all* should know better."

The newswoman was stumped again. She hadn't even touched the salad that sat in front of her. "How well did you know J.J.?" she asked, changing her direction. She wasn't sure if Annette knew about his murder yet, but she assumed Annette did.

Annette went soft immediately with sad eyes and a heavy heart. "That man always needed some help, in my opinion. He just seemed so . . . *lost*, like he missed his calling or something."

"I thought he was *out there* myself," Judy interjected. "I think he was even *high* when I first met him, but I didn't necessarily read him as a bad person, just misguided."

"That's just the thing. Getting high and drunk and all of that can mask a lot of other issues. Like that Kevin Hart movie, *Laugh at My Pain*—J.J. had a lot of *pain* inside of him that he didn't know how to deal with."

"But who would want to *kill him* like that?" The question just rolled off of Judy's tongue, surprising even her. She wanted to know more about everything.

Annette shrugged. "Who knows? I thought you were here to talk about *Shawn* though. I have no idea what kind of people that man was involved with."

"You're right. That's off subject. But they're all a big part of Shawn's world. He seems to be really connected to all of his friends from Michigan. He didn't make any new friends down here in Atlanta?"

"Friends in the entertainment business, yeah. He knows all of the music, television, and film people. But who really comes to Atlanta to be involved with the regular people? We're all down here trying to do something extra. I'm originally from Memphis myself, and I thought I would have a singing career. But nope. I stopped that shit years ago. I met one too many *fools* down here that forced me to change my whole tune. Now I'm strictly about handling my own business in real estate."

Well, I definitely met her on her business grind, Judy thought. *I don't even know how much of this I can even use. She makes too much sense for television.*

"You know, you are *nothing* like I thought you would be," Judy had to admit to her.

Annette smiled, chewing on her salad. She said, "You don't have a microphone or cameras with you either. So Shawn told me to keep it all one hundred."

Judy laughed and asked her, "Do they a
Michigan?"

"The ones that I know. That's how they say *real*—one hundred. But yeah, it's very *tiring* to have to put on a show all the time for that celebrity stuff. That was another thing I didn't like about being around Shawn and trying to cut records. I just wanted to be *me*, you know? Not a 'Nutty Nettie,' but just *Annette*. But if you put a microphone and camera in someone's face, they'll turn into something else for you, especially down here in Atlanta."

"Girl, I can't agree with you *more*. Everybody wanna be somebody," Judy stated.

Annette gave her a high-five across the table. "You know? But at the same time, I learned how to do that *to get the results that I need down here*."

Her last comment struck a chord with Judy. For the rest of their conversation, Judy couldn't get that phrase out of her head.

"Do I need to plan on Shawn being so *guarded* about his life? What's the deal with that?" she asked as they wrapped it up. Judy had a plastic to-go box for her uneaten salad.

"Yeah, he's an actor for the cameras only. But *off* camera, Shawn is *all* Michigan, like, 'Who are you? I don't know you. What do you want from me?' That's just how they are. They're like, 'What's the purpose of me knowing you?' But he'll come around. He obviously trusts you. That says *a lot*."

Judy extended her hand as she stood up to pay their bill. "All right, well, we've talked for an hour. I know you have to run, but I thank you for doing this. It's given me a much clearer, mature view of who Shawn is and who he deals with."

"Yeah, but I can't speak for Rhonda," Annette reiterated. "He was dealing with her *before* me, so I guess you can say that he *learned* from it."

They shared another laugh as they headed for the door. Annette exited, but Judy didn't make it outside. The colorfully dressed blog girl had bumped into her . . . again.

"Hey, how are you? Judy Pierce, right? I'm YellowGirl1. Remember me from outside the courtroom?"

"Yeah, I remember you, but I'm on the run. I have to pick up my two kids," Judy told her.

144

"So, you're doing an in-depth story on Shawn Blake now?" the young woman pressed.

Judy froze. "Why would you think that?"

"Well, I saw you just talking to one of his baby mommas. And you were in court with him, but you weren't covering him there on camera. Sooo . . . I'm assuming you're doing something much *bigger*, right?"

"That doesn't necessarily have to be the case," Judy countered.

"Well, it's either *that* or you're getting incredibly comfortable with his *peeps* for some reason."

Judy didn't appreciate her line of logic, her rude intrusion, or her rapid-fire tongue. So she snapped, "You know what? You really need to learn some professional *manners* if you want to be a part of the real *media*. What are you, a student at Georgia Tech?"

"Grad student, actually, but thanks for the compliment. Looking mad-young keeps it all interesting."

"Well, *acting* mad-young does *not*," Judy barked at her. "So understand who can help you out here, because you'll need it one day for a real *internship*."

As Judy hit the sidewalk and marched up the street to her car, YellowGirl1 stared at her through the glass doorway in deep thought. "In-teresting," she hummed. "I must be onto something. I'll need to look more into this."

10... DEEPER AND DEEPER

Shawn took his time before calling Benny. He wanted to get all of his thoughts and information together first. By that afternoon, he had spoken to Alex, Devon, Larry, and Toot about the death of their friend. They all seemed surprised by it.

"I just dropped him off last night, man, before this shit happened," Devon said over the phone. He was stunned the most. "Had I fucking known that somebody was waiting for him last night . . . *Shit!* I'm just torn up right now, bro'. I don't even know what to say."

"I should just come down there to the hospital with y'all, man. I haven't even been out the house all day," Shawn told him.

"Naw, Benny said to leave you alone about it. We all know you 'bout to start working on that new movie. And you got cops trailing you now. So, we'll just see you at the funeral."

"What would that look like? I don't show my face until the funeral? That's crazy," Shawn complained.

"We just don't want to make it worse than it already is by getting you involved in it, bro'. You being here ain't gon' bring him back," Devon argued. "We all know you got love for J. So don't even worry about that. I'll hold it down for all of us."

"His funeral might not even be here. Won't his people want

him back home in Flint?"

"Yeah, we'll all head back home to The Factory then. That ain't no biggie."

"I just don't like this feeling, man, like y'all secluding me out or something," Shawn said. "I don't have Ebola just 'cause these cops are following me."

"But you know they're still looking for anything to pin on you. Just talk to Benny first before you make any moves. He can explain everything better than I can, especially right now. I'm just hurtin' over here."

"How are Larry and Toot taking it?" Shawn trusted Devon's opinion on the matter more than theirs. Devon was the closet to James.

"You know how Larry is, man. He ready to find out who did it. And Toot, he talkin' 'bout putting out a dedication song or some shit. But you already talked to them."

"I did, but I wanted to hear what you felt. Nobody was closer to him than you."

"Nope. But call up Benny, man. I'm assuming you haven't talked to him yet, right?"

"He hasn't come down to the hospital yet either?" Shawn quizzed him.

"Naw, he was here *first*, but he left out as soon as we got here. You know how Benny is, man. He like to overthink things. Who knows what's on his mind right now. Just call him up. I'm sure he would tell you more than he would tell us."

"Why you say that?"

"Come on, man, he love you like that. But J. . . . J.J. was startin' to fuck up too much."

Shawn was tempted to ask Devon if he felt Benny would sacrifice James to protect him against any pending murder charges like Alex had suggested, but he decided against it.

Naw, let me just talk to Benny first, he thought. "All right, I'ma call him up right now."

"Yeah, and just check in with me later on."

Shawn took a deep breath to settle his nerves before he called

Benny. "I guess I do feel like something's going on. I never feel comfortable talking to him anymore," he mumbled. "Yo, what up though, B.? You're the last person for me to talk to about J.J.'s murder last night."

"Yeah, it's fucked up, fam', but I didn't want to bother you about it today. I know what you working on."

Shawn said, "Come on, man, J. is *family*. You should've been called me today."

"Yeah, well, it's a whole lot going on in my mind right now. You didn't call me up either, so I figured that you were busy."

"I was just trying to figure everything out, that's all."

"Well . . . we gon' do the funeral back home in Flint next week. I've already been on the line, talking to his people."

Shawn nodded. "That was fast."

"What do you mean?"

"You already making funeral arrangements?"

"Well, what do you think happens when people die? You think you got a *month* to do it?"

"Naw, but I figured his family would handle all that."

"They gon' handle some of it, but he down here with us, so I had to get it started. That's just taking care of your responsibility. I gotta get him back home first."

"I guess you would have to do my funeral too then, huh?" Shawn cracked.

Benny paused. "Yo, what's this about, man? I always take care of y'all. What other family you got back at home, distant cousins? What they ever do for you but jump on the bandwagon once we got it started? What, you forgot? I keep telling you, man, it's us against the world out here. We all we got. Hollywood don't care about us unless we making them money. Even then they don't care. It's the *people* who buy the tickets."

Shawn heard that and knew he was barking up the wrong tree. Benny had a way of making him feel guilty after looking out for him. Guilt was how he secured his loyalty. So once again, Shawn backed down from a confrontation with him.

"It's all good, man. Everybody's a little stressed right now."

"That's why I told them to leave you alone. You got that director's meeting coming up today, right?"

Shawn looked down at his watch. "Yeah, in another hour."

"That's what you need to be focusing on. You being distracted ain't gon' make J. come back to life. The best thing you can do now is use it for a stronger performance. Dedicate this new movie to our man J. You feel me?"

Shawn was speechless. Benny had a way with words indeed."Yeah, I hear you, bro'."

Benny paused again. "There's a big difference between *hearing me* and *feeling me*, Shawn. Black people want to *feel you*, not just *hear you*. They love you when they can *feel you*, but when they only *hear you*, they ignore your ass. Make sure you remember that. You gotta make the people *feel you* more in this next movie. The news about you got 'em wide open now."

Shawn couldn't help himself. He smiled and asked, "What, you read that somewhere?"

Instead of being offended or defensive, Benny answered him calmly. "You'd be surprised, bro'. I actually read a lot now, as much as *you* do. Reading kills a lot of the extra noise around me so I can think straight. That's why I don't want them bothering you when you're reading."

"Yeah, I feel you," Shawn said.

"That's what I'm talking about, right there," Benny told him, excitedly. "Have a good meeting with that director today. Let me handle everything else. That's what good management is for."

Shawn hung up the line and felt more confused than ever. He felt duped, emasculated, and angry. He stared into empty space and growled, "Damn! This motherfucker ain't no *manager*. He's a *conman*. He's *good* at it too."

Still angry with himself after a cowardly exchange with Benny, Shawn gave the gray-haired and energetic movie director a passionate and fiery script read in his living room.

150

"I would *never* do that to you. I'm offended that you would even *say that* to me. I love you more than you could ever imagine. But you can't *see it*. You can't *feel it*. And you only hear what you want to hear. So I'm *tired*. I'm just tired of caring anymore."

The director flipped through his script while seated on the sofa. He looked for the words Shawn had just delivered and couldn't find them.

"I added some of that in," Shawn told him. "I needed to put some more *teeth* in it."

The gray-haired director nodded, enthused. "Jesus! Well that was *great*! That was very passionate, Shawn. We'll have to add some of that."

"Thank you. I've been working on it."

"I can see that. It's a good thing too, because you're gonna have to blow this role out the ballpark. This film could really catapult your career to that next level. We're talking Denzel Washington here."

Shawn shook his head and chuckled. "No offense, Eddie, but you white guys are gonna have to find another name outside of *Denzel Washington* to compare us all to," he commented, while forming quotation marks with his hands.

"Yeah, like *who*?" Eddie challenged him. "We're talking *serious* acting here, Shawn, not comedies. Denzel is one of the few black men that even *white* women are moved by. That's where we need *you* to go with this. So, we've decided to change the script a little.

"We wanna make the antagonist a rich white guy now. And we want to have you die as a result of an accidental shooting. Or maybe not *die*, but almost die, you know? We want more sympathy for your character."

Shawn froze. The climactic scene from the critically acclaimed film *Fruitvale Station* came to mind. "So, you want the people to cry for me?" he asked.

The director grinned at him and opened his palms. "We're seeing eye to eye on this, Shawn. I *love it*. The climate in America is just right for it."

"But haven't they seen that before with *Fruitvale Station?*"

"Yeah, and it *worked.* Michael B. Jordan is getting called for lots of new *crossover* roles now. So if we can really get the audience to sympathize with you, you can grab them by the balls for a major upswing in your career."

Shawn nodded and took a seat next to him to think. "If I go in that direction, I would have to change the kind of movies I make, right?"

Eddie read his concern and sighed. "Shawn, I have to level with you. I've had to fight tooth and nail to keep you attached to this project. I'm not gonna lie to you about that. With your name in the news so much, a few of our producers have been looking at you as a loose cannon, a time bomb."

"So, it's hurt me more than helped, huh?"

Eddie wavered. "Not necessarily. My point is, you could *use* some of that recognition to give the audience a bigger piece of you on screen. Adding the necessary *teeth* to the role is important. I also like the sympathy we could generate from black injustice in America right now. We want to use that to our advantage as well."

Shawn smiled. "And make the people feel me more, right?"

"Exactly."

Shawn shook his head and laughed again.

"What's so funny?"

"I just had that same conversation an hour ago. It's funny to hear you saying it too."

"Yeah, it's true. It's about *more* than just acting. You want to use this film to put an imprint on people's minds, and that's done more *emotionally* than it is intellectually, particularly for actors. Directors get kudos for how intellectual a film is, but you guys have to draw on the emotional connection. I really think you can do that here."

"So, I'm no longer the bad guy?"

Eddie negotiated his words. "Well, you still have an *edge* to you. We don't want you to change that. But we want you to play it more *conflicted* rather than *sinister.* You know what I mean? We want more Two-Face and less Joker."

"I know exactly what you mean," Shawn told him. "That's like my real life right now. I'm caught in between two extremes and flipping coins to figure this shit out."

"Well, just make sure that coin lands on *heads* every time," Eddie joked.

"I know, right?" Shawn agreed. "I need to keep winning."

That night at home, Judy pulled all of her facts together and went to present them to her husband in the den. Marlon was still refusing to return to their bedroom, so she had decided to come to him. She plopped down next to him on the sofa and said, "Okay, so, I met up with his daughter's mother today over lunch, and this woman was straight *business*. There was nothing crazy about her at all. She's into Atlanta real estate."

Marlon eyed his wife peacefully. "Judy, everybody's straight business now. Television makes them *look* crazy to make money. These people know *exactly* what they're doing."

"Yeah, but his son's mother, Rhonda, she really *is* crazy."

"Did you talk to her too?"

"Not yet, but I can imagine. She was ready to come at me inside the courtroom."

"Because she's not getting the kind of money she wants yet," Marlon concluded. "Obviously, the second woman is smarter. She's making her own money now. So, she doesn't have a *reason* to be vengeful. But the first mother is still trying to figure out how she wants to deal with her own life and finances, because he's not in it anymore. And all of her frustrations are making her act out."

"That's a very clear way of looking at it."

"It's the *only* way to look at it. That's what's going on," Marlon insisted. As he spoke, his cell phone lit up again. He had it face-down on the sofa, but Judy could still tell when a new message or call came in.

"Are you gonna answer that?"

"Are you gonna bring your work home to talk about every night, even though I don't agree with it?" he countered.

"I asked you first."

Marlon exhaled. "Why are you bothering me right now?"

"Why am I *bothering you*? You're my *husband*. I'm trying to *talk* to you."

"About your *work* with some guy that I don't want to hear about. What don't you understand about that? Yet you keep bringing it up to me."

"Because I want you to know that everything is all right. I didn't even see him today."

"It doesn't matter if you saw him or not, you're still talking about him. You're trying to pitch me a damn *soap opera* every night now. I don't wanna hear it."

"You're not gonna distract me from what's going on with your *phone*, Marlon. Now I will give you my damn phone because I don't have anything *extra* going on. But I can't say the same about *you*, can I? Are you cheating on me?"

Despite her tough woman stance, Judy's heart was beating like crazy. She had been telling herself not to ask him that question. Lord *knows* she didn't want to hear the wrong answer from him. But in anger, the question had jumped out of her mouth, so she was forced to deal with the anxiety of receiving a reply that might make her explode.

"No," Marlon barked at her. "When, where, and how? I just don't feel like talking about your *work* every night."

Judy exhaled. "So, you're talking to another woman about something else? Because it's *obvious* you don't want me to see whose calling and texting you at this time of night."

"And what if I was? You would want to divorce me for that?"

"Nobody said anything about a divorce."

"That's what people do. You get into any friction at home, and they start dialing up the lawyers."

Judy faced him and snapped, "Marlon, don't you do that. Don't you *dare* fucking do that to me! You do *not* compare me to that *bullshit* out there! I didn't say anything about a *divorce*. That's *crazy*! Is that what *you* want? Just because I wanted to do something more with my career?" Again, her heart started to race.

Marlon could read the pain and hurt in her eyes and hear it in her voice. He shook his head and backed down. "I don't feel that way at all. I just feel . . . disrespected right now."

Judy calmed down and continued to work it all out in her mind. Her husband was forcing her to wrangle with a tough decision. "Marlon, you know that I've never backed down from anything . . . but if that's what you want me to do . . ."

Tears began to build up in her eyes. One drop escaped, and she wiped it away. Marlon found himself forced to make a tough decision as well.

He looked at his wife and mumbled, "I don't want this to look like I'm *forcing* you not to do what you want to do."

"But you *are*," Judy argued. "That's why I talk to you so much about it, so you'll know what I'm doing every step of the way. It's important to me that you *trust me* on this. It's nothing like what you think it is."

He glanced at the television before looking back into her pained eyes. "I need you to trust me too then. There's nothing going on. It's only talk."

Judy paused, trying her hardest to let it slide, but couldn't. "Talk about what?" she asked.

Marlon shrugged, irritated by his revelation and the difficulty of the truth. "Just regular life stuff, Judy—funny and simple shit. You don't even do that anymore. Everything is straight business with you too now."

Judy frowned and felt defensive. "Well, it's not like *you've* been a ball of fun either lately. You come home every night and act like you don't want to be bothered with me. So it goes both ways. You have to *be* fun to *get* fun. I try a lot more than *you* do."

He shook his head, worn out from the discussion. "All right, we both got stuff to work on. So we'll work on it."

Judy continued to think about her husband's cell phone and his fun conversations with another woman, but she decided to call a truce. There was only so much truth that she could take in one night.

At least he's not cheating on me . . . yet. I'll need to deal with that real soon. I just have to get my mind back together now . . . and get some rest.

She stood up from the sofa and made her way back to the door. Then she stopped and looked back at him. "I wish *I* was still fun," she said with emphasis on her way out.

Marlon sat on the sofa and cracked a grin, like an adolescent boy. He knew good and well he couldn't deny his wife that evening. She hit him with just the right amount of charm and vulnerability to cut open his hard shell. He had gotten what he wanted from her that night, or at least *partially*. He had broken Judy down a bit from her high horse, and it was time for him to treat her for it. Maybe she would remember for next time.

He grabbed the remote control and mumbled, "Yeah, let me go on in there with her," before he turned everything off.

Alex arrived at The Factory Studio that evening to meet up with the remaining Michigan crew, all except for Shawn. He was determined to give Benny a piece of his mind in front of everyone.

"I know how you think, bro'," Alex told him. "So I'm not putting J.'s death past you. And we can keep it all in the family and all that, but I don't appreciate one of our own being allowed to go out like that, man. That was *fucked up!*"

No one spoke up as Benny responded. "Look, we all hurting right now, Al. But I can't protect y'all every minute of the day. Shit happens, man. If they knew where J. lived and were laying low to get him, then what do you want me to do? I don't have ESP to know everything. So we all gotta deal with it now."

"How do we know somebody else won't be next?"

Benny shook his head in their small, private meeting room. "You can't allow yourself to get all paranoid, Al. You too big for that shit."

Larry smiled and caught Alex's eye.

"Ain't shit in here funny, L. You think this a fuckin' *joke?*"

Devon had to step in between them. "Calm down, Al. Nobody

feels worse than me about this shit, man. But us fighting each other won't do no good."

"I'm just saying how ironic it is that J. goes out like that right after these cops start following Shawn around. I mean, that shit sounds a little too convenient to me, man," Alex insisted.

Benny frowned at him. "So, what are you saying? You think *Shawn* had something to do with this? Come on, man, that's crazy."

"J. was always hatin' on Shawn anyway. Let's just be honest," Toot interjected.

"That don't mean shit," Devon snapped at him. "Fuck you talkin' 'bout? We all *family*. That music shit done went to your head."

"Clearly," Larry agreed. "This ain't no album beef. This is real fuckin' life."

Alex couldn't believe his ears. They were all heading in the wrong direction off of Benny's clever insinuation. "I didn't say shit about Shawn setting him up. Benny said that shit."

"Didn't you say it was ironic? Fuck you bring that up for then?" Benny challenged him. "You know something we don't know?"

All of a sudden, all eyes were on Alex, and not in a good way. It forced him to explain himself. "All I'm saying is that we all know J. was the shooter at that after-party. So, if the cops and the news are all trying to put Shawn's name in it, then it makes sense for J. to take the fall for it to protect Shawn."

Devon looked sharply at Benny. Alex was on point.

Benny said calmly, "You're assuming we're the only ones who *know* that J. pulled the trigger. But if somebody else out there saw him do it, you really think they care about pinning it on Shawn like the cops and the media?"

Benny paused to let everyone think about that. "Real-ass gangstas don't care about that celebrity news shit. They just want *revenge*, bro'."

"They know they can't go after Shawn like that anyway. That's a much harder fuckin' target," Larry added.

Devon looked back at Alex for his counter. Benny and Larry both made sense.

"That's my *point*," Alex responded. "This all went down too easy for comfort. That's all I'm saying. This shit just don't feel right."

Devon looked back at Benny, still trying to figure out what to believe.

Benny said, "So, you want to come back here and blame that shit on us? After how long we been together? Does that make sense to you, Al? *Really?*"

All eyes were on Alex again. He no longer had a response.

Benny shook his head in disappointment and spoke to wrap things up. "Like I said, we all hurtin' right now. But this ain't the time for us to start pulling apart. We gotta stick together. Shawn ain't here with us tonight because I told him not to come. He already got too much on his mind as it is. He need to focus on that movie shit. We all know that.

"Not only that," Benny continued, "we already know that if the cops are following him around, waiting for him to fuck up, then they're following *us* too. And you know we don't need that shit. None of us. So, he need to stay away from *all* of us for a while, until we see how this shit go down."

Devon nodded, temporarily satisfied with Benny's logic. Alex wasn't. Nevertheless, it didn't make sense to keep arguing about it if the others didn't believe him. So he kept his silence for the moment.

Yeah, we'll see, Alex thought. *It'll all come out soon.*

11... PIECES COMING TOGETHER

Marlon read it first at UPS headquarters after he was bounced a link to the *American Celebrity Media* website. There was a source in Atlanta claiming that Shawn Blake's friend James "J.J." Pendleton had been killed in retribution for the murder of Anthony "Tone" Jacobs on the early morning of Sunday, October 26th. The source further claimed that Blake was never implicated in the murder. It was supposedly all media hype planted by the Atlanta Police.

Marlon read the full article on his smartphone and shook his head. "Okay, now someone's working overtime to get him off," he said to himself as he walked into a restroom at work.

This stuff is way too easy, Marlon thought. *I'll let Judy bring this up tonight and see what she has to say about it. I'll just act like I don't know anything.*

At the downtown Atlanta precinct, Police Chief Clarence Wallace called Detectives Todd and Weinberger into his office and closed the door to discuss their case. He was a robust black man with a healthy head of dark hair, cut sharply like a military vet. The two detectives took a seat in the pair of chairs that faced his desk while the chief stood tall behind it. He tossed a printout of website reports in front of them.

"Have you read this?"

Todd leaned forward to take a look before peeking over at Weinberger. Weinberger smiled. She didn't need to look. She already knew what was coming.

"Yeah, we read about it," Todd answered.

The chief sighed. "This celebrity news shit is a real pain in the ass. That damn report is on five or six different websites already. How do they keep managing to get this stuff?"

"They pay for it," Weinberger answered casually.

"Hell, they don't even have to pay for it now," said Todd. "When one of these so-called *sources* comes forward with groundbreaking news, they become celebrities overnight themselves now."

"Well, I want these sources *found* and brought in," Chief Wallace barked. "*Immediately*. This shit makes us look like *fools*. What's next, criminals getting paid to confess their crimes to websites too? That should be unconstitutional.

"It's one thing to pay for videos and celebrity pictures, but once these guys start paying people for tips on criminal information, that's something totally different," the chief continued. "Now they're allowing some damn *source* to accuse us of framing the news. I had a bad feeling about this as soon as all of those people came forward on the night of the first murder. It seemed like they all just wanted to be out in front of a camera.

"So, what's this kid been up to lately?" he finally asked them of Shawn Blake. "Any leads?"

Weinberger shook her head. "He's been all work and no play."

"Yeah, we'd be better off following the other guys at this point. He's trying to be a choir boy now," Todd added.

"Maybe you all should have thought about that before you made that loud splash out in front of the courtroom," the chief said.

Todd looked confused. "You said it was a good idea to see if we could get him to crack."

"Well, maybe you should have told me I was *wrong*," Chief Wallace countered. "Public shame doesn't seem to embarrass these people anymore. I figured it would at least hurt his pockets, with folks being afraid to hire him for new film roles, or something."

"Or, it could make him more popular for easier marketing," Weinberger suggested.

The chief shook his head. "I want this *source* and the shooters *found*. So get right on that and give our movie star a longer leash to let him make some mistakes again. He might come out of hiding to celebrate. So back off him a minute."

"Yes, sir," Todd answered, rising to his feet with his partner. "It'll all come out in the wash. It always does."

Alex flipped his wig when he saw the latest blog and social media reports. He stopped everything and called Shawn right away. "Now what?" he said over the phone. "I *told you*, bro'. This shit is too predictable. The only problem is, that's the same thing Benny's gonna say. It's like, too simple to make any sense, right?"

Shawn leaned back in bed, listening. He was barely up after another long night. His beautiful, half-naked companion brought a glass of orange juice from the kitchen, wearing nothing but his crisp white T-shirt. He took the glass and nodded toward her, taking a sip before he responded to Alex.

"Yeah, I heard about it. But I don't know what to say about it yet."

"How'd you hear about it?"

"Toot text me a link about it earlier. Then I searched it online."

"Wait a minute. *Toot* hit you up this morning? Of *all* people, right? That boy ain't cared about nothing but his album for the last couple of months. I don't even think he *cares* about J. getting blasted. He started talking about how y'all didn't get along the other night."

"He said that?" Shawn asked curiously. His companion began to rub his manhood under the sheets, but he stopped her to concentrate on his phone call.

"Yeah, Toot was all about the friction, not the love. So hearing that he was the first one to call you up about it sounds fishy to me too."

Shawn shook his head and didn't bother to respond to him. Instead, he said, "I'm just trying to focus back on my work these days, man. The director Eddie Sankosky told me the other day that he made some changes to the script to try and make me a major star now. He even accepted the changes I wanted to make."

"Man, that's all good," Alex said. "I ain't mad at it. You *need* to reach that next level."

"Yeah, but then he started talking that Denzel Washington shit again. That's like the only black actor they really respect."

"Yeah, nobody's on Denzel's level, not even them white boys. He murders all of 'em now. But it's good to see you back doing your thing, man."

"You ready to fly back home to Flint for the funeral?" Shawn asked him, changing the subject. He wasn't up for another long conversation.

"Yeah, we not flying in the same plane as Benny, right?" Alex asked. "Toot and Devon not flying at all. They want to drive in that orange Lambo. I don't agree with that shit either. That's way too much attention. But that's what Benny's allowing them to do."

Shawn grumbled, "I'ma hit you back later, man. I'm still try'na rest up over here."

"All right, I'll talk to you later then, bro'. Go ahead and get your rest."

When he hung up, Shawn's female companion said with fascination, "Your life is so full and different. It's very interesting."

Shawn eyed her wearily. "Trust me, a lot of people may *think* they want to be in this life, but this shit is like walking on a giant eggshell, where every day you feel like it's ready to crack wide open and you'll fall in the yolk and drown."

His pretty companion stared at him with sparkling bright eyes and wild hair. "That's deep." She didn't know what else to say. She was just happy to be there to share quiet moments with him. In fact, she felt inspired to reach out and hold him, to show her full dedication.

"Anytime you need me . . . I'm here for you. I mean that."

She had all of the sincerity of the world in her starstruck eyes, but Shawn looked away, not wanting to make that connection. He didn't want to commit himself to the lie that he cared about her. He had too much going on. He at least wanted to thank her for her support though. He felt it was the right thing to do. So he looked back into her eyes and said, "Thank you. I appreciate that."

By the time Judy and her co-anchors were off the air that morning, the web reports on James "J.J." Pendleton's death as retribution had spread everywhere, including the comments that Shawn Blake was not implicated in the murder.

Bob Truesdale read the reports himself and called Judy into his office to have her explain what was happening with her story. He was definitely more pressed about it than he had been before.

"Where are you with your report? Has he opened up to you yet?"

"He had been, but then this murder happened with his friend, and he's had to do some script readings this week with the director of a new film he's slated to star in that goes into production in January," Judy rambled. She felt incompetent, but there was nothing she could do to speed up the pace.

"So, you haven't had access to him?" her boss concluded.

She thought about bringing up her conversation with Annette, but she knew it wasn't what Bob wanted to hear. Instead, she told him, "As a matter fact, I plan to call him to meet for lunch today."

"That sounds as if you don't have an appointment already," Bob countered.

"Well, yeah, I have to wait and see what his day looks like."

Bob folded his hands on his desk while eying Judy doubtfully. "This isn't going the way you expected, is it?"

Judy sighed and spoke the truth. "It's taking *longer* than I expected, yes. But I *do* have his trust and confidence, and he has warmed up to me. He's even allowed me to meet up with his daughter's mother over lunch the other day in Midtown."

"Oh really? What did she have to say?"

Judy cringed. "Not anything that would move the needle of the ratings. There was no drama with her at all. She's a very sound and logical woman, who only plays the role of a single mother in distress when she *needs* to. Apparently, she does well for herself by selling real estate in the area."

Bob exhaled and leaned back in his chair, restless. "I'm starting to get the feeling that Shawn is a very well-protected man. I've seen cases like this before with several American stars, not only in film and television, but in sports and music too. The powers behind them make sure they remain on track. So, we'll just have to wait it out a little longer and see what happens. I still have a bundle of faith in you."

Judy smiled, but she didn't particularly like his choice of words. "Thank you," she told him graciously. *But a bundle runs out though, doesn't it? How come he just didn't say he has faith in me, period? Anyway . . . I know what I have to do.*

"It's getting really hard these days to compete with the obscene methods of *American Celebrity Media* and the gossip sites," Bob said. "The one thing traditional news stations have over these guys are the interview features. Most real stars won't talk to these salacious bloggers and carnivorous websites. I was hoping your new model of insight could give us a leg up on the competition. You know, like a *Barbara Walters Special* or *Oprah* even."

Judy heard him loud and clear. *Get the story done by any means necessary!*

"That's the general idea," she said, agreeing with him. "I just have to make it happen."

With his point made, Bob changed the focus of the conversation. "How's everything at home with your family?"

Judy shrugged. "We're good. How's your family?"

"Stressed over money," he answered surprisingly.

Judy was stunned by his honesty. *Do I go in on that or leave it alone?* "What, you all don't have enough?" she joked.

Bob sighed. "Apparently not. My son wants me to invest in a new technology project he's involved in, and my daughter wants me to help her to make hundreds of thousands of dollars' worth of improvements to her vacation home in Myrtle Beach. I told her only if she rents it out for nine months with a management firm. But she doesn't want to."

Judy nodded. She didn't know how to respond. "It'd be nice to have that problem."

Her boss chuckled. "My wife just wants me to pay up, but we don't have it to spare right now."

Okay, I'm definitely not going in on that, Judy warned herself. She nodded and sat there silently, waiting for him to dismiss her or change the subject.

Instead, he asked her, "What about you? Do you have family members who are always in need of money?"

As an only child, Judy could only think of her mother. "Ahhh, I basically give my mom and dad whatever they want. They spoiled me as a child growing up, so I like to spoil them as an adult to show my appreciation."

Bob nodded. "That's good. As long as they're not asking you to buy them a new million-dollar home, right?" he joked.

Judy laughed with him. "No, they're not doing any of that. I've actually been *blessed* with parents who are very self-sufficient and supportive. They both like to work, and they don't ask me for much."

Finally, Bob was ready to let her go. "All right, well, you get back out there and do the best you can. That's all we can ask of you."

"I'm on it."

"All right, well, good luck."

Judy couldn't wait to leave his office. "Shit," she grumbled to herself down the hall. She was ready to call Shawn Blake and force the issue. Things were getting crucial.

Why would he talk to me about his money and family issues? she wondered about her boss. *Does that mean he trusts me more now, or is he sending me a message not to fuck this up?*

"Shit," she cursed herself again.

On cue, Brenda Avant made eye contact with her from the hallway.

Okay, I don't have time for her sour grapes this morning, Judy thought.

"Hey, Brenda, I'm on my way out," she announced.

"I can see that."

Judy smiled and kept it moving. As soon as she was alone in her car, she jumped on her phone to call Shawn.

"You are *not* getting off the hook today, mister," she prepped herself as the line rang.

"Hello," he answered sheepishly.

"We need to meet up for lunch today. *Seriously.* There's just too much going on with you now to discuss. And good morning. I hope you've had a good night's sleep."

Shawn laughed. "Aw'ight, I feel you. I could use an update myself. Let's say we meet at one o'clock."

"Same place?"

"Naw, at a coffee shop closer to me in Buckhead."

"Oh, okay. That's better for me to get back home afterwards."

"Good. I'll text you the address."

"*Please* don't be late," she pressed him. "I have to pick up my kids afterwards."

"I'll surprise you," Shawn responded.

Judy pulled up in the small parking lot of a coffee and bakery shop in the affluent neighborhood at a quarter to one. She was shocked to see how empty the place was at lunchtime.

"Oh, wow, this is a nice little hideaway," she noted as she climbed out of her car. She was further impressed to find Shawn already seated at a table in the back.

"Oh, my God! I'm in *heaven*," she exclaimed as she walked back to join him.

Shawn stood up to greet her with a hug. "I told you I'd surprise you."

"So, why have we been meeting at the other place?"

"I know it better. I'm just trying this place out. I heard it can get crowded in here."

Judy sat down at the small table and got straight to business. "Okay, so, what's going on? Have you read all these new reports online?"

Shawn exhaled. "It's all crazy, man. I gotta fly back home this weekend for the funeral."

Judy's eyes popped open with concern. "That's why I needed to talk to you. You can't keep stalling the process, Shawn. Every time something new happens, it makes me look unprofessional, like I'm a damn *groupie* and not doing anything."

Shawn smiled. "Naw, you're not a groupie. Everybody knows you're a pro."

"But I don't have any *results* yet. So when you get back from Flint next week, I'm ready to do this, Shawn. That's all one hundred," she told him.

He heard that and laughed hard. "I see you've been hanging around my people."

"Yeah, but I'm still not getting what I need from *you*. They all say you trust me now, so what's the problem? Let's just set this up and go with it. If we need to create a script to stick to, like a movie, then let's do that. But I need to have *something* on camera *soon*."

Shawn grinned as if her urgency were humorous. "Your producers are on your ass now, huh? 'Where *is it?*' " he cracked, mocking urgency.

Judy stared him down across the table. "This is not a fucking *game*, Shawn," she snapped. "I've gone out of my comfort zone to follow you around and meet with you, and even met up with your baby momma, while you're still toying with my *time*. And I don't appreciate it.

"And to answer your question, it's *more* than just my producers on me; it's my *boss* on my ass. The owner of the company wants it. You promised me you would *do it*. So now you got my ass all out at work with no skirt on. Do you know what they do to women on the job with their asses out and no skirts? They fuck you. They don't give you money like they do at the strip club. No, they fuck you or fire you at the job and most of the time, *both*. Then they don't have to worry about the guilt of seeing you around every day."

The middle-aged blonde, who worked part time at the Buckhead coffee shop, overheard Judy from behind the counter and thought, *Jesus Christ! But that's true. That's what they do to us.*

Embarrassed, Shawn looked the woman straight in her eyes and grinned at her. Then he looked back across the table and lowered his tone. "You got missing marbles, man. That's why I like you, though. You don't take no prisoners. But what I have to tell you right now is off the record. Okay?"

"This has *all* been off the record. I haven't reported anything."

"All right, keep your cool. I don't need you making another scene in here," he warned her.

Judy held up her open palms for forgiveness. "Okay, I apologize. You just really got under my skin with your little joke. But I'm fine now."

Shawn leaned in closer to speak with confidentiality. "Aw'ight, well . . . with all that's been going on, my boy Alex, the big dude, he's been talking all this craziness about Benny controlling the media to blow up my career. Can you actually do something like that?"

Judy leaned back and thought about Shawn's question. Then she leaned forward to speak. "Well, we've been called the Fourth Estate because we're supposed to be out of reach of influence from government, business, or the general public. But let me tell you, with all these new websites, blogs, and webzines or whatever, we don't really know what their standards of ethics are. A lot of them are able to slip in under the guise of presenting, quote-unquote, *entertainment* news. So they'll turn around and report some nonsense from unknown *sources* and call it *entertainment* to prevent getting sued. The real news media can't get away with that. We would find ourselves in trouble with the FCC, the journalism code of ethics, and everything else. No one would take us seriously anymore.

"So, *technically*, your friend can't control the *real* media, but with all this other stuff going on that influences public opinion, it ultimately affects us all anyway. So in a roundabout way, he *can* control the people's *perception*, which means everything now. I've even heard of people calling the paparazzi on purpose to follow celebrities to create more news. Then these people act like it's such an atrocity.

"*Please*. They know they're getting free media attention," Judy went on. "The paparazzi are a new form of marketing now. So yeah, Alex is right. If you have the right contacts, manipulation can happen all day long. And these people get *paid* for it."

Shawn nodded and leaned back in his chair to take everything in.

"Why? Is that what you think is going on?" Judy asked. She was thinking fast now herself. She thought back to what Annette had told her: *I try to do anything I can to help keep him out of jail.*

"Let me ask you something. Did you get Annette involved in real state?" Judy questioned.

Shawn shook it off. "Naw, she did that on her own."

"With money that *you* gave her? Because she never really said that."

Shawn paused to consider her suggestion. "You're saying that she got the money from somewhere else?"

"Does she know Benny and have a relationship with him? She knows the rest of your guys, right? Would Benny give her any keep-quiet money? He *is* the businessman of the group, right? Or are *you* giving everybody money?"

Judy was going a mile a minute with her questions while reflecting on a half-dozen ideas her husband had alluded to.

"Damn, slow down a minute," Shawn said. "Of course she knows Benny. But she didn't like him. Just like you don't."

"Or, is she only *acting* as if she doesn't like him? I was shocked that she didn't hold more animosity towards you."

Shawn frowned. "Naw, she's cool with me and all, but she definitely has her blowups. Don't let all that businesswoman shit fool you."

"That's my point, though. She's originally from Memphis, right? She told me that she learned how to do what she needs to do to get the results she needs *down here*. That means *acting*. A lot of people do that in Atlanta."

Shawn shrugged. "That's how America is in general. Everybody fakes it now."

"Do people fake it like that in Michigan?" Judy challenged him.

Shawn had to pause again. He shook it off and said, "Naw, not in Michigan. You don't have anywhere to go to fake it. Everybody knows you up there. You are who you are."

"That's how it is in Indianapolis too. But if we're gonna call Atlanta the new Black Hollywood, then you tell me what's going on. This place has the most black reality TV shows than any other city in the country."

Shawn chuckled to lighten up the mood again. "You fake it down here on your job too."

"Yeah, on my *job*, but not in my real *life*," Judy insisted. "Think about it. Why are you even sitting here with me, Shawn? Because I keep it *real*, right? Otherwise, you wouldn't trust me. So, come on, let's do it already."

Shawn nodded. It was time for him to give up the goods.

"Aw'ight, as soon I get back . . . we'll set that up."

"Thank you," Judy said. "But can we at least get back to your childhood years, while we're sitting here? I at least need to know that much about you before you head back up to Michigan."

Shawn sighed. "I basically had to do a lot on my own. I had to figure it all out before I became a teenager. I didn't have a supportive family like that, so a lot of things I had to do were out of necessity.

"I wasn't no bad kid," he pleaded. "I just didn't have no other options. It was either survive or go under."

"Survive by doing what?"

Shawn spewed from across the table, "You know what we gotta do out there. You're not naïve!"

"But are you willing to tell me that on camera?"

"Like a confession? Come on, man. Is that what you expect me to do?"

"I mean, it's all in the past now, right? Or is it?"

"It doesn't matter if it's in the past or not. Some people can't take the *truth* like that. I feel like I'm in the prime of my career, ready to break out in a new film. *Shiiiddd*, you're not getting any confessions like that from me."

Judy responded, "A lot of black men were out there in the streets and turned their lives around. Look at all these rappers who were previously drug dealers."

"Yeah, on a *record*. Ask me how many I believe. That's why these smart rappers don't do that shit anymore. You don't make no money in jail."

"What about your friend, *Toot*?"

"What about him? This ain't his interview. And he don't rap about *trapping*. He made sure we kept his album all about ho'ing, flossing, partying, and the daily grind."

Judy grinned. "Well, isn't that nice of him?"

"Yeah, we don't want that shit coming back on me. You know how the media do me. *You* included."

"I was just doing my job, Shawn. But this is different. You'll have a chance to really impress the public with your story and get them to accept it."

"Yeah, that's what you *say*. But you can't predict these people."

"I mean, come on, Shawn. How bad can it be? You still ended up graduating from MSU, right? How many guys off the street can claim that?"

"That's because I was smart," Shawn boasted.

Judy didn't expect to hear that from him. Obviously, the man was talented, but looking at the group of guys he hung out with, boldly claiming his intelligence didn't strike her as something he would readily do. Once she had been around him long enough, Shawn seemed more apologetic about his position than boastful, especially in regards to his relationship with Benny. He seemed passive even. So she asked him about that.

"Is that what you say around your friends?"

He immediately backed down. "Naw. You don't try to show up your people like that, you know?"

"That's how you really feel though."

Before Shawn could answer, a customer in line at the counter recognized him. "Oh my God! Shawn Blake! Someone told me you lived in this area. I love *all* your movies."

In a hot second, the full-bodied African-American woman in her thirties was all over Shawn and Judy's small table. Shawn looked up, smiled, and nodded. "Thank you."

Then she recognized Judy. "Oh, my *God*! Aren't you Judy Pierce from the cable morning news?"

"Yes," Judy confirmed. "Nice to meet you."

All of a sudden, a crowd of late-lunch customers in the shop were all paying attention. With her back turned to the front door, Judy hadn't noticed them until it was too late. Before she knew it, the woman was asking them both to take pictures.

"You don't mind, do you?"

Judy looked at Shawn, knowingly.

Now I know why you like the other place, she thought. *This is not gonna work.*

12... CHAOS

A few tips to the Atlanta police led them straight to the seedy apartment complex in Decatur, where they could find the three suspects from the recent shooting. Eight squad cars pulled up with more than a dozen armed officers from Atlanta and DeKalb County, all wearing bulletproof vests, including Detectives Todd and Weinberger.

"All right, we don't need any loose cannons," Todd announced. "We have other residents to consider, including children and the elderly. Okay? This is *not* an abandoned building."

The racially mixed group of officers all agreed with his directions and prepared themselves for an organized raid. They separated into four smaller teams to cover three exit stairwells and the main elevators of the four-story complex. The remaining officers were stationed outside the building to provide additional cover, in case the suspects attempted to jump out of the windows.

Inside the barren third-floor apartment, Che, Marcus, and a friend watched music videos on a flat-screen television in the living room. With two sofas, a coffee table, video games, DVDs, and plates of old food and drinks spread around the room, it looked like a college dorm. The three of them passed around a thick-rolled blunt of marijuana, while Dave, the grizzle-haired older man, made himself a turkey sandwich in the kitchen.

His cell phone went off in his pocket as he spread mustard on white bread with a butter knife.

Dave stopped to pull the phone out of his pocket. "Hello."

"Yo, dawg, I don't know if they coming after you, but it's cops all over your building right now."

Dave casually walked over to the window and looked through the cheap egg-colored blinds. "Oh, shit," he commented, keeping his cool. "Thanks. I wish you would have called me earlier though. Ain't shit I can do about it now."

"Man, I just happened to look out the window. It ain't like the cops give us *warnings*."

"They damn sure don't. But aw'ight, pimp. It is what it is."

As an older man who had been in and out of jail, Dave didn't panic. He knew they would have to prove everything they charged him with. He also knew he had a payday coming. So he relaxed and thought about how he would respond.

If these motherfuckers bust up in here, they're ready to shoot at anything that moves, he figured. *I need to stay calm and unthreatening. In fact, I'm not even leaving the kitchen.*

He stripped down to nothing but his boxer briefs. Then he laid everything neatly over a chair.

"I was up in the kitchen making myself a sandwich, about to get dressed, when they bust up in here," he mumbled to himself. That would be his story, and he was going to stick to it. Who would shoot at an undressed, unarmed older man?

A minute later, the Atlanta and DeKalb police force burst through the apartment door as expected.

BOOM!

"FREEZE! DON'T MOVE!"

The sudden and violent explosion of noise alone would startle the average person enough to make them jump out of their damn skin. Add the paranoia from smoking marijuana in the early afternoon, with three armed men who were already jumpy, and you had another police nightmare on your hands.

Che jumped up, turned, and spotted the police, who were running through the door behind him. In surprised confusion, he accidentally stumbled backwards into the coffee table while attempting to grab his gun so it wouldn't go off inside of his pants and shoot his balls off.

However, the police didn't know what the young man was thinking. Reaching is reaching. For all they knew, the man was attempting to fire back at them. So they shot him in the chest.

BOP! BOP! BOP! BOP!

Che fell back and collided into the television as it crashed to the floor.

With bullets flying past their heads over the sofa, Marcus tossed the blunt and dove to the floor, praying he wouldn't be shot in the back of the head.

"Don't shoot! I'm down!" he screamed into the floor. In a hot second, the aggressive police force was on his back, pressing him down, where Marcus had a gun at his belt.

"Ahhh!" he squealed as the gun pressed into his pelvis.

They locked his hands behind his back, handcuffed him, and flipped him over.

"Check his belt!"

When the closest officer reached for the gun inside of Marcus's pants, the automatic pistol went off rapidly.

BOP! BOP! BOP!

"AHHHH!" Marcus screamed again in agony. The bullets hit him right in his private parts.

Their unfortunate friend was the only one who didn't move from the sofa. He was too *shocked* to move.

Five pistols were aimed at his face.

"Dammit!" Detective Todd yelled. "All right, stand back and cover him," he told the arresting officers as they gave the final suspect some space. The man did exactly what he was told, allowing them to arrest him safely.

Meanwhile, Dave raised his hands up high in the kitchen, wearing his boxer briefs, his tattooed chest out. There was nothing left for the police to do but turn him around and place handcuffs on him.

"It looks like you boys just made another big mistake in here," he commented slyly.

All eyes locked in on Detective Todd for his response. However, Todd waited for them to find the shotgun from a locked closet door before he spoke. Then he pointed and grinned. "It looks like *you've* made the big mistake. That's exactly what we were looking for."

Dave shook his head. "I have no idea what you're talking about."

"We'll see," the detective commented. "Take him away," he told his men. "And get those paramedics up here."

"It's too late for that now," Dave mentioned as they led him to the door. "It looks like a couple more reckless casualties of young black men from the police."

Detective Todd eyed his partner Weinberger and decided again to hold his tongue.

This business is getting way too political these days, Todd mused. *It's best to leave all that extra talk to the lawyers. I'll need to smoke a cigarette after this shit.*

"Just take him out to the car," Todd barked.

When Marlon arrived home from work that evening, he was furious. His family was surprised to see him so early. It was barely after five o'clock.

"Hey, Dad!" his sons cheered from the kitchen table. They were doing homework.

Marlon nodded to them and remained tight-lipped.

Judy smiled at him from behind the kitchen counter. She felt good about her day and had just begun to cook dinner in her apron.

"You took off a bit earlier today?" she asked him. "What a pleasant surprise."

Marlon eyed her skeptically and remained stoic. "Let's ahh . . . talk for a minute."

Before Judy could respond, he walked out of the kitchen in haste and headed toward their bedroom.

Judy wondered what was going on. Marlon was breaking her happy groove. She decided to get his urgent conversation out of the way and return quickly to preparing her meal.

"What's going on?" she asked him inside their bedroom.

Marlon closed the door and held his cell phone up to her face. "Have you seen this?"

Judy focused her eyes to read the caption: *Are Shawn Blake and Judy Pierce an Item?* Her heart jumped immediately. The article included a picture of them leaning over their small table, as if ready to share a kiss.

Judy eyed her husband defensively as she considered the story's insinuation. "That's ridiculous!" she snapped. "Come on, Marlon, you know me better than that. They can make a picture look like anything."

"Well, what was going on here?" he questioned.

"I couldn't hear him, so we both leaned in for privacy. We probably shouldn't have even met there. The place we usually meet at is less crowded and more secure."

"Secure to do what?"

"To interview, Marlon. What are you talking about? This is a public location. I'm not trying to hide anything. What is wrong with you? We need a more secure place so people like this can leave us the hell alone! What site is this anyway?"

"Does it matter?" Marlon asked. "You're bringing shit in our lives that we don't *need* right now, Judy. I don't want to be a part of this shit. I have a *job* to go to every day. Now you're telling me you didn't know about this before I came home?"

"It just happened today, Marlon. I'm wearing the same damn clothes." She stepped back so he could see. "I came home, put my phone away, and started cooking dinner. I was in a good damn mood and didn't want to be bothered today."

"Yeah, I see why," Marlon quipped. "But you don't think about *me*. I can't just turn my phone off and hide from this shit. I don't even know when it's coming."

Judy paused and became concerned. "Someone asked you about it at work?"

"Not yet, but you know it's coming. This is only the first site that I saw it on. You know how everybody picks up the same story and runs with it."

Judy felt conflicted. Her husband had a valid point. Pierce was his family name. "Well, I can assure you, there is nothing going on between us but conversations about his life."

"And now is the perfect time for you to step away from it all," he suggested. "Just make a clean break and say that it got too crazy for your family."

"What?" Judy snarled. "Marlon, I am far too close to finally getting this story done to just step away like that. We are finally ready to—"

"You don't have a *choice*," Marlon snapped.

Judy cringed. "I don't have a *choice*? What do you mean?"

"The buck stops here. You're not doing it anymore."

Judy eyed her husband incredulously. "I know you're not telling me what to do. Now we can discuss it, but—"

"We're not discussing a damn thing! It's not up for discussion. You're not gonna have me going to work every day looking like a damn *fool*."

"Well, you just tell whoever at your *job* that it's the nature of the business," Judy advised him. "You have to ignore all of that nonsense. People just like to talk and don't know what the hell they're talking *about*."

Marlon couldn't believe his ears. "Look at you," he said. "You're sitting here making all kinds of excuses. It's over, Judy. Like I told you in the beginning, you don't need to do it."

He walked away and started taking off his work clothes as if the decision were final.

Judy took a deep breath, exhaled, stepped back toward the door, and marched out of the room toward the kitchen.

"I don't know *who* the hell he thinks he's talking to," she mumbled, "but I'm the one who pays the big fucking *bills* in this house."

By the time she reached the kitchen, Judy was no longer in the mood to cook. Instead, she pulled her phone out of her bag on the countertop to check her messages. She found that it had been blowing up for the past few hours.

"Shit! So everybody knows about this but me."

"Knows about what?" Marlon Jr. asked from the table.

Judy glared at him.

Taylor chuckled.

"Shut up," Junior barked at him angrily.

"I didn't say anything to you."

"You *laughed.*"

"Look, I am not in the mood for this," Judy fumed at both of them.

Taylor looked baffled. "You said you were in a *good* mood."

"I *was* in a good mood," she snapped at her baby boy. "Now I'm not."

"Just because I was ear hustling?" Junior pleaded. "You don't get mad at *Taylor.*" He looked genuinely hurt by his mother's suspected favoritism.

Judy shook it off and calmed herself. "I'm not angry at you because of that, but you do need to stop doing it. Mommy has a lot on her mind right now. A lot of *grownup* stuff."

"Okay," Junior whimpered with a nod.

Judy felt guilty about coming down on her boys so harshly, especially after being in such an enjoyable mood a few minutes earlier. Before she could openly apologize to them, she spotted Marlon Sr. in casual clothes, walking back out from their bedroom. She was instantly pissed off again. She took her cell phone out onto the patio in the backyard.

"Dad, did you make Mom mad?" Junior asked his father.

Marlon Sr. looked through the patio's sliding glass doors and grinned. "Yup. So I guess we'll be ordering more pizza tonight."

"Yaaayyeee!" Taylor cheered.

Judy walked down the steps of her patio onto the lawn as she continued to eye messages and missed calls on her phone. She wanted to read everything before jumping to any conclusions. What she read aggravated her even more. She called Alexandria to rant.

"Who the hell is this YellowGirl1? Do you know who this little girl is?" Judy blasted.

"Oh, she's on her way to becoming a big-time blogger. I've seen a lot of her stories online," Alexandria answered. "She's written about Chris Brown, Karrueche Tran and Rihanna, Kanye West and Kim Kardashian, Jay Z and Queen B, T.I. and Floyd Mayweather Jr. That girl has been *on it!*"

"And now she wants to write about *me?*" Judy questioned. "How do I compete with *those people?* I'm not on their level. And where did she even get this damn *picture* from?"

"Come on, Judy, you know you can grab any pictures online these days. All she has to do is a name search, and if somebody posts something new on you, she hits the jackpot."

"That's exactly what happened too," Judy admitted. "We met up at a new place today in Buckhead. There were too many damn people in there with camera phones."

"Well, why would you meet him in *Buckhead* of all places? You already *know* how many people like to stargaze up there."

"He asked me to. Or I pressed him to, really. I wanted to talk to him face to face before he left for his friend's funeral in Michigan."

"Well . . . you gotta deal with it now. We all know what you're doing, so it shouldn't be that much of an issue. It'll all blow over."

"In the meantime, this little girl is fucking with my family *and* my career. Don't let me get in contact with this damn girl."

Alexandria paused. "You don't wanna do that. That's the worst thing for you to do."

"Yeah, I know. I'm just *pissed* right now. She got my damn husband over here telling me to drop the whole story. You believe that shit?"

"I mean, you gotta look at it from *his* perspective. He's not a public figure like you are. So it bothers him more than you."

"But I'm almost done now. Shawn agreed to finally go on

camera."

"Your husband doesn't know that. He only knows what people bring to his attention."

"No, my husband knows *everything*, because I *tell him*, every damn night, whether he wants to hear it or not."

"Did he know about this?" Alexandria quizzed her.

"Of course not. I didn't know about this shit either."

"Well, there you go. That's the lack of control that *he* probably feels right now."

Judy remained defiant, determined, and angry. "Well, I'm not stopping my damn story over some bullshit. Marlon is just gonna have to deal with it. Crazy-ass girl," she complained again of the young and aggressive blogger.

"Do you see how this girl dresses?" Judy continued. "I bumped into her outside the courtroom and again at The Greek Cafe. And she needs to get a damn *stylist* and stop wearing all those bright-ass colors."

"So you *do* know about her then."

"I don't really know the girl like *that*. I just bumped into her a couple of times. Now she's decided to fuck with me and my family. And she's very *rude* and disrespectful."

"That's how they all are nowadays. They can't even help themselves. They have to be loud and rude to be heard over all the other noise out there. But don't take it personally. She just sees you and Shawn as her next meal ticket. He's the biggest talk of the city right now.

"You know they caught the guys who shot his friend in Decatur earlier, right?" she added.

"No, I didn't know that. I was offline and in my own world with my kids today. Sometimes it's better to do that. Just go offline and find some peace."

"I *wish*," Alexandria cracked. "But you aren't into Facebook, Twitter, or Instagram like I am. I guess it's another generational thing."

"No, I get enough of the news already," Judy countered. "I

don't need more of the gossip shit all day. But I know plenty of older people who use that stuff all day long. Even my husband uses it more than I do. Maybe *he* needs to go offline."

Alexandria laughed.

"All right, girl. I feel better already," Judy said. "I just needed to clear the air and talk about it. I'm still not backing down from my husband on this interview. So if I end up with a black eye that you have to cover with makeup in the morning, you know what happened."

"Girl, you *crazy*. All right, I'll see you in the morning. Be safe."

The conversation was far from over that night concerning Judy's all-access assignment with Shawn Blake. After the boys' homework, pizza, and bedtime, Marlon Sr. was back at it as his wife tried her best to avoid him.

"So, you do understand me, right?" Marlon said as he walked into the bedroom.

Judy continued to ignore him as she watched her favorite TV show in bed.

"Do you hear me?" he pressed her.

Judy eyed him. "Marlon, *please*. Let it rest."

"Let it *rest*? That's easy for *you* to say. I'm not the one who did anything."

"I didn't do anything either," Judy snapped. "Do you think that I don't have to deal with this now too? Because I *do*. I'm gonna have everyone at work looking at me funny tomorrow before I explain to them that nothing's going on. Then we'll get back to normal. You need to go to work and do the same."

Marlon sighed. "You're one hardheaded-ass woman, you know that?"

For a second, Judy, stunned, didn't know how to respond. "Whatever," she mumbled. "I know I still pay the big fucking *bills* in here too, so I can *afford* to be hardheaded."

It was all ego and defiance talking, mixed with an element of truth.

Marlon overheard her and stopped on his way out the door. "What was that?"

"Marlon, I don't want to get into this."

"You said you still pay the big fucking bills. I heard you."

Judy looked away from him and back to the television.

"This *is* about money then."

"No it is not. It's about me finishing what I started."

"So, why you bring up that shit about the *big bills*?"

"Because I'm still paying the fucking *mortgage*," she blasted him. "And you are not gonna tell me not to work."

Marlon shot back, "This ain't even about your *work*. This is about your *ego*, Judy. You gotta know when to let shit go. I'm tired of telling you that. That's how you got yourself involved in this in the first place. But all right, you wanna learn the hard way."

He walked back out of the bedroom and slammed the door behind him.

BOOM!

Still dressed casually in blue jeans and a white thermal shirt, Marlon pulled on his leather boots in the hallway, grabbed a jacket from the closet, and headed for the door.

By the time he reached his SUV in the driveway, Judy was calling him on his cell phone.

"Yeah," he huffed over the line.

"Where are you going?"

"I'm going out to get a drink."

"Where?"

"Wherever the hell I end up. I can *afford* to pay for a *drink*," he cracked. *And for a hotel room,* he thought.

"Marlon, I didn't mean it like that," Judy explained.

"It don't matter how you meant it, you're still thinking it. So maybe you need a man who can pay all the *big bills* now, since I can't."

"Marlon—"

"I'll see you tomorrow," he said and hung up.

He opened their security gates with the remote and was off toward the road. Then he made a phone call.

"Hello," a familiar voice answered.

"I need you to meet me off of 85 North and 285. I'm on my way there now."

"Why? What happened?"

"I'll tell you about it when I get there. I'm too upset right now to talk. I just need to drive and concentrate on the road. Okay?"

She paused. "Okay. I'll see you when you get out here."

When Marlon arrived at a low-key hotel off of I-85, just north of the 285 loop in North Atlanta, he walked into the bar and sat down at an empty table to order drinks.

"Can I get you a glass of water?" a waitress walked up and asked him casually.

Marlon looked up and already knew what he wanted. "Naw, give me a Crown Royal Black with Coke, and a large order of buffalo wings with ranch dressing."

The waitress nodded. "O-kay." *He knows what he wants,* she thought.

After she brought out his drink and placed it down on the table in front of him, Alexandria showed up from Judy's job at WATL Cable. She squeezed Marlon's left hand and sat down in the chair beside him.

"You know you two have to work this out."

With her smooth brown hair loose and wild, Alexandria looked more enticing than normal. It was a sexy bedtime look.

"Damn," Marlon responded to her.

"What? My hair? You caught me off guard tonight. I wasn't expecting to go out anywhere."

Marlon reached out to touch it. His fingers cut straight to her scalp. "It's soft," he said.

Alexandria grinned and tried to ignore his comment. "Yeah, so . . . what's going on?"

He shook his head as the Buffalo wings arrived. "You want

something to drink?" he asked Alexandria.

"Heck no. I have to get up at five o'clock in the morning. You forgot where I work?"

"But it's only after ten now."

"And? I would have to drink before eight or even seven to get it all out of my system."

Marlon took his first sip and said, "Anyway . . . your girl is really starting to get under my skin. She just wants to do anything she wants. She doesn't care about anyone else."

"Yes, she does. Judy loves her family. You guys mean everything to her."

Marlon drank again from his short, wide glass. "She sure don't *act* like it. She's just hardheaded. Are you that hardheaded?"

He softly knocked on Alexandria's head with his balled left fist. "Shit. You might have to thicken up your hair to protect your scalp more."

"I know, right? My hair has always been thin like that."

"But it feels good though," Marlon said, massaging his fingers through it.

Alexandria finally moved his hand away from her soft mane. "This is so weird. Imagine how she would feel if she knew we had become friends?"

Marlon smiled. "Shit, you've been keeping me sane for the past few months. You don't know how many times I've thought about straying. I'd probably be with a woman right now if it wasn't for you helping me."

Alexandria smirked. "What, you got one on speed dial?"

"No, but I could find one."

She shook her head. "That's even worse. You would go out and find a woman out of the blue?"

"Men have been doing that for a thousand years."

"Cavemen, maybe," Alexandria quipped. "But that's just *foul*. You don't know where these women have been—especially when you have a wife and kids at home."

"Especially if a man has a young cutie on the side like you too, right? Why would he want an ugly stranger?"

She grinned and shook her head again as the aroma from the hot Buffalo wings floated up into her nose. She reached out and took one.

The waitress brought her a glass of water with lemon.

"Thank you," Alexandria offered.

Marlon chomped on a wing. "Let me ask you a question. I know what I get out of this. I get a chance to go back to my youth when I was still courting your girl. But what do you get out of it? I don't have any big money. Judy just reminded me of that tonight."

Alexandria stared into his face and shook it off. "It's not about the money. I've been around plenty of guys with money who don't know how to act. So has Judy. It's about finding a genuine guy who really cares about you. She knows that too."

"Well, why would she say some shit like that tonight?" Marlon asked. He was still hurt. A woman could never speak about a man's lack of economics without hurting him. Even joking about his *lack of size* hurt less. A man could pay a woman to lie to him. But without money, he had to do a whole lot of crafty talking, which Marlon wasn't up for.

Alexandria sighed—she felt his pain. "Your wife is not the kind of woman you can back into a corner. If you do that, she's gonna pull out her claws. A lot of women in her position would, really. Judy's a fighter. She didn't mean it."

"What about you?" Marlon asked. "Would you do something like that?"

She shook it off. "I'm not really vindictive like that. I'm more of a loving person. I would probably ball up in a corner and cry."

Marlon listened while he finished up his first drink and called for another.

"Don't drink too many of those. You still have to make it back home tonight," Alexandria warned him.

"I'm not going home tonight."

Alexandria paused, concerned about him. "Where are you going?"

"I'm staying right here. And if you wanna keep a strange

woman out of my room tonight, you need to stay with me."

"You know I can't do that," Alexandria shot out.

He eyed her curiously. She was a beautiful young woman—a potential homewrecker, for sure. It was undeniable. He knew it before he responded to her on Facebook; but he never expected her to *continue* responding to him.

"So, I'm gonna ask you again: What do you get out of this?"

She shrugged, absently. "I don't know. I'm just learning from it, I guess."

"Learning what?"

"How to make it work with a man who's worth it."

Her response shocked him. It turned him on too. "So, you think I'm worth it?"

"Of course. That's why Judy Pierce loves you," Alexandria answered slyly.

Marlon took a sip of the second drink as soon as it arrived at the table. "I'm not talking about my wife right now, I'm talking about *you*. Do *you* feel that I'm worth it? I don't feel that way at home. I feel like a utility man, a plumber or something."

"She's just very focused right now, that's all," Alexandria explained. "It takes a lot to do what she does. She even tried to link me up with a job to do some interviews. And I was so nervous that they had to keep telling me to calm down and relax. Judy can just go on camera and do it all in one take. It's *amazing* watching her work. She's so natural at it."

Marlon listened intently and immersed his left hand into her soft, wild hair again. He nursed his drink in his right. "You wish you could do some of the things that she does, huh?"

"Definitely. I just admire *both* of you guys. I'm just trying to learn, that's all."

"Ain't nothing wrong with that," he told her as he continued to stroke her hair. "Ain't nothing perfect out here either. We all find what we need to feel whole. You know?"

The gentle strokes of his hand in her hair began to feel good to her, too good for comfort. So she stopped him again.

"Don't do that," she whined. *I don't want to be bad,* she told

187

herself.

Marlon grinned sheepishly as the alcohol began to hit him. "I thought you said you wanted to learn something," he hinted.

Alexandria smiled back, catching it. "I already know about that."

"I'm sure you do," Marlon teased.

Judy looked down at her cell phone in bed and refused to keep calling her husband to check on him. "I'm not gonna be that crazy woman," she said aloud. She even thought of calling Alexandria back to talk, but she didn't want to give her young coworker too much of her information. It was one thing to joke about her husband, but it was entirely different to share too much of their personal business.

"She don't need to know all of that. I tell her enough already," Judy grumbled. Instead, she broke down and called her mother in Indianapolis.

"Hey, Mom. What are you up to?"

Her mother paused, skeptically. "What's going on?" she asked. It was close to eleven o'clock at night, and her daughter rarely called her just to say hello.

"Oh, I've just been meaning to call you, that's all. I know I've been extra busy lately."

"So you decide to call me at eleven o'clock at night when you have to get up early for work tomorrow?"

"Better late than never, right?" Judy cracked. Even her laugh was unconvincing.

Her mother stalled her out for the inevitable. "I guess," she mumbled, waiting.

Finally, Judy sighed and gave it up. "Okay, Mom . . . Marlon and I just had a fight."

"What kind of fight?"

"A disagreement."

"About what?"

"My work. I'm still developing this big story that the gossip people started talking about, and he doesn't like it."

"Shawn Blake again?" her mother asked her. They had spoken about him briefly before.

"Yeah. So now the rumor is that I'm sleeping with him."

Her mother paused again. "Are you?"

"Mom, come on. No. But Marlon doesn't even want to hear the *gossip* about it. So he tried to put his foot down and told me to stop the whole story. You know I can't do that."

"Why not?"

"Mom, I finish everything I start, you know that. I would feel like a quitter, especially now that I'm so close. I've been working really hard for this."

Her mother exhaled. "Baby, look . . . in just a few more years, you're gonna look back at some of these things you fight about now and laugh, because you'll understand how small they are in the big picture. Now I already read about this nonsense with this man earlier, and I was just waiting for you to call me about it."

"So, you already know?" Judy sounded surprised.

"As old as you may *think* we are, all of this new technology stuff makes everything instant and easy now. I have friends—some of them older than me—who read about everything you do and then call me up to talk about it. I've learned to taper my own emotions until I talk to you about these things. A lot of this stuff is like the new television. These people don't have anything better to do."

"So, every time I do something, you already know about it before I call you?"

"Just about."

The grown woman, wife, and mother of two boys felt like a teenager again. She had no idea her career had gotten that deep. "Well, damn. I don't think I like that," she complained. "That sounds as if I don't have any privacy."

"You wanted a career in television, now you got it. With that being said, you don't have to do *everything* with it. Save something for yourself and your family. That's all Marlon's concerned about. He has to hear about it just like *we* do. His family in Maryland hears it too, I'm sure. You have their name now. So, whether you realize it or not, it's not just about *you* anymore. We *all* have to deal with your lifestyle."

WOW! Judy thought. She was blown away by her mother's mature and honest perspective. "Mom, sometimes the simplicity of the truth just smacks you right in your face. I didn't even realize it was this big."

"I know you don't, because you just go out there and do it. And we're all proud of you for that. But then we all have to deal with the fallouts too. So there's a positive *and* a negative to it. That just goes with everything you do."

When Judy hung up, she had a much wider view of things. "I've been really selfish, but you *have* to be to succeed," she argued to herself. She raised her fingers to her temples. "Damn!"

However, she still didn't know what to do. She was caught in the middle of her story and wanted to finish it. Quitting was not in her blood.

"Maybe after this one I'll leave it alone. But I am *this* fucking close," she grumbled with her index finger and thumb. Then she looked at the time. It was now close to midnight with no word from Marlon.

"Fuck, let me call him." After trying three consecutive times with no answer, she finally left a message: "Marlon . . . I'm *wrong*, okay. I talked to my mother about it, and I didn't realize how much my job affects everybody around me. I mean, I'm not in your shoes, so I can't feel it the way you do. But I love you and my family, and I'm willing to work it out.

"I understand now that I just can't do everything," she acknowledged. "So please . . . come home."

13... AND MORE CHAOS

Marlon was determined not to come back home that night, and he didn't. As a result, Judy couldn't sleep. Not only was she concerned about where her husband was, who he was with, and what he could be doing, she was also concerned about him not being home with their two young sons when it came time for her to head to work in the morning.

By 4 a.m., with no word from him, Judy paced from the bedroom to the kitchen. She was losing her mind.

"Mother*fucker*!" she shouted, swinging angry air punches with tears in her eyes. Her heart raced. With pain and fire in her chest, she felt ready to fight the world. "That little fucking *bitch*!" she cursed again, referring to YellowGirl1. "This is my real *life* she's fucking with!"

Against advice and wisdom to ignore the frivolous nonsense of the social media world, Judy thought again about contacting YellowGirl1 and strongly reprimanding her. She looked her up on her smartphone, and the colorful young blogger popped up with ease.

"Oh, so you *are* blowing up, huh, bitch?" Judy spoke to her phone.

Apparently, the young woman had been writing about a host of celebrities and getting plenty of attention for it, just as Alexandria had told her. Judy started typing furiously in the blogger's comment box: "Watch your back, because karma is a motherfucker," along with a bunch of other wild things with adult language attached.

She reread the comment, editing her words for tact, maturity, and clarity, while possessed by her goal of striking back hard. Then her cell phone rang in her hands and startled her.

"Shit," she cursed and fumbled with it. It was Marlon calling her at a quarter to five in the morning. "Oh my *God!*" she responded to the time. She had no idea how long she had been preoccupied with writing the perfect response to the young blogger.

"Marlon, I have to go to *work*," she barked as she answered her phone. "And the kids have to get to *school*."

"I'm on my way home now," he told her casually.

"From where?"

"From sleeping."

Judy thought about it. "With *who?*" she said, automatically assuming things.

"What? Why I gotta be sleeping with somebody? You're getting off on the wrong foot again, and I'm not even back home yet."

Marlon had a point, and Judy had to get ready for work.

"I'll see you when you get here," she told him. "I have to get dressed."

By the time Marlon arrived home, Judy had taken a quick birdbath and put on a charcoal-grey skirt suit. She forced herself to keep a cool head. She still had a job to perform on the public airwaves of Atlanta. She planned to get her rest after work, if she could keep her husband's night of mystery off of her mind long enough to discuss it with him later.

This is not a hot-headed reality show, she told herself. *This is real life and my real family. So we'll talk it out later.*

At the moment, her non-emotional course of action made the most business sense. But she had no idea how she would act later on in the day.

Marlon walked into the door, expecting another verbal spar. He didn't get one. Nor did he get a hug or a kiss, which he wasn't expecting.

"We'll talk later," his wife told him, ready to head out.

"We'll see," Marlon grumbled.

Judy stopped at the door and turned to face his back as he continued walking.

Leave it alone, she thought as she walked out. *I have to get to work.*

Judy's lack of sleep was apparent on her usual car ride to work. She felt drained and sluggish behind the wheel. Once she arrived at the station, the bright lights of the studio and makeup room felt like knives jabbing into her head.

"Wow, the lights seem really bright this morning," she complained to Alexandria.

The young makeup maven was perky and energized as usual. She shrugged and said, "They're the same as they always are."

Judy rubbed her eyes to try to stop squinting.

"I was ready to cover up your black eye this morning, like you told me," Alexandria joked. She wanted to appear as normal as possible, but the timing and subject of her humor was ill-fated.

Wendy hurried into the room, having overheard. "Oh my God. Don't tell me your husband's abusive." Genuine shock and concern covered her face.

"No he is not," Judy responded promptly. "She was joking, Wendy."

"So . . . is everything okay between you two?" her co-anchor probed.

It was the worst feeling in the world for Judy to have Wendy questioning her personal life, particularly with the stereotypes that continued to dog black men. Nor did Judy trust the woman's motives. She assumed that Wendy had read YellowGirl1's blog about her and Shawn Blake online as well. So she reached for a low blow to explain herself.

"We are not the Ray Rice family. Okay? I don't get knocked out in casino elevators."

Judy hated the statement as it rolled off of her tongue, but she knew that Janay Rice and her football-player husband had become a new talking point for America and domestic violence, whether it was fair to the young, black couple or not.

Wendy responded in awkward embarrassment, just as Judy expected. "Oh, I wasn't insinuating—"

"Yes, you were," Judy snapped. "It's another American stereotype for us to fight now."

Michael walked in and added to the tension without saying a word. In fact, his silence made their squabble more awkward. He was admitting that he had overheard them and didn't know how to deal with it. He didn't even tell them hello.

Brenda Avant walked in and asked, "Is everyone on the ball in here?"

Judy eyed the veteran producer, knowingly. *Shit, she read it too. She's always looking at shit online.*

"All systems are a go," Michael perked. "I just need a touch of powder to take the shine off this morning."

Alexandria looked mortified by the whole situation as she attempted to work her way through it. "Well, Judy doesn't need much makeup. Dark grey is a great color to absorb the lighting."

"It doesn't feel like it," Judy complained again. She figured saying anything was better than sitting there like the victim of a hit-and-run.

"You probably have a lot on your mind today," Brenda hinted.

Yeah, she knows, Judy thought. *I'll deal with her later too.*

When the team of anchors ran through their morning stories, Judy was pleased that she had been pulled from reporting the new information on the recent arrests in connection to the murder of Shawn Blake's friend. Che Torrence, the first suspect, died from gunshot wounds to his chest during the arrests. A second suspect, Marcus Berry, had apparently died in the hospital overnight after sustaining fatal gunshot wounds to his groin.

Wow, this is getting deeper by the minute, Judy thought. She hadn't bothered to reach back out to Shawn concerning all of the new developments, including the minor shake-up in her personal life. She didn't know if she would even continue to pursue the story.

I guess I'll know what I need to do by the time he gets back to Atlanta next week.

However, Brenda Avant wanted to know now. During the break, she called Judy in for another private conference.

"Close the door," Brenda commanded.

Judy did as she was told, took a seat in front of Brenda's desk, and waited for the sermon. She knew it was coming.

Brenda eyed Judy from across her desk, tolerantly. Meanwhile, Judy tried her best to remain calm and not give away her anxiety; but Brenda could read her impatience through the artificial stillness in the room. She knew it was unusual for the fiery anchor to remain so tranquil in the middle of her family chaos.

Come on. Just get it over with, Judy thought. *Say whatever it is you have to say.*

Finally, Brenda told her, "I hope you don't think I'm picking on you, because I still like you. Like the late Maya Angelou once wrote, you are a phenomenal young woman."

But . . . Judy thought without voicing it.

Brenda continued, "But this world really hasn't changed that much for us, not philosophically at least. Sure, we have more money and opportunities now, but we still have to fight some of the same battles that we've been fighting for years. And that's what you're going to come up against, the same black-community-in-crisis stories. I'd rather see you covering more about the new regime of black *excellence*."

"Shawn Blake *is* excellent," Judy argued. "He just happens to be wrapped up in a bunch of other nonsense."

"That's my point," Brenda countered. "When do we get to air stories that *don't* have the black nonsense? They *do* exist. We now have more well-trained and experienced broadcast journalists all over the country just so we can air more stories about the same troubled entertainers, uneducated rappers, desperate women, and reckless athletes."

"Well, if it's so bad, why do you keep working here?" Judy asked. She couldn't take it anymore. No one was forcing the old woman to remain on the job, especially over forty years. But Judy felt guilty about voicing it. Brenda had been her rock-steady champion, ally, and troubleshooter at the station.

"Because I need to *train* someone who's strong enough to carry the torch, if not *here*, then somewhere else," Brenda explained.

Judy wasn't expecting that. She sat still and dumbfounded as Brenda continued.

"You've now put yourself and your own family right in the middle of this craziness. And if you think it's going to end here, it's not. I've seen these violent train wrecks before. They just keep stopping and going until eventually, everyone on the train dies."

Judy didn't want to hear it, but she didn't have a choice.

"I warned you about this *weeks* ago," Brenda poured on. "I knew this would happen as soon as you got involved in this mess. Now I'll have to help you clean it up. So, I'll pull together a cease and desist letter to stop her from using your name and likeness in any more of her fabrications."

Judy remained speechless. What could she say? She wanted to downplay it all, but she still didn't know how big of a deal it was yet. So she held her tongue until she had more information.

"Now, you know that Bob is out of town until next week at an international conference in London. So we have a few days and a weekend to figure out how this goes before he gets back," Brenda concluded.

Judy felt like a child again, the same as she felt the night before, after speaking to her mother. The old veteran producer was still an asset after all. Judy nodded and exhaled, accepting her help. "Thank you," she mumbled. There was no more to say.

When Judy returned to the greenroom near the makeup area, Alexandria was anxious to apologize for her slipup that had started the ball rolling downhill earlier. First she looked around to make sure that they were alone.

"I'm so sorry about this morning," she whispered.

Judy blew her off. "It's not your fault. I got myself in this mess—me and Ms. YellowGirl1," she cracked. She tried her hardest to laugh, but it didn't work.

Alexandria couldn't laugh either. She no longer saw any humor in it. She didn't even want to talk about it anymore. She only wanted to apologize.

Feeling the clumsiness between them, Judy quickly changed the subject. "I heard you finally met up with Chase and Walter."

Alexandria didn't want to talk about that either. "Yeah, and I totally bombed it," she answered distastefully. "I was so *nervous*."

"At least they liked your look," Judy mentioned on the bright side.

Alexandria looked as if a brick had just slammed into her face. "I am so *tired* of hearing that without having any talent to do anything *with* it," she huffed. "I don't even know how to dance for a video."

"You don't want to do that," Judy said as she poured herself a cup of water. "We've had enough pretty girls in swimsuits doing that nonsense already. You just need to learn to stay calm in front of the cameras. That's all. Just imagine they're not even there."

"But they *are*. And I can't help thinking about what everything looks like on the other side. You know?"

Judy frowned. "You need to stop thinking so much and just do it. The more you think about other people's reactions, the less you'll want to do. That's the situation I'm in now," she hinted. "And I don't like it."

Alexandria smiled. "You're just used to doing *you* no matter what."

"Exactly," Judy agreed.

Her young friend paused. "I wish I could be that way about

some things."

"Yeah, but you know what? Maybe *I'm* learning that I can't always get away with what I want."

Alexandria heard that and left it alone. She still felt too guilty to respond.

Minutes later, Marlon climbed out of his SUV in his UPS uniform at his son's elementary school. He had no idea what he was walking into, and he didn't like it. All he knew was that the principal had called and asked if he could make an emergency visit to the school regarding his oldest son. So Marlon left the UPS headquarters and headed right over, like any good father would. But he remained apprehensive about what he would hear.

"Yes, I'm Marlon Pierce, here to meet with the principal about my son," he announced at the front office.

"Oh, yes, right this way."

The school secretary, a middle-aged white woman, led him back to the private office of the principal, an attractive black woman in her early forties. The principal stood up and smiled to greet Marlon immediately and shook his hand across her desk. She then took a seat in her large leather chair as Marlon sat to the right of his son.

When he looked into Junior's face, he could see that his son had been in a fight. So he waited for the principal to explain it all.

"Mr. Pierce, I'm terribly sorry to have to call you here with this, but we have a rather complicated issue on our hands," she began.

Marlon looked at his son's bruised face. "I can see that. It looks like he was in a fight."

"Under the circumstances, I honestly can't blame him," she explained. "Apparently, a fifth-grade student had gotten a hold of some adult information online at home, and he brought that information to school today and proceeded to humiliate your son with it."

"Jesus Christ," Marlon said, embarrassed.

"Yes," the principal confirmed with a nod. "The student was calling your wife—" she stopped and looked down at the notes on her desk, "an H-S-H, for Hollywood Sleepin' Ho, and had made up a song about it."

As she continued to explain it all, tears began to roll down Marlon Jr.'s bruised face.

"So, your son went ballistic out in the schoolyard. This kid is much bigger than him, so Marlon took the worst of it," the principal explained. "I've already called the student's parents, had a meeting earlier with his mother, and suspended him for five days."

Marlon Sr. nodded back at her. "This is ah . . . *damn*."

The principal also had to deal with the adult side of the issue. "Now, I did call and leave your wife a message, but I do understand that she is still at work at this hour, and I know that your office is a lot closer than hers."

"Yeah, she can't break away like I can either," Marlon added. "So a *fifth*-grade student came in here after reading that?" he asked rhetorically.

"He's actually the *youngest* of four children in his home," the principal explained. "But he would not admit where he got it from, at least not here. So they will have a very interesting conversation at home tonight."

"So will we," Marlon promised.

"Mr. Pierce, I understand that we all live in an incredibly public world these days. With all of these social media outlets, people can say or post anything they want, whether it's true or not. Parents are really being forced to figure out how to manage it all, for ourselves and for our kids, and at a much faster rate than I think we're prepared for."

"You can say that again," Marlon agreed. "We don't even allow our boys to have cell phones yet, but some parents do. So, what happens now with our son?" He figured he would deal with everything else later.

The principal felt uneasy, but it was still her job to explain the school's position. She looked at his son and said, "Well, I want to give Marlon at least three days to recuperate from all of this, either at home or through in-school suspension. I'm also going to make a note on his record that he did not instigate or carry out a fight without reason. He won't be viewed as a problem child or anything, if you're concerned about that."

"I'm just trying to figure it all out for when I tell my wife, that's all."

"If she can still come in after work, we can all discuss it again together, if you'd like," the principal advised.

"Yeah, we'll see," Marlon grumbled, ready to leave. He felt like ramming his entire body through a wall. He was so angry.

"Ah, if you don't mind, can I ask your son to step out of the room so I can speak to you alone for a minute?" the principal asked.

Marlon looked at his son. "Oh, sure, not a problem."

"Marlon, take a seat out on the bench in the main office. Your father and I will be right out in a minute. Okay? Close the door back when you leave."

Once he walked out of the room and closed the door, the principal said, "Your son is really a good kid, and I feel sorry for him. He was only trying to protect and honor his mother. But I also have to worry about you and Judy now. I didn't want to bring that part up in front of him."

"Oh, of course not," Marlon agreed. "The truth is, I told my wife not to get involved in this story at all. This guy, Shawn Blake, seems to have bad karma with everything. So now we *all* have to deal with it."

"And how exactly do you plan to do that? I have to ask," she said apologetically. "I have phone numbers of several good marriage counselors that I can offer you. I would be *remiss* if I didn't at least *ask*. It may be a private issue for you, but once it comes into this school, I have to do my job."

Marlon felt as if he were back in school again himself. "Yes, ma'am. I understand. You have to cover all of your bases."

"I do. And I'm also asking because I *care* about you guys," she stated. "I care about *all* of the parents and students at this school, including the fifth grader, who I hope and pray will learn a viable lesson of his own from this.

"So, just to make myself clear, I totally understand the anger that Marlon displayed in defending his mother today. But as adults, we have to learn how to channel our anger into resources that can help us deal with whatever issues we may have."

Marlon grinned and cut to the chase. "If you're asking me if there'll be any more *violence* at home with my wife tonight, then you can put your mind at ease. I *do* know how to act like a mature man, husband, and father."

The principal held up her hands in surrender. "I'm just doing the best job I can to safeguard each and every child who enters our doors. And the issues of the parents *always* affect the children in some form or another. I *do* love you all. That's why I stick my nose in."

Marlon didn't feel *loved* when he left her building though. He still felt *angry*, he *and* his son. He didn't know what else to say to Junior as they drove back toward the UPS office in his truck. So he said the best thing that he could come up with.

"I'm proud of you, son. And I don't care how big a kid is, you try to kill his ass for your mother. Well, not exactly *kill* him, but you know," he clarified. "You try to just beat his ass, like you did."

His son grinned, surprised. It was a great way to break the ice. He told his father, "He just kept saying it, Dad. I tried to ignore him at first, but then other kids started repeating it. 'Your Mom is a H-S-H.' So I just went crazy on him."

"Well, first of all, you know it's not true, right?" Marlon asked. "You just got a lot of people out here who want to write shit to get attention. And they don't know how many people it affects."

"But why would somebody do that?" Junior asked from the passenger seat. "They're just hating?"

Marlon took a deep breath and sighed. "They're doing a little more than just hating. Believe it or not, son, people actually *make money* by making up things now. There's a lot of sad people out here today who find joy in knowing somebody else's personal business, whether it's true or not. And most of the time, they only care about the terrible stuff. That's just the America we live in now, son. We have a very sick society."

14... HOTTER THAN JULY

On their way home to Flint that Thursday morning, Shawn and Alex found themselves stuck at the security checkpoint of Hartsfield-Jackson Atlanta International Airport.

Shawn leaned in and whispered to his friend, "You don't have that in your luggage, do you?"

Alex turned and frowned at him. "Hell no. I wouldn't do that to either one of us."

Shawn looked backed at the TSA staff and wondered what was taking them so long to move their luggage through the monitors.

"Is this your bag, sir?" a staff member asked as he pulled Shawn's black leather bag aside.

Shawn answered skeptically, "Yeah, what's the problem?"

"You have something liquid in your separate compartment?"

"Not that I know of."

They opened the top zipper compartment and pulled out a large bottle of cologne.

"Shit, I forgot about that. I shoved that in there while running to my last event. Can I put it in the Ziploc bag with the other stuff? That's where it would usually be."

The TSA agent was already ahead of him. He grabbed Shawn's Ziploc bag of bathroom items and pushed the cologne bottle inside.

Then he ran the bag back through the monitor.

"Thanks," Shawn told him.

A tanned brunette with sculpted curves smirked as she collected her luggage right behind him. Recognizing who he was, she was determined to speak.

"I thought you'd travel in a private jet or something," she commented.

Shawn looked her over and grinned. "Not when the schedules don't match. What about you? Where's your private jet?"

She smiled and said, "I'm not that privileged."

"Why not? You look good enough," he flirted. "Tell your man to splurge before somebody takes you away from him."

Alex gathered both of their things and chuckled.

The young brunette stopped to continue the conversation. "Someone like who?" she asked.

Shawn looked back at Alex, knowing better.

Leave it alone, man. We got shit to do, he told himself. He looked back at the young woman and warned her, "You gon' get yourself in trouble out here."

"I think I can handle myself," she told him boldly.

As the three of them moved away from the security area, Shawn became more apprehensive. "Do you know who I am?"

"Of course," she said. "Why wouldn't I know? You've been all over the news."

"Not for good things. That doesn't concern you?"

"I know it's not all true. Otherwise, you'd be in jail now, right?"

Shawn nodded. He didn't trust her. She was far too forward and out in the open in front of hundreds of people. As far as he knew, she could have been an undercover cop. So he casually dismissed her. "Yeah, you have a nice trip."

The young woman seemed surprised. "Well, maybe I'll bump into you again sometime."

"Yeah, maybe," he grumbled and walked away behind Alex. All of a sudden, Shawn was on full alert. He felt like everyone in the airport was watching him with ulterior motives. "You can't trust nobody out here now, man. That shit felt like another setup."

"It damn sure did. She was *fine* too," Alex admitted and laughed. "You see that body on her? She had that Kim Kardashian look. I guess they think you Kanye West now."

Shawn chuckled. "Yeah, they're trying to do something. But I think you're rubbing off on me now, Al. You got me all paranoid in here. I don't even feel like getting my usual Pinkberry yogurt today."

"I'm just saying, man. You put all these pieces together, and what do you come up with? Two of the guys the police arrested yesterday are dead."

Shawn shook it off as they headed down the escalator toward the trains for the terminals. "You're not trying to blame that on our boy too, are you?"

"Naw, he can't set up everything. But it's just ironic though, ain't it? Things are dropping into place like a jigsaw puzzle. That's why I'm glad you're flying up here with me today so you can think about it. You even got your reporter girl in trouble with that social media shit now," Alex joked.

Shawn winced. "Yeah, that was fucked up. She won't even take my calls now. I feel sorry for her, Al. She's been straight professional the whole time. I left her a message and told her that this morning. Maybe she can let her husband listen to it if she needs to."

Alex frowned. "Nobody cares about being professional anymore. They just want that bullshit. You know that by now. She'll have to figure this out for herself. And her husband ain't gon' believe no shit coming from *you*. How many women you dug in now and called them your friends? Come on now. We all know that game."

"But it's true though," Shawn insisted as they reached the bottom platform. "She's just been real cool with me."

"You know *I* know that, but how many people out here want to believe it? Being friends ain't sexy enough. They wanna know if you're knocking her. And if you're not, then they don't even care."

As they stood and waited for the shuttles to arrive, Shawn

rubbed his goatee and didn't say another word. Instead, he continued to watch the people who glanced at him. How many of them could work with celebrity websites? How many could work with the police? And how many of them were regular citizens who judged him for everything?

Shit, maybe I should have taken the private jet with Benny and L., he mused in silence. *Or maybe we should have rode with Toot and Devon . . . in a less attention-getting car.*

On their drive up to Michigan in the flamboyant burnt-orange Lamborghini, Toot blasted his music from the passenger seat while Devon drove. They headed up Interstate 75 North and had almost reached Lexington, Kentucky.

"Look, man, I'm not gon' listen to your shit the whole way up here," Devon complained. "I've heard it enough already. I want to hear some of this new T.I. album."

Toot looked disgusted in his gold fronts. "You wanna listen to T.I.? Man, don't you know that's the enemy?"

"Says who?"

"We don't really get down with Atlanta like that," Toot commented.

"Why not? We've been living down here for years now."

"Naw, we just been gettin' this money. We don't like them like that."

"You mean, *you* don't. You don't speak for me," Devon argued. "I got plenty of friends in Atlanta now."

"Yeah, 'cause your people from down there."

"My people from Alabama," Devon corrected him.

Toot shrugged. "It's the same thing, one state over. It's still country as hell."

"And where are your people from?"

"Come on, man, you know we from Chicago," Toot barked with pride.

"And before that, y'all came up from Mississippi, right? Ain't that what you told us? Your people got country roots too, and you look like that shit right now."

"Aw, man, stop hatin'. You need to get you some gold fronts," Toot teased him.

Devon shook his head. "Everything you do is contradictory, man. You're like a walking, talking oxymoron."

"Yeah, I'm bad, man . . . and it's all good," Toot responded on cue.

Even Devon had to laugh at that. His rapping friend may have looked and acted crazy sometimes, but he still understood everything that went on around him.

Devon returned to concentrating on his speed at the wheel. The car alone drew enough attention, so he made sure not to be pulled over for speeding.

"Yo, turn that shit down, man, we passing a state trooper," Devon warned.

Toot looked out the window at the police car up ahead and snapped, "Fuck the police!" But he turned the stereo system down anyway. That made Devon suspicious. He had complied too easily for comfort.

"You don't have any weed on you, do you?" Devon asked.

His friend eyed him passively and said, "Of course I do."

"Shit! I told you not to bring that shit in here. You know how long we gotta drive."

"I know, man, but that's why I needed it for the trip."

"You're not smoking that shit in here," Devon barked. "I will put your ass on a Greyhound bus in a heartbeat."

"Aw, man, don't act like you don't smoke weed," Toot argued.

"I won't do that shit on a long road trip in a Lamborghini. That's just how black people make the news—over stupid shit."

Devon was heated. "We'll get pulled over for a simple license and registration check, and they'll smell the weed on you," he continued. "Then you'll act up and they'll arrest us, claiming that we resisted, with eight more cops called to the scene. Then they'll beat you in the fucking head, and I'll be forced to respond to it. So they'll beat me down too. Then the whole community ends up in an uproar when they report the shit on the news, when you shouldn't have been smoking weed in the first fucking place."

Devon had their whole story already.

Toot chuckled. "You tripping, man. I got an album to sell now. I'm not going for that shit. I know how much attention this car brings. But I'ma get me some Diesel as soon as we get home."

Devon shook his head as they approached the state trooper, who had parked on the right shoulder of the interstate.

"Just keep your cool and don't look at him," Devon warned.

Toot looked anyway to see what the officer was up to. As soon as they drove past him and were fifty yards up the road, the state trooper pulled into traffic behind them.

Devon eyed him in the rearview mirror the whole time. "Shit, here he come," he panicked.

Toot looked back and said, "We ain't did nothing."

"I told you not to look though. We don't have to do nothing. We already did it. We black, and we driving in an expensive car. That's why you don't smoke no weed in this car. You're *asking* for trouble."

They drove forward within the speed limit, expecting the police cruiser to pop on the flashing lights behind them at any moment.

"This shit is nerve racking, man," Devon complained.

"You want me to drive?" Toot teased him.

"Aw, hell no. At least I know how to stay in my lane and do the speed limit. They'd really pull us over if *you* were driving."

"But we still ain't did shit," Toot insisted. "So he ain't got nothing on us."

Nevertheless, the two black men remained in terror as the Kentucky police cruiser followed behind several cars, including theirs.

Toot said, "He could be following anybody out here, man."

"Yeah, we'll see."

After another mile up the road in suspense, the police cruiser finally pulled aside and parked on the shoulder of the road again without bothering them.

"Whewww! Shit!" Devon let out.

Toot laughed. "I told you he ain't have shit on us. Now let me turn my music back up."

"Naw, he might call another state trooper up the road from us," Devon responded cautiously. "So just chill. This gon' be a long-ass ride."

Toot frowned and mumbled, "Man, next time I'm taking that ride in the jet with Benny and them."

Bernard "Benny C." Chavis stood outside of a familiar northside storefront on Pasadena Avenue in the cold air of Flint, Michigan. He wore a brown rabbit-fur coat with a hood while reflecting on how far they had all come from the streets they once ran on. The depressed business area had once been buzzing with endless hustle and bustle back in his youth of the 1990s. Benny remembered the hot days of summer when he didn't want to leave the action out on Pasadena, Saginaw, Martin Luther King, DuPont, Stewart, and Pierson. But that seemed like another lifetime now. As he stood there on the frigid and empty block of boarded up buildings and silence, he realized that there was nothing to return to but the memories.

"What you having, flashbacks?" Larry asked, walking up beside him in his long black leather coat.

Benny smiled and confirmed that he was. "It seems like a hundred years ago, man. There's so many people I knew from this strip who are no longer here now."

Larry shrugged. "That's life, man. That happens to everybody. We all wish we could go back to them times when we were young. Shit was way simpler then. You took your lumps and kept it moving."

Benny grinned. "I gave some lumps out here too."

"Oh, no doubt. It goes both ways. You know I did my dirt out here," Larry said. "But we the survivors now, B."

Benny extended his right fist for a pound. "That's what's good."

Larry gave him a pound back as a call came in on his cell phone. He pulled it out of his coat pocket and looked down at the number. "This shit in Atlanta is really heating up now, man. How you calling it?"

Benny shrugged. "It's the same old game of chess, L. You know how we do. You pay for another hand to move the pieces. And you never tell anybody where the original orders came from. You hear me? You just pass that shit down the line and stay untouchable."

"What if this dude already spent the money?" Larry quizzed.

Benny looked and frowned. "Then you tell his ass he better find some more. Fuck we look like? This motherfucker think we sugar daddies? He better come up off that shit. Go ahead and handle that."

Larry finally answered his phone. "Yeah, what's up?"

"Yo, the player want that money, man, like now."

"Well, give it to him. We gave it to you already," Larry responded.

"I'm saying though, he wants more than that."

"Aw'ight, so this what you do: You negotiate with him, you get the lowest price you can get, pay him off, and then I'll reimburse you for it."

Benny looked at Larry sideways before he nodded. "Okay," he mumbled.

However, the caller didn't like the idea. "I'm saying, man, I'on know about all that. Just give him what he wants, 'cause I'on wanna be in the middle of it like that."

Larry told him, "You already in the middle of it. He ain't talk to *me*, and I'm not trying to know him. I know *you*, and that's how I'm trying to keep it. So you need to hush 'em up with something, and then we handle our own business from there. You should have never told him that you getting shit from me. 'Cause now he try'na count my pockets and don't even know me. That's bad business. People start naming all kind of prices when they don't know somebody. So you need to pay him something and get him to come back down to earth. You feel me? That's business one-oh-one."

There was a long pause over the line. In the meantime, Benny smiled his ass off and gave Larry another pound on the Flint city sidewalk.

The caller said, "I'ma see what I can do and call you back."

"That's what's good," Larry told him.

As soon as he hung up the line, Benny said, "Now that's fucking thinking. He needs to handle his business and then we'll handle *him* . . . however we need to. That's how the game is played. If he's *smart*, he'll figure out something on his end, then we'll make the next move on ours."

With no time to stop and gloat, Larry changed the subject. "So, how long you planning on standing out here, man?"

"Not long at all. I just wanted to see it and think for a minute, before we're surrounded by all these people tonight. Like you said, we the survivors out here. So I'm trying to have a moment of silence."

Larry nodded. "Then we pick up Shawn and Al from the airport around two, right?"

Benny nodded back at him. "Yeah."

With that said, Larry returned to their black limo, which was parked at the curb. He looked back at Benny as he reached for the door. "Shawn been spending a lot of time with Big Al lately," he commented casually.

"Somebody gotta protect him, L. Al don't have a record like the rest of us. So the cops can't fuck with him."

Larry cracked another grin. "Everything is a chess move, huh?"

"And if you don't know that . . . you lose."

Back down in Atlanta, Keith huddled up in his southwest apartment with two of his trusted friends.

"I don't like that shit, man. What if they decide not to pay you back?" his first friend commented.

"They paid me every time before," Keith responded

thoughtfully.

"You should have squared this guy away when you had the chance the first time," his second friend complained.

"Shit, Dave headed to jail now anyway. And Che and Marcus just got murked. So, we'll give him like three or four thousand and tell L. that we gave him six or seven," Keith explained.

"What if they find out?" the first friend asked.

"How? He just told me he don't even want to know Dave."

"Yeah, that's what he *say*, until you start talking real money. All it takes is for them to send somebody to snoop and find out," the second friend argued.

"You need to stop being so greedy, man. Just pay this guy some money and get it over with," said the first friend,

They were both against Keith's faulty moves, but the lead man remained defiant.

He said, "Look, they got money like that, man. They just don't want nobody being able to finger them. That boy Shawn Blake is at the root of *all* this shit. So if we really want some paper, we go after *him*. Then they'll *really* pay up."

Keith's first friend looked baffled. "Are you *crazy*? If they're doing all this shit just to keep him out of jail, what you think they gon' do if you try to hurt him? They'll come down here with a whole *army* from Michigan."

"Well, bring that shit then!" Keith barked. He pulled his gun out and said, "I told y'all, I'm not afraid of *no*-fucking-body! Fuck Michigan!"

"It's not about being afraid, man. It's about making *sense*," his second friend snapped.

Keith insisted, "I *am* making sense. I got an army too. Y'all think I don't know more people in Atlanta? And I know how to get to these boys now. I'm telling you, Shawn Blake is their weakness."

His first friend shook his head and moved to rub his temples. "I'm about to go lay low, man, 'cause you trippin'. You see how the media covers this dude? Anybody who even deals with him ends up on blast. You see how they're doing that reporter woman now, right?"

"Yeah, Judy Pierce," the second friend filled in. "They're doing her grimy."

"Well, that's her fucking problem," Keith barked. "They're only doing that shit to her 'cause they know she got a family. The media don't deal with us like that. The streets don't give a fuck about the media. We got our own rules."

However, the media *did* care about the police. The Atlanta and DeKalb police forces were both taking heat for the clumsy handling of the recent arrests and deaths in Decatur.

Police Chief Wallace had Detectives Todd and Weinberger in his office again. This time, he remained seated behind his desk. He sighed. "What else can happen with this case? Did you get anything valuable out of the two remaining suspects in custody?"

"Not a thing," Todd answered first.

Weinberger said, "The young man doesn't seem to know anything about it, and the older man is trying to pin it all on the two deceased."

"Of course he is," the chief grumbled. "What would you expect him to do? But we know that it was three of them, and that shotgun is a grown man's gun."

"Yeah, but they thoroughly wiped down the fingerprints," Todd informed him.

The chief sighed, disgusted by the case. "He's not going anywhere. He has a record as long as California. We just have to find someone to point him out from the scene as the shooter. We also know that he's related to Anthony 'Tone' Jacobs, who was killed outside the nightclub."

"So was one of the two deceased," Weinberger added.

"That's *two* of them with motives then," the chief assessed. "So, our guy Blake is headed out of town this morning for his friend's funeral in Michigan, right?"

"He was just spotted at the airport," Weinberger confirmed.

"Now we have a local news reporter, Judy Pierce, intertwined with him," the chief mentioned.

Todd looked at his partner Weinberger to respond to that as well. So she did.

"We can't confirm any of that. We only saw her with him during lunch meetings, and it seemed to be all professional."

"But now she's being sucked into the storm with him," the chief commented.

"That's what it looks like," said Detective Todd.

"When he gets back in town, you keep an eye out on both of them to see what pops up. As far as these two deaths from yesterday's arrests goes, honesty is the best policy. So just explain it exactly how it happened and express sympathy for their families. But we still have a job to do, and they were both armed and dangerous suspects."

Todd and Weinberger accepted their orders. "Yes, sir."

15... FIGHTING WORDS

As soon as Judy's longer than usual morning was over at work, she made it out to her car in the parking garage, where she could listen to her phone messages in private.

First she listened to Shawn Blake's message:

"Hey, Judy, it's Shawn. I don't even know where to start with this, really. I tried to call you a few times yesterday, but . . . of course, you didn't answer. So I'm just gonna leave you this message before I head out of town this weekend.

"It's messed up how they did you in that article. But that's how people are nowadays. They don't care that we're just doing interviews; they only care about getting a rise out of the people. And people fall for it every time. So I apologize for that.

"I don't even know if you still wanna meet up with me and do this anymore. I can't blame you if you don't. But I just wanted to apologize. You've been the perfect professional with me. Peace."

His message was good and straight to the point. Judy appreciated it. She even saved it to listen to again if she needed to.

"We just need to do the damn interview for the cameras now," she mumbled to herself in the driver's seat of her car. "There's nothing else for us to talk about."

Then she listened to the message from her sons' school:

"Yes, good morning, Mrs. Peirce. This is Dr. Eleanor Stafford, principal at Manor Road Elementary. I wanted to give you a ring this morning and have you to call me back at the school at your earliest convenience regarding your son Marlon Jr. Knowing the nature of your work, I do understand that you may not be able to get back to me as promptly, so I am going to call your husband, Marlon Sr., as well. I hope to hear back from you shortly. Bye."

Judy didn't know what to think of the principal's call.

If Marlon was sick, I would have gotten a call from the nurse's office, right? she thought. So she jumped back on the line and returned the principal's call, assuming it was something urgent.

"Manor Road," the secretary answered.

"Yes, this is Judy Pierce, calling the principal back in regards to my son, Marlon."

"Oh, yes, your husband just came and took him home," the secretary told her.

Judy grimaced. "Is he sick?"

"No, he isn't sick. Let me see if I can put you through to the principal's office. Hold on." The secretary clicked over to the principal's line, only for a recorded message to pop on.

"Shit!" Judy huffed impatiently. She hung up without listening to the rest of the message and called her husband instead.

"Yeah," he answered, expecting her.

"What's wrong with Marlon? The school said you just picked him up."

"Yeah, I did."

"Well, are you home? Where are you?"

"I'm back at work."

"Where is Marlon?"

"He's doing his schoolwork in an empty office here."

Judy remained dumbfounded. "Why? What's going on?"

Marlon exhaled. "He was suspended from school for fighting today."

Judy frowned, disappointed. "For what?"

"A kid was talking about you, so he went off."

"A kid was talking about *me*?" Judy couldn't figure it out, and she had quickly grown tired of the guessing game. "Marlon, *what the hell is going on?*"

"I'll let you come and pick him up from the office, then you can ask him about it on the way home. I need to get back to work."

"Marlon, *really?* You're not gonna tell me what's going on with our son? This is *petty*. I would never do something like this to you."

Marlon paused. "You'll find out when you pick him up," he insisted.

Judy took a deep breath to calm herself. "All right, I'm on my way." She hung up, pissed. "I don't fucking *believe* him. I am not sleeping with this man, and he's acting like a damn *fool* about it."

She started up her car and headed toward her husband's job with an axe to grind. "I can't believe I married somebody this damn *childish*," she continued to rant while she drove.

When Judy arrived at the UPS headquarters, not far from their home in Alpharetta, she wasted no time rushing her son out to the car for a one-on-one talk.

"I can't believe your father made me go through all of this without telling me," she continued to complain. She cupped her son's face in her palms to get a closer look at his bruises. "Okay, it's not that bad. So, what were you fighting about it? Your father said something about a kid talking about me."

Marlon Jr. was hesitant. He didn't want to deal with it anymore, but he knew he had no choice. He looked his mother in her eyes and said, "A fifth grader read some news online and started calling you a H-S-H."

Judy frowned at him, bewildered. "An H-S-H? What is that?"

"A Hollywood Sleepin' . . ." Marlon didn't want to say the last word. He was unsure if he could get away with it in his mother's presence. But he didn't need to say it.

Judy repeated the phrase in her head and . . . BOOM! The final word hit her like an explosion. "Oh, shit! *Ho?*"

Her son didn't need to confirm it. He even looked away from her, embarrassed. As Judy fell into a deep spell of silence, Marlon looked back at his mother to see how she was taking it.

It felt as if someone had stuck a fiery hand inside of her chest and ripped her heart out while it was still beating. Judy could only imagine what her son must have felt like at school. How he had to interpret what it all meant, as well as whether the information was actually true.

She could imagine how important it would be for Marlon to defend her reputation, particularly while in front of a bunch of his peers. It was the kind of family reaction that people who wrote such articles could not have thought about before writing them. How do you even explain the complicated slander and insinuations of the adult world to a nine-year-old child whose mother still means the world to him?

The anger and helplessness that Judy felt from not being able to the stop the nonsense before it reached her son forced tears to roll from her eyes.

To soothe his mother's pain, Marlon spoke up. "Dad said it wasn't true. He said people just try to make money off of stuff. It's not true, right?" her son asked for confirmation.

The realization that Junior had to even *consider* it as factual only made Judy cry harder. "No, of course not," she barked. "Your father's right. People are just trying to . . . create stories."

Junior nodded eagerly and said, "Okay," as if a giant burden had been lifted from his shoulders. Now he would have to explain it all to his classmates and confirm that it was false. What would the students tell their parents about it?

He's too young for this shit! Judy blasted in her head.

She wiped her eyes and face with her hands. Not being able to take it, she opened her car door while still in the parking lot. She told her son with a cracked voice, "I need to take a walk."

But once she stood outside of her car, she realized the UPS parking lot was not the place to cry and definitely not the place to throw a tantrum. So she stood outside of her black Mercedes and breathed deeply, attempting to gather her thoughts.

218

I feel like whipping this girl's ASS for writing that bullshit! she seethed inside.

She realized that adults could not settle *their* issues through violence without repercussions, but Judy still wanted to throw a fist at someone. Fighting was how she handled everything.

I can't fight everybody, she mused. *I have to grow up from that.*

"She's gonna have to retract that shit. That's all there is to it," Judy mumbled. She wiped her eyes again and sat back in the car to check her makeup in the vanity mirror. "So how many days did they suspend you for?" she asked her son.

"Three days. But I can do an in-school suspension too."

Judy looked at him and nodded. "I don't like you doing a suspension at all, but we have to deal with it now. I'm sorry that this even happened." She leaned over and gave her son a hug and kissed him on the forehead.

"It's okay, Mom."

Every word Junior spoke made her cry again. "If Mommy would have just *listened*, this wouldn't have happened," she sobbed. She looked back at her son. "It's my fault. I shouldn't have done it. Mommy can't take every job."

"It's okay, Mom," Junior repeated. "I know I shouldn't fight. I just didn't want him to keep saying it."

Judy cried into her son's small shoulder. "I know. I don't want anyone saying that either."

"And he was trying to make a song out of it," he added.

"Okay, that's enough," Judy said to stop him. "I don't want to hear anymore about it. Okay? He was *wrong*. And his parents need to whip his ass."

Marlon Jr. grinned and kept going. "The principal suspended him for *five* days at home."

Judy wiped her face a third time before she noticed several UPS staff members peeking at them as they made their way in and out of the building.

"Okay, we need to go on home before they start thinking

something else out here," she mumbled. She didn't want her husband's UPS coworkers thinking he had done something vengeful to her. That was the last thing they needed. So she sat up straight, put her seatbelt on, and started the engine.

"We'll all talk about it with your father at home tonight," she told her son on their way out of the parking gate.

"With Taylor too?"

Judy thought about that for a few seconds. "Does he know that you were in a fight?"

"No, we have different lineups."

"But he could hear about it in school, right? And then he'll know that you weren't in school when I go to pick him up today," Judy debated.

"I could go with you."

"Yeah, but he'll still know . . . unless you go back in the building before he comes out."

"We could go meet with the principal first. She wanted to talk to you about it anyway."

Marlon seemed to have gotten over it all. Judy hadn't.

I don't even know if I want to meet with the principal now, she thought. *What is she even thinking about us? And I know Marlon probably said something to her. I hope he didn't tell that woman I'm hardheaded. I bet he did.*

Judy stopped her hyper thoughts and shook her head as she drove home on the winding roads of Alpharetta. "This is ridiculous," she mumbled.

"What?" her son asked, curiously. He couldn't help himself.

"Nothing," she barked.

This is grown folks' business, and now I have to include you in it, she admitted to herself. *Shit! I hope Taylor doesn't find out. He's only six.*

Fortunately, Taylor Pierce was not a part of the grapevine of gossip that afternoon at school. Judy had him sent to the main office before the final bell rang to make sure the older kids never got the word to him. Her agreement with the principal was that Marlon Jr. would do an in-school suspension without it being written up. That way, none of the students could question getting into fights without repercussions and Marlon would not sustain a permanent record for the incident. Judy also didn't include her son in her conversation with her husband that evening.

"So, what are you planning to do?" Marlon asked his wife skeptically inside the bedroom.

"I was gonna write this girl a response letter to her blog, and Brenda wants to send her a cease and desist letter. She really needs to retract this shit. It's gone too far."

"You think she's gonna do that?"

"She doesn't have a *choice*. So, before I sue her ass, and everyone else who runs it, she needs to do what's right. This is not some damn college newspaper. And it's not *cute*."

Judy climbed into bed while Marlon continued to stand at the foot. He was ready to head back to the den.

"Where are you going?" she asked him.

"To watch the highlights. It's November. The new NBA season has started."

Judy paused. "You can watch the highlights in here," she said. "We're not done talking about this. This is *serious*. Our son was suspended from school today."

Marlon frowned at her. "Oh, *now* it's serious. It takes your son getting suspended before you want to listen to me?"

"Marlon, I said that I was sorry."

"Yeah, you're sorry now, after I had to sit up there in that office with a principal who thought I would go home and put my hands on you. It made it worse that she's a *black woman* assuming that shit."

"And what did you tell her about *me*?" Judy asked. "Because I know you went up there and defended yourself."

"I told her that I advised you not to do it."

"I knew you said some shit like that."

"It's the *truth*. I'm not gon' sit up there and hide this shit.

We're both being judged now, Judy. This whole family is being judged. So of course, I'm going to defend myself. Did you walk in there and tell her you had an affair with Shawn Blake?"

Judy looked appalled. "Marlon, stop it."

"What did you tell her?"

"I told her that I was reporting for my damn *job*."

"Exactly. You defended yourself. But I'm supposed to walk in there and say, 'Oh, my wife can do whatever she wants. It's her career, and I don't have anything to say about it. She pays all the big bills and the mortgage.' Is that what you wanted me to say?"

"Marlon, you're being a smart-ass now."

"I'm asking you. What did you want me to say? Because I'm still pissed off right now about all of this shit. I'm trying to find my own way of dealing with it. What, I gotta make more money for you to listen?"

"Obviously, you're still upset about—"

"You damn right I'm still upset!" Marlon shouted. "The same way you're upset about this blogger girl, I'm upset about how you treat *me*. The only reason I even gave you my support on this Shawn Blake thing originally was to see how far you would try to go with it. And you tried to push for that extra mile, like you always do, with no consideration for me."

"Oh, so you were only testing me with that? I tried to back down from the story, Marlon. I tried *several* times."

"Bullshit! When you don't wanna do something, you don't do it. You would have told your boss no from day one, just like you turned down that job at ABC to work for cable. So don't even give me that."

Judy reflected on her opportunity to work at ABC years ago. "That was a lot more complicated than this," she said. "They wanted me on the late news shift and on a weekend trial basis, and I just didn't feel like I fit in well with them."

"You didn't want to do it, so you turned them down," Marlon insisted. "This whole celebrity interview idea is on a trial basis too, isn't it? It's not what you normally do. They're not paying you for it. You were trying to put it on the table as something extra."

"And?" Judy piped. "What's your point?" She was tired of talking about her job. She wanted to talk about *their lives.*

"*And* it was what you wanted to do," Marlon answered. "So don't sit up here now and tell me that. Everything is about *control* with you. You're only mad now because you can't control this shit. Well, real life don't let you control everything, Judy."

She was done with this argument and more concerned about their family at the moment. So she calmed down and said, "What's important now is how we move on from this."

"That's more important for *you* right now. I'm still simmering. I *can't* move on yet."

Judy was ready to respond with something defensive, but she caught herself.

"What, I need to get over it?" Marlon asked, reading her eyes. "Well, you don't get to tell me what to do, just like I don't tell you what to do. I'll get over it when I damn well please."

He stormed out of the room and left his wife speechless. He avoided all of her questions about where he had been the night before. Maybe that wasn't important anymore.

"This has been a long-ass day," Judy told herself aloud as she rubbed her weary eyes. It felt as if she hadn't slept in a week. "I just need to take some Tylenol and go to bed now. I'll handle this girl tomorrow."

When tomorrow came—a much needed Friday morning to end a hectic work week—Judy found that YellowGirl1 had added another layer to her story, questioning whether Shawn Blake would receive more favorable news coverage from WATL Cable than he would from Atlanta's Big Four networks—ABC, NBC, CBS, and FOX. Judy hit the roof again.

"Okay, this little girl is toying with me now," she complained inside the greenroom.

"Judy, you just have to ignore it. She's obviously—"

"How are you gonna bring this story to my attention and then tell me to ignore it, Wendy?" She was at it once again with her co-anchor.

"Someone just bounced it over to me while we were on air," Wendy replied.

"And you felt this would be the perfect timing to tell me? I've been ignoring my phone on *purpose*, but all of a sudden you're paying that much attention to *yours*."

Michael and the rest of the production staff wanted to evaporate from the small room, including Alexandria. It was a heated round two.

Wendy's face turned red. "I didn't think that you would respond to it like this," she argued. "We're professionals, and you're letting this amateur girl get to you."

"Look, you don't have a husband at home and kids in school, Wendy, so you have no idea what this feels like."

Michael interjected, "Come on, Judy, kids are used to all of this stuff now. They know it's all talk. They do it all themselves on Facebook, Twitter, Instagram, and now Snapchat."

"Ask me if my sons even have a cell phone, Michael," Judy snapped. "They're not teenagers. I don't want them getting used to this kind of stuff. It's *wrong*, plain and simple."

"Judy, in my office. *Now!*" Brenda's voice boomed. She seemed to drop out of nowhere. Judy didn't like her tone, but at least she would get to rant in private. She followed Brenda back to her office with no hesitation.

Brenda closed the door behind them and warned her tersely, "You need to get yourself together before you lose your job. Do you know what you sound like out there?" she lowered her voice and whispered.

Judy didn't want to answer, but she did anyway. "People have fights at every job," she said calmly.

"And guess who's the first to get fired after those fights?" Brenda countered. "I told you before, when you allow your emotions to dictate your actions—"

"You're emotional yourself," Judy argued, cutting her off. "You just showed your emotions out there too."

"Because I *care* about you," Brenda snapped. "Do you not

understand that? But you make me feel like I'm wasting my time and energy. You're too *experienced* for this. This isn't anything *new*. Do you remember LaVonia?"

"Yes I do, but she didn't have a family like I have," Judy answered.

"She had your same ambition, but she was too raw," Brenda reflected. "She thought she could get by on momentum alone. But momentum comes and goes. You are far more *talented* than she was, but it won't mean a *thing* if you let it all get away from you.

"Now, I've already given you my support to work through this," she continued. "I'm sending the cease and desist letter today, particularly since she's now naming the station and questioning our integrity at WATL. But *you* have to allow the process to work its course."

A page went off on Brenda's phone, signaling her to get back to work. So she cut their passionate talk short.

"Understand that a black woman's *tone* will *always* be considered angry. So you get back to smiling," she advised Judy. "Just because we're forced to smile doesn't mean we're not thinking."

Brenda smiled broadly to remind her young sage how to do it before she left her office. It worked. Judy had not seen Brenda smile like that in so long that it seemed cartoonish. She thought about it and chuckled down the hallway.

"Okay," she mumbled to herself. "Let me get back to doing my job." She floated back into the makeup room with Alexandria and said, "Hit me with a touchup."

Alexandria didn't know what to think. But it was much better to have a perky Judy than a spicy one. "Okay, I'll touch you up."

Judy sat back in the elevated makeup chair and smiled. "I have to remind myself to keep smiling in here, like you do," she told Alexandria.

Alexandria, filled with her own anxieties, chuckled. "Yeah, you got that right."

Judy closed her eyes as Alexandria applied powder to her face.

"But you're still thinking a lot, aren't you?" Judy asked.

Her young friend paused, caught up in a muddle of emotions. She said, "Of course. We're always thinking."

"I know we are," Judy told her.

Alexandria watched as the talented and fiery anchor returned to the news desk with her two white co-anchors, and went right back to her broadcast with a smile.

"Atlanta, we're now in the month of November, which means colder weather, jackets, hats, scarves, and a new NBA basketball season, featuring the Atlanta Hawks, new draft picks, and free agents . . ."

Alexandria witnessed Judy's effortless transition from anger to joyfulness, all for the sake of professionalism. She marveled at it.

Amazing! she thought. *I wish God had given me some of that. All I can think about now is how she would kill me if she ever found out about Marlon.*

16... BACKSTABBERS

In Grand Blanc, Michigan, fifteen minutes southeast of Flint, Shawn and his guys met up inside the large lobby of their hotel late Friday morning.

Benny hugged Shawn excitedly and hollered, "What up though? We got people waiting to see you back home today, fam'." Benny was still sporting his flamboyant fur and hood.

Shawn smiled, dressed casually in a dark-blue pea coat and a knit hat. "I know, right?" he said. "I ain't been back home in a minute. I gotta make sure we hit Big John's for a Philly Cheesesteak. Then hit up Coney Island's for breakfast Sunday morning."

"Yeah, that's what's up," Larry agreed. "Get that Big John's sauce on it too."

Alex looked around and asked, "Where's Devon and Toot?" Like a reminiscing football player, he had pulled out his dark-blue and gold Michigan University jacket with his letters and jersey number stitched on the sleeves.

"They out doing interviews and making runs to sell that album," Larry answered. "This ain't vacation time up here for Toot. He got that money to get."

"He damn sure do," Benny agreed.

"I know he happy to do it in that Lambo up here too," Shawn

mentioned.

"Like that private jet y'all flew up here in," Alex hinted to Benny and Larry.

"Well, y'all take the jet to Atlanta with us on the way back," Benny responded casually.

"What about my roundtrip ticket?"

Benny looked to his right at Larry and shrugged. "Let Larry use it."

The guys broke out laughing.

"*Shhiiiddd*, Larry don't look nothing like me," Alex cracked.

"Yeah, I look way better."

As they prepared to walk out the door, a light-brown cutie slid up next to Shawn and grinned. "I hate to bug you in the lobby like this, but can I take a picture with you?"

She was too cute to be turned down, and she knew it. She had a tall brown girlfriend on the side, waiting for his answer with a camera phone. However, Shawn was still leery about folks taking pictures with him for the wrong reasons.

He peeked at Benny and remained skeptical. "I don't know if you wanna take pictures with a wanted man," he told the young woman.

She frowned. "We know they've been making up a bunch of stuff about you in Atlanta. But I'm from Flint, and I got'chu. I don't even get down like that."

Benny said, "Yeah, B, you home now. Cut that shit out. Go 'head and take a picture with her. She ain't gon' bite you."

"I might," she joked as her girlfriend giggled. They both looked to be in their mid-twenties.

Larry smiled and said, "You can bite me all you want. That's my style."

Alex shook his head and held his comments to himself as Shawn begrudgingly took the pictures.

Benny told the young woman, "You might wanna leave us your number too. We may be having a little get together for him later on."

Alex looked at Shawn intentionally. Then he looked back at Benny. "I thought we were all here for a funeral."

Larry didn't like his negative response, but Benny kept his cool. He said, "The living still gotta live, Big Al. J.J. would understand that. How come you don't?"

"I'd rather just respect the dead for a minute, that's all," Alex said, "if that's all right with you."

Sensing the tension between them, the young woman slid away without leaving them her phone number. Larry didn't like that either. He wanted to be able to talk to her more. "What's your problem, man?" he complained to Alex.

"What's *your* problem?" Alex snapped back.

Shawn stepped in between them. "Kill that shit, fam'. Don't y'all know they got people watching me every minute now?"

Alex looked around inside the lobby and noticed the extra eyes that were on them. "Aw'ight, you right. Let's go get something to eat."

"We're not heading to Corunna Road Mall though. There's too many people out there," Shawn stated on their way out the door.

"Now, why would we want to do something to you like that?" Benny asked from the back.

"I'm just letting you know. I'm not signing a hundred autographs today. And I don't want to look mean."

"Word," Alex grunted.

Larry gave Benny a look and kept his silence for later.

Something's going on with these boys, Larry mused. *They act like they beefing with us.*

They headed outside to the black limo and climbed in with plenty of legroom.

"Aw'ight, Flint, here we come," Shawn announced with his feet up.

The limo driver pulled off slowly.

—Did you see it?—

Marlon thought for a second about lying to her. He didn't want to see that picture, nor the article that came with it. He wanted to act as if it didn't exist. He was fucking dreaming, right? It was all a dream, like the Biggie song. Or more like "Nightmares" from Dana Dane. That's how blown his mind was, jumping back in time to find references from any and everything to try and cope with the shock.

He saw a flash of Halle Berry saying, "Love After all of the unexpected events of the week, Marlon Pierce had to force himself to get comfortable again at work. Now that it was Friday, he figured his family would take the weekend off to recuperate.

We'll make it through this, he thought. *It'll all blow over when these people move on to someone else to fuck with.*

Then he received another urgent text message from Alexandria.

—*Oh my God! What are we going to do?*—

She attached a link to a new website article for him to view immediately.

Without going to the link, Marlon assumed he knew what it was about and texted her back.

—*I already read what they said about the networks. They're just reaching now to keep the story going. I'm over it.*—

—*No, this is about US! They have pictures of us from the bar at the hotel!* —

—*Oh my GOD!* —she texted him again.

—*WHAT?* — Marlon texted back. — *How? Are you joking?* —

—*No. Go to the link!* —

In the middle of the UPS workforce, Marlon maintained his calm and took a walk toward the restrooms to find out what was going on.

"Hey Marlon, how's everything going? Is everything all right?" one of the managers asked him.

That made Marlon instantly suspicious. Did the manager know something already?

"Yeah, I'm good. I gotta hit the restroom right now though. When you gotta go, you gotta go," he responded with a smile. He never broke his stride either. The link on his phone was more critical than chit-chat.

He strolled into the men's room, found an open stall, hustled inside, closed the door, and took down his pants and drawers as if he really had to go. Then he found the link that Alexandria had sent him.

There was not only a clear shot of them sitting at the hotel bar table together late Wednesday night, but the article had posted a picture of Marlon's left hand all up in her hair as he stared at her adoringly. The caption read, "Do Judy and Marlon Pierce Have an Open Marriage?"

SHHHIIIIIIITTTTTT!!! Marlon panicked. Nothing was coming out of his body, but his mind was having diarrhea. *WHAT THE FUCK? WHO DID THIS SHIT? FUCKKKKKK!!!*

He had no idea what to do, how to feel, what to say, how to react, where to begin—or how to even process it all. His mind was a *mess.* He was *floored.* Caught off guard. Humiliated. And he didn't want to move from the damn toilet. It was the perfect irony of the situation. Someone had caught him taking a shit with his pants down, and they had posted it all over the Internet.

In the middle of his real-life horror, Alexandria startled him with another new text.

shoulda brought your ass home last night," from the movie *Boomerang.*

"You know you done fucked up, right?" Bill Duke's detective asked in *Menace II Society.*

Back in reality, Alexandria was still pressing Marlon to respond to her texts.

—*Are you still there? I don't know what to do!*—

Marlon didn't know what to do either. He started thinking about self-preservation.

"I did not have sexual relations with that woman," President Bill Clinton insisted. Under pressure, that's the response Marlon decided to go with.

He texted back—*We didn't do anything. Those are just pictures.* —

Alexandria responded—*I know, but . . . why were we even there together?*—

She was asking him to provide her with answers for their story, but Marlon was thinking more about who took the damn pictures.

—*Did you see anybody following you that night?*— he texted.
—*No. Did you?*—
—*Of course not.*—
—*Well, what do we say now? Oh my God!*—

Marlon could read the panic in her text messages. He imagined her crying all over the place. That's what she admitted she would do, especially since she and Judy had become good friends. But Marlon had only started communicating with Alexandria regularly over the past few months, mostly through social media.

I should have just left all that shit alone! he thought.

He came up with something and texted her again.

—*Just say I was helping you work through a breakup with your boyfriend or something. You know, it was just platonic.*—

There was an extended pause after that. Then Alexandria responded—*That won't work with Judy. She knows that I didn't have any boyfriends. And why would I come to you.* —

Well, shit, girl! I don't fucking know! Marlon barked to himself.

"This is *crazy!*" he finally mumbled inside the stall. He felt a headache coming on. Then the paranoia set in.

Did this girl fucking set me up? He panicked. *Is she trying to get something out of this? But why would she want to do that to Judy?*

He wondered what his wife would think of the article and the principal at his sons' school. What if she had been alerted to the story? He was certain the principal was following it.

Marlon sank his face into his hands and squeezed his forehead and temples with his fingers in prayer. *God . . . what have I just done?*

Judy inched forward in the car line to pick her sons up from school that Friday afternoon as if nothing had happened.

I have a whole weekend to deal with this now, she thought. *Just get the kids, order them some pizza, and let them do whatever they want to do tonight while I get this all worked out.*

After reading the new website article—this time in the

National Urban Report—about whether she and her husband had an open marriage and viewing a compromising picture of Marlon with Alexandria, of all people, Judy was determined to hold on to her sanity.

I'm gonna work it all out and let Marlon explain himself at home, she decided. *Then I'll figure out what to do with Alexandria.*

As she approached the front of the line to scoop up her boys, Ms. Hamilton looked more rose-cheeked than usual. Judy figured it was out of embarrassment. *I know she fucking knows already,* she thought. *She follows everything I do.*

"Oh, hi, Mrs. Pierce," she choked up. "How are you today?"

Judy read right through the young woman's anxiety. *Cut the bullshit, girl,* she thought. She couldn't help herself. "I feel miserable right about now, but I'll make it," she admitted.

Ms. Hamilton damn-near swallowed her tongue. "Oh, uh, uh-"

"I bet you don't want to be a newscaster anymore, do you?" Judy poured on her.

The young woman shook in her stance and looked for a rock to climb under, but there was nowhere to hide. She uttered nervously, "Ah, well, umm . . ."

"Don't even worry about it. I'll be all right," Judy told her. "You don't need to have sympathy for me. I'm stronger than that. It's all lies."

Her two boys climbed into the backseat and buckled up as Judy drove off. After shocking Ms. Hamilton with the truth, she actually felt better about it . . . for a minute.

Marlon Jr. asked, "Mom, were you talking to her about *that?*" He was using code language to keep adult business away from his little brother.

"About what?" Taylor asked on cue.

Judy shook her head. *These damn people have no idea how these bullshit-ass articles affect your whole life and family.*

"I was telling her how I was gonna order you guys pizza for dinner tonight," Judy lied to her son.

"Piz-zaaahhh," Taylor cheered.

Marlon knew better, but he smiled and let his mother get away with it. It was grownup stuff.

Marlon Sr. headed home in his Range Rover with his cell phone glued to his right ear. "No matter what happens, don't ever break from what we talked about. Okay?"

"O-kay," Alexandria whimpered over the line. "I'm so sor-reee."

"Look, it was both of us. Okay? I just needed someone to talk to. That's all it was. You understand that?"

"Yes . . . but what if she tries to hurt me?"

Marlon paused and thought about that. Alexandria had a point. Judy had a history of violence. He said, "You're gonna talk to her before this weekend is up. You have to. You can't go back to work without this being settled. Neither of you can."

"I don't know if I can go back to work at all," she whined. "It's a very tightknit circle at the station."

Marlon thought about that as well. "They should be able to understand it then. Or just let Judy explain it to them while you keep quiet."

Marlon realized his wife was five times stronger than Alexandria was, and she was older. Judy had also been at the station longer. She had seniority.

"But she can't explain it for me when she's not around. I do makeup for two news teams, not just hers," Alexandria mentioned.

"Just stick to the story. Tell it like it is, get it over with, and move on. Okay?"

Alexandria paused. "I'll try."

"You'll *try*?" Marlon snapped. He was losing his patience. "Look, just say what we talked about, and you'll be fine. Okay?"

Alexandria was so unstable that Marlon was afraid to hang up the phone. But he was almost home, and he was anxious to prepare himself for his wife.

"Look, I'm gonna do my part and you have to do yours. Now I'm almost home, so I need to hang up. Get yourself together and stay ready," he advised her. "She might want to call you up in the middle of it, and you have to answer your phone. We cannot prolong the issue."

"Oh my *God*," Alexandria repeated. She sounded fearful and frustrated.

Marlon shook his head, doubtfully. *This girl's gonna fuck up. I can see that already. So I need to protect myself, and my family more than anything. I can't really help her.*

"All right, I gotta go now."

When Marlon hung up, he was so relieved to end their feeble conversation that he decided to give up on worrying about discussing it with his wife. What was the use? The conclusion was out of his hands. So he was calm about it.

"I'm just gonna say what it was," he insisted aloud to himself.

He entered the security gate code and drove in to park next to his wife's black Mercedes in the driveway. Then he took a deep breath and exhaled before climbing out of his SUV. "All right, here we go," he mumbled.

All was quiet when he walked into the house, and Judy and the boys were not in the kitchen. Marlon headed to the bedroom, but his wife was not there either. Then he walked into the den, where he found his two sons playing video games with plates of pizza spread around the room as Judy watched them quietly.

"Hey, Dad," Taylor greeted him.

Marlon Jr. followed his brother's lead and spoke to his father as Judy made eye contact and stood. Then she walked out of the room without a word.

Marlon followed her back into their bedroom for the showdown and closed their door behind him. Judy sat on the bed in silence and turned to face him, giving her husband her undivided attention.

Oh, I wanna hear this shit, she told herself. *Every minute of it.*

Marlon said, "I guess you saw that new website article today."

Judy took her time to respond. "And I'm still trying to understand it," she said. "Are you interviewing Alexandria for something?"

All right, she's loving this, Marlon thought. *I look like the biggest asshole in the world now.*

"I just needed someone to talk to who understands your business, Judy. It's not like I have a bunch of friends who have wives on television. They can't relate to that. So I needed an inside perspective, that's all."

Judy nodded calmly. Marlon's explanation actually made sense. However, they were just getting started. She planned to toss the kitchen sink at him with all the dirty dishes.

"Okay, well . . . your hand in her hair gave you an extra perspective? Or was that some kind of camera editing trick?"

Marlon took a deep breath. "I mean, her hair was all out and wild that night, and I just . . . reached out and touched it for a minute. It wasn't like it looks at all."

Judy stared him down with Superman's x-ray-like vision. "You mean the same way it looked as if I were going to kiss Shawn Blake across the table?"

Marlon shrugged. "I guess so. Yeah."

"But I never *touched* him," Judy snapped. "In fact, I don't think I shook this man's hand but once. But you got your hands all up in a black woman's *hair*. Do you know how intimate that is? You may as well have stuck your hand in her panties."

The temperature in the room was starting to heat up, five degrees at a time. It felt like a slow torture.

Marlon frowned. "Come on, now. It wasn't even like that."

"Oh, it wasn't? Well, how did it feel? I know she got that Indian grade shit. And you just had to have it, right? 'Let me see what this shit feels like. It looks so *soft*,' " she mocked him. "You think I was born yesterday, Marlon? Everybody wants to fuck that girl. She talks about it all the time."

"Everybody wants to fuck Shawn Blake too," Marlon countered.

"And if they're hanging out with him late night at some hotel bar, *alone*, they probably will get fucked. So let's start with the meeting place. How did you even meet up with her there? Was it all by coincidence?"

Marlon was back on the spot. "What if it was?"

Judy faked surprise. "Oh, that would have been a hell of a

coincidence. 'Hi, Marlon, funny meeting you here. Why don't you sit down and have a drink with me and put your hands in my hair. I don't mind.' Is that how it went?"

Shit! She's loving this, Marlon repeated to himself. *I gotta cut this shit short. I'm not gon' do this all night.*

Judy's slow grind was more aggravating to him than her fast explosions. And Marlon was certain that she realized it.

He said, "Okay, look . . . we started hitting each other up on Facebook a few days after that last network party you had downtown at the Marriott over the summer. She helped me to understand and cope with all of the things that you were going through. But once you started doing this Shawn Blake story, I started talking to her even more, because she was telling me that it would be all right. Then this whole website thing broke, and I told her that I was getting tired of this shit. So out of the kindness of her heart, she came out with crazy hair to meet me at the bar that night and to talk about it, knowing that y'all both had to be to work in the morning. Okay? And the whole hair thing was one fucking second, Judy, but you catch something like that on camera, and it looks like you were there for an hour. That wasn't the case."

Judy stared him down again. "So . . . you mean to tell me that you've been talking to her for *months* now, and I haven't heard about this not *once*? That girl works with me *five* days a week, Marlon. Then she calls me outside of work. So does it sound *normal* to you that she would never once tell me she's been having Facebook conversations with my fucking *husband*?"

Marlon frowned. "She didn't want you to trip about it, like you're doing right now. How would you take her giving me advice about you?"

Judy had to stop and think. "Giving you advice about *me*? Marlon, that girl barely knows if she's coming or going half the time. She knows her *makeup* and that's about *it*."

"Exactly," Marlon countered. "You don't think she knows anything, so why would you want her talking to me?"

"Well, why would you want to talk to her in the first place, Marlon? How did you even start off on Facebook?"

" 'Your wife is wonderful. I admire her so much,' " Marlon quoted.

That sounded just like Alexandria. Judy had to admit that herself.

"So, she gets all close to you because she admires me?" she commented. "And then she decides to keeps this away from me for *months*, while she's blowing up your damn phone every night? No wonder she doesn't like people looking at her cell."

Judy shook her head. She didn't like any of it. "I don't trust her at all now," she told her husband.

Instead of leaving Alexandria out to dry, Marlon attempted to toss her a rope to save her. "That girl worships the ground you walk on, Judy. But now she's feeling *crushed*, because these crazy-ass website people are after you, and apparently they are following me now too. It's all crazy. Think about it. We don't have no damn open marriage. They're trying to rip us apart with anything they can find."

Judy cringed. "Marlon, don't stand here and blame shit on the cameras and the media. The point is I wasn't doing anything with Shawn Blake, and you knew everything about it. I was doing my damn *job*. But what did I know about you and Alexandria? She had plenty of time to come clean with me if it was all *innocent*. But she *didn't*. So let's move on to the next line of questions. Did you fuck her? You had to ask *me* that question, right?"

Here we go, Marlon told himself. She was hitting him with layer after layer.

"No I did not," he answered. "We're both getting caught up in this thing."

Judy aimed her x-ray vision eyes on him again. "Oh, so now we're *both* caught up. At first, you thought *I* was the one who was crazy. Now you're getting some of your own medicine."

Marlon even wondered if she had been the one to hire someone to follow him. However, he left that thought unsaid.

"So now I have to talk to Alexandria, right, to get her side of the story?" said Judy.

Marlon was already prepared for that. "I didn't talk to Shawn Blake," he said. "I took your word for it."

Judy frowned. "Excuse me, does Shawn Blake work with you at UPS? Because I'm quite sure if he did, you would ask him about it. And you'd be ready to whip his *ass* if he didn't have the right answers too."

Marlon couldn't even argue with her, so she continued.

"We can call him up right now if you want to talk to him. In fact, he left me a message yesterday."

Without hesitation, Judy put her cell phone on speaker and played Shawn's message for her husband. "Hey, Judy, it's Shawn. I don't even know where to start with this, really. I tried to call you a few times yesterday . . ."

As Marlon continued to listen, he worried again about Alexandria's side of the story. *She's gonna fuck this up, but there's no way around it. Judy has to work with her. So I have to see what she says and get ready to protect myself.*

When Shawn's straightforward message ended, Judy asked Marlon, "Now, do you have one from Alexandria that I can listen to? Because she surely hasn't called *me* today, and that feels like guilt already. She *knows* she's wrong."

Marlon remained careful. "I don't have a message."

"Did you talk to her?"

"Of course, I talked to her," he admitted. "She's terrified now. She doesn't know *how* to talk to you. All she kept saying was how sorry she was."

"Sorry for what, having a secret relationship with my husband? Her ass *needs* to be sorry. You have no idea how much *restraint* I've had over the past few hours not to call that girl up or go looking for her ass, because I needed to hear it from *you* first."

"That's why she hasn't called you. I told her I would talk to you first."

"What, so you can try and calm me down with the right *lies*?" Judy blasted. "You *know* she got an ass-kicking coming to her. That girl sat right up in my face for the past *two days, knowing* that she was with you, and didn't say a damn thing. Now, do you wanna change your story before I call her?"

Marlon thought about that. *Ain't shit I can do now. It's all up to her.*

He shrugged. "It's your call, Judy. Go ahead and call her."

For a second, Judy hesitated. She expected him to at least try a different story. But since he had called her bluff, she followed through and dialed Alexandria's number. She put the speakerphone on from the bed.

"Hello," Alexandria answered in a weak and scratchy voice. It sounded as if she had been crying for hours.

"Alexandria, you know who this is, and you know what we're going through right now. So, I need to ask you some questions, and just so we're clear and transparent, Marlon is standing right here with me."

"Oh my *God*, Judy, I'm so sor-reee," Alexandria broke down immediately. "We were just talking, just talking," she stammered.

Judy looked at Marlon to read his every emotion. He shook his head, breathed deeply and waited.

"I don't understand. If you were only talking, then why are you so sorry?" Judy asked her.

"Because I never told you that we were friends. I didn't know how you would take it. But now that someone took those pictures, you can read anything into it."

"You got that right, especially late at night with my husband's hand all in your hair."

"That was only for a second, because my hair was so wild. But it wasn't like it looks." Alexandria's voice cracked with every syllable. "Judy, you know I would never want anyone to see my hair like that. But we were in a hotel sports bar with panoramic windows, so it wasn't like we were hiding from anyone. I love you guys too much for that. And I admire everything that you do. I was only there to try and help you."

Her voice was so pitiful with emotion that Judy felt sorry for her.

Okay, she's making this hard now, she told herself. *But she was wrong!*

Marlon couldn't look anymore. He forced himself to avert his eyes from her. *This is crazy!* he thought. *All because she wanted to get into this celebrity interview shit. Now my whole damn life will end up in the news.*

"You're telling me you got up out of bed to meet him there with crazy-ass hair just to *talk*?" Judy pressed her.

"Yes . . . I did it for *you*. I did it for *both* of you."

Judy was so angry and twisted she started stuttering. "Girl, st-stop saying that shit. You didn't do it for *me*. You did it for *you*."

"Nooo," Alexandria wailed like a child. "I didn't have anything to do with what you were going through. I was in bed, and I got up only to try and be helpful."

"Helpful by doing what? Seeing my husband behind my *back*?" Judy snapped. The pain and anger were pouring out. The calm charade was over. Judy yelled, "That's not fucking helping *me*! Your ass would have been better off *hiding* with him!"

Alexandria went silent. Marlon looked back at his wife in apprehension. He expected Alexandria to crack at any minute.

Oh my God! Here we go! Marlon panicked.

"Would you rather he called somebody who didn't care?" Alexandria asked.

That caught Judy off guard for a second, but then she said, "I would rather he had talked to *me*."

"And sometimes you don't hear him," Alexandria countered.

Judy froze and looked up into her husband's eyes. She had no idea the young makeup artist would hit her upside the head with that. She expected to have her way with a weak and insecure younger woman, but it didn't quite turn out that way.

Marlon was surprised. It wasn't part of the script, but it was honest.

Shit! Judy cursed herself. *This got damn girl! What we do in my house is none of her damn business!*

"So, what are we gonna do about this?" Judy huffed with Alexandria still on the line. "Because we don't have a damn open marriage."

"We just say that we don't, and that this is all nonsense," Marlon suggested with a shrug. He felt amazingly relieved. Alexandria had done her part.

"Yeah, you *would* say some simple shit like that if it's

241

convenient for *you*," Judy barked at him. She still wanted to be mad at something, or some*one*.

"What do you think *I've* been going through at work this week?" Marlon asked her. "You just keep it simple. 'It's my wife's job, man. They make up a lot of stuff. But you know me better than that.' That's been all week long, Judy. Now that it's *your* turn, you got a problem with it."

"Because she has to *work with me*," Judy repeated. "How do you think that's gonna look every day?"

"Well, maybe I just won't work there anymore," Alexandria interjected.

Judy and Marlon eyed each other again.

"Yeah, and then they'll really think you did something," Judy countered.

"Well, what else do you want her to do?" her husband asked her.

It was the driving question.

Judy exhaled. "I don't know. I need more time to figure this shit out."

"Well, I'm sorry about everything," Alexandria told them. "I feel horrible."

Yeah, you need to feel horrible, Judy thought. *And I don't trust you now. Nor do I believe you . . . bitch!*

17... TRUSTWORTHY

Back up in Michigan, in the middle of a crowd at a Buffalo Wild Wings sports bar, Shawn received the third call in a row from Kenya, his fellow MSU Spartan alumnus. He realized that it was urgent.

"Hello."

"Hey, how's it going back home in Flint?"

Shawn walked near the restrooms and adjusted the phone to hear her clearly through the racket. "It's crazy. But I'm trying to focus on this funeral in the morning and not get too caught up in it."

"Okay, do what you gotta do. I just sent you a link earlier. Did you look at it?"

"Naw. What about?"

"Your reporter friend, Judy Pierce, in Atlanta. What's going on with that? I like her."

"Yeah, you know how the media game is these days, man. They're trying to do her dirty just from being around me."

"Really? For what? What did she do? It seems like somebody's out to get her or something. They're going after her husband now too."

Shawn grimaced. "What? Her husband?"

"Yeah, you need to read the link. They had some bullshit article talking about an open marriage and catching her husband out with some young floozy the other night. I know Judy don't get down like that, do she?"

"Naw, I doubt that."

"That's what I'm saying. Does Benny know what you're doing with her?" Kenya probed.

"What, the whole interview thing about my life?"

"Yeah, did you tell him that?"

Shawn thought about her question and grinned. "I forgot—you never liked him either."

"Well, I don't know how you forgot. I don't even like saying his damn name. But to each his own. I just wanted to see if you knew what was going on with all that. Have you talked to her about it?"

"Naw, she won't answer my calls now."

"Oh, well that tells me a lot. If somebody didn't want her to talk to you, this is damn sure how to do it. I would flip out if somebody fucked with my family too," Kenya said. "That's why I couldn't stay married with a whole bunch of extra shit going on. I need *peace*."

"So, what are you trying to say? Somebody don't want her to interview me about my life? You're starting to sound like Alex now. He thinks all this shit is being set up by you know who."

"Well, if it walks like a duck and quacks like a duck, then you tell me, Shawn. Is it a *wolf*?"

Shawn laughed as he looked back through the sports bar crowd and caught Benny's eyes on him from their corner booth, as if they were wondering about each other at the same time. Then he looked away and returned to his conversation.

"I mean . . . what do you want me to say? He's been looking out for me for years. He never did anything bad to me."

"Of course not, you're his meal ticket. Why would he want to do something to you? But if anybody else tries to get too close to you . . . you know what I'm saying? Just watch yourself," Kenya warned him. "You're too intelligent and talented for that; but whenever you get around him, I always notice that you start slipping. That's not the Shawn I know. Don't change your last name and get soft on me. Stand your ground."

Shawn grinned at how well Kenya knew him. "I'm already ahead of you," he said. "But all right, let me read this article you sent me."

"Yeah, you really need to do that."

Shawn stepped into the men's room and searched his smartphone for the latest article on Judy Pierce's husband. Once he found it, he winced. "Damn, they caught his hand in her hair," he mumbled. Even he knew how intimate that was for a black woman. He carefully read the article. "Shit!" he piped. "Let me send this to Al."

When he returned from the restroom, he was curious to see how Benny would feel about Judy's attacks. He walked right over to him with his phone.

"Yo, check this out."

A bit wired from his drinks, Benny looked at the mini-sized article with bloodshot eyes and squinted. "Damn, he got his hand in her hair. She must got that natural shit," he cracked.

"What do you think about all that?" Shawn asked him.

Benny gave him an absent stare. "What about it?"

"First a bullshit article comes about me, now they're going after her and her husband."

Benny remained a blank wall. "And? Fuck you want me to do, tell them to leave her alone? I don't have shit to do with that."

"Are you sure?" Shawn pressed him.

Suddenly, their private conversation became intense.

"Man, don't accuse me of no bullshit like that," Benny said. "That's petty shit."

"It may be petty, but it got me a lot of fucking news. People are talking about it, right? That keeps me hot in the 'hood, like J.J.'s murder."

"Yo, man, what's going on?" Larry spoke up.

Alex jumped in place to protect Shawn. That made Toot, Devon, and the rest of The Factory crew take notice from the other booths and tables around the restaurant.

Benny told everyone, "Hold on, hold on, everything's all right. We just drinking in here. Calm down and hold your liquor. We got a funeral to go to in the morning."

"We shouldn't have come here in the first place then," Alex complained.

"Where you want us to be, Al, in a church?" Toot jabbed. "We can't stop living because of J. He wouldn't stop living for *us*. Would he Devon?"

"Why you putting me in it?" Devon whined.

"Because you knew him the best."

Larry shook it off and said, "Yo, we all in here looking crazy, talking about some dumb shit. Let's just eat, drink, have a good time, and get up early for this funeral tomorrow."

Benny nodded, loving his conclusion. "I couldn't have said it better myself."

Shawn grinned and kept his silence. However, the homegrown Factory members were unsettled by the friction.

"You all right, B?" a few of them asked Shawn. The death of J.J. struck a chord with them, and they heard his hint loud and clear. Maybe Benny C. had something to do with it.

Shawn nodded and said, "Yeah, I'm good. Like he said, we all been drinking."

Benny laughed loudly and gave him an overbearing hug. "I got nothing but love for you, fam'. A little argument ain't hurt nobody."

Alex watched it all with his usual skepticism. *Fake ass!* he thought. *Little by little, Shawn is starting to see it now.*

"What you think now?" Larry asked Benny inside the limo. They had dropped everyone off for the night.

Benny calmly stroked his goatee. "We gon' deal with it all when we get back to Atlanta. What's your boy talking 'bout down there now?"

"Oh, Keith? He said he gon' get a price and let us know."

Benny thought about that for a moment. "What you think he'll do if we don't give him the money? Is he that serious?"

Larry paused. "He about the only one who is."

"Oh yeah? I guess we'll find out then. And we'll bring a few more killers down from The Factory."

"How you think Shawn'll take that?" Larry asked.

Benny gave him a stern glare. "He don't need to know about it. It's better for him that way. He startin' to act too paranoid now. He need to stick to acting and let us handle everything else."

"What about Al?"

Benny paused. "We'll handle it when we get back to Atlanta."

Emotions were considerably tame at J.J.'s funeral that Saturday morning. There was no reckless crying or hysterics over his open casket. The proceedings had a business-as-usual feel, with a typical speech about a young man whose life had ended too early to make the necessary changes he could have made to become a more productive citizen and father. His three children and their two mothers weren't even emotional. The man had never spent enough time in their lives to elicit such sentiments from them, particularly after receiving a promise of acquiring new money to hold them over in his death that J. had never provided while he was alive.

Their graveyard march, however, signified a loss of innocence. The finality of J.J.'s body being lowered into the ground allowed Shawn to understand more than ever that they all had *one chance* to live . . . and their clocks were forever ticking.

"You all right, B?" Alex quietly asked his friend inside the limo. In their separation from the group, he could tell that Shawn was in deep thought.

He nodded. "I'm good. I'm just mapping this all out in my head."

Alex looked out the window at the others to make sure he and Shawn still had a few minutes of privacy. "You believe Benny didn't have anything to do with your girl Judy Pierce and her husband?" Alex had some ideas of his own about that.

Shawn eyed him and said, "I'm gonna find out. Usually, somebody tips you for shit like that. These photographers don't just pop up randomly. They had to know that he was there."

"Or they followed him," Alex suggested. "That's just what I'm saying. If he didn't want you interviewing with her, all he had to do was *say it*."

"Yeah, but that wouldn't create any media attention," Shawn countered. "This shit does. Everything is about creating a buzz now."

Alex shook his head. He couldn't believe the motive. "This media shit is that big now? That's unbelievable, man. You'll ruin somebody's family just to get in the fucking *news*?"

"With millions of new people becoming popular through cell phones and computers these days, you gotta find other ways of standing out," said Shawn. "That's just how he looks at it."

"In that case, we may want to check into who tipped that blogger, YellowGirl1, to start this shit up in the first place. You think she did that on her own?"

Shawn thought about that and said, "That's a good point."

"Yeah, I saw that loud-ass girl outside your court case. And I'm sure she saw Judy there too," Alex added.

Shawn looked surprised. "Oh, yeah? How come you didn't tell me that earlier?"

"I wasn't even thinking about it, really. It just hit me when you started talking about people having tips." He peeked out the window to check on everyone else. "All right, here they come."

Larry climbed back in the limo first. "What y'all doing in here—making out?"

"Yeah, and now we got you in here for the threesome. So bend your black ass over the bar," Alex joked crudely.

Toot climbed in and cringed, overhearing him. "Fuck y'all talking 'bout in here, man? What, I'm in the wrong limo or something? Kill that gay shit."

"Word, right?" Devon agreed, climbing in behind him. "Have some respect for the dead out here."

Benny climbed in last. He kept his cool in a long brown trench coat. "I feel like a father who just put one of my son's in the grave," he said. That put a stop to the playful mood inside the car and left them all with more thoughts than jokes.

Yeah, like the Godfather, Alex thought. *And you just had your own son whacked.*

That Saturday afternoon at home in Alpharetta, Judy continued to wrap her mind around a viable solution for her personal and family concerns. She ignored all of her incoming phone calls as she cleaned up her house and brainstormed. However, she did check her phone repeatedly to see who was calling.

"Taylor, I want all of your toys back in the toy box, and that includes the ones you throw in the closet," she barked to her youngest son as she peeked in his room from the doorway. It was a clean-house day for all of them.

"Awww, mannn," Taylor whined.

Judy eyed him with reprimand. "Let me hear something else. When I tell you to clean up your room, that's what I mean. And I mean *all* of it."

As she walked away, another call popped up on her cell phone. It was from Brenda Avant. Judy paused and decided to take that one. "Good afternoon, Brenda," she answered with light-blue rubber cleaning gloves on her hands.

"Good afternoon, Judy. Are you able to talk to me today?"

"Yeah, let me get situated and I'll call you right back."

Judy went to take off her cleaning gloves and wash her hands in the bathroom before making the return call in the den. She closed the double doors for privacy.

Brenda shocked her when she said, "We're letting Alexandria go from the station. I don't know exactly what happened between her and your husband, and frankly, I don't care. But I do know when to draw the line, and disrupting someone's family is definitely it."

Judy was speechless. *Damn!* she thought. She was still trying to figure it out in her head. Again, she felt sorry for Alexandria. *All of this, just because I got involved in interviewing Shawn Blake.*

Brenda said, "That *was* Alexandria with your husband in the pictures, right?"

Judy exhaled. It was a suffocating experience, especially with her history of bulling through matters unscathed. Now she was stuck in a much more delicate situation.

"I was trying to decide how to deal with this in a way that makes sense for all parties involved," she explained. "If we fire her, doesn't that make it look like something was really going on?"

"Well, what would you suggest?" Brenda asked her calmly. She made it sound as if she was open to other ideas.

"We could say that we're all good friends and that there was really nothing to it," Judy answered. She couldn't believe her own words. Nevertheless, she was attempting to manage it all as best she could without being led by her emotions. A major part of their jobs at the news station was emotional management.

Brenda paused, cautiously. "Judy, we're all going to have to make some incredibly tough decisions here, but there has to be some repercussions for this. That's just the way it is. If I were you, I would seriously think about taking a two-week leave to get away from it all and recharge my batteries."

Judy heard that and shook her head defiantly. *No fucking way!* "And how would that make me look? That would make me look *weak*," she stated.

"You have to stop thinking so much about how it *looks* and think about how it really *is*," Brenda countered. "People have very short memories these days. If we handle this all correctly, they will forget about it in a few months and move on."

"Yeah, and in the meantime, Wendy goes after my job as lead anchor," Judy blurted.

"Actually, Michael would lead in your absence."

"Oh, so you've already thought it out?"

"I had no choice. When Bob gets back next week, it's imperative that we have all of the answers lined up and ready to go. Otherwise, I wouldn't be doing my job."

"Well, I thought you said that you were trying to help me," Judy whined. The deck of cards seemed to be stacked against her.

"I am trying to help you. But even my cease and desist letter to this blogger girl doesn't mean much now that the *National Urban Report* has gotten involved with these new pictures of Alexandria and your husband. If we don't nip this avalanche in the bud correctly, *American Celebrity Media* will be next to jump on board—I'm sure. They would make this story an even *bigger* headache.

"Trust me, two weeks is less than a *minute* over the span of a forty-year career, if you're able to last that long," Brenda said. "The key is to get this done right."

"Yeah, but we don't know what *right* is yet," Judy argued.

In the middle of their antsy conversation, a new call came in from Shawn Blake, which Judy promptly diverted to her voicemail. *I don't have time for more of his apologies right now.*

"So, this is your idea of help?" she continued to bicker with Brenda.

"Judy, I told you a month ago when you first came up with this great plan of yours, that I didn't think it was a good idea. In fact, I told you that it was *terrible*. These people have gotten far too desperate for attention. I never trust their motives anymore. It used to be that they would only do interviews when there was something specific they were trying to promote. Now it's gotten to the point where there's so much nonsense being covered, we have no idea of knowing what's real or what's being fabricated.

"So yes, you got yourself into this mess, and this is the only way that I can help you out of it," Brenda concluded.

Judy sat there blankly. She was angry at everything, including herself for not heeding the older woman's wisdom earlier. *Well . . . I guess there's no more to talk about,* she conceded.

"Can I at least ask you not to make up your mind until I give this some more thought?" Judy asked calmly.

"I haven't locked in a decision yet, I'm only presenting the options to you," Brenda responded. "There aren't many we have at this point. So, how long would you like me to wait?"

"Just for a few more days," Judy pleaded. "We were all just hit with this yesterday."

Brenda took a pregnant pause. "I would need to speak to you and Alexandria both in my office at no later than five fifteen, Monday morning. So you get your story together by then, and I'll decide if it's strong enough to sell to Bob."

"Okay," Judy agreed quickly. She didn't have any other choice.

When they hung up, Judy reflected on how she'd gotten around Brenda to cut a deal with Bob, only to find herself in a bucket of nonsense. Now she was willing to back up and let Brenda get her out of it.

"I don't think I trust that rich white man. He makes me nervous," she mumbled. "Like Brenda said, once they have you out there, they can change on you *quick*. So I need to let her handle this."

Out of curiosity, she checked her phone messages to listen to what Shawn Blake had to say: "Hey, Judy, this keeps getting crazier by the minute, right? I read that new article on you and your husband, and I've been thinking a lot about what's been going on now.

"I can't do it, because you know they're following everything I do now, but maybe you could find out if that blogger, YellowGirl1, was tipped or paid to write an article about us that led to this.

"You and Big Al got me thinking a lot now that all this is not just by coincidence. But it won't look right for me trying to dig it up. You even got me thinking about Annette now. I'm ready to ask my man if he gave her some money on the side. He's into property and real estate like that too.

"But all right, I'm just giving you some more inside information to work with. It'll sound crazy unless you can bring it all together. So, I wouldn't even talk about all this unless you're sure."

Shawn's loaded message pushed her thinking into overdrive.

YellowGirl1 wrote an article a few weeks ago about "Ricky Slim" and his music, right after his court case with Shawn too, Judy thought. *Was that by coincidence? Now Shawn tells me that*

252

Benny's into real estate? He didn't tell me that before. Maybe I do have some more investigating to do. But I can't just send this girl a damn letter. I'll need to step to her ass face to face and catch her on campus somewhere.

"I just need to ask this girl a few questions and see how she responds," Judy insisted aloud. "I probably won't even be able to catch up to her."

Her anxious energy was building up, like a runaway train.

"Hell, I got nothing to lose at this point. Let me just go down there and see."

"Where are you going, Mom? I thought you said today was clean-up day," Marlon Jr. asked an hour later. Judy was dressed and ready to head out the door, but they were only halfway finished cleaning their large house. They hadn't cleaned it as feverishly since the end of summer.

"I have to make a run," she informed her oldest. He didn't need more information than that. It was grown folks' business. She headed out to the backyard to tell her husband, who was blowing leaves to collect in several Hefty trash bags—a tedious, all-day process. Under the circumstances, however, Marlon didn't mind. It allowed him to focus on something other than his wife, Alexandria, his coworkers, and all the new mess he was involved in.

"I need to make a run," Judy told him.

Marlon Sr. stopped what he was doing and looked confused. "Something came up?"

"Yeah," she answered with a nod.

That was all he needed to know.

Marlon backed down and mumbled, "All right." *You're not gonna do anything reckless, are you?* he wanted to ask. He had no idea what was on her mind, but he didn't trust it. Nevertheless, he was still not in a position to question her, so he let his apprehensions go.

Judy marched out the front door, climbed into her car and hit the road toward Georgia Tech's campus. "Probably won't even find this girl," she mumbled as she drove through clear and sunny weather. "I'll look up a few private investigators after work on Monday."

With a bunch of questions and ideas on her mind and no home football or basketball games to jam up the Atlanta traffic that Saturday, Judy arrived in the Midtown area much faster than expected. She parked in a lot on Georgia Tech's campus and got nervous.

What if I find this girl and she acts a fool out here and tries to write something else about me? she wondered in a panic. Determined to at least try, she headed back to The Greek Cafe, where she'd bumped into YellowGirl1 before.

The popular restaurant was not as crowded as it had been during the weekdays at lunchtime, so it was easy to identify the patrons sitting in each area. When Judy spotted the colorfully dressed grad student in plain view in a booth to the far right, she froze and panicked again.

Oh shit, she's here! What's the chance of that? Unbelievable!

She was so shocked to find the girl that she spun away as if trying to avoid her. Then she calmed herself. *Okay, just keep your cool and do what you came to do. You're a professional.*

The young woman was so into her laptop and salad that she never saw Judy coming.

"I hope you're not writing another article about me," Judy cracked and took a seat across from her.

YellowGirl1 looked up from her usual writing spot at the cafe and jumped when she saw who it was. "Shit! What do you want?" she asked defensively.

Judy forced a smile. "Calm down, I only want to talk to you."

"I'm not writing about you anymore," YellowGirl1 responded, looking around nervously.

"Good. Unless of course you want to retract what you already wrote. That would be nice."

Judy couldn't help herself. The opportunity to pitch a retraction was perfect.

YellowGirl1 looked around again and appeared ready to break for cover. Either that, or she was looking for witnesses.

"I mean, I only asked a question," she stated. "It's my right of free speech to do that. But like I said, I'm not gonna write about you anymore. So . . ."

"Why did you write about me in the first place, Riquan?" Judy pressed her, using her real name. "Did someone tell you to do that? Was it an assignment from ATLHeat.com? Were you paid to write it? It looks like you're eating well."

Judy's journalism and research skills were on full display. But it was more of an interrogation than an interview. Obviously, the young woman was rattled and ready to flee, so Judy didn't expect her to answer the questions; she only wanted her to realize who and what she was up against.

Oh my God! I knew I shouldn't have come here today, YellowGirl1 reflected. *I should have just played it safe and stayed at home.*

"Yeah, whatever," she responded, while frantically grabbing her things to leave. "I don't see you badgering the *National Urban Report* about what they published. Everyone wants to attack the little guys. It's so typical."

"Oh, don't worry, they're gonna get theirs too," Judy informed her. "You people all need to know who you're fucking with."

The young woman stood up, leaving her barely eaten salad on the table. With her laptop in hand, she decided to retaliate. "If you ask me, I think you really *did it*—you *and* your husband. You're *disgusting* and you're only mad now that you got *caught* and someone's writing about it."

As a few onlookers began to tune in, she added, "You know you *did* Shawn Blake, and your husband *did* your coworker. Why don't you just be woman enough to admit it instead of bothering *me*?"

At that moment, all of Judy's professionalism went out the window. She barked, "Girl, I will kick your fucking *ass*! You don't know shit about me."

As soon as Judy stood up, YellowGirl1 raised her hands to her face in defense and stumbled backwards. Judy read it all as a flop and was angry enough to attack her for real.

This damn girl knows she's wrong! she thought. *Now she's in here acting, and trying to make a damn scene.*

"Why don't you admit that you got *paid*, you fucking media whore?" Judy snapped and pushed her.

Startled, the young woman reacted and threw her laptop bag and computer at Judy's face. With quick hands and anticipation, Judy caught it in mid-air, like a volleyball player, and threw it back. Not as quick or as athletic, the younger and smaller woman was not prepared for the volley. The rectangular bag and computer crashed into her face and head.

"AHH! Oh my God! Help me!" she screamed to any and everyone inside the restaurant.

Judy looked around and panicked. All eyes were on her. *Oh, shit!* she cursed herself. "Why would you throw your computer at me?" she yelled back, to explain her actions.

The young, colorful woman ignored her and continued screaming while holding her injured head, "Oh my *God*! *Security*!"

Fuck! Judy fumed. "You shouldn't have thrown the computer at me."

"You *attacked* me!" YellowGirl1 barked back.

By that time, calls were being made to the campus police, while the restaurant manager walked out from behind the counter to investigate the scuffle.

"What's going on here?" He was a towering, heavyset man with thick black hair.

"She's exaggerating," Judy told him.

The manager inspected the scene and shook his head. "I think you need to leave," he advised Judy. She looked like the obvious aggressor, and she was not a college student.

Judy wasted no time to heed his words and made a mad dash for the exit. She was determined to get away from it all.

"Okay, this was a huge mistake," she admitted as she crossed the street toward the parking garage. It was a block away and around the corner.

Two campus police cars arrived at the scene as Judy turned the corner. Feeling like a fugitive, she hustled into the parking garage with a racing heart to find her car and escape to safety. She quickly climbed in behind the wheel and exhaled.

"Shit!" she cursed, sinking her face into her hands. "This is getting crazier by the minute. Let me just get the hell out of here."

She started up her car to head out of the garage for home just as the two campus police cruisers blocked the entrance gate with their flashing lights and sirens.

WHHRRRRPP! WHHRRRRPP!

Judy jammed her breaks and froze with both hands on the wheel. "Oh my God!" She didn't know what else to say or do as they zeroed in on her. She closed her eyes and listened, afraid to even look.

"Could you step out of the car, please?"

She opened her eyes and climbed out of her driver's seat while shielding herself from the glare of the flashlights with her hands inside the dimly lit garage.

"Were you inside The Greek Cafe, ma'am?" a young campus officer asked.

"Yes, I was," Judy admitted. There was no sense in lying. More than a dozen people could identify her at the scene, including the manager.

"And did you assault a woman by throwing her computer?"

"She threw it at me first," Judy protested.

The next thing she knew, the officers were calling for backup.

Fuck! she cursed herself again. *Now what?*

18... LIGHTS, CAMERA, ACTION

At close to seven o'clock that Saturday evening, Marlon received a phone call from his wife. He had finished cleaning up the leaves in the backyard a while ago with thoughts of taking a long hot shower as soon as Judy returned home from her extra-long errand. She had been missing in action for four hours.

"Marlon, I need you to take the kids over to the neighbor's house and come get me," she told him solemnly. There was no emotion in her voice. She had run out of it.

"Where are you?" Marlon asked. "You crashed the car? Are you all right?"

Judy paused. "I'm in jail. I'll tell you all about it when you get here."

Marlon was speechless. Of course, he wanted to say more, but not over a prison phone. So he withheld his questions and thought about it all in silence.

"Okay. Where do I have to come and get you?"

After a brief conversation about the address and the bail amount, Marlon hung up and took a breath.

"I knew I didn't have a good feeling when she left the house today," he mumbled. "I should have said something earlier."

The gravy kept getting hotter and thicker. He changed into

fresh clothes, with no shower, and made a phone call to their neighbors, who lived a mile up the road.

After dropping his boys off, Marlon was anxious to call Alexandria and check in on her.

"Hello," she answered, cautiously.

"Hey, are you all right?"

She was still dragging and depressed. "Yeah, I'm all right."

"Judy didn't come after you today or anything, did she?"

"No," she answered with more vigor. "Why would you ask that?"

"She's been arrested for something. I'm headed downtown to bail her out. She wouldn't tell me anything over the phone."

"YellowGirl1," Alexandria mentioned immediately. "Her real name is Riquan Stills. She's in grad school at Georgia Tech. I bet Judy went after her."

"Why in the hell would she do that? You don't go after a young writer who's already looking for attention," Marlon ranted. "That's professional suicide. You know it's gonna end up in the news again. This shit right here will make the *real* news."

"Oh, my *God*, you're right," Alexandria agreed. "*American Celebrity Media* would pick up on something like this. They like to use more than just pictures. They usually buy video footage for their *ACM TV* show."

"God dammit!" Marlon snapped as he drove. "That's all we fucking need right now!"

Alexandria paused. "You need to keep calm, because if they end up with video cameras down there at the police station, you don't want to give them more material. *ACM TV* loves stuff like that. They specialize in celebrity arrests."

"Shit, are you kidding me? They'll have cameras down there already? This just happened."

"No, I'm not kidding. So get yourself together before you get down there. If someone was following us to take pictures at that hotel, then don't think for one minute they won't be on this story. That's what's so crazy about it. It's like, once this stuff starts, they don't leave you alone until the money runs out or the interest in the story dies off. This one is just getting started. So you'll get new people piling on."

Marlon hadn't even thought of live cameras being there on the scene for his arrival at the police station. Alexandria was right. Cameras seemed to pop up out of nowhere with arrests, even for regular citizens. It made him not want to bail his wife out at all to avoid more of the chaos. But calling a lawyer on a Saturday evening was not an option. He couldn't even imagine the possibility of waiting too long to get Judy out. He wanted her back home for their boys as quickly as possible before it could get any worse. Calling a lawyer would only prolong the issue.

"Yeah, thanks for telling me this," he commented to Alexandria. As much as Judy may have thought of her as a pretty-faced airhead, she sure knew about the media industry. "And you did pretty good with Judy yesterday too," he mentioned. "You came up with a totally different approach to it. I appreciated that."

Alexandria exhaled noticeably over the phone. "I was only telling her the *truth* though. I love what you guys have, and despite what people may think, I would never want to see you guys fall apart. You give me inspiration. So just . . . keep your cool down there. Okay?"

"Will do," Marlon agreed. When he hung up, he mumbled, "Damn, she's cool. No wonder I got involved with her."

Judy's young friend had been anti-drama, and Marlon had pulled her right into the middle of the craziness. Yet, Alexandria refused to blame him for it and was still willing to help.

I guess she is telling the truth, he thought. *I'm glad I called her. I feel a little more prepared for this now. I could have been walking right back into an ambush down here.*

Sure enough, when Marlon arrived at the Atlanta police station, there were at least a half-dozen people camping out with cameras to record the action—professionally and unprofessionally. As soon as he parked and climbed out of his vehicle in the adjacent lot, the vultures noticed him and asserted themselves on cue with cameras, lights, microphones, and a series of antagonizing questions. No matter how prepared Marlon attempted to be, the first question nearly got a heated response out of him.

"Marlon Pierce, how does it feel to be married to an angry black woman?"

Feeling a rush of anxiety, Marlon looked at the desperate man and quickly turned away. *Nope! Just keep on walking,* he reminded himself. *They want to piss me off on purpose.*

"Do you guys really have an open marriage?"

Does your mother have an open marriage? Marlon thought as he walked passed them.

"You just wanted a younger, happier woman, right, Marlon?"

Yeah, just like your father does. He's tired of your ugly-ass mother.

"Hey, show a little respect," the lone woman in the group of men commented. There was no chance they would listen to her.

A young black man, wearing a DC baseball cap, attempted to slide Marlon his business card. "I'm Chase. I work with Judy. Tell her we need to get this all on camera for her own defense. She hasn't been returning our calls."

Marlon took note of the man and his dread-headed partner, but he never stopped to take his card. He had a one-track mind. He walked inside the station and went right to business at the reception desk. "I'm here to bail out Judy Pierce."

"And you are?" the robust policewoman asked him from behind the counter.

"I'm Marlon, her husband."

The officer smiled, pleasantly. "All right, let me find the paperwork for you."

After paying her bail, Marlon watched his wife emerge from a holding cell with a calm and respectful officer at her side. She appeared unfazed, which shocked him. He expected to see more uneasiness or agitation from her, but he didn't. She was only relieved to be free.

"You okay?" Marlon asked. He didn't know whether to hug her or not.

She exhaled and nodded, standing there in front of him. "Yeah, I'm good. Let's go," she said and headed toward the exit. "I've been in here long enough already. That seemed like the longest few hours of my *life*. I don't know how people can do that for *years*."

Marlon stopped and warned her inside the doorway before they made it back outside. "I just wanna tell you, they got cameras waiting out there for us."

"Yeah, I know. As soon as I walked in here, they were all gawking and talking about me. I knew it would get around to the media somehow. At the arraignment building, they had people in there asking me for autographs. *Crazy*," she snapped. "Which way did you park?"

"In the lot to the right," Marlon told her as they walked out together.

Judy stepped into the hot, bright lights of the cameras and ignored them all while making a right turn, in step with her husband.

"Judy Pierce, are you guys getting a divorce? Is the open marriage now over with?"

"How many writers and reporters do you plan to assault now?"

Even with her years of training, Judy felt just as uncompelled to respond as her husband. *These assholes know just what to say to make your temperature rise,* she thought. *That's why I'm so glad I don't have to be out here with them.*

"Will you be back on air Monday at WATL Cable?" the lone woman asked her.

"No comment," Judy answered as she and Marlon approached his vehicle.

Chase and Walter appeared. They cut in front of the others to block their cameras like a security team.

"What the hell?" a cameraman complained.

Chase said, "Judy, we need to get up and do an interview with you. You need to do this for yourself. Call me."

Judy said, "I will," and climbed into the passenger seat of her husband's Range Rover.

"You've been saying that for weeks now," Chase responded sourly.

Judy shut and locked the door as Marlon made his way to the driver's side.

"All right, let them out of here! The show is over!" an irritated police lieutenant barked. The aggressive camera crews backed away and allowed them to leave.

"So, *you do* know those guys?" Marlon asked his wife, in reference to Chase and Walter.

She nodded as they made their way up the street toward the highway. "Those are the two young guys from DC, who I started this whole thing with."

"And now you don't call them back anymore?"

Judy breathed deep and gathered her words. "My boss told me very clearly that he didn't want me involved with reporting things that would decrease my name value. So, you know, Shawn Blake is definitely *A-list* with real talent. But I'm not interviewing Tom, Dick, Jackie, and Suzy from the reality TV circuit. It's hard for me to keep telling them that, because I know how badly they want to create something.

"I even tried to set up . . . Alexandria with them," she stated with an irritated pause. "And now I guess—after everything that's happened to us—they want *me* to be the guinea pig now. And I *definitely* don't want to do that."

"Okay, so . . . what happened down here with YellowGirl1?" Marlon asked, changing the subject. That's what he really wanted to know. "Do you even know this girl's real name?"

Judy looked surprised. "What, you heard what happened already?"

Marlon frowned. "Well, what other writer are you gonna

assault? It's obvious. What I *don't* understand is why you would drive down here and do that. That didn't make any sense," he fumed at his wife.

"I didn't drive down here to assault her," she argued. "I just wanted to ask the girl a few questions, and I got the answers I needed. Then she started spazzing out and threw her damn computer at me. To be honest, I didn't even expect to catch up to the girl. Obviously, she must hang out at The Greek Cafe."

"She's a college student on campus. Where do you think she's gonna hang out?" Marlon countered.

"Actually, she's a grad student in mass communications, and her name is Riquan Stills. She's from Shreveport, Louisiana. After doing my research on her, I'm quite sure she has some kind of agreement with ATLHeat.com. It's a database marketer that sends email blasts out to millions of people to view certain websites, support businesses, and read highlighted blogs and articles online. And they don't do that for *free*. So either she's paying them for their marketing services—which I doubt she can afford—or they could have paid *her* to write certain articles and then helped her gain traffic.

"Then I searched more, and found that this same database marketer has been pushing a lot of traffic on Shawn Blake, and everything that surrounds him, including *us* now," she concluded.

Marlon listened to her and added it all up as they entered Interstate 85 North. "So . . . let me get this straight. You're saying that this marketing company is sending out emails to people to read articles about Shawn Blake, and that they may have paid YellowGirl1 to write those articles about us?"

"Yes. They also push traffic to the *National Urban Report* and *American Celebrity Media* followers, particularly for the articles attached to Shawn. So, in other words, if someone wanted to blow him up or bring him down, ATLHeat.com would be the smoking gun. They're essentially providing the hot numbers for everything that has his name attached to it."

Marlon nodded. "Okay. So obviously, someone's paying them

to do that, unless they're doing it all for *free*. But is that a crime? That just sounds like promotion of hot news. We just happen to be a part of it now."

"Yeah, and all to benefit *who*? That's the question. Who gets the most out of this?"

Marlon shrugged and responded, "Whoever hates Shawn Blake, I guess. This has all been a bunch of crazy news connected to *him*, right?"

"And people are buying it up too," Judy said. "I came down here to find out if I was onto something, and this little girl confirmed it. Why else would she throw her damn *laptop* at me, of all things? That's like a movie director throwing a hundred-thousand-dollar camera. She was obviously trying to make a scene and get paid, because she knew she was busted."

"And you just helped her do it," Marlon said. "I mean, I get everything that you're saying, but you got a lot of dots to connect here for it to mean anything to the public. That company ATLHeat.com could just say that Shawn is hot news and good for business right now; and that they have nothing to do with what he does in his personal life, *or* what we do in ours. Then what?

"You still have a boss to deal with on Monday," Marlon answered his own question. "I still have UPS, looking at me sideways. The principal at our sons' school is apprehensive. Our kids have to deal with crazy-ass songs and what have you, and *now* you have a pending assault case. But you're sitting in here all excited, thinking you're playing a game of detective. I mean, *come on*, Judy. What are you doing?" he snapped.

A mountain of frustration was building, and Marlon saw no way that his wife's far-out theories would help them.

"Actually, I thought about hiring a good private detective on my way down here today," Judy responded calmly. "We can't allow this to happen to us and not fight back. Somebody's fucking with us, Marlon, and it's not right."

Marlon shook his head and sighed. He couldn't believe his ears. Judy hadn't changed a bit. After everything that they were going through, she remained hardheaded.

266

She said, "I know what you're thinking—that I'm still stubborn and hardheaded. But I know a lot more about what's going on now. And you're *right*—there are a lot of pieces to connect here. But now we'll get to see if ATLHeat.com pushes any new articles about this assault. Then we'll know that *I'm* right."

"Judy, everyone's gonna cover this assault charge now anyway. We'll be on the damn news *tonight*," Marlon fumed. "What do you think those cameras were there for? They already got the footage they needed just from us walking out of the police station. It's been one thing after the next with us. So, of course, this marketing company is gonna push people to these new articles. They would be foolish *not* to. They've been following the story this whole time."

"What if they *created* it?" Judy hinted. She seemed genuinely convinced, as if a lightbulb had gone off in her head.

Marlon smirked. "Okay, so now according to *you*, some marketing website company just created everything that happened to us and Shawn Blake? Is that what you're saying? And they made you assault this girl with her computer too?"

It all sounded ridiculous to Marlon. He waited for his wife to respond.

Judy kept her calm. "Marlon, you'd be surprised at what manipulated information can do to people's perceptions nowadays. If you report it, say it, and show it enough, they'll believe anything you want them to believe."

Marlon decided he had heard enough. *I see why she wasn't fazed by going to jail,* he thought. *She's got another pipedream idea in her head, and she doesn't even care if we both get fired in the process.*

"Do you even care about the potential fallout from all this?" he forced himself to ask her.

Judy nodded, steady as iron. "I have thought about it. I had a couple of *hours* to think about it in that damn jail cell. Let me tell you what I already know:

"Brenda Avant called me earlier today and told me that

267

Alexandria is being fired, and that I need to take a two-week leave while everything blows over. Michael is supposed to take over my lead anchor position instead of Wendy. But I already know that Bob likes *women* as the lead anchors, because our research has shown that we have more female viewers who appreciate us. So, Wendy would get a chance to go after what she's always wanted— my job—and the writing is already on the wall that I may not make it back.

"So instead of me waiting around to bend over and eventually get fucked, I've decided to be proactive and solve this shit for myself. Because the station is not going to help us do it."

She added, "I also know a lot more about what's going on with Shawn and all of his friends from Michigan. I have some buttons to press on that shit, too."

His wife was impossible. She also had a point. There was an awful lot of information out there to deal with, and the odds were all stacked against them, unless they could figure something out on their own.

Marlon said, "I sure hope you know what the hell you're doing. It's a big-ass world out there you're playing with, and you're only one woman."

Judy sighed and allowed herself to contemplate her husband's reservations. "Marlon . . . at this point, we don't have a damn *choice*. If we don't make any sense out of all this, these people will make it look uglier than it already is, unless we come out swinging to win. And that's what I plan to do."

19... NOW I KNOW

As expected, the latest news on Judy Pierce hit the media fan and spread like wild pollen in the springtime. Like Marlon had stated, his wife's assault charge became another falling domino in all of their recent misfortunes. Everyone was talking about it, including Detectives Todd and Weinberger. They were having a late drink at the same hotel bar where Marlon and Alexandria were photographed.

Detective Todd watched and listened to the breaking news report on the FOX network as he took another sip from his glass. When the report was over, he eyed his partner.

"Does she seem to be rapidly falling apart here or what? I thought this woman had much tougher skin than this."

Weinberger continued to stare up at the small television that hung above the bar. She was still trying to process it all as she nursed her own glass.

"This is ah, very interesting," she responded. "But at a bar like this, with windows everywhere, I don't see how her husband was trying to hide anything."

Todd grinned. "Why hide if you have an open marriage?"

"You really don't believe that, do you?" Weinberger asked him seriously.

"You don't seem to believe *anything*," Todd countered, finishing his glass.

"I would think it would be obvious to even you at this point that someone's definitely out to ruin her and her family."

"And what would be the motive for that?"

Weinberger shrugged. "Getting too close to Shawn Blake—obviously. Maybe someone's afraid he may tell her something incriminating. She's a reporter, right?"

She took a sip of her drink and allowed her senior partner to ponder what she had said.

Todd nodded thoughtfully. "Who would have enough money and sophistication to pull this kind of a thing off?"

"Bernard 'Benny C.' Chavis," his young partner answered casually. "You're not underestimating him because he's an ex-con are you?"

"Not at all," Todd responded. "I told you he was the ringleader *weeks* ago. But now . . . this just seems too obvious. Shawn has to know his partner is manipulating things behind the scenes, right? Or do you believe that this *actor* is that innocent?"

Weinberger grinned. "*Nobody's* innocent. *Nobody*," she quoted. "That's The Kingpin's line in *Daredevil*. It was one of Jennifer Garner's best movies. The follow-up, *Elektra*, was horrible."

Todd smiled. "That sounds like a line I would use. I liked Michael Clarke Duncan. You ever see him in *The Green Mile*?"

"Of course. It's a classic."

"All right, so . . . Judy Pierce is now a ripe turkey who we need to talk to," Todd said, redirecting the conversation. "If she *does* know something, we may have to surround her with some protection."

"Well, someone believes that she's dangerous, because they're definitely out to shut her down," Weinberger said. "And they're making plenty of news out of her in the interim."

While still peeking up at the weekend stories on FOX, Todd's young partner got him thinking. "So . . . breaking news is a valuable commodity for the networks, right?"

270

Weinberger nodded. "Of course. It's how they build their viewer numbers and establish their advertising rates."

"And the same thing applies to websites, right?"

"Everything is based on the viewer numbers. Your *eyes* are the customers."

"So . . . let's say, like a boxing match, I have Floyd Mayweather Jr. on the right side, and he's already popular. Then I go out and find . . . I don't know, David Garcia, who's a local boxer and not as popular on a national level. Then I put both of them together, and—"

He clapped his hands loudly and made his partner flinch on her stool. "BOOM! I make money while promoting *both* of them. It's showtime, right? Does that make any sense to you, or am I just drinking too much?"

Weinberger leaned back on her stool and grinned. "You may be giving them a little *too* much credit, but . . . it's viable, yeah. But you would have to know that David Garcia is *marketable*."

Weinberger began to contemplate that. The idea actually made sense. She said, "Well, if Shawn and his guys know that she's reactive in that way, then—"

"You lead a loose cannon to a war, and you watch her explode. Then you sit back and make money off of the fireworks," Todd suggested. It made sense to him too. He cracked, "Shit, I need to order me another drink."

Weinberger laughed. "She's definitely a Type A personality, that's for sure."

"And I can't wait for us to talk to her either. I already know her type. It's fireworks all day long with her."

"Yeah, but how would they know about her husband?" Weinberger questioned.

Her bald, old partner scowled at her. "Shit, that's easy. Once a man finds out his wife may be cheating with a known celebrity womanizer, you follow him around and see what happens. And that's what they did. But now, to find him with a *coworker* of hers, and with his hand in her hair, that there was a damn *bonus*. I'm sure they didn't even expect *that*. They probably just wanted to get a picture of him drinking or sneaking out to a strip club or something. And *boom*, in walks the coworker, so they ran with it."

"This is all a hypothesis," Weinberger responded, amused. "You're not telling me they suggested the spins on the article too, are you?"

"They don't have to do that. These crazy bloggers are creative enough to build a story on their own. We're in the *hype* generation now," he answered. "I bet you this YellowGirl1 is ready to sue Judy for some change in a civil court case. You know that's coming. So, that's another article to write. In fact, they got a *few* of them coming now. Judy has to go back to work this week, right? That's another story. So we'll catch up to her on Monday afternoon, right after she goes off the air."

"*If* they even let her work on Monday, after this," Weinberger suggested.

Todd continued to grin. "Then she'll have even more of a reason to talk to us."

Back up in Flint, Michigan, Larry received word on the Judy Pierce news in Atlanta and called Benny about it from his smoky hotel room.

"Yo, man, shorty wildin' out down in Atlanta," he said in a scratchy, weed-filled voice.

"What? Who? Who you talkin' 'bout?"

Benny sounded preoccupied and inebriated himself. Larry grinned, imagining a hot and ready woman in his room . . . or maybe two.

"That reporter girl, Judy Pierce. She done fucked around and assaulted YellowGirl1 today."

That got Benny's attention. "She did *what*?"

"She assaulted that blogger girl. They had it all over the Atlanta news tonight."

Benny paused, then said, "Damn, I didn't know she was gangsta like that. I need to have her on *our* squad." He laughed. "Aw'ight, fuck it, man. We'll handle all that when we get back down there. We getting out of here tomorrow afternoon."

Larry frowned. "What happened to Monday?" He had expected to stay a day longer.

"We got too much to do, man. We gotta get this money right. It's too much going on now to stay up here. I'll hit you back in the morning."

When he hung up, Larry mumbled, "Damn, I was just startin' to get comfortable. I guess I need to call me a shorty too tonight."

He went back to smoking and looked through his cell phone for old Michigan numbers. He stopped at Nicole Riley. "There you go. Let me see what you up to tonight."

That Sunday morning at home in Alpharetta, Judy struggled to figure everything out again. Her thoughts were so discombobulated that she pulled out a notepad in her bedroom to jot down the things she needed to do, not necessarily in their order of priority.

Call Mom. Explain things to Chase. Research private investigators. Think about a response to Brenda. What about Bob? What if I'm fired? Talk to lawyers about this assault case. What if YellowGirl1 tries to sue me? Follow more ATLHeat.com stories. Counter all of the news reporters. Explain my theories. Find out more on Benny. Call Shawn back. Talk to his baby momma, Annette.

"And what else?" She stopped and thought before returning to her list.

Prepare myself for work tomorrow. Protect my boys and family. Think about the response at school. And . . . love my husband.

When Judy wrote her final note at the bottom of her long list, she became conflicted, emotional, and angry. She thought again about Alexandria and felt that she was letting the young makeup artist off the hook.

"I should have beaten *her* ass instead of going after

YellowGirl1," she grumbled. "That girl Riquan is just young, dumb, and desperate for a big story, but Alexandria *knows* better than what *she* did."

Judy still didn't have a confession from her coworker or husband, but she surely had the evidence. Yet she couldn't get Alexandria's pitiful whining out of her head. *I love you guys so much. I admire everything you do. I was only trying to help. I would never want to see you guys fall apart.*

Judy couldn't remember her exact words, but she knew the essence of them, and the recollection stirred up fresh anger and tears. "Yeah, you wanna help me by fucking my damn *husband*," she grumbled with sniffs.

Alexandria's whiny voiced popped right back into her consciousness. *Would you rather he called somebody who didn't care? Sometimes you don't hear him.*

That part hurt Judy the most. Had she failed her husband by not compromising with him when he needed her to? Marlon had always been there for her. Whenever she had complaints about anything, he was right there to listen, advise and support—even when they disagreed. He was never missing in action.

However, when pushed against the wall, Judy was quick to shoot a dagger at his heart and manhood by boasting about the superior money she made. She cried about how tough it was to commit, sacrifice, and love unconditionally.

"Maybe I just need to shut it all down for a minute and reevaluate my family, like Brenda told me to," she cried. "I've just been going so hard all these years that I don't even realize my selfishness anymore. That's what Marlon was trying to tell me. Now we have all this bullshit to deal with."

The thoughts didn't hit her that hard while in jail, but in the privacy of her own home, Judy was allowed to process the real impact of it all. With her bedroom door locked, the kids in the den, and Marlon out to retrieve her car from the police impound, she was able to be bluntly honest with herself. But there was no going back now. There was only forward. So she wiped the tears from her face and looked back at her notepad to refocus.

"Okay, just call Mom back first."

Her mother didn't even say hello when Judy called. Instead she asked her daughter, "Are you okay?" That only made the hurt and tears resurface.

Judy took another moment to wipe her eyes. "I was fine until I made my list this morning," she cried.

"Baby, your list won't make it go away. You need to cry now, because it *hurts*."

Judy heard that and cried like a baby. "What do I need to do now, Mom?" she wailed.

Her mother paused to allow the grief to pour out of her system. She said, "Judy, you need to take this one step at a time, and do all that you can do. Then you leave the rest in the hands of the Lord. You can't fight everything, and you're not gonna win every battle. So you go ahead and do everything you have on that list in front of you, because you *need* to do it to feel whole. That's just the way you are. But after you do, it doesn't mean that everything is gonna turn out the way you want it to, or expect. Even if you have to move on to a new job, you do it."

Judy listened in silence.

"But you need to look at the things that are most important to you. That's your kids, your health, and your family. That includes *Marlon*, because I *like* Marlon. He's your *family*. Do your hear me?"

"Yes," Judy whimpered.

"Now . . . I don't know what really went on, and nobody's perfect, but I *don't* believe that Marlon is the kind of man who would get up and leave his wife and kids. So unless he proves me wrong, I'm not jumping on anybody's bandwagon to give up on your husband."

Judy cried, "I'm not giving up on him either. I love him. He's just tired of me always doing my own thing. I really pissed him off this time."

"Well, you all need to take a vacation together. You've *always* been one to overwork yourself, Judy."

"I know," she admitted. "Everyone tells me that."

"And you remember that, no matter what happens, you are *loved*. Do you hear me? You do not come from a family that doesn't love you. So don't act like you're out there by yourself, because you're *not*. We are all here with you."

"I know, Mom. I know."

"Hold on, your father wants to speak to you."

"Okay."

"Judy," her father answered the phone gruffly, "if it gets too crazy for you down there, you, Marlon, and the boys can come on back home. I never liked Atlanta that much no way. There's too many people down there trying to climb on top of each other just to stand up and beat their chests. And that ain't never been good for black folks to do. So before I have to bring my shotgun and rifle down there, you come on back home to Indiana."

Judy couldn't help but smile at her father's old-school approach and candor. He didn't say a lot, but when he said it, he meant it.

"Okay, Daddy," she told him and chuckled. "I don't want you bringing your shotgun."

"I know you don't. Here's your mother back, 'cause I'm still angry right now."

Her mother came back on the line and said, "That's where you get it from, right there. He just can't wait to go out and shoot somebody. But it don't always work that way."

"It's gon' work that way if you make it like that," Judy overheard her father argue.

"Look, you let me finish talking to her before she gets into more trouble. Now what was I saying?"

"You were saying to hold on to the things that are most important to you," Judy answered.

"Yeah, don't you let this stuff make you lose your common sense," her mother huffed. "Nobody cares more about you than your family. So you go on back to your list and put family next to every last thing on there. Family trumps *everything*."

Judy smiled when she hung up and did exactly what her mother told her, marking family above everything. The process cheered her up and made her list feel a lot less crucial. So she moved forward and finally returned a call to Chase. He was good and ready for her with his pitch that morning.

"Thank God, Judy! We're just trying to help you now," Chase told her excitedly. "The best way to do that is to fight their stories with your story. You gotta be able to control your own statements and media, just like we wanted to do with Shawn."

"Who would interview me?" she asked him.

"I can do it myself. You can write all your own questions for me to ask."

Judy shook her head and shot the idea down. "That's not gonna work. We have to have a respected reporter to do it or no one will take it seriously. It'll do more harm than good."

"So, who could we get to interview you?"

That got Judy thinking again. "Let me come up with a list. Then I would have to prepare myself for every possible question. So it's not as simple as you think. Each person I choose would have a different line of questions and a different delivery. I would have to adjust my approach and practice for each one of them."

Chase fell into a spell of silence.

Judy asked, "Are you still there?"

"Yeah, I'm still here. I'm just thinking about what you just said. And you're right; it is more complicated than I thought. It's almost like casting different actors to play the same role. They're all gonna be slightly different."

"Yeah. Each anchor or reporter has their own individual style, when they're good. And this wouldn't be some three-minute soundbite. You're talking about a good fifteen, twenty minutes to edit down. Oh no, I would have to prepare for that."

Chase laughed. "No wonder Blake didn't want to finish it when he shut down on you. You were killing him. Remember that?"

Judy reflected on that and felt remorseful. "Yeah, now I know much better," she moaned. "It really makes you think when you're on the other end of it."

"But you are willing to do it though, right?" Chase pressed her.

Judy hesitated. She didn't want to put her foot in her mouth. She looked back at her list and thought about her family. "It really depends on how this thing goes, Chase. I mean, if I don't need to come out and talk, then why would I do it? But, if it *does* come down to the point where I *need* to, then I'll have to be prepared to make that decision. But right now I feel like we would be jumping the gun."

"Yeah, I see what you're saying. We have to see how it plays out first," he agreed. "But in the meantime—"

"I'll get prepared for it," Judy interjected. "Trust me, I'm already doing that. I really have no choice at this point. This is my real life we're talking about."

After hanging up with Chase, she looked down at the next item on her list. But instead of taking the energy to start researching private investigators, she scrolled all the way down to calling Shawn back and thought about giving him a sincere apology.

"Now I know just how you feel," she mumbled in reference to the embattled actor and his chaotic life in the media. That realization forced her to take a break from her list. She sighed and stood up from her bed to stretch. "Yeah, I need to call him up and give him an apology. But first let me go hug my babies. This is a long-ass list to get through."

She left her list on the bed and headed for the bedroom door to return to her treasured role—a loving mother of two young boys.

"These two little guys will always love me," she mumbled to herself. When she left the room, her smile was huge.

20... THE RETURN

As promised, Alex got a chance to fly back to Atlanta from Flint that Sunday afternoon on the rented private jet with Benny, Larry, Shawn, and a pretty new assistant named Zola, who was from Detroit. Zola, an irresistible and professional woman, was Benny's idea to help soften up their image.

"It's been too much of just us guys down here for way too long, man," he explained. "And Zola was looking for a change of scenery."

The perfect medium-brown, tall, and curvaceous model type, there was instant skepticism as to who and what Zola was really there for, particularly from Shawn and Alex. Zola put their assumptions to rest right away in the intimate and comfortable courters of the soft leather seats.

"I know you're all thinking that I'm somebody's fuck buddy, but I'm not. I'm coming to Atlanta to do a job and deal with all the media that's been getting out of hand for you guys. I've been speaking to Bernard about it now for *months*."

"Bernard?" Alex asked her sarcastically.

"Yes, I call him by his real name, Alex," she answered. "That's all a part of being professional. And just to get this out of the way, I like pretty girls as much as you do. But I don't let them interfere with my job."

Larry looked around and started chuckling. She was new to him too. Benny hadn't spoken a word about her. The woman just popped up at the airport that morning with her luggage.

Shawn asked her, "So, you're looking for a wifey?"

Larry laughed even harder, still buzzed from smoking the night before.

"If I find a woman I like that much, then yeah, I'll think about it," Zola answered. She was dressed in a bright-green skirt suit with black stockings and gold and black heels, as if she were looking for style points.

"How old are you, if you don't mind me asking?" Shawn questioned.

"Oh, not at all. I know I may not look it, but I'm thirty-two, and I've definitely paid my dues while working in the music and sports industries. Then I went into a marketing position with the casinos for the past couple of years and just got tired of it. I've been watching what's going on with your career in Atlanta, and I begged Bernard to give me a shot at cleaning some things ups."

"And you just up and walked off your job like that at the casinos?" Alex asked.

"I took a two-week leave as soon as I knew you guys were coming back to Flint this week for the funeral."

Shawn looked at Benny and asked him the obvious. "How come you didn't introduce her to us yesterday? I saw her at the funeral, but I didn't know who she was. I thought you were a member of J.'s family or something."

"Everybody's mind was on the funeral yesterday, fam'. And I figured she would have three straight hours to talk to us today on the plane," Benny explained.

Shawn said, "I already have PR and marketing people."

"Yeah, but they deal with the *promotions* side more than crisis management, correct?" Zola interjected.

Shawn grinned, sheepishly. "They've been having to deal with everything lately."

"That's my point," she countered. "I'm here *specifically* to help get the whole *train* back on the tracks, not just some of the pieces."

"Yeah, she's gonna work with us this whole week to see how we like it," Benny said.

Alex frowned. "But shouldn't Shawn keep a separation from us, man, on a business and professional level? You know the police are watching everything he does now."

"He ain't had no separation from *you*," Larry barked. "When *you* gon' separate from him?"

"I don't have a *record*, either," Alex countered. "So he don't need to separate from me."

"Aw'ight, calm down," Benny told them both with raised hands. "This isn't permanent. I just wanted to bring Zola down and try this out for what she calls 'damage control,' especially with Shawn having another court case coming up this week. Instead of us just talking about it, I wanted her to see it and feel it out.

"So just calm down. No decisions have been made yet," he promised them. "She has a lot of experience dealing with people who have records too. That's why I like her. She talks about working this from every angle. So just listen to her for a minute."

As the crew sat quietly, everyone had their individual thoughts.

Yeah, his ass is full of surprises, Alex said to himself. *Now he brings in his own media expert from Detroit? I mean, how obvious can you get?*

Shawn smirked and mused, *I wonder what Judy and Kenya would think about her. We'll see how much she can handle in a minute . . . once Rhonda and the ATL media gets around her on Tuesday.*

On Larry's side of the plane, he thought, *Shit, Benny didn't tell me nothing about this girl. She bad as all outdoors and freaky, but what is he doing with this media shit? Is he trying to throw us all off and do the opposite of what we need? We need more privacy than talk right now. But maybe that's his game plan to mix it all up. I'll talk to him about it later.*

When their jet arrived in Atlanta, it was nearly six o'clock that evening. The sun had headed west and Shawn was glad to be back, eager to return to his own space.

"I've seen enough of you guys these past few days. So, if y'all don't mind, drop me off at the taxi booth. I need my space back to think a minute," he announced as they climbed into another awaiting limo.

"Well, tell Big Al not to cry then, 'cause I ain't even been around you like that this week," Larry cracked. "Maybe you tired of feeling his shadow on you."

Alex only stared at him. He didn't like the idea of Shawn traveling alone, but he was a grown-ass man, so he held his tongue.

Benny smiled and shook his head at their constant bickering. "You sure you good with that, man?" he asked Shawn.

Shawn shrugged. "It's a taxi ride home. What you think—I'ma get kidnapped? Ain't nobody after me like *that*. Even the cops take a break on Sundays."

Larry said, "The strip clubs don't. They do great business on Sunday nights. I'm ready to take Zola out and introduce her to ATL's strip club scene tonight, since she like pretty girls."

Zola grinned at him. "The only stripping for me tonight is climbing out of these clothes and into a comfortable hotel bed. I'm exhausted."

From what? Alex wanted to ask her. But he left it alone.

Benny shrugged. "Aw'ight, we'll drop Shawn off for a taxi then. No biggie. He's going straight home like a regular man."

When Shawn climbed out of their limo and said his goodbyes, he found an awaiting taxi, jumped in, and immediately checked his cell phone. He saw that Judy had called him earlier and left a message. He plugged in an earpiece and listened to it privately.

Once he heard her humble apology, he smiled and thought of calling her back.

"Naw, it's Sunday night," he mumbled. "She's probably in the middle of something with her family. She's had a lot to think about this weekend." Then he listened to the rest of his other messages, including one from Rhonda:

"Shawn, you know good and well you can afford to pay us

more than twenty-four hundred dollars a month. I know you're flying around, jet-setting with limo rides and shit. And you treat Annette a lot better than you treat me, and I have your *oldest*. But I have to keep taking you to court like this, and I'm honestly getting tired of it."

"Well, stop doing it then!" Shawn barked at his phone, as if she could hear him.

He was so passionate about it the driver looked back in his rearview mirror to make sure everything was all right.

Shawn grinned at him and shook his head, embarrassed. "I'm good, man. It's just these women out here with their demands, that's all. Once you lay down with them, they think they own you. So please don't have a child with them unless you planning on getting married."

"That's what marriage *is for*," the gray-bearded, hat-wearing taxi driver told him. "Why would you want to have a child outside of marriage? It's much cheaper to raise them when you're all in the same household. That way you can share everything instead of buying everything *twice*. Two houses, two cars, two beds. It's all too much."

Shawn nodded and chuckled. "That's a good way of looking at it. You're right. But what if you can't stand the damn girl?"

"Then don't have a child with her," his driver answered. "Don't date her. And don't ask for her phone number. Just leave her alone and let her be angry with someone else."

It made common sense to the taxi driver. He couldn't understand why people made their lives so complicated. The stories he had heard from the back of his cab were impossible. And they all made him feel blessed to have a life of simplicity.

Shawn told him, "You're right again. We all know that. But then life sneaks up on you and you end up making decisions that you're stuck with . . . unless you can get out of them."

His driver nodded as he looked into the rearview mirror. "Well, good luck with that," he said. *But real life doesn't let you get out of anything,* the bearded man thought. *It all comes back around sooner or later to find you.*

Back in Alpharetta, after taking a break to spend quality time with her two boys, Judy got back to her list on the bed and contemplated her return to work that Monday morning. She hadn't called Brenda back and didn't want to. Nor did Brenda call her to speak about the new assault charge from that Saturday evening.

I guess we'll get to everything in the morning, Judy figured. Their big face-to-face meeting was set for 5:15 a.m. sharp. Now they had a few *more* issues to discuss between them. *After this damn assault yesterday, what if they decide to fire me too now?*

Judy had no idea what to expect. She also didn't expect for Alexandria to call her on cue that Sunday. She viewed the young makeup artist's number on her cell phone and mumbled, "Is this girl trying to read my mind now?" She was hesitant to even answer. She did anyway.

"Hello." She had no desire to say much more than that. *We really don't need to talk or see each other until tomorrow when we have a mediator in the room,* Judy thought.

Apparently, Alexandria had been thinking as well and wanted to throw in the white towel. She opened up and said, "Judy, I know we have that meeting tomorrow in Brenda's office, but to be honest with you, I'm ready to take the fall for this and just get a job somewhere else." She sounded civil and mature.

Judy heard the alarm beep from the front door and realized that Marlon had made it back home with her car. Wanting more privacy to listen to Alexandria, she made sure her bedroom door was locked as Alexandria continued:

"I wouldn't even feel right working there anymore. It's not like they were paying me a lot of money anyway. Maybe I'll head down to Miami to work in the fashion industry or something."

She made it seem as if being fired from the station was already the conclusion. Her added talk about Miami sounded like she was trying to escape the drama that everyone else would be forced to stay and deal with.

Judy said, "Well, I still need you to be there to allow Brenda to understand what happened, for *my* sake. Otherwise, she won't respect me anymore." *And I need to look you straight in your damn eyes anyway,* she thought. *Your ass ain't getting off that easy! Oh, no!*

"Oh, I'm still going to be there. I owe that to you, Marlon, and your family," Alexandria responded. "But there's no sense in me trying to keep my job or sway anybody's decision. I mean . . . I was wrong for not telling you."

"You got that right," Judy said. "You had plenty of time to tell me." *I'm still waiting for everything else to come out too,* she thought. "So, I'll see you in the morning," she told Alexandria. She wanted to cut off any further conversation before she got angry again.

Under past circumstances, Alexandria would have been a marked woman, but the complications of adult life, family, and a profession in the public eye no longer allowed Judy to handle her situations with force.

I'm already in hot water with this Riquan Stills girl now, she thought. *But we'll see what happens with this tomorrow.*

With nothing else to be said, Alexandria mumbled, "Okay."

Judy couldn't wait to hang up on her. She said to herself, "This is going to be a sleepless night. I don't need to hear anything else from this girl. Now her ass wants to run off to Miami. I bet she does."

On the southwest side of Atlanta, Keith was anxiously awaiting his phone call from Larry. "I know this boy better hurry up and get this money to us," he told his trusted friends as he sat in the front passenger seat of their black Yukon. "It ain't like they don't have it. So they need to give that shit up before things get ugly out here."

They all sat outside in the parking lot of an Atlanta strip club as cars began to pull up. Enthusiastic customers were climbing out for the "Free Before 11" promotion deal.

"Is that that fool, Ricky Slim? What Ricardo doing out here?" Keith's driver commented from the wheel.

"Yeah, that's him," his second friend said from behind the driver in the backseat. "You can spot them crazy-ass clothes he wears a mile away."

"That's that new producer with him, right? What's his name again, Drive Time?" the third friend asked from behind Keith.

Keith rolled down his passenger-side window and yelled, "Ricky! What's up, boy? What you doing out here?"

Ricky Slim peered at the truck sideways until he noticed them. "Oh, what's up, Keith? What's up, y'all?" He walked over and gave them all handshakes through the window as his beefy music producer stood behind him. "We over here trying to see how these girls respond to this new single."

"What, that 'Pants Down' song?" Keith asked.

Ricky Slim said, "You know it, man. It's that freaky deeky with the 8-0-8 kick behind it."

"But why you showing up so early though?" the driver asked.

"Oh, we just checking in to make sure the DJ got the vinyl and the CDs, then we gon' come back later. We hittin' several strip clubs tonight."

Keith nodded at him and grinned, pulling his baseball cap down to his eyes to look more sinister. He said, "I guess that new green paper from Shawn Blake people came in handy for you, huh? If he beat ya' ass down again, you can push another single."

Ricky chuckled nervously. That wasn't a subject he wanted to discuss out in the open.

"It's all about that music, for me. I'm past all that, you feel me? And money can't help you if you don't have nothing hot to push."

Keith frowned. "Shit, you can have the hottest music you want out here; if you don't have no paper for them DJs, your shit ain't getting played. I know the game better than you do. You play the front door while I play the back. But it's that back door that gets shit done, so you can walk in the front like the Jeffersons. But if ain't no paper popping off in the back, they'll treat your ass like

Urkel when you walk in."

His friends broke out laughing inside the truck.

Ricky Slim smirked and said, "All right then, man," before walking off with his producer.

"Yo, why you try'na crush that boy's dreams like that, Keith?" the driver asked while still chuckling.

Keith frowned. "I just hate when these fake-ass artists forget how these deals are really made out here. You know how much money it takes to push a single? To make a movie? Or promote some comedian? Then they turn around and act like they don't know you, hanging out with these new people, like they did it all themselves. I just wanna remind that boy what time it is."

His friends continued to laugh as Keith's cell phone went off.

"Hold up, quiet down," he barked before he answered. "Hello . . . Yeah, what's up? I'm waiting on you. Tell me where to meet you at."

When Keith hung up, he nodded to his friends and pulled out his loaded pistol from under the seat.

"It's showtime, man. I'm not trying to use this, but they need to have my money."

"But you didn't even pay nothing yet," his driver confessed.

"They don't need to know that. I'm not putting no money on the table until they put *my* money on the table," Keith countered. "They the ones who wanted to kill their own boy. What kind of friends are they? If that's how they do each other in Michigan, I don't trust them no way."

Larry prepared himself for a money drop-off, while calling Alex, of all people. "Big Al, I need to make these money runs tonight and Devon and Toot ain't make it back yet from Flint. So I need to take you along with me," he explained.

Alex hesitated. "Money runs to where?"

"You know we still do strip club parties, right? Well, we got a couple of show promotions going on tonight. That's why we needed to get back here. I got a couple bags of ones to drop off."

"And these clubs can't supply their own money?"

"They can, but the more we do for them, the more we get back. And these deals are what keeps us all eating. It ain't just about Shawn's movies," Larry hinted.

Alex thought, *It ain't ever been just about Shawn. Benny's using Shawn as the anchor for all his other shit. So maybe I should go, just to see what's up. He wouldn't even ask me this if Devon was still in town.*

"You can't go by yourself?" Alex quizzed him.

"Come on, man, with a bag of fucking money? What I look like, an old lady with a new purse walking through the alleyway? I'm headed your way now, man. It'll only take a couple of hours."

Alex sighed and grumbled, "All right, man. Whatever. Come on, then."

Forty minutes later, Alex and Larry pulled up in a black Cadillac Escalade to a meeting spot in southwest Atlanta's university area.

"They got a strip club around here now? And when you get this ride?" Alex was skeptical of everything, including the black leather gloves that Larry was wearing.

Larry looked at him from behind the wheel and frowned. "I needed something to get around in until Devon and them get back. And they always got strip clubs around colleges. These school girls gotta pay their tuitions, don't they?" he cracked.

Alex didn't like that. "You think that shit is funny? Every young black woman ain't trying to strip to go to school. What's wrong with you?"

"It was a fucking *joke*, Al. Stop taking everything so seriously."

"Well, stop saying stupid shit!"

Alex barked.

Before he realized it, Larry had pulled into a small parking lot and stopped the truck. Then he jumped out with the first dark trash bag of money and walked over to a black Yukon that was parked on the right.

"This ma-fucker 'bout to drive me crazy tonight, man," Larry complained as he handed the bag of money over to Keith's driver through the window. "He's always arguing about some petty shit."

Keith grabbed the bag from his friend and wanted to count it up, but all of the ones inside threw him for a loop.

He winced. "What the fuck is this—stripper money?"

Larry faked confusion. "What? What are you talking about?"

Keith grabbed his gun from under the seat and said, "It's nothing but ones in here. You trying to fuck with me?"

Larry looked back at Alex, who was still sitting in the passenger seat of the truck, guardedly.

What the hell is this? Alex thought. He had his hand on his own gun inside of his jacket and was prepared to protect himself.

Larry yelled, "You gave me the wrong fuckin' bag?"

Alex looked bewildered. "What? Man, what are you—"

BOP! BOP! BOP! BOP!

Larry shot him four times through the glass window with a pistol that quickly appeared from his right coat pocket. Everyone inside the Yukon froze, shocked.

The driver recoiled from the wheel. "What the hell?" *Did he just shoot his own friend?*

Before they could decide how to respond, Larry shrugged it off. "Sorry about that. Keep counting the money." He put the gun back in his coat pocket as if nothing had happened.

Keith glanced at his guys inside the vehicle and tightened the grip on his gun. *Is this motherfucker crazy or what?* He had no idea Larry could be that malicious.

In their brief moment of confusion, Larry pulled out a second pistol from his left coat pocket and shot Keith three times through the open window.

With his gun out and ready, Keith never even pulled the trigger as the bullets struck him in the face and chest. Larry then shot his driver, who was a sitting duck at the wheel. The young man had nowhere to escape.

The two friends in the backseat were so terrified and confused, they thought only of ducking for cover while attempting to flee. However, the friend who sat behind the driver was trapped as well.

Larry shot him through the window as soon as he moved.

"Ahhh!" the young man moaned as the bullets struck him.

The third friend, who sat behind Keith, fell out of the back door with plans to run.

"Oh, shit!" he cried as he scrambled for his life. He stumbled to his feet, but with his pants hanging down low with no belt, he was forced to reach down and pull them up too many times to get away.

Three bullets caught him in the back. The first struck him in the head, the second hit his left shoulder, and a third bullet lodged in the middle of his spine. The young man had no chance of living as his face crashed to the loose gravel of the parking lot.

Larry ran back to the Yukon and reached through the window to reclaim the bag of money. He tossed the first gun onto the driver's lap to set him up for Alex's murder. He then grabbed the second bag of money from the back seat of the Escalade and sprinted across the street, where he jumped into the back of a dark sedan with a getaway driver ready at the wheel.

"Let's go!"

They peeled off behind the smooth purr of a V8 engine as the car accelerated from the scene and approached Interstate 20 East, long before the police arrived.

21... FIREWORKS

A crowd of Atlanta police officers and forensic investigators showed up at the murder scene in the southwest university area to try and piece together what had happened. Detectives Todd and Weinberger were there too, having been called to the scene out of bed after Shawn Blake's friend, Alex Cunningham, had been identified as one of the murder victims.

Todd looked around and exhaled. "This must have been one hell of a conversation. And it looks like these guys got the worst of it," he said in reference to the three men in the Yukon. All five of the deceased bodies, including Alex's, were still there to be studied thoroughly.

"But why would they leave their truck here?" Weinberger asked, referring to the Escalade. "They didn't even try to get their friend to the hospital?" she said, referring to Alex.

Detective Todd took a closer look at the Cadillac and shook his head, gravely. "He wasn't gonna make it to the hospital. They would have been driving dead weight. And if the suspects didn't want be known, a hospital run is out of the question."

"They must have plenty of money to leave a *Cadillac*," a uniformed officer suggested.

"Looks like most of the shooting took place from right here, in between the two vehicles," the forensic investigator commented. He stood in between the two SUVs.

Detective Todd looked down at the spent shells that were circled in white chalk on the ground. "Those are two different shells?" he asked to be certain.

"Yeah, we found one of the fired guns in the driver's lap, but he didn't have any gun powder residue on his hands or on his clothes. So the gun was most likely dropped in his lap. And it looks like the other guys in the vehicle didn't bother to even shoot."

"They were all taken by surprise?" Weinberger questioned. She started thinking of a police officer hit, which she couldn't comment on at the moment.

"It looks like only two guns were fired, and we have one of them," the forensic investigator commented. "So unless these guys all used the same gun, it may have been just one man."

Detective Todd listened to it all without comment. He had some ideas of his own.

"We have no fingerprints on the steering wheel or the driver's side door," an assistant mentioned from the Cadillac. "The driver must have been wearing gloves."

Todd walked around to the driver's side door of the Cadillac and climbed in behind the wheel.

"What are you doing?" the investigating assistant asked him.

"Well, I'm about six foot two, and I like to sit comfortably when I drive. So whoever drove this truck is definitely shorter than me," Todd said with his knees bent up. "I'm predicting he was under six feet."

Weinberger smiled, knowingly. "That's a good idea."

Todd climbed out and grinned at her. "You're getting nothing but the best from me, baby girl. I've been doing this for a long time. And it looks like a double hit to me, nice and neat."

Even the forensic investigators were impressed with his methods. "So, if we have a hit on our hands, which one of the guys on your case list fits the bill?" the lead forensic investigator asked him.

"Larry 'Little L' Bradford," Detective Todd answered with

confidence. He had studied the Flint, Michigan, files and memorized them all. "But we don't have anyone left out here to point him out. That's the hard part. We gotta prove that he was here."

He turned and looked around at the late-night bystanders, who watched them all from behind the police ropes. He wondered if any of them had witnessed anything.

"Anyone speak up to identify anybody?"

"Not a one," an officer answered and shook his head.

Todd looked back and said, "Yeah, it's the no snitch rule . . . unless the police were involved. That's when *everybody* snitches and starts pulling out cameras."

Weinberger grinned and remained silent. *I'm not touching that,* she thought. *Only David can get away with saying stuff like that.*

"What about their cell phones?" she suggested. "Someone had to call them all first, right?"

Todd grinned back at her. "Good idea. Let's check that out."

Judy and Alexandria sat in front of Brenda Avant's desk inside of her office with the door closed.

Brenda opened her palms, sitting comfortably in her tall leather chair behind her desk. "Okay, so what's your story?" she asked them both.

Judy took the lead. "Of course, we all know each other, and my husband had a tough moment where he wanted to reach out and understand more about what was going on. Since I wasn't listening to all of his concerns at the time, he reached out to talk to Alexandria about them. And without any of us knowing that someone was trailing him, he momentarily put his hand in her hair at the sports bar—where they met up to have their conversation— and we have another sensationalized story on our hands," Judy explained calmly. "But if there was no momentum built up around my name and family from the first articles with Shawn Blake, then this whole open-marriage nonsense would have had no legs to stand on.

"And for the record, we don't have one of those," she stated. "So obviously, someone's out to ruin my career and family, and I've now decided to take a two-week leave to figure this all out and get away from the heat for a minute."

Judy had worked to perfect her opening statement during every minute of her drive to work that morning, and she planned to say no more until she was asked.

Brenda took it all in and looked at Alexandria. "Is that what happened?"

Alexandria nodded. "Yes."

"Do you believe you can deal with all of the chatter you're about to hear inside these hallways and the stares you're going to receive because of this—enough to keep doing your job?"

Alexandria was surprised by the question. She figured she was out the door before she even walked in that morning. However, Brenda made it seem as if there was still hope for her.

"I am not a homewrecker," Alexandria answered. "I would never do that to anyone. But certain pictures can make people think anything. So that will never happen again."

Brenda kept her eyes on her. "And you're telling me that you've never slept with her husband?"

With Brenda's hard stare, Judy's heart jumped in her throat from the sudden spell of anxiety. *Shit!*

"No, I have not," Alexandria answered convincingly.

Brenda looked back at Judy. "Do you believe her?"

Judy exhaled, pleased with Alexandria's answer. "I have no choice," she responded. "Either I believe her . . . or I have to whip her ass."

Brenda smiled and chuckled at Judy's usual candor. She looked back at Alexandria and pointed. "Unless someone publishes new pictures of you in bed with her husband, don't you *ever* change your story, and don't you *ever* go around her husband again. Do you hear me?"

Alexandria felt like crying again. She was getting another chance. She nodded and said, "Yes, ma'am."

Brenda continued to glare at her while she thought about it. Finally, she said, "Okay . . . you go back to work this morning, and we'll see how it goes."

Alexandria was so happy, she felt like doing cartwheels inside the hallway. With her hands folded in prayer, she stood up and looked back at Judy. "This will never happen again. I swear to *God*! I am so sorry about this."

"Look, go on out the room, girl," Judy barked at her. She didn't want to hear it. She realized that Brenda had a much deeper conversation prepared for her that morning. Once again, she felt like Alexandria was getting off the hook.

Wisely, Alexandria read her irritation and left the room without another word, closing the door back behind her.

With just the two of them left, Brenda asked Judy, "So, what happened with you on Saturday?" She was obviously asking about the assault of YellowGirl1.

Judy went right into it without a blink. "I went down there to ask the girl a few questions, and she didn't like them, so she tried to insult me and leave. Then, I foolishly pushed her on her way out, so she tried to throw her computer at me. I grabbed her computer and threw it back, but she didn't catch it or deflect it like I did, so it hit her upside the head and face. Then she started yelling for security.

"At that point, it was obvious that I had made a big mistake by even going down there," Judy admitted. "Then the manager walked up and told me that I needed to leave, so I left. By the time I reached my car in the parking garage, here comes the campus security, and they detained me until the Atlanta police arrived to arrest me."

She couldn't get any more thorough than that.

Brenda said, "Well, what did you have to ask her?"

Judy took another breath. "I went online and did some research on all of these crazy stories coming out, including hers. I found that this marketing database company called ATLHeat.com has been sending out email blasts, apparently on everything that Shawn

Blake gets involved in, which obviously includes me and my husband now. So I asked her what her relationship was with this company, and whether they had paid her to write these articles. She didn't want to answer that question.

"In fact, she started saying that she wasn't going to write anymore articles about me and complained that I was going after the 'little guys' instead of asking questions of the *National Urban Report*," Judy added. "That's when she started acting out, calling me *disgusting* for having an *open* marriage with my husband and for sleeping with Shawn Blake and all that nonsense. She wanted to create a smokescreen and instigate a fight to keep me away from the real answers."

Brenda stared across her desk and listened calmly. Judy had no idea what Brenda was thinking. She was just trying to keep it simple, with the truth.

"I know it may all sound crazy to you, but that's what I was doing," Judy concluded. "I wanted to be proactive instead of reactive and ended up *reacting* to some nonsense anyway."

Out of nowhere, Brenda cracked a wide smile. "I have always been very impressed with you," she said. "Where most people would sit back and gripe, whine and complain, you have always gone that extra mile. Well, I've been doing some research of my own."

Brenda held up a file of printouts that she had set on her desk and left unopened. She said, "You're absolutely right. This ATLHeat.com and a few other smaller websites have all been working in tandem to promote various articles and events that all connect to Shawn Blake, his friends, strip clubs, rap albums, and a gang of other Atlanta parties. It all looked random until your stories came up, which have nothing to do with strip clubs and music.

"However," Brenda continued, "if the same people who go to strip clubs and listen to rap music are interested in reading slanderous stories about celebrity hook-ups, open marriages, relationship conspiracies, and all that kind of stuff, then you now get a chance to build up a database of satisfied customers in that same demographic. So I asked a young friend of mine, who still promotes these parties and things, to tell me anything about these websites and their marketing. He told me that over the past few months, ATLHeat.com has become one of the fastest growing database companies in the whole southeast region because of Atlanta's popularity with music, strips clubs, and all of these reality TV shows.

"So, you're absolutely *right*," she repeated passionately. "These people have found a way to create the kind of news that allows them to market to all the folks who love *ratchet*."

Judy began to smile and feel vindicated. "That means I'm not crazy then," she commented.

"No, you are not," Brenda told her. "Furthermore, whenever crooks move into new businesses and start to get greedy, they often get *sloppy* about covering up their tracks. These websites have so many obvious ties to Shawn Blake that it makes your head spin. Some of the articles are from people who are supposed to be his enemies. It's like they all climbed in the same boat together and decided to make money off of Shawn.

"I pulled together this detailed file over the weekend to share with the proper authorities to get you out of this *mess* that you got yourself in, because there is *definitely* a method to the madness going on," she said. "Next, they need to find out who's behind the financing of these companies. That's when you'll really get to the truth."

Judy felt so relieved. She could have jumped up and did cartwheels herself. It was Christmas morning again for the little girl from Indiana.

She told Brenda, "I *really* appreciate you. You have no *i-dea*."

Brenda said, "I'll have a sit-down with Bob about all of this when he gets back in tomorrow. I'll explain to him that some people's desperation to build an audience has gone to extreme and dangerous measures. That's why I never wanted you out there in the first place. You're too good to waste your career on that nonsense. But you still need that two-week leave so you can rest

297

your mind, heal your family, and allow us to clean all this up."

Judy nodded and breathed easily. *Now I can finally get some sleep tonight,* she thought. *I need to go back home and get some sleep right now*

"I also thought about the Alexandria issue, and you were right about that as well," Brenda said. "It wouldn't make strategic sense for us to fire her right now. That would only add to the speculation of what may or may not have happened with your husband. These drama lovers wouldn't care about how it was reported. They would continue to believe whatever they want to be true. But if we keep her here, and her story holds up with no more pictures to talk about, then that'll blow over with the rest of it."

Judy continued to smile. She said, "I'm very impressed with you too. You're adapting your old-school ways to the new tricks that are being played."

Brenda sat back in her chair and chuckled. "Well, maybe you'll listen to me next time. I still know some things."

When Shawn found out about Alex's murder that morning, he was as angry about his news as Judy was overjoyed about hers.

"FUCK!" he yelled into the empty space of his condo. He watched the news story unfold right there on Judy's WATL Cable station. Then he called Benny immediately. "Yo, you see this on Al? How this shit happen, man?"

Benny paused. "We need to meet up and talk about it. You know where."

"What time? Right now?" Shawn asked him urgently.

"Give me like two hours."

"Two hours for what?"

"So I can pick up Zola."

Shawn frowned and snapped, "Yo, this ain't no fucking media issue, man. This is *family*! We going right back up to Flint now for *another funeral*? How is that even gon' look?"

Benny said, "We obviously in a war down here now, B. But

you need to calm—"

"I'm not fucking calming down!" Shawn blasted. "I've been calm for too long about this shit already. What are you doing, man? What the fuck are you doing?"

Benny didn't respond. He said nothing at all.

"Hello?" Shawn asked, to see if he was still there.

"Are you trying to say something to me?" Benny asked him calmly.

Shawn recognized his dangerous tone and thought about his question for a moment. "What if I am? Are you denying it? This shit has gon' too far, man. Way too far."

"Look, let's just meet up and squash all this."

"You mean, *kill it,* right?"

"What?" Benny barked. "Come on, man, don't play yourself. You too smart for that."

"All right, well, let's just meet up in two hours then," Shawn huffed.

"That's what's up," Benny agreed.

When Shawn hung up, he remained a man on fire. He marched right into his bedroom and pulled out a silver and black Glock pistol from the hidden compartment inside the box spring of his mattress.

"If we're at war, then I need to be ready for it. Who's to say I won't be next?" He had an hour and a half to burn before taking off for his meeting with Benny. He thought about Judy being absent from the air that morning, and all of the chaos that she and her family had been going through on account of him . . . and Benny.

He called her up impulsively, only to get her voicemail again and decided to leave her with some of his thoughts. "Yo, this is Shawn, calling you back. I got your message yesterday, but I figured I got in too late to call you . . ."

In the middle of his words, Judy rang him on his call-waiting line. Shawn clicked over to answer. "Yeah, I'm sorry to call you back so early like this, but—"

"I just saw the story about your friend Alex on the news," she said, cutting him off. "That's *crazy*."

"Ain't it though? It's crazy what's been going on with *you* too. But now you know how *I* feel, huh?" He was referring to the confession Judy had left him on his voicemail.

"Yeah, I really do now," she admitted. "Sometimes you really can't understand until you're forced to go through it yourself."

"That's what I was trying to tell you from day one. This is what life is like in the bubble," he said. "You wake up in the news every other day just because somebody wanted to tell a fuckin' story, and you didn't have shit to do with it."

"But that's the nature of the news, Shawn. That's the industry that I'm in," she reminded him. "We don't just cover stories on people who *want* to be in the news. We're not a PR firm. Most of what we cover are stories from people who *didn't* ask for it."

"Yeah, and then you make money off of it with the ratings. But do we get a cut of that?" he asked her rhetorically. "No. Do we even get a chance to explain our side of the story fairly, without ya'll pushing questions down our throat? No. So now I'm glad you finally see how it feels to be on the other side of it."

Judy hesitated before she spoke. "Shawn, I understand how upset you are right now. Look at what just happened to me over this weekend. I get it. I was angry too. Now, I haven't had any *friends* killed out here like you have. I can't say that I've experienced that. But when my oldest son was suspended from school last week for protecting my honor while some kid was calling me a 'Hollywood Sleepin' Ho,' I really felt like killing somebody myself.

"That's the kind of thing that kids remember for the rest of their lives," she continued. "There's nothing we can do to erase their memories. So imagine how bad a mother would feel after some shit like that."

Her story forced Shawn to chill for a minute. "Damn, that really happened?"

"Yes, it did," Judy confirmed. "A damn ten-year-old *fifth grader* made up a song about it, and he was singing it at school around my son after reading stuff online with his older siblings. So I get it, Shawn, I do. Trust me!"

Shawn looked down at his watch and thought up something spontaneously. "Look, I know you probably don't want to finish up that interview with me now, but I have more to tell you . . . in person. I feel like I'm running out of time to tell it now, to be honest with you."

"You think somebody's after you next?" Judy asked him curiously.

"Why not? You really think I'm untouchable?"

"Well . . . where would you want to meet me? The last place we met didn't work out so well."

"Yeah, well, we can't meet at my other place now either," he said. "It's too obvious." *Plus, the cops are probably following me around again,* he thought.

With his Glock pistol still in hand, Shawn looked out of his condo window down to the street, mimicking the iconic home defense image of Malcolm X with his assault weapon.

I don't even know if I should talk on the phone in here anymore, he thought. *Benny might have bugged my place. I should have dealt with his ass a long time ago. This is all my fucking fault! Now my boy Alex is dead.*

"Well, where could we meet then?" Judy questioned.

"Ahhh . . . let me hit you back on that. I gotta make a couple other calls first."

"All right, call me back."

As soon as Shawn hung up, he texted her.

—I don't even know what I can say on this phone now. So I'll probably text you back a location.—

—Okay.— Judy responded.

Back at home, Judy stripped down for bed, turned her lights off, and closed her blinds and shades for darkness to allow her mind, body, and eyes to rest. She still had the television on to watch her station's morning news and see how it would pan out with just Michael and Wendy. Once she had hung up the line with Shawn, she felt conflicted about agreeing so fast to meet him.

Do I really want to meet with him again? I'm just now starting to pull all of this craziness together. We already know what's going on with him now, so I really don't need to talk to him about anything. We know his friend Benny C. is behind it. We just need evidence. But maybe Shawn is ready to give me more information for proof. He's tipped me so far on everything else. But I need to get it on tape this time.

Judy had so many different thoughts running through her head that she didn't get any rest at all.

"Shit! If he has somebody after him, why would I want to be out there with that?" she mumbled. "I got a damn *family* to raise."

Her cell phone rang again with a call from the offices at WATL Cable. She looked at the call and wondered. *I hope this isn't Brenda and Bob calling me for a conference, because I'm not ready for all that.*

She flirted with not answering it before she decided to pick up the line on the fourth ring. *I'll just fake it and tell them I'm still trying to recuperate from being up all night worrying.*

She then remembered that Bob wouldn't be back in the office until Tuesday.

"Shit, what am I thinking? I really do need some rest," she mumbled. "Hello?"

"It's Brenda. I just wanted you to know that I've spoken to an Atlanta police detective, who's already on the case. He wanted me to give him your number, but I told him you would call him back once you were ready, and I took down his number instead. Are you ready for it?"

Judy didn't know if she was ready for *anything* this morning. She thought the hardest part was already done. Apparently it wasn't.

Shit! Now a detective wants to talk to me? I guess that's the next process.

"Ahhh . . . let me get out a pen." She scrambled through her nightstand drawer to the left of her bed, where she had placed her long list. "Yeah, I'm ready."

Brenda read off the phone number and said, "The detective also advised that you should have no more discussions or contact with Shawn Blake. Did you know his second friend who was killed last night?"

"Yes, I did," she answered somberly. "Alex wasn't a bad guy either. He was actually the first one I met, and more like a big protector."

"Well, Shawn doesn't have that protection now. The police are trailing him for his own safety. You need to stay away from him while they do their jobs. Has he tried to call you at all?"

"I haven't answered him," Judy lied. "But he did leave me a few messages."

"About what?"

"Basically, to apologize. I saved them."

"Good. The police might want to hear those."

Shit! Judy panicked. *I should have never said that.*

"But what about our journalistic integrity?" she questioned. She started thinking about how much the police would want to ask her, but didn't know how much she wanted to tell them. *This is getting more complicated by the minute.*

Brenda told her, "You need to tell them everything and wipe your hands clean from this. He didn't give you much of a story to protect anyway, right? If he had, this may have all been over with *weeks* ago. So just let it all go. Your family is more important."

"What about my *own* safety? I mean, he told me some things that—" Judy stopped herself and thought about it. *I don't need to reveal all that either.*

Brenda read through her hesitation, "Those are the kinds of things the police are gonna want to know. People are being *killed* out there. This is about more than slander, libel, and journalistic integrity, Judy. Real *lives* are at stake. So it's for his own good that they be able to solve this case. And if you can help them, then you do it."

Judy could see there was no point in arguing with her. Brenda had her mind made up to follow through with a simple solution. She said, "If these officers believe that you'll be in danger, then surely they'll have you and your family protected."

"Yeah, but do I really want to deal with all of that?" Judy asked instinctively.

Brenda paused and spoke with caution. "This is going to be a hard process, Judy. That's why your two-week leave was so necessary. There are a lot of moving parts here that all need to be figured out."

SHIT! Judy cursed herself again. *When is this all gonna be OVER?*

"All right, I'll deal with it," she said to end the call.

"Judy, do not make this more difficult than you need to," Brenda insisted. "Just answer whatever they ask you."

Yeah, that's easy for you to say. Your family isn't in the middle of this shit. Despite her thoughts, Judy realized that Brenda *had* warned her against taking on the story from the beginning.

Judy forced out a sigh and repeated, "All right . . . I'll do it."

When Judy finally hung up, she was even more conflicted. She stood up out of bed and hollered, "Shit! I guess I can forget about catching up on my sleep today. I may even need to call my mother back. The plot just thickened again."

22... POLICE WORK

Believing the police were trailing him again after Alex's murder, Shawn tossed on a dark hooded jacket and sunglasses and snuck out the side exit of his building. He walked over to the parking lot of a neighboring housing complex and found the silver Pontiac Camaro that Alex and Devon had left there for him a week ago as a getaway car.

Shawn climbed into the car and turned on the engine while keeping his hood and sunglasses on until he had driven out of the lot and into the street without anyone trailing him. He then took off the hood and retained the sunglasses on the bright and sunny morning.

Parked in the opposite direction, Detectives Todd and Weinberger sat in their unmarked car across the street from Shawn's condo, still waiting for the first sight of him in his black Mercedes SUV.

Todd checked his watch from the passenger seat while Weinberger sat behind the wheel. She stared down at a police computer conveniently placed on a rotating stand right below the dashboard.

"Yup, they're at it again," she commented. "They have an ATLHeat.com update that reads: 'Judy Pierce Goes Ballistic on

YellowGirl1,' and—get this—they also have 'The War of Flint Versus Atlanta'."

That got Todd's attention. He looked over and said, "You're kidding me."

"Look at it," Weinberger said.

She spun the computer screen in his direction so he could take a look for himself. Todd read the captions and clicked on the links. The bloggers had new pictures of the WATL Cable anchor enraged, as if she were charging forward in a fight. They also had impoverished neighborhood pictures of the city of Flint next to pictures of the rougher areas of Atlanta.

The detective shook his head and grimaced. "So these guys basically hire a bunch of desperate bloggers and then send them loads of new traffic, as long as they're writing the nonsense stories that this company wants to promote."

Weinberger winced. "*Hire* them? They don't have to hire these bloggers anymore. If you're gonna offer them a million hits of traffic, most of these guys will write articles for *free*. They just want the exposure. That's what's going on these days."

"Yeah, but they still have to be professional enough to get the right information," Todd argued. "They can't all be amateurs."

"Why not?" Weinberger countered. "These guys are not professional journalists; they're clever bloggers with articles that are snap short. It's an easy formula. All you need are the right stories to follow."

Detective Todd read a few of the random responses online and commented, "This reminds me of *Vibe* magazine back in the nineties with the whole Tupac Shakur and Biggie Smalls beef. You had East Coast and West Coast, Bad Boy Records and Death Row. Back then you had to wait once a month for the nonsense. Now these bloggers, websites, and search engines can update this shit every hour."

"And you literally have people waiting around with their cell phones in hand or at their laptops to get the new updates," his partner added.

Todd continued to shake his head. "That sounds like a new damn crack drug—crack news on a cell phone."

Weinberger chuckled. "They call it *ratchet* now."

Todd pondered her white skin and cultural background. He didn't know how he felt about her knowing so much about the African-American community's habits and dirty laundry. Nevertheless, cultural knowledge was part of their police work, so he let it slide.

"What was one of your favorite ah, rap groups, coming up?" he asked her slyly.

"Tribe Called Quest," Weinberger answered and giggled. "I liked more of the old school stuff."

Todd frowned. "That ain't old school. Well, I guess it is for *you*. Old school to me is Run DMC, Grandmaster Flash, Kurtis Blow, the Sugar Hill Gang, and folks like that. But you were barely born when they were around."

"Yeah, but I still know about them—LL Cool J, Big Daddy Kane, Rakim, Queen Latifah, MC Lyte, all of them."

Detective Todd eyed her again. "And what white rock groups can you name?" he quizzed.

Weinberger smiled and said, "Red Hot Chili Peppers, Kurt Cobain and Nirvana, Guns N' Roses, ah—"

Todd cut her off. "Those are the same white groups that black people know. And it sounds like you're struggling to name them."

"Yeah, I didn't really listen to rock like that."

"But you listened to rap music?"

She shrugged. "Yeah, we all did—Snoop Dogg and Dr. Dre, DMX, The Pharcyde, Sir Mix-A-Lot, Eminem, Outkast. I mean, come on, rap music was more popular. We even listened to 2 Live Crew from Miami with Luke Campbell and the whole strip club music thing. That's not anything new. So when I look at these bloggers and websites now, they're basically tapping into the whole trap music, strip club, ratchet lifestyle that so many young people are into."

"But now they're attracting *older* people with this stuff," Todd said.

"They're expanding their demographic. What do you expect them to do?" Weinberger replied. "The television networks are doing that with the reality shows. The older generation doesn't go out to strip clubs and parties. So what do they do? They watch the nonsense on ratchet TV instead. They may not call it that, but that's what it is."

Before Todd could comment, a call came in from the central Atlanta police station from Chief Wallace. They put him on speaker.

"I just spoke to our FBI guys about this Shawn Blake case, and it's gotten much bigger now with this whole website thing. They were already onto these guys, so we'll let the FBI handle this ATLHeat.com thing. That's more their expertise and a lot more sophisticated than we want to deal with right now. Our part is to solve these Atlanta murders and find out *how* or *if* Shawn Blake was involved in any of it. The phone records from last night's murders didn't turn up much. A lot of these guys are using burner phones to do their dirt."

"So do you still want us to question Judy Pierce, or do you want the FBI guys to do that now?" Todd asked to make sure.

"Nooo, we still want to question her. She has a lot of information on Shawn. The FBI doesn't really need her now. They're going right after these Internet companies and bloggers to seize their computers, bank account records, and all of that. They have trails of money coming in from all over the country. So the FBI guys have their website technicians and all that stuff on the case now. But we still need to talk to the key witness about Shawn, and that's definitely Judy Pierce."

"All right, we're still waiting on her to call us," Todd informed him.

Chief Wallace said, "If she doesn't call you by two o'clock, you make plans to drive out there and knock on her door. We don't have time to waste."

When the chief hung up, Todd looked down at his watch. It was fast approaching noon. "She has two more hours. After that, we'll drive out to her."

Weinberger nodded and looked forward. Shawn Blake's black Mercedes SUV was still parked in the lot in plain view. "What about Shawn?" she asked.

Todd shrugged. "Either he's not coming out, or he gave us the slip already. But I know one thing: I'm getting hungry. And there's a Subway right up the street from here."

Weinberger smiled. "As soon as we leave, he's gonna come out. You know that right?"

"Then we'll drive out to question Judy and catch up to him later."

Weinberger nodded. "Sounds like a plan."

Still nervous about talking to the police or meeting up with Shawn again, Judy made plans to conduct her own investigation from home. She wrote another list of things to do at her kitchen table that included a follow-up phone call to Shawn's baby momma, Annette.

Before she could get started on it, Shawn texted her again.

—All right I'm driving out to you now. I'll hit you back with a good meeting spot off of 285 West.—

Judy cringed as she read the text. "Oh no, don't come out here," she said to herself in a panic. "Did I ever tell him where I live?"

Everyone knew Judy lived in Alpharetta in the northwest. She spoke about it often. But they didn't know exactly where. *However, if somebody followed my husband, then why wouldn't they be able to follow me?* she thought. That made her more nervous.

"Shit! I need to come up with something to tell him," she huffed at the table. She stood up to pace the room and think and came up with something feasible.

She called Shawn back on his phone and received his voicemail. She left an urgent

message. "Hey, Shawn, I just got a call from the nurse at my sons' school less than ten minutes ago, and it sounds like one of my boys has come down with some kind of hundred and two degrees fever. So I'm on my way to run over there and scoop him up right now."

"I'm sorry, but I won't be able to meet up with you today. I don't even have the time to sit down and text you back right now. I'm getting myself together, and I'm out the door."

She hung up and breathed comfortably. "Okay, that should work. Let me see if he hits me back."

She walked over and opened up the back patio door to add the elements of the November weather to the background, as if she were actually driving. But Shawn didn't call or text her back. So she called Annette with the same background noise to fake driving to school.

"Hello," Annette answered after a few rings.

"Hey, Annette, I'm sorry to call you out of the blue like this, but this is Judy Pierce, remember me? Shawn's reporter friend from WATL Cable."

"Oh, yeah, you don't need all the formalities with me. How are you doing with everything, being all over the news and all?"

"I'm hanging in there, you know. Shawn and his friends have been in the news a lot too," Judy said. "Have you been watching everything?"

"Yeah, girl, it's umm . . . I don't even know what to say. Two murders in two weeks."

"*Eight* murders if you count the four other guys from last night and the two who were killed by the police."

"*Nine* murders if you count the guy from the club a month ago," Annette added.

"How 'bout that?" Judy said.

"Yeah, it's all crazy."

"Well, have you talked to Shawn about it? He just called me to try and meet up with him again, but my son just came down with a fever at school, and I'm rushing over there to pick him up."

"Shawn doesn't really um . . . talk to me about too much. He'll talk to *you* before he talks to me. So I don't really bother him like that."

"Even after two of his friends were killed? He was telling me something about Benny last week."

Annette hesitated before saying, "What about Benny?"

Judy smirked with her hook and bait dangling in the water. "I mean, does Benny have a lot of money like that? Because Shawn made it seem like it was Benny's responsibility to pay for the funeral. I don't mean to get into their business, but is Benny financing everything? I thought Shawn was the one with the money. He's the Hollywood star, right?"

Annette clammed up quick and didn't go for it. "I don't know, and I don't really care. Like I said, I just do my own thing with my real estate. I don't get into all that stuff with them."

"Well, last time I talked to Shawn, he said that Benny was into real estate and properties too. So they never gave you any tips or anything?"

"Why would he do that? I never associated with him like that," Annette responded sourly. "I mean, what are you trying to say? Are you reporting on some shit again? Haven't you gotten in enough fucking trouble as it is? Now you wanna fuck with me. Child, please."

She hung up the line and that was it. Judy stood there on her patio in the cold and thought about it. She was not convinced.

"She got upset a little too fast, which means that she knows where I was going with it, and she didn't want to talk about it. So we need to check into her real estate money," Judy mumbled.

She walked back into the kitchen to look at the next phone number to call from her list—Gene Whiteside at Peach Cobbler Records. That's when Shawn's next follow-up message came in.

—I hope I'm still here to get a chance to tell you more.—

Judy froze and knew that she couldn't respond. *I wonder how much he has to tell me now,* she wondered. Nevertheless, she didn't dare respond to him until later. *But what if he fucks around and gets killed?*

She was tempted to call him back, but she fought against it. "He'll be all right. I'll call him back in another hour—or text him. Now let me get back to what I'm doing . . ."

311

Shawn randomly drove around in the silver Camaro, as if he couldn't make up his mind on what to do. He was also running out of gas, not having enough in the tank to begin with.

"I don't believe they didn't fill up the fucking tank," he barked.

The first gas station he pulled into off the beltway had two police cruisers present. The first officer filled up at the fuel island, while the second was parked out in front of the convenient store, talking on his cell phone.

"Shit!" Shawn cursed. He felt like a wanted man, even though he wasn't. However, he did have a loaded gun inside the car with him. His probation terms from several years ago did not allow him to legally own one. "Do I chance it?" he asked himself.

Instead, he spotted another gas station up the street and decided to play it safe by filling up at that one.

He looked down at his watch again as he fueled up and found that his two hours had run out. He had less than thirty minutes to make it to his meeting with Benny on time. He finished pumping his gas, climbed back into the car, and contemplated.

"Fuck, let me just set this up," he said.

He pulled the car into a parking spot and called Judy Pierce back. He waited for her voicemail to leave another loaded message. "Yeah, this is Shawn calling you back. Sorry to hear about your son. But I need you to hold on to this message for me in case I don't make it out tonight.

"I don't really trust anybody right now, but I gotta tell *somebody*. This whole thing with Benny has been about fear and loyalty the whole time. Now that he sees that I'm trying to focus strictly on my acting career, it's like he's getting more reckless; a girlfriend having a nasty tantrum before the breakup, you know?

"But to be honest with you, I don't even know if he needs me around anymore. It looks like he's got the perfect formula now. He'd probably get more value out of me if I died."

Shawn left the message at that and hung up without another

word. He had said all he felt he needed to say. He backed out of his parking spot and turned into traffic with urgency to make his meeting with Benny. He inadvertently ran through a red light, right in front of the police cruiser from the first gas station that he had driven away from.

"Shit!" he cursed again as he watched the police cruiser in his rearview mirror.

The officer shot out into traffic behind him. WHHRRRRPP! WHHRRRRPP!

"FUCK!" Shawn spat and immediately pulled over to the right. There was no way that he was running. He had been pulled over and arrested plenty of times before. He knew that he could survive another one. However, the police cruiser blew straight past him and sped up the road for another destination.

Shawn watched the cruiser take off and head onto the beltway as he exhaled behind the wheel. "Damn, that was close."

He sat there a minute longer and began to read the close call as an omen. *Maybe I shouldn't even go to this meeting. Let's see how Benny responds to that.*

Back at Judy's home, she started sweating her own next move. She listened to Shawn's desperate message *twice* and proceeded to fight with her conscience.

He's just trying to manipulate you and get his way, she thought. *I am not going back out there to meet with him. I barely even want to pick up my kids now. But what if he gets killed out there for real and I didn't try to help him?*

"He's not gonna get killed," she mumbled out loud, unconvincingly. "He's worth too much. This whole thing is established around him."

But like he said, Benny may have the Internet formula Back at Judy's home, she started sweating her own next move. She listened to Shawn's desperate message *twice* and proceeded to fight with her conscience.

He's just trying to manipulate you and get his way, she thought. *I am not going back out there to meet with him. I barely even want to pick up my kids now. But what if he gets killed out there for real and I didn't try to help now without him. There are plenty of celebrities out there who get into trouble. ATLHeat.com has strong momentum now.*

"That damn thing isn't gonna last," she said aloud. "The police know all about it and they're about to shut that party down. I'll help make sure of that. They are *not* getting away with this shit!"

Okay, but what about Shawn? This man is practically begging for your help, and what do you do? You lie to him and hide behind your phone. Her thoughts persisted.

"I *am* helping him," Judy barked. "But I have a *family* to think about. I can't go back out there with that shit. He's gonna have to figure this out on his own."

At their usual bar hangout and meeting place on the west end of Atlanta, Benny stood next to Zola at the tall counter with fresh drinks in hand. They were both dressed like corporate executives at Happy Hour.

Zola sighed, standing tall and stately in black suede heels. "This is horrible. As soon as I get down here there's another murder." She couldn't even enjoy her drink. She was only holding it there like a statue.

Benny nodded calmly beside her and raised his short glass to his lips. The golden tint of the liquor matched the accents in his richly colored tie. "No matter what happens, we gotta stay focused," he advised. "Everything in life is a test of your stamina. We can't let nothing break us. That's what I need to tell Shawn today. No matter what, it's all good."

Zola observed his calm, solemn stance and optimistic words of reserve before she nodded back at him. She fully believed in the man. He seemed built to last. So she forced herself to drink anyway.

Benny took another look at his watch. The time approached

two o'clock with no sight or word from Shawn. He was already twenty minutes late. *Did his ass just stand us up, or did he get stopped somewhere on the way?*

When Benny looked up again toward the entrance, an ambush of police officers rushed into the room with their weapons drawn, wearing bulletproof vests and helmets.

"Put the drinks down on the bar, get your hands up, and don't move!"

"What the hell?" Zola responded nervously.

"Just do what they tell you," Benny advised her with ice in his veins.

They both set their drinks down on the tall counter and raised their hands up slowly as the officers approached them with handcuffs.

"You have the right to remain silent," the rugged lead officer announced.

However, Benny had one question to ask them. "What's the charges?"

"Conspiracy to commit murder."

That answer led to a second question. "To murder who?"

"Alex Cunningham."

"What? That's crazy," Zola responded fervently.

Benny looked back at The Shot Bar manager, who shook his head grimly behind the counter. There was nothing he could do. The police had staked them out.

"What are you arresting *me* for?" Zola complained, following behind him.

"You're an accomplice."

"Oh, this is bullshit," Zola barked.

"Ay," Benny snapped at her, "*focus*, right? Keep your calm. We got lawyers for this."

"You're gonna need them too," the lead officer cracked.

23... THE HEAT IS ON

Detectives Todd and Weinberger arrived at Judy's home security gate and buzzed her intercom at 2:27 p.m.

"Who is it?" Judy sounded like an innocent maid.

Detective Todd looked around the premises and spotted several cameras pointed straight at them from inside the gated property. Then he smiled, knowing that she could see them. So he spoke as if auditioning for the cameras.

"I'm Detective David Todd, and this is my partner, Laura Weinberger. We've both been waiting around for hours to hear back from you today. So, once it reached two o'clock, the chief told us to come on out here and ring your doorbell. As you already know, this case is a very serious matter. We have had several murders over the past couple of weeks, many of which remain unsolved. If you have any detailed information that we could use, we would love to hear it."

Judy paused as if she needed another minute to consider what Todd had said. "Okay, but umm . . . I have to run out and pick up my sons from school in less than thirty minutes."

"We understand. We'd just like to get this conversation started, if you don't mind," Todd said.

Judy buzzed them in. As the gate slid back slowly, the

detectives climbed back into their car and drove up to park in front of the garage.

"Well, here we go," Todd told his young female partner as they approached the front door. He was openly excited.

Weinberger grinned without a word. She was only curious to hear what Judy had to say.

The embattled newswoman opened the door, shook their hands, invited them in, and led them straight to the kitchen table. "Would you like something to drink?" she offered.

"We're not allowed to have anything stronger than water while on the job," Todd joked. "Unless we're undercover, of course."

Judy grinned back at him. "You'll both have water then."

By the time she brought their half-filled glasses of water, Todd and Weinberger had both noticed her notes of names and phone numbers that were deliberately placed right out in front of them.

"What's all this?" Todd asked her, pointing.

Judy sat down across from them and answered, "My investigation."

Todd looked at Weinberger and chuckled. *Here we go,* he repeated to himself.

"So ah . . . what did you find out?"

Judy answered, "Well, I think we all know by now that Bernard 'Benny C.' Chavis is behind everything. After I attended Shawn's court case last month with Ricardo 'Ricky Slim' Morgan, it was pretty obvious that he was paid off to change his story in court. So I called his executive producer today, Mr. Gene Whiteside. He immediately wanted to get off the phone with me when I started bringing up the irony of his artist 'Ricky Slim' promoting his new songs at the same Atlanta strip clubs that Shawn, Benny, and the rest of their Michigan crew frequent."

Weinberger sipped her water and set her glass down on the table. "They all frequent the same clubs here in Atlanta," she said. "You have to give us something more than that."

Judy eyed her and said, "Well, YellowGirl1 also did a story on him that was marketed with traffic provided by ATLHeat.com, just like the Shawn Blake articles that she wrote in the past, and the nonsense articles she recently published on me. But that may all be a coincidence too, like how Riquan Stills—that's her real name—acted a complete *fool* when I asked her about any money she may have been paid to write these articles."

Weinberger was still unconvinced. "A lot of these bloggers are not getting paid," she commented. "Many times they'll negotiate for a tradeoff of traffic."

"I understand that," Judy countered, "but typically, when people provide services for *free*, they are quick to say, 'Oh, I didn't get paid for this. I did it because I *love it*,' or whatever the case may be. But when you actually get *paid* and try to turn around and keep it a secret, and someone finds out about it, that's when you have *issues* and want to fake a fight because somebody knows your business. You don't start fights over anything that's *free*, because free is not worth anything."

Detective Todd smiled, enjoying it all. He looked down at Judy's list and asked, "So, what's Annette's story? That's Shawn's second baby's mother, right? What did you talk to her about?"

"Oh, I had a good conversation with her, the *first* time. She basically told me that she'll do whatever she needs to do to keep Shawn out of jail. She also told me that she doesn't sweat him for money because she does her own thing in real estate. So I was curious about where she got the start-up money. I wondered if she had gotten any advice from Benny, because I understand that *he's* into real estate and properties too now.

"Well, she didn't like me asking that question too much when I called her back about it today," Judy continued. "That's when she got aggravated and hung up on me."

"Well, you know, a lot of people don't like talking to reporters," Todd stated. "They always have the feeling that you guys are gonna misquote them."

"The same way they avoid talking to police officers," Judy cracked. "Particularly when you get in their personal business. Nobody likes that. Not even me," she admitted.

"I see you also have Rhonda written down here. That's his first baby momma, right?" Todd said.

Judy nodded. "She's a totally different case. I didn't even have to talk to her. I just wrote her name down to understand the difference between her and Annette. They are night and day. Annette can be paid off to play her position, like a true professional. You can't even *pay* Rhonda to keep her mouth shut. She's gonna complain, bitch, gripe, and run her mouth no matter what. She was even doing it in court. That's why Benny didn't take care of her. He doesn't like people who run their mouth. So Rhonda will end up taking Shawn to court forever, and she *still* won't be satisfied. They're supposed to have a family court case for child support tomorrow morning."

Todd was speechless, marveling at her. She was a qualified anchor indeed, wrapping up every story and applying nametags. However, she hadn't said one word yet about Shawn. That's what the two detectives were there to hear.

"All right, so ah . . . we can definitely use all of that," Todd said, "and we thank you for it, but what about Shawn? What did he tell you?"

Weinberger grinned. Her old partner was back to work.

Judy said, "Well, before I go into that, let me solve your murders for you."

Todd glanced at Weinberger again and grinned. "All right, be my guest."

"Okay, well, J.J., AKA James John Pendleton—he was high as a kite the first night I met him, and it was obvious that he was uncontrollable, a loose cannon. So he would be the first one you would want to get rid of to keep your crew tight. He's almost like a male version of Rhonda, with a substance abuse problem to boot. So his murder was, for lack of a better word, *expected*.

"But Alex, now he was a good guy. He was big, straightforward, protective, and very respectful from the first moment I met him," she continued. "The problem was, Alex wasn't afraid of anyone either. So once he started calling Benny out for things and bringing them to Shawn's attention, well . . . that was another *problem* for Benny, and he just solved it.

"Now, this kid *Keith*, who was murdered last night with Alex—I remember seeing him sitting on Ricky Slim's side of the courtroom last month. He walked out of court *angrily* once it became obvious that this kid was changing up his story. So again, it looks to me like another case of a loose cannon. If Benny started doing business with Gene Whiteside and Ricky Slim to protect Shawn from going to jail, Keith would eventually have to be dealt with for running his mouth as well. His poor little friends followed right behind him like they did in court."

Todd asked her, "So, who's the triggerman?" He was fully immersed in her story. Not even Weinberger could argue with her conclusions.

"Well, let me tell you," Judy started, "when I first met Little L., or Larry, there were no stories coming out of him at *all*. Do you hear me? Our introduction was like two seconds flat. He was dressed in all white and was completely icy. He let me know quickly—*Do not play with me. I am not here for your games.* Shawn pulled me away from him like a hurricane was coming. So if I had to choose anybody as a killer, Larry would be the one, because we all know that Benny can't go around doing it himself. As for Devon and Toot . . ."

Judy shrugged. "You have a wannabe rapper and a roll dog. They're both pretty much harmless."

Weinberger finished up her water and was ready to ask for more. *Damn, she's pretty good,* she thought. *I'm impressed.*

Todd said, "Okay, so . . . now we get to the grand finale. Tell us all about Shawn Blake."

Judy looked down and checked her watch. It was five minutes to three and time for her to leave to pick up her children.

She folded her hands in front of her face as if she were in prayer and struggled with her words. "You know, as much as I want to believe that he's all naïve and innocent, it just doesn't add up to me. I mean, he's around these guys all the time, so he *has* to know what's going on with them. If I could figure all this out in a *month*, then, come on. He's been around these guys for *years*. But he really hasn't told me much of anything. It's like his whole life is in a bunch of small pieces."

"Did he tell you his last name was Tasker before he changed it to Blake?" Weinberger asked.

"No he did not. And let me just say this before I have to get up and go. When I last sat across the table from Shawn, and I asked him how he was able to graduate from college amidst all of the chaos that he was supposedly raised in, he told me it was because he was *smart*."

She looked directly at Weinberger. "Now, I can't speak for your culture, but using the term *'smart'* in the black community becomes a very loaded term. It creates a clear separation between *you* and the rest of the people. A lot of us *really* don't like that word. We don't *trust* it. It's like you're automatically suspected to be selfish, while leaving the rest of the people behind. It's like, conspiratorial.

"So he immediately told me that he doesn't say that around his friends," she continued. "But yet . . . whenever he gets around Benny, he turns into the complete *opposite*, like a little boy with a water faucet behind his ears. I just find that very hard to believe. So, that's my story on everything. I'm telling you guys all of this because I am *not* going be a witness. So you can take everything I just told you and go be cops."

She stood up from the table and was ready to leave. "I'm going back to my family now, if you don't mind. If you can't solve this case with all of the information I just gave you, then you don't deserve to be detectives."

Todd stood up with her, followed by his partner. "We'll see," he said.

"Not with me you won't," Judy insisted. "I've gotten way too involved with this thing already. So it's time for me to go back to what I do, and that's reporting the news."

Weinberger said, "Well, if you ever think about becoming a detective at some point, we could really use some more good women."

Judy smiled. "Thanks for the compliment. Now let me go get my sons."

"So, what do you think?" Todd asked Weinberger inside the

car as they headed back to Atlanta.

Weinberger grinned from behind the wheel. "Now I see why Benny went after her too; she's dangerous and well informed."

"Yeah, but she created more news for him too," Todd suggested.

"Okay, but here's how I'm looking at it: Out of all of the different reporters here in Atlanta, why did Shawn Blake pick her to tell his story? Or *not* to tell his story as the case may be?"

Todd thought about that. "Well, why did she pick Shawn Blake? It takes two to tango, right? And she did this outside of her regular work."

"Do you think she's had any more contact with him?"

"What, over the past few days?" Todd said. "He's probably called her. Yeah."

"But she didn't talk about that."

"We didn't get a chance to ask her, either."

Weinberger pondered that. "You think she still wants to finish up his story in some capacity?"

That made Todd pause and think about the situation too. "Her story on him seems ah . . . incomplete, right? I mean, she's figured out everyone else *but him*. And he was the only one she was assigned to cover."

"So, what's your take on Shawn?" Weinberger asked.

"Ah . . . I was hoping to find more of that out from her," Todd cracked and laughed. "This guy is really a mystery. It's like he's right there in front of us, but we can't quite place him. Now, he does have those real charges on him: possession of an illegal firearm, petty drug possession, and a couple of domestic violence disputes with Rhonda years ago. But most of his stuff has been either thrown out of court or reduced to misdemeanors, which has only given him probations and restrictions. Never any jail time. It's like he knows exactly what he can get away with and what he can't. We'll just have to figure this out over the next few days. But at least we have Benny in custody now—for as long as that lasts. And we'll see how he reacts when he gets out."

Shawn remained in the area of the 285 West Beltway as he tried to figure out what to do. He paid for more minutes on two non-traceable cell phones to set up his plans for the evening. Then he called Annette back on his regular line.

"Did you get my message about Judy?" she asked him, irritated.

"Yeah, I got it. So she's playing detective now, huh?"

"And I don't appreciate it," Annette piped. "Why is she after me with that? I didn't do anything to her."

"All right, we'll talk about it later," Shawn said. "But after Alex got killed last night, it's way too much going on around me now. So I need you to do me a favor."

Annette hesitated. "You're right, it *is* a lot going on. What do you need me to do?"

"I need to crash at your place tonight. The cops been sitting outside my condo all morning to fuck with me. I don't feel like being bothered with that. It seems likes they're ready to knock on my door at any minute."

"All right, you know what time you're gonna be here?"

"Naw, not yet. But I'll let you know. Just wait up for me."

Gene Whiteside was trapped in a quagmire with everyone else. He couldn't even think about listening to new music at his Atlanta studio. He called his top-priority artist, Ricky Slim, into his private office for a meeting instead.

Ricky closed and locked the door behind him and sat down with trepidation.

Gene eyed him and said, "You know what's been going on lately, right?"

The young artist exhaled. "How could I *not* know? We just saw Keith and those guys last night before it happened. But . . ."

"But what?" Gene pressed him.

"He was running his mouth about us dealing with these guys, so . . . I guess they dealt with him," Ricky commented honestly. "I mean, that's the code of the streets, right? No snitching. We all know that."

"That's the damn problem. These guys are still too much in the streets," Gene complained. "I thought I knew Benny better than that. I didn't sign up to get involved with no murders. I tried hard to avoid that shit. Now I got this damn reporter, Judy Pierce, calling me up and asking questions like she knows something. So I'm figuring that Shawn told her."

"But why would he tell her that?" Ricky cringed. "That doesn't make any sense. Does he *want* to go to jail?"

"Well, who else would tell her?" Gene barked, frustrated. "He's been hanging out with her right? Anyway . . ." He quickly calmed himself down. "I think we need to hold off on promoting this new single for a minute, until we allow all of this to—"

"What? Not right now, man. This single is just starting to take off," Ricky argued. "They were loving it at the strip clubs last night. We got a hit on our hands."

"Your ass'll be right in jail, dancing to it too with your damn *Pants Down*," Gene cracked at him sourly. "Now you listen to me. If this reporter woman is already asking me questions, then it won't be long before the cops come around here too. So we gotta get our stories together.

"I don't know what this woman's plans are," he continued. "But I *do* know that social media has been all over her ass for the past couple of weeks, especially with—"

Gene stopped in mid-sentence to think about what he'd just said. "*Shit!* She got it off ATLHeat.com. These assholes promote everything together, sometimes in the same emails. I told them to stop doing that shit. They needed to use disassociated databases and email blasts to promote everything separately."

"They can't do that," Ricky said. "ATLHeat.com is what everyone knows and respects. If you promote from some other sources, the people won't care as much. That's like trying to promote something from Beyoncé without using her name or face."

"Shit, it's done all the time," Gene argued. "You don't need to have some big celebrity website right in the middle of everything. You just need a great marketing plan. That's what makes these celebrity's heads so big now. Look at Kanye West. The boy's head so big they gotta fly him into open-air arenas with a helicopter. And his head still gets stuck in the lights."

Ricky Slim laughed, but Gene was dead serious.

"This shit ain't funny, Ricardo," he barked. "The police are gonna put a big-ass spotlight on every business promoted by these guys now. You watch what I tell you. We need to shut everything down and get our story straight. Right now!"

Ricky sighed, and his shoulders slumped in defeat. "If we don't use something that's popular like the *Heat* to promote us, it's gonna cost us a lot more money and it may not even work," he said. "That's why a lot of artists are not making it now. It's hard to build buzz with so many people fighting for the same space and attention."

"Well, we don't have a choice right now, Ricky. I'm not going to jail over this shit. So we're gonna shut down until we have a grip on this whole situation."

In Stone Mountain, Georgia, to the northeast of Atlanta, five dark sedans pulled up in the parking lot outside of an old tattoo parlor as a website technician smoked a cigarette in front of the small, storefront building.

"What in the world?" the shaggy-bearded middle-aged white man responded. He watched as a team of FBI agents jumped out of their cars and pulled their guns on him.

Two of the agents wore dark suits and ties, while the rest donned dark-blue FBI jackets.

"Drop the cigarette. Stomp it out and walk us inside," the suit-wearing authority figure told him. "This is the FBI." He pulled out his badge for proof.

"Yes, sir," the man said. He dropped the cigarette to the ground, stomped it out with his right shoe, and turned toward the tattoo parlor door. The FBI agents followed right behind him with their guns drawn.

Inside the small one-story building, a staff of computer technicians of all nationalities and both sexes worked at various computer stations on advanced equipment throughout several open rooms.

"Oh my God!" a young woman yelled as the agents quickly flooded into the computer offices and surrounded them with their pistols.

"This is the Federal Bureau of Investigation! I need your hands up where you are and don't move!" the FBI authority shouted, holding his badge up high. There was not one threatening-looking man or woman inside the building. It looked like a typical nerd-based staff at Google, Apple, or Facebook, but with more African-Americans, Latinos, and women involved.

"Now stand where you are and keep your hands up high," the FBI man told them.

The staff of about fifteen did as they were told as the agents began to search them all for weapons.

"What is this about?" a Latina woman asked them, confused.

"Where is Ganesh?" the FBI man asked her.

"I'm Ganesh," a late thirties East Indian man stepped up and responded from the back.

"Is there any reason why you haven't changed the name outside the building to Free World Interconnections, LLC?"

Ganesh tried his best to look and sound innocent. "We just haven't gotten around to it yet. We're still designing our new sign," he answered. "Is there a problem with that?"

The FBI man returned his pistol to his shoulder holster and shrugged. "I don't know, you tell me. Haven't you made enough money to design a fucking sign by now? You've made *millions* off your ATLHeat.com database alone, right? Did you set that up or not?"

Several staff members began to fidget, nervously. It was obvious to the experienced FBI agents that more than a few of the company's workforce were in on it.

"Are you all aware that you've been receiving payments from individuals and businesses that are involved in criminal activities, including money laundering, bribes, and conspiracy to commit murder?" the FBI man asked them all.

"*Murder?* We haven't conspired to murder anyone?" Ganesh protested.

"Yeah, you just helped to pay for it and then promoted it all online," the FBI man countered.

A collected groan of dread filled the room.

"I just started working here last *week*. I don't even know what you're *talking* about," the same Latina woman complained.

"Tell it to your attorney," the FBI man told her. His team lined them all up and marched them outside in a single file to wait for the local police to arrive with handcuffs and vans.

"Shit! I knew this was too fucking good to be true," the middle-aged white man spat as he walked back outside the building.

"I'm sorry to hear that for ya'," the FBI man told him. "You should have kept your job at Best Buy."

The decision to allow Bernard "Benny C." Chavis to make bail had already been made. Chief Wallace informed his detectives about this on an updated call from the phone in his office.

"Once we let him out, we need to trail his every move and every phone call he makes. We're sending security detail out to Alpharetta to protect Judy Pierce and her family, whether she agrees to be our star witness or not. If Benny now believes that his hometown friend has conspired against him, we can't just have this reporter floating around. Especially if she's out here making her own investigative phone calls, like you guys have said.

"The FBI will help us out as well now," the chief added.

"They've already raided the website office out in Stone Mountain. We should have more incriminating information on this guy any minute now."

"So, why even let him out then?" Weinberger asked the chief over the line.

Wallace nodded and agreed with the young detective's suggestion of caution. "Laura, I hear what you're saying, but if this guy is as impulsive as we all *believe* he is, he'll make some more desperate moves that'll make this case easier for us."

"Yeah, but we might get a few more people *killed* in the process," Todd argued. "Even Shawn."

Chief Wallace sighed. "This guy has powerful lawyers and plenty of money to get himself out. So I'd rather do this early, while he's still a little hot under the collar, than to have him wait it out and think too long about it. You want him playing a game of *speed* chess, where he can make more mistakes and force us to counter. Let me call you guys back once I have some more information on it."

When the chief hung up, he still felt a bit uneasy about Benny getting out of jail, but he was willing to take the gamble.

"This police work is never safe," he mumbled to himself, "for any of us."

24... THE BOARD GAMES BEGIN

Marlon arrived home from work before six o'clock that evening after another worrisome day of darting eyes and muted whispers at UPS. He found an unmarked sedan parked outside of their security gate with two men sitting inside. He thought about stopping to ask them who they were, but figured he would ask his wife instead, once he made it into the house.

"You know we have two men sitting in a car outside of our gate?" he asked Judy inside the kitchen. Their two young sons were out of the room at the moment.

Judy grimaced, wearing her cooking apron while fixing another family meal at the stove.

"Two men in a car? Do they look like cops?" She placed down her long cooking spoon and went to have a look at the security monitors. "Shit," she cursed. "Two Atlanta detectives came out here to talk to me today after I didn't call them earlier. I told them that I didn't want to be a witness in a case against Shawn Blake. So I guess they sent a security team out here anyway. Did you say anything to them?"

"No, I figured you knew what it was about. That's why you couldn't talk to me at lunchtime today?" Marlon asked. He had called to check in on her earlier that afternoon.

"I was making some other calls at that time," Judy said. "I

wanted to have enough information on this case for them to leave me alone."

"How did they get in touch with you anyway?"

"Brenda gave me their number after she had put together a file to present to the police about ATLHeat.com. She came up with the same research that I had, and she found out even more about it. So I know that I'm not crazy now."

Marlon nodded, taking it all in. "What all happened at work today? I saw that you weren't on air this morning."

"I took the two-week leave, Marlon. I didn't have a choice. It's not even safe for me to be out there now until all of this craziness is settled. But get this: Brenda decided to keep Alexandria around so it won't look like they fired her on account of us."

Marlon listened and kept his poise. He didn't want to appear too sympathetic about Alexandria. "Okay," he responded blandly. "So, now they got us on security watch?" he said quickly to change the subject.

Judy shrugged. "I guess so. But as long as they're not bothering us . . ." *Then again, I wonder if they can bug our phone calls or something,* she wondered. "Why, is it bothering you? You want me to call up and complain about it?" she suggested.

Marlon stopped and thought about that. "If we need it, we need it. Somebody was following me around the last few weeks, right? So they probably know where we live already."

Judy spotted their sons headed back toward the kitchen and whispered, "Okay, that's enough. Have you both washed your hands?" she asked her two boys. Once they made a U-turn for the bathroom, she told Marlon, "We'll talk more about it later."

Devon and Toot arrived back at The Shot Bar that late Monday afternoon from their overnight stop in Cincinnati. They were caught off guard by the whirlwind of news the manager had to give them. He led them out back to tell them in private.

"Man, this shit is crazy," Toot said. "Alex got shot and killed last night as soon as they got back? That's why nobody been answering their damn phones today?"

"Well, Benny got arrested today too," the manager told them.

"*What?*" Toot overreacted. "Fuck out of here!"

"Yeah, they arrested him right at the bar today. He was in here waiting on Shawn to show up. That's why I was trying to warn y'all. They charged him with Alex's murder."

Toot looked at Devon, who had been listening to it all with no comment.

"You believe this shit, man?" Toot asked him.

"So, where's Shawn and Larry at?" Devon asked the manager.

"Like I said, Shawn was supposed to meet up with Benny over here, but he never came through. Then the cops popped up, so it was a good thing he *didn't* come. And Larry . . . *who knows* where he is?"

Devon said, "All right, Toot, we need to get rid of this loud-ass car and split up to cover more ground."

Toot winced and said, "Man, you know I can't drive nothing. If they pull me over, it's *curtains* for me."

"You need to call one of your lady friends or a cab or something then. I've been around you for too long the last few days already," Devon complained. "I need my space to think right now. We'll stay in touch over the phone."

"Aw, man, you ain't say you needed space last night when I hooked you up with that bad-ass girl in Cincy."

"Yeah, but this is serious shit now, Toot, and you too fuckin' irritating. So just tell me what girl you need me to drop you off with, and I'ma get the other car to find out what's going on."

"We supposed to stick together now, if anything, not separate. That's when everybody get killed in the horror movies," Toot cracked.

Devon looked at the bar manager for empathy. "You see what I put up with from him? Everything is a joke. I need to think seriously right now."

"Don't spend too much time around here doing it," the

manager advised them. "I don't know if they have a lookout or what, but it's not safe around here right now."

"Say no more," Devon told him. "Let's go, Toot. Start calling your girls up to get dropped off."

"Shit, you can drop me off at the crib then instead of all that."

"Not with that orange Lambo I'm not. I'm getting rid of this shit, *quick*. That's like driving around with an infrared beam on your forehead," Devon explained. "I'm ready to leave that car somewhere and take a taxi myself."

Toot frowned. "You're not serious, are you?"

"Hell yeah, I'm serious. In fact, you can do what you want to do with it."

Devon tossed him the keys as if the Lamborghini were a worthless get-around car.

"I just told you I can't drive in Atlanta, man."

"Well, catch a cab like I'm about to do."

Devon started jogging through the alleyway without even looking back.

"Where you going?" Toot asked him, confused.

"It may be cops out there now. I'm getting out of here."

Toot looked back at the manager. "It's serious, *like that*?"

The manager nodded. "They ran in here for Benny like the SWAT team today."

Toot nodded back and said, "Take these keys then and keep that ride safe." Then he ran off up the alleyway behind Devon.

Benny was arraigned from jail after four hours of waiting and thinking, and he walked out a man possessed and still focused. Zola had been let out two hours earlier with much less complications.

"There's a lot going on out here," Benny's well-dressed attorney advised him as they headed to an awaiting Lincoln Town Car. "You might want to hibernate like a bear for a few days, at least," the attorney advised. He looked like a Wall Street tycoon.

Benny didn't appear to be listening to him as he climbed into the back of the vehicle with a driver up front. He had a one-track mind. As he sat down, his attorney began to scribble down notes on a piece of notepad paper.

The FBI arrested Ganesh and his whole staff today.

Benny looked down to read the note and breathed deeply. He said, "We gotta make sure everybody gets their proper representation for that."

"We will," the attorney responded.

Then he wrote, *Judy Pierce is calling around seeking information.*

Benny nodded. "A lot of us need to learn our lessons in life, man. This has been a big lesson for me today."

"I hear you. I'm sorry I couldn't get you out earlier."

His attorney wrote another note. *No one's heard from Shawn. Police are staking him out.*

Benny said, "I can't believe they're trying to charge me with this. I got nothing but love for my Flint family. Shawn has brought all of us together, man. I love him like a little brother."

Larry relaxed in the living room of a fully furnished house in Union City, just south of Atlanta's international airport. There were four other guys from Flint, Michigan, there with him who had arrived earlier that day.

"Whenever the word comes, man, we just ready to go at it. It's whatever," one of the more talkative members of the group informed Larry as he rested on the cream-colored sofa.

"Yeah, just stay cool, man. That call will come soon. He still gotta get out and get situated first," he said, referring to Benny.

After a combination of taxi and train rides to make sure he

wasn't being followed, Devon arrived at a midnight-blue sedan that he had parked in a lot in Buckhead. It was fully prepared for emergencies. He found the key that he had placed conveniently under the windshield wiper and climbed inside the car, immediately pulling out a non-traceable phone from the glove compartment.

He powered up the phone and sent out a text message.

—I got the car. Tell me what you need me to do. It looks like it's on now. Sorry I got back so late. —

He started up the engine and drove out of the parking lot as he anxiously awaited a response. He was relieved when he finally got one.

—That's all good. I'll hit you back once they make a move. Delete every text after you get it.—

—Cool. Are you all right?— Devon texted back.

—Yeah, I'm good. Just stay ready for whatever.—

By nine o'clock that evening, everything remained calm and peaceful at the Pierce house. Judy put her sons to bed and checked her camera monitors to see if the security team was still watching over them. She was no longer bothered that they were.

When she returned to her bedroom to unwind for the evening, she felt an unexpected sense of tranquility from not having to prepare for work and deal with the thoughts and speculations of her coworkers for a few weeks. Marlon waited for her inside the room.

"So, what's going on now that you couldn't tell me earlier?" he asked.

Judy smiled and shrugged, feeling good. "Everything is pretty much over with. The police have all the information they need. My job knows what happened. No one got fired. And I'll get a little break now to clear my head and recharge my batteries while the process works itself out."

After dealing with all of their issues and pushing them into a locked suitcase in her mind, Judy began to strip down from her clothes for bed.

Now I'll need to figure out how long it'll take for me to feel intimate with you again after whatever happened or didn't happen with Alexandria, she thought of her husband.

"What if it doesn't all work out like you think?" Marlon questioned.

Judy thought about that herself, but she wanted to stay on the bright side. She said, "I wish all the people involved the best, but I just want to get back to my normal life now. I'm forcing myself to not even think about it. That's why I gave the police a truckload of information today, like Brenda told me to do. It's up to them to solve it now."

Marlon watched his wife climb into bed and felt more comfortable about things himself. *I'm really blessed to still have her,* he mused and grinned. *I love this woman! And I almost fucked it all up.*

He realized that it would take at least a few weeks before he could touch his wife again intimately. *But that's all right. I deserve it,* he thought.

As he stepped into the bathroom to brush his teeth, a call came in on Judy's cell phone. With no intentions of answering it, she looked to see who it was.

Alexandria? What the hell is she doing calling me?

"I hope this girl's not thinking we're gonna be friends again," she mumbled. "She must be out of her damn mind."

Alexandria hung up without leaving a message, then called right back. Irritated, Judy grumbled, "Shit. Let me see what this damn girl wants." She answered her phone with an attitude. "Hello." Alexandria was disturbing her peaceful night.

"Judy, I'm sorry to call you like this, but . . . I just can't do it anymore."

The broken speech and tears were all back again, but Judy cut her off this time. "You know what? I don't even want to hear it. Brenda told you to stick to your damn story, and that's what you need to do," she ranted, assuming the worst. "So, why are you even

337

calling me with this shit?"

"Because what I told you wasn't *truuue*," Alexandria wailed like a baby.

That was all that Judy needed to hear. She hung up the line and cursed, "Got *dammit!*" In a violent rage, she threw her cell phone across the room and hit the middle of the TV screen with it.

Marlon dashed out of the bathroom frantically. "What's going on?"

Judy jumped out of bed as if she were ready to pounce on him like a tiger. "You tell me what the fuck happened with her!" she shouted at him.

Before Marlon could defend himself, Judy started throwing closed-fist punches, striking her husband in the face, head, and shoulders with rapid fire before he finally ducked down and tackled her onto the bed.

"What are you talking about?" he pleaded. "What's going on?"

Judy yelled, "You know who the hell I'm talking about! Alexandria just called me!"

She continued trying to fight with him as Marlon struggled to pin her to the bed with his superior weight and strength.

"She called you about what?"

"To tell me what *really* fucking happened that night, Marlon! The little bitch is breaking down just like I *knew* she would—even when she had this cleared! All she had to do was keep her fucking mouth shut! Now tell me the got damn *truth!*"

Judy stopped fighting with him and killed him with her laser eyes and spiteful voice instead. Once he relaxed, she kicked him off of her, expecting to hear something that she would hate.

Marlon regained his balance in the room as his wife sat up in bed and awaited his confession. He took a few needed breaths from their fierce scuffle before he could even speak.

Just when I thought this shit was over, he thought. *Now what?*

Alexandria sat up and balled her eyes out in a straight-back wooden chair. Her legs and torso were duct-taped tightly to it.

Only her arms were left free, so she could dial Judy's number and speak on her cell phone.

"Call her again," a man's gruff voice demanded. He wore nondescriptive black clothes, from the black ski mask over his head down to the black boots on his feet. He sat five feet away in a chair in front of her, where a black pistol dangled from his black-leather-gloved hand.

Alexandria looked up and around the room at three other imposing men, who stood and flanked her with more guns out. They were all dressed in identical black clothes and ski masks inside of a dark and empty storefront space.

"Why are doing *thisss*?" Alexandria cried. Tears streamed down her face.

"Why are *we* doing this? Why did you fuck her husband?" the ringleader asked her from the chair. "That's what *we* all want to know."

"I told you, it was just in the moment. He needed it," she whined.

One of the men standing laughed. "Shit, we *all* need it. Especially from a bad-ass girl like you. I see why he fell for you. This is what he got in trouble for, right?"

The man ran his gloved hand through her long, wild hair as the others laughed.

"All right, leave her alone," the ringleader barked from his centered chair. "Now call her again and tell her everything you just told us," he insisted of Alexandria.

"She's not gonna answer *meee*," she wailed. "I called her three times already."

"Yo, give her some more tissues to wipe all that snot and shit off her face," the ringleader commented. "You're too damned pretty for all that. She reminds me of Ciara."

"She damn sure do," the others agreed as they handed her more tissues. Under the critical circumstances that she was in, they were all prepared for her to cry.

Alexandria wiped her face again.

"All right, now call her again," the man in the chair demanded. "We want to hear you tell her the details, like you told us. It made me hard in this chair just listening to you," the ringleader cracked for another laugh.

Alexandria stared at him defiantly as fresh tears ran down her face. She wiped them away with her bare hand as if determined to stand her ground with new courage.

"You're not gonna call her?" the man asked her casually.

Instead of answering him, Alexandria allowed her right arm to dangle limply with her cell phone in hand before she dropped it to the floor.

Unfazed by her rebellion, the ringleader shrugged it off. "All right, fuck it then. Let's just kill her and get this over with."

A cold, hard pistol was quickly placed to her right temple as Alexandria leaned forward and went into hysteria. *"O-KAAAYEEE!* I'LL CALL HER! I'LL CALL *HERRR!"*

Her arms shook violently at her sides as she realized her disobedience could end her life. These men were serious.

"Give her the fucking phone back," the man barked to his guys. "We're not playing with you. If you need to call her back *twenty times*, you do that shit until she answers . . . then you tell her everything that happened. And don't spare her none of the details either."

Judy got dressed at home as fast as a tornado and picked up her phone from the floor in front the television. It remained usable, having protective casing and shatterproof glass. The television was fine as well, with a minor scratch in the middle of the flat screen. However, Judy's tranquility that night had been eviscerated.

"Where are you going?" Marlon asked her, concerned. After telling her more about his mysterious night out with Alexandria, he felt hopeless all over again.

"Did you tell me where you were going when you ran the hell out on me?" Judy barked. "Well, don't ask me shit about where I'm going."

She packed an overnight bag.

"This is not the way to handle this," Marlon pleaded.

She ignored him and opened up the bedroom door to walk out. "You take the kids to school tomorrow like you always do," she said. "These security guys outside the house will probably follow me around all night anyway. I just need to get away from your lying ass so I can think straight."

"That's unfair," Marlon whined, sounding unmanly.

Judy stopped out in the hallway and repeated, *"Unfair?* What's unfair about it, Marlon? You *lied* about shit. I didn't. I *knew* that you were lying too."

"It only happened—"

Marlon spotted his oldest son, Junior, peeking out of his door and into the hallway, so he stopped himself from saying more.

"Where are you going, Mom?" Junior asked his mother.

She looked at her son, then back at her husband. "You ask your father," she answered as she headed for the front door.

Enraged, Judy stormed out of the house with her bag and never looked back. She didn't care if the security guys followed her.

"They can wait outside and protect me at my damn hotel room," she grumbled. But when she drove her car out of the gate, she didn't see them parked there anymore.

I guess they went back home until the morning, she assumed. *Either that or they're hiding somewhere else.*

She looked in her rearview mirror as she drove out to see if their unmarked car would pop out and trail her to the freeway. It never happened. In the meantime, Alexandria continued to call her cell phone nine straight times.

Judy looked down at her phone as she drove and snapped, "What the hell is wrong with you? I do *not* want to hear your damn *confessions*! Just leave me the hell *alone!*" She couldn't understand what had gotten into Alexandria. "This girl is turning into my *worst* fucking nightmare!"

When Alexandria called her for the tenth straight time, Judy answered the phone just to curse her out.

"What the hell is *wrong* with you, Alexandria?" she yelled. "We are *not* friends, and I do *not* want to talk to you right now. So just go the hell away and stop calling me!"

"I didn't want to do this either," Alexandria whined. "But I *have* to. I have to tell you what really happened."

"No, you do *not*! Marlon already *told me*, so I don't need to hear shit else from you! Okay? So good fucking *night*!" she fumed. Her veins were bulging out of her neck and forehead as she swerved at the wheel.

"Nooo, waaaittt!" Alexandria wailed.

Judy hung up on her and was confused as ever. The girl seemed to have lost her damn mind. Judy shook her head. "What in the fucking world is wrong with her?!"

The thought suddenly hit her as she drove south on Highway 19, back toward Atlanta. *I didn't want to do this either, but I have to.* Judy reflected on her words. *Did somebody force her to—*

"Oh, SHIT!" Judy cursed. *What if somebody . . .*

She became so alarmed by her radical thoughts that she pulled over on the shoulder of the road to consider them. "Did somebody *make her* do this?" she asked herself over the steering wheel. She smashed her hands into her face, filled with grief.

"Oh my *God*! What if somebody really . . ."

She didn't even want to say it. Instead, she decided to call Alexandria back.

"Hel-lo," Alexandria answered in her pitiful whine.

Judy asked her calmly, "Are you okay? Is everything all right with you tonight?" She may have sounded calm, but while she imagined a scene of insanity, Judy's heart was racing as loud and strong as thunder.

"No, I just feel terrible about what I did to you *guyyys*," Alexandria broke down and cried again.

Judy held her cell phone tightly as she experienced a rush of anxiety. She needed more information to validate her thoughts. "Okay, but where are you? Are you at home?"

"Ahhh . . . I don't know. Umm, *nooo*, I'm not at *hoooome*."

Judy closed her eyes, forcing herself to keep her composure. "You don't know where you are?" she asked her, on the edge of panic. Before she could get another word out of her, Alexandria clicked off the line.

"Hello?" Judy responded. "Hello? Shit!"

She called Alexandria's phone right back and got no answer. She called again. Her anxiety and heart rate continued to rise after the third time with no answer. She imagined all of the atrocities that could happen to a young, pretty woman in the hands of ruthless people.

Alexandria's final words were all the confirmation Judy needed. She began to shed desperate tears of her own. As her feelings of hopelessness and sympathy converted into more frustration and anger, she began to scream and beat on her steering wheel.

"These mother-*FUCKERRRS*! *GODDD*! I can't *BELIEVE THISSS*!" she yelled, gritting her teeth and wiping her eyes. With no time to waste to save Alexandria's life, she immediately thought of calling Shawn. He had essentially admitted that his friend Benny was behind it all. What was he waiting for? He needed to stop his friend from this madness. Immediately!

When she got nothing but his voicemail, Judy decided to let Shawn have it. "You fucking *coward*! Your friend is fucking with people's lives, and you think it's all a got damn *game*! People are dying out here, and now they have Alexandria, you *asshole*! I don't give a fuck about your *street loyalty*; you better turn his ass in *right now*! Or I'm telling the police everything about *all* of you!"

Judy began to search her purse for the phone numbers of the two Atlanta detectives before remembering that she had placed them in her nightstand drawer at home. She thought of calling her husband and telling him to find the numbers and read them off. As soon as she started to call home, Shawn Blake called her back.

"Hey, are sure you know what you're talking about?" he asked her calmly.

343

"Yes, I'm fucking sure!" Judy blasted him. "I just talked to her, and she's crazy out of her mind right now."

"Well, if somebody has her, why would they let her talk to you?"

"They wanted her to confess what she did with my husband to get back at me. They probably knew that the police had security at my house, so they went after Alexandria instead. Now where are you? I need you to call your friend *right now* and put a stop to all this *shit*! RIGHT NOW!"

"Calm down, man, we can't talk about this over the phone. I'll text you where to meet me. They're after me too now. Are the police around you?"

"No, they're coming back tomorrow. I'm sitting on the shoulder of the road now on Highway 19."

"All right, I'll text you where to meet me."

"Just do it then," she barked. Judy hung up the phone and awaited Shawn's text. "We're getting to the bottom of this shit *tonight*, or somebody's gonna have to kill me too," she insisted to herself, wiping tears.

When the text came with his location from a foreign phone number, Judy read it and grumbled, "Good. That's only ten, fifteen minutes away." She pulled back onto the highway and took off for his destination in haste.

25... COUNTER MOVES

Shawn Blake sat up in a reclining office chair in a small room at a nearby hotel off the 285 West Beltway with three cell phones in front of him on the desk. After texting Judy on one of them, he called Devon on another.

"Hey, man, make a call to Benny and Larry and ask them about a kidnapping and hostage situation at that southeast Atlanta property he bought recently."

"What? A kidnapping and hostage situation?" Devon asked, surprised. "Is that what they're up to now?"

"I don't really know, man, but I just got a crazy call from Judy Pierce about that girl Alexandria."

"The one they caught with her husband?"

"Yeah, Judy thinks somebody's forcing her to confess some shit over the phone to get back at her. It sounds crazy to me, man, but call them and check it out. Don't go over there or anywhere *near* them until you talk to me first. All right?"

"All right, I got it."

"And don't tell them I told you this either. Say you got it from a source off the streets."

"All right, I'll make them calls right now."

"When you say it, man, you gotta make it sound like you

already know what they're up to, because if you don't, they'll blow you off. You know how they play that game."

"Yeah, you right. They'll try that *know-nothing* shit on us."

"Exactly.

"So make sure you call Benny about it first. If I'm guessing right, Larry won't give you the right information unless Benny tells him to. Benny may even tell him to lie to you, like nothing's really going on. So call Benny first and leave him a message if he don't answer. Then you wait like ten, fifteen minutes before you call Larry."

"But won't Benny be pissed off if I leave him a message on his cell phone like that?"

Shawn grimaced and barked, "Do you really think that shit matters at this point, man? Who the fuck cares what he's pissed about. He's knocking us off one by one right now. You don't see that shit?"

"I mean, I got you but . . . he would never knock *you* off," Devon reasoned.

Shawn contemplated that for a moment. "What if he thought I went to the cops to dime him out? Would he kill me then?"

"But you would never do that, would you?"

There was confliction in Devon's voice that Shawn needed to snuff out. "Come on, man. Fuck no! Of course not," he answered strongly. "But it doesn't really matter what I would do. It only matters what he *thinks* I would do. Would Benny go back to jail out of love for *me*, or would he kill me to look out for himself? I've been asking myself that question ever since I woke up and heard the news about Alex this morning. So if push comes to shove, and it's his gun against your gun . . . what are you gonna do?"

After a beat, Devon said, "Yeah, you right. I don't trust him now either . . . ever since that shit went down with J."

"Well, go ahead and call him, man. Since he hasn't heard anything back from me, he'll definitely wanna talk to you now. You won't even have to leave him a message. Watch. He'll answer your call. Then he'll ask if you've heard anything from me. And you haven't. All right?"

"All right."

"And remember, don't make any other moves until after I call you later."

Benny sat in deep thought on a comfortable lounge chair at his luxurious downtown condo. His lovely friend Sekoya brought him a drink while wearing a curve-hugging dress that accentuated her body like a light-brown chocolate Easter bunny in tall heels.

With her legs crossed on an adjacent sofa, Zola watched Sekoya's every move. She was obviously attracted to the young woman.

"Do I get one of those too?" Zola asked.

Sekoya turned to her and smiled, innocently. "Oh, of course. No problem."

Benny caught onto the magnetism in the room and grinned in silence. *I should let them get it on right in front of me, just to have something to do while I think all this shit out,* he mused. *I know Sekoya wouldn't mind. She'll do anything for me.*

Zola returned to the business at hand. "That arrest tossed me right in the middle of the fire today," she commented, snapping Benny out of his daze. "I deserve a good drink."

He nodded to her, calmly. "Trust me, I wasn't expecting that today either. But I did want you to be a part of the craziness instead of just talking about it. A lot of people don't understand the difficulties of trying to turn your life around while surrounded by a circle of enemies who want you to fail. Now you know how that feels."

"I sure do," Zola said as Sekoya mixed her a drink at the minibar near the kitchen.

"I expected us to have a candid conversation with Shawn today. That way you could hear some of the things that he goes through on a regular basis and give him some suggestions. I like the way you talk about handling things. But now this Alex murder . . ." He stopped and shook his head, then said, "It's always something, man. That's why staying *focused* is a key word for us. "

"I'm sorry about losing my poise out there, but that just came out of nowhere for me," Zola said, sounding embarrassed.

Benny chuckled. "That's the way it always is for us, especially for Shawn. Some new shit fucks with him every day."

When Sekoya returned from the minibar with another short glass of liquor and cranberry juice, Zola made sure to caress the young woman's hands with hers on the pass-off. "Thank you very much," she gushed.

"You're welcome."

Benny smiled again, distracted by Sekoya's curves himself. "I think you may see something you like in here," he hinted back at Zola.

She smiled and admitted he was right. "Oh, definitely. You have very good taste in women. You're not offended by my interest, are you?" she asked with a sip of her drink. "Forgive me for being a little stressed right now and acting out."

"We're all stressed right now," Benny countered. "That's why I decided to just chill tonight. I know they're trying hard to get a rise out of me. But I'm too experienced for that at this point. That's what our enemies are not understanding."

He looked over again at Sekoya, who posed sexily near the bar with nothing under her dress but smooth skin and exotic scents. That was just the way he liked her.

"And I'm not offended by what you're attracted to at all. Sekoya is very ah . . . tasteful," he emphasized to Zola.

Zola raised her brow, intrigued. "Oh, is she?"

"Yes, she is," Benny teased with another sip of his drink.

Sekoya looked back at both of them curiously from the bar. *Is something kinky about to go on in here?* she asked herself. She already realized that Zola was eying her there in the room. Although she had never been with a woman before, she was attracted to Zola as well. *She definitely raises my temperature,* she admitted.

Benny nodded and said, "Sekoya . . . go sit on Zola's lap while we talk. And don't be shy with her."

Sekoya looked hesitant for a second, but only for a second.

"Okay," she told him submissively. *Anything you want,* she thought. She walked back across the room to sit on Zola's left thigh and adjusted her loose dark hair out of the way. Zola wrapped her left arm around her to hold her steady.

"Now, where were we?" Benny asked Zola.

"You were talking about how hard it is to rebuild yourselves as legitimate businessmen while surrounded by enemies who always assume that you're involved in something else."

Benny grinned. "That's a great way to put it. That's exactly what I mean."

Zola smiled back and bragged, "That's what I do. I make things easily understood."

As Benny watched them both on the sofa, Sekoya began to run her index finger through the outline of Zola's hair and around to her left ear. Zola responded by caressing Sekoya's pert breasts.

"These are just *perfect,*" she commented. She couldn't help herself.

"You wanna taste them?" Sekoya asked, pulling her perky, light-brown breasts from the cleavage split in her dress. She dipped her index finger into Zola's drink and rubbed it around her nipples.

"Oh, my," Zola responded, leaning in softly with her tongue.

Benny relaxed comfortably and said nothing. Their business conversation was officially over as far as he was concerned. He was already wondering how he could join in with them on the sofa. He even ignored the incoming call on his cell phone.

Fuck all that gangsta shit tonight. I'm getting laid up in here, he told himself. But he at least wanted to see who it was. He looked down at his phone—Devon. That made him take notice. Devon rarely ever called.

Does he have something important to tell me, or is it just about Alex or that damn car? he wondered. *I should have gotten rid of that Lamborghini a long time ago.* Nevertheless, he understood how important image was for rappers like Toot and the music industry in Atlanta. *Then again . . . I wonder if he's talked to Shawn.* He decided to answer the call anyway.

"Just keep doing what you're doing, ladies. I'm not even here .

349

. . until I want to be," he teased. Sekoya and Zola paid him no mind, too immersed in their curious seductions.

Damn! Benny thought as he watched them. *Let me get this call out the way.*

He jumped on the line and said, "Hey, D., y'all got back safely with that car, right? I was out of commission for a minute, if you couldn't reach me earlier. It's been a lot going on out here, man. I guess you heard by now about Alex."

"Yeah, I heard about it. I also heard that they arrested you today. That's why I left the car parked outside at The Shot Bar," Devon said. "I didn't know if the police were after all of us now or not. But I know I'm not riding around in that car if they are. Did anybody go down and identify Alex's body?"

Obviously distracted by what was going on in front of him, Benny responded, "Naw, the police got us all scrambling right now, man. They're trying to pin that shit on me. And I don't know where Shawn is right now. You talked to him? Where's Toot?"

Benny was all over the place, but was not inclined to rush anything. He wanted to let it all play out. He didn't plan to stay on the phone long with Devon either. He was only touching base with him.

Devon told him, "I haven't talked to anybody but the bar. But yo, get this—I heard on the streets a few minutes ago that we supposedly snatched up that girl Alexandria to get back at Judy Pierce, and took her over to that new storefront you got on the southeast. Is that true? The streets are talking, man."

Benny frowned, disturbed by the information. "What? Where you get that crazy shit from?"

"Man, I don't even know these people, they just know me. After that shit happened last night with Alex, the streets are talking like crazy now. I'm just getting back, so I don't know what the hell is going on. That's why I'm asking you. I ain't heard nothing back from Shawn yet either."

Benny barked, "Well, the streets need to shut the fuck up and keep our names out of shit, because I don't know what the fuck they're talking about. I'm relaxing up in my spot tonight after just getting out of jail. Like I told you, they're trying to get us all scrambling out here, so you gotta stay focused and ignore all that shit."

"All right, you sure? So, Larry don't know nothing about it either?" Devon pressed him.

Benny thought about that. *Why is this motherfucker talking all this shit over my regular phone like this? Is he crazy? Or is he working with the cops now?*

Suddenly, Benny clammed up and said, "Yo, enjoy your night, fam'. I don't know nothing about that shit. I'm about to get into something."

By that time, Sekoya had taken half of her dress down while still sitting on Zola's lap. The dress hung down around her waist, with her nipples, shoulders, and flat stomach all free to enjoy. Zola worked her like a patient masseuse.

Shit, I'm definitely getting in on some of this, Benny plotted. *Let me call Larry about this shit first.*

He used a second non-traceable phone to call Larry and walked toward the kitchen for more privacy.

"Yo, what's good?" Larry answered, anticipating his call.

Benny told him, "I've been busy pressing the chill button tonight, fam', after getting out of jail on that Alex shit. But it's all good. They got nothing on it."

"That's good to hear. So, what's the next move, man, just chillin'?"

"You already know it," Benny confirmed. "They just waiting for us to do something stupid now, and it's not gon' happen. But check this out. I think Devon just turned Benedict Arnold on us, fam'. He just called me up talking some shit about the streets telling him that we snatched up that girl Alexandria to get back at Judy Pierce, and that we was holding her at that new property on the southeast. I don't know what the fuck he talking about. Then he tried to put your name in it. I know *I* didn't tell you to do no shit like that. I love women too much to kidnap them . . . unless I'm planning on making them my personal sex slaves or something," he cracked while still watching the seduction take place in front of him across the room.

Sekoya stood up from Zola's lap and dropped her dress to the floor, standing butt naked in heels. Zola spun her around and slowly began to kiss down her naked back and lick around her curvaceous ass and hips.

Oh, shit! Benny thought excitedly. As he watched, his pants began to tighten and moisten. *Let me get the fuck off this phone!*

He said, "Yeah, so um . . . have them boys check that out at the southeast spot and see what happens. Don't go over there with him, just in case it's a setup. And if Devon calls you up on this shit, act like you going to check it out with them. In fact, tell him we *both* showing up just to see how excited he gets. We'll see what happens in a minute."

"All right, that's what's up. I'll handle that right now."

Benny couldn't wait to hang that phone up. He continued to watch the two beautiful women make out as Sekoya turned back around to face Zola and kiss her on the lips while starting to undo her clothes.

All right, I'm gon' wait until they're both butt naked and licking each other out before I jump up in this shit with my dick, he told himself with discipline. *Damn, this shit is hot!*

"All right, we finally got something for y'all to do," Larry told the eager Flint Factory crew at the hideaway house in Union City.

"Just say the word, man. What is it?" the young ringleader stood to his feet next to Larry and said.

"All right, I'ma text y'all the address to find on your GPS. It sounds like somebody kidnapped some girl, and they're trying to frame us like we did it. I don't know if that shit is true or not, but y'all need to check it out."

Two of the four Factory members looked at each other and frowned at the idea.

"Why would somebody do that?"

Larry shrugged. "That's what I'm saying. I don't even know if it's true. So ya'll go over there and find out."

"You not going with us?" one of them asked him.

Larry shook it off, casually. "The cops know my face out there already, so I gotta lay low for a minute. They don't know y'all yet. Take that car out back with the Georgia plates on it. Don't go out there in that Michigan shit. The keys are right there on the kitchen counter."

As soon as his guys left to investigate the scene in Atlanta, Devon called Larry right on cue from another non-traceable phone. Instead of waiting for his friend's outlandish pitch, Larry went straight for the jugular.

"Yeah, man, I heard about this bullshit-ass kidnapping. So, I'm about to leave out and meet up with Benny over there at the new property to see what the fuck is going on."

"Benny's going over there with you?" Devon asked him. He sounded surprised.

"Yeah, dog, he's tired of people putting our name in shit around Atlanta, especially now. So he wanna see who it is, up close and personal. And he want me with him. You trying to meet us out there too?" Larry suggested.

"Yeah, let me think about that," Devon responded. "I was about to unwind and smoke something for a minute. All this crazy shit that's been going on can make your head hurt."

"Well, Toot ain't call us up about no shit like that," Larry said. "Where is he at right now? And what people were you hearing this from?"

"I mean, Toot came back and probably hooked up with them girls, man, you know how he is," said Devon. "And I know different people than he does."

"All right, well, I'm leaving out now, so me and Benny'll call you back later on, once we find out what's what."

"Ya'll do that. I just wanted to let y'all know what people were saying," Devon replied.

Larry hung up and mumbled, "Yeah, his ass is lying. But we'll find out what's up in a minute."

With Judy on the way to meet him at his low-budget hotel off of 285 West, Shawn snuck out the side exit of the building and into his silver Camaro. He wanted to see if anyone was following her when she arrived. As soon as he got comfortable in the driver's seat, Devon called him back.

"I just did it, man, and told them what you told me. But get this: Larry just said that he *and* Benny are going over there *together*. I wasn't expecting all that. Were you?"

Shawn thought about that for a moment. *He's onto it,* he assumed. *Benny ain't showing up for no shit like that. That's like the king making queen moves. If you play chess, you know the king can only jump two spaces at a time.*

He didn't want to explain it all. Devon wasn't a king *or* a queen, but he was more than a pawn. He was like a knight on a horse, moving forward and sideways in small open spaces. If used correctly, he could be a wicked surprise.

"All right, well, like I said, stay away from them until I tell you the next move," Shawn advised him. "I just called some other lookouts I know in that area to see if anything is going on. As far as we know, Larry could be there right now. Did everything sound quiet when he talked to you?"

"As quiet as a mouse," Devon joked. "I didn't hear nothing in the background."

"So he's probably already there. I bet he ain't tell you where he was, did he?"

"Naw, but he said he'd talked to Benny as soon as I got on the phone with him."

"Yeah, I told you that. Benny and Larry always have their stories together, but they don't tell the rest of us *shit*. Don't even worry about what they're saying. Just wait on me."

"All right, that's what's up."

Shawn hung up and continued to look out for Judy—the real queen piece. She had the courage, intellect, and moxie to move everywhere. He remained impressed by her.

Judy pulled into the parking lot of the hotel to meet up with Shawn right as her husband called her. "Should I answer this?" she grumbled. She parked and sat for a minute to debate the question. With so much going on, she decided not to answer. "Let me see if he leaves a message." She wondered if Alexandria had been forced to call Marlon that night as well.

After waiting a moment longer, she listened to her husband's message.

"Judy, when you left here tonight, you somehow got past the security guys while they made a run to the gas station. They're asking me where you are to catch up to you. It's their job.

"So, call me back when you get a chance. I need to know what you want me to tell these guys."

Judy shook her head and said, "Well, that's their damn problem. I'll call back once I know what's going on with Alexandria."

She called Shawn back while rushing out of her car toward the hotel entrance, only for him to text her back from the foreign number again.

—*Walk back outside. I'm right behind you.*—

Judy did an about-face and walked out of the hotel to find Shawn waiting for her at the curb behind the wheel of the silver Camaro. "Get in," he told her as he leaned toward the passenger-side window.

She jumped into the passenger seat and shut the door. She buckled her seatbelt and asked him, "So, what did you find out about Alexandria? Where do we need to go and who do we need to talk to? Let's go to Benny right now."

Shawn looked into her eyes to see if she was serious. She was.

He said, "I'm not even trying to see Benny like that. You just want me to drive right to him because of Alexandria?" He pulled away from the hotel entrance as he asked her.

Judy barked, "Your ass needs to stand up to him, Shawn. What he's doing is *wrong*, no matter how much *loyalty* you have. Don't you understand that? You're not some damn *child*. You're a

355

grown-ass *man*! So call him up and ask him about Alexandria, *right now*. I am dead fucking *serious*!"

She was highly frustrated. Shawn could read it through her reckless body energy. She was a human volcano ready to erupt.

As they pulled out into the street toward the beltway, he asked her, "You think you could pull the trigger and kill him if you needed to?"

Judy paused to consider what he was asking her. She said, "If it's between him or somebody I love . . . then what *choice* do I have? What choice do *you* have? Are you willing to die for his loyalty? Would he die for *you*? I seriously doubt it.

"He's just *using* you, Shawn," she snapped. "You're like the new fucking street drug, and you don't even get it. So where are we going? Do you know where they're holding Alexandria or what?"

Shawn breathed deeply as they jumped on 285 and headed east. He made another non-traceable call and put it on speaker inside the cup holder.

"Who are you calling?" Judy asked.

Shawn held up his right hand and said, "Just listen . . . and keep your mouth shut."

"Hello," a man answered after a couple of rings.

"Do we have a deal?" Shawn asked.

There was a pregnant pause over the phone. "I'm only doing this 'cause I got love for you, man. But you gon' have to deal with Benny if we walk away, you know that right?"

Shawn exhaled as he watched the traffic out on the beltway. "Yeah, I know. It's just no way around it now."

"Nope. He gon' keep doing what he wanna do until you deal with him. Now you gon' put us in the middle of the heat. So you gotta end this shit the hard way and make it look like self-defense somehow."

Judy looked at Shawn and understood for the first time how serious the situation really was for him. *Oh, shit!* she thought. *This is really happening!*

Shawn said, "All right, just um . . . leave the girl there for me

356

to get her, and I'll deal with Benny later."

"You gon' have to do that then, man. You know you the only one who can get that close to him. If I have to do it, it'll be an all-out war that I'm not trying to be in. But if *you* do it, The Factory will understand that shit better, fam'. That's all one hundred. Just explain it to them. At the end of the day, nobody from our 'hood wanna hold back your success. We all wanna see you shine and do bigger and better things. But Benny, he gon' keep poisoning your fucking soup until you die, man. So it's best to kill him now, while you still young and healthy, player. For real."

"All right, I got all that, man. Just um . . . leave the girl there," Shawn said.

"Yeah, she safe and sound. Her face all messed up with tears and snot and shit all over it, and she pissed and shit on herself in the chair, but she'll be all right. We ain't do nothing to her. Her nerves may be shot for a couple of weeks, but she'll live through it. So go on and get her. We outta here."

Judy heard that and sighed in relief.

"That's all love, man. Thanks," Shawn concluded.

"Yeah, you got it. Just handle that other business."

When Shawn hung up, Judy was speechless. What else could she say? She was only happy that Alexandria would live through it. As for Shawn, he had some serious sticky shit on his hands to wash off. It wasn't going to be easy. So he concentrated at the wheel in silence as they hit 85 South toward downtown Atlanta.

He looked over at Judy and said, "You see what my life is really like now? This ain't a movie, television show, social media, or all these corny-ass blogs creating a bunch of bullshit to sell to people like Benny does either. This is my real fucking *life* right here, Judy. You got all access for real now. You wanna put this on *camera*? On *tape*? You wanna package this shit with commercials and all that?

"I gotta kill a man who I grew up with and who looked out for me for *years*," Shawn confessed to her. "He *know* I don't wanna do it too. So he been keeping his hooks in me *deep*, that 'hood *poison* that my man just talked about. We all in this together, fam'. It's us against the world. We all we got.' And all that bullshit.

"But I can't go to the cops and tell *them* that shit," he continued.

"What, I'm supposed to be in protective custody for the rest of my fucking life? They don't have a budget for that. So you wanna ask me all these personal questions and then say, 'Oh, Shawn isn't telling me enough. He's so mysterious.' I always hear that shit from reporters. Well, how *real* do you wanna get? You really want *this*? This shit right *here*? Well, now you gon' get it."

Shawn returned to concentrating at the wheel of the car as they quickly neared downtown Atlanta and the southeast. He said, "Now you gon' wish you could go back to them fairytales."

Judy took a deep breath and exhaled. *I'm already wishing that,* she admitted to herself. *This is absolutely crazy! All of it! I will never get myself involved in any shit like this again. But for right now, I just wanna see Alexandria safe. Then Shawn can handle all of that 'hood shit with Benny on his own. I have nothing to do with all that.*

26... CHECKMATE

Shawn received a text on his non-traceable phone right as they reached their exit to the southeast.

—*They just pulled up. Be careful out there. Go hard!*—

It was perfectly timed information. Shawn pulled off the exit and texted his response.

—*Good. I'm here now too. Thanks.*—

Shawn rounded a few corners toward their destination as Judy became extra anxious and nervous.

"You all right?" he asked, taking in her prolonged silence.

She forced herself to nod. "I'm as all right as I can be in this situation," she answered honestly. "Are you sure this is safe?"

Shawn pulled into a parking spot near a seedy area of new business developments and storefronts that remained incomplete.

"Naw, it's not safe. That's why I brought this with me." He pulled out his shiny silver and black Glock from beside his seat.

Judy saw the gun and panicked. "What do you need that for? I thought he said they were leaving and it was all good to go in and get her."

Shawn gave her a look of serious intent as he opened the door to climb out. "There's always surprises when you're dealing with Benny," he said. "I gotta be prepared for anything."

Judy was immediately conflicted. She wanted Alexandria saved, but not by shooting people. "Can't you just go in there and talk it out with them? Benny has the ultimate love for you, right?" she asked him frantically. Shawn grinned and said, "We'll see." He shut the car door and started walking with the gun concealed in his jacket.

"Oh my *God!*" Judy panicked again inside the car as she watched. She tossed her hands to her face and blurted, "What in the hell have I gotten myself into?"

Shawn quickly rounded the corner of the developing storefronts. He headed toward the back alleyway to get inside of Benny's new building at the corner of the block. As soon as he hit the alley, he spotted one of Larry's new guys from home, who was apparently guarding the door. Not recognizing who Shawn was, he aimed his gun at him.

"Yo, fam', it's Shawn Blake," the hometown actor announced.

"Oh, shit! What you doing out here?"

"I heard about this shit too, and I wanted to get this girl out," Shawn explained to him.

"Oh, all right, cool. They're in there trying to cut her free now."

Shawn walked past him and headed inside, where three more of Larry's guys were trying to cut Alexandria free. She panicked, as if they were there to finish off the job with more torture. She didn't believe anything they had to say.

"Oh, my *GOD!* Please don't kill *MEEE!*" she wailed.

One of the guys grabbed her mouth to stop her loud crying. "Shut the fuck up, girl! Nobody here to kill you. We trying to *free* your pretty ass. Who did this to you?"

Shawn walked in behind them, taking them all by surprise.

"What the fuck are y'all doing in here?" he yelled in their direction.

Instinctively, the young men turned and pulled their guns on him, but Shawn already had his out, aimed and ready to open fire.

BOP! BOP! BOP! BOP! BOP! BOP!! . . .

There's no way around this, Shawn told himself as he gunned all three of the young men down with superior aim and the advantage of surprise. *I gotta do what I gotta do.*

He then turned to deal with their lookout man at the back door. As expected, the young man heard the gunfire and ran back into the room, confused, with his gun aimed.

"What the fuck?" he shouted.

Shawn kneeled on one knee and waited for him. The man rushed into the room, standing tall. He never had a chance.

BOP! BOP! BOP!

Shawn put his gun on safety and slid it into his jacket pocket. Then he finished cutting Alexandria free from the chair. She recognized him immediately and began to cry her eyes out all over again.

"Thank you, thank you, thank *youuu!* Oh *Godddd!*"

"All right, now be quiet. I still have to get you out of here," he told her as he picked her up to carry her out. He also grabbed a cell phone from one of Larry's guys.

By the time he reached the back door with Alexandria in his arms, Judy had rushed into the building from the alleyway and startled him.

"Shit! How come you didn't stay in the car?" he barked at her.

"I fucking *couldn't!* I couldn't concentrate," she yelled back at him.

She spotted the lookout man, who had been shot and killed near the back door, and she could only imagine what happened to the rest.

"How many guys was it?"

"Don't worry about that. Let's just get her out of here. I'll drop y'all both off at the hospital."

They rushed Alexandria through the alleyway toward the car, passing a few onlookers who wondered what had gone on.

"Is she all right? Was there a shootout back in there or something?" an old homeless woman asked them.

"Yeah, tell the cops once we get her out of here," Shawn answered. "We don't want them slowing us down with a bunch of questions. She needs to get to the hospital, right now. Somebody kidnapped her."

"Well, you hurry up and get her to Grady Memorial then. I'll get the police," the woman responded, running clumsily in the opposite direction.

Shawn and Judy stretched Alexandria out in the backseat of the Camaro and made a U-turn, taking off for the hospital. Alexandria had lost circulation in her limbs. She was still numb and shaking in her state of delirium.

Judy leaned her seat back and turned around in her chair to reach into the back and rub Alexandria with her left hand. "Don't worry, girl, we'll get you to the hospital, and I'm gonna stay there with you all night. Okay?"

Alexandria moaned and mumbled something incoherent while Shawn rolled the windows down. The stench of Alexandria's fear was smelling up the car.

Judy sighed and shook her head, feeling terrible. She touched Shawn's right arm as he drove and told him, "I really appreciate this, Shawn. You have *no i-dea*. You finally stood up for what you needed to do."

Shawn didn't respond, at least not immediately. He paid strict attention to the road again. Then he grumbled, "It's not over with yet."

Judy didn't want to say too much more with Alexandria still in the back of the car. However, she had to. "You're not really gonna do that, are you?" she asked Shawn in code.

Again, he ignored her. Once they neared the hospital, with the emergency sign lights up ahead of them, he said, "You got my back on this in court, right? I'm gonna need you for this. I'm not even supposed to have a gun anymore; but if I didn't have one for this, she'd be dead right now. They weren't trying to hear no negotiations in there. They had strict orders."

Judy had no choice. She nodded and agreed to his request. "Of course I will. I totally understand now. So yeah, I got your back."

When they pulled up into the emergency entrance, Judy got a paramedic to run out with a wheelchair for Alexandria. Then she grabbed Shawn by his left arm through the opened driver side window before he could drive off.

She looked into his determined eyes and pleaded, "Shawn, is there any other way?"

Once again, he looked away from her. "You already heard what time it is in the car earlier," he responded, staring straight ahead through the windshield. "There ain't no other way." He looked back into her eyes and said, "The fairytales are over. This is the real shit right here. This is my real life."

Judy nodded and squeezed his arm, filled with grief. "Be careful then," she said. "You have two kids who love you. You have to make it back home for them."

"Roger that," he cracked and grinned.

As he drove off into the night to handle his unfinished business, Judy thought again about her own two kids at home . . . and her husband.

"Thank *God* I have them."

Shawn made it back to the highway on 85 North and headed toward home in the northeast before calling the last number on the cell phone that he had confiscated. He figured that either Benny or Larry would answer.

"Hello," Benny's right-hand man spoke up.

Shawn recognized Larry's voice and smiled. "Were you expecting to hear somebody else?"

Larry hesitated before saying, "I damn sure was. What you doing with it?"

"I'll tell you what—don't answer the rest of those phones when the cops find the other three," Shawn hinted.

Larry hesitated again. "So you killed all four of them?"

"Did you kill five last night, including my man Alex?" Shawn asked him back. "Why hasn't anyone seen you today?"

"I heard nobody seen you *either*."

Shawn cut to the chase and said, "All right, man, here's the deal . . . if I turn up dead, you'll still be serving a fake king whose got nowhere to go but down without *me*. But if you back off, I'm gon' keep rising with the dead weight finally off my ankles. You feel me?

"Now you can act like you don't know what time it is if you want, but this whole game of eating off my back is *over*. I'm ending that shit *tonight*," Shawn promised. "The Factory already chose my side. They all know what's going on back in the 8-1-0. So if you fuck around and make the wrong decision, you can forget about *ever* going back home again. Somebody'll find you. But if that's how you want to live, then make your move. 'Cause I'm gon' make mine. You feel me?

"Your fake king taught me that," Shawn instigated. "You want the people to *feel you* more than just *hear you*. I'm learning that now myself. In fact, I learned a lot of good things from him. But we can't go down this ugly road no more, man. I'm not gonna allow it. So what are you gonna do?"

Larry thought about Shawn's words for what seemed like an eternity. Then he said, "You really think you gon' get away with this?"

"I'm already set up to get away with it," Shawn answered boldly. "Every finger in the room is pointed at your man now; and a dead man can't argue. But let's say you take me out instead. He gon' have even *more* fingers pointed at him. On top of that, he'll have to find a new meal ticket to eat off, or go straight back to the street game. He'll tell you himself that the street shit don't work like it used to.

"You gotta upgrade your game now, fam'," Shawn concluded. "I know how it all works now. My vision is clear as crystal."

"All right, so . . . what are you trying to get me to do, man?" Larry asked. "'Cause all of this fucking talking in circles is giving me a headache right now."

Close to midnight, Benny, Sekoya, and Zola were all butt naked in his king-sized bed, exhausted. Benny was stretched out on the left, Sekoya was squeezed in the middle, and Zola was flopped on the right.

They had had so much fun together the past few hours that no one bothered to answer their phone calls . . . until it was all over. That's when Benny finally reached over to his nightstand and grabbed his phones to check for missed calls.

Larry received the first call back while the two angels continued to rest in his bed.

"Yo, man, what happened out there tonight? Was it anything?" Benny asked him.

"Man, I was trying to call you earlier. Things didn't go well out there."

"Yeah, I was umm . . . a little busy with something. What you mean, things ain't go right? What happened?"

"The cops shot up my whole team, man," Larry said. "I told them to go over there to see what's up like you said, and it turned out that girl *was* really in there. Somebody *did* kidnap her. The cops showed up right after my guys got there, and they thought *we* did that shit. So everybody panicked with the cops and got all shot up."

"So Devon *is* our Benedict Arnold then. They're probably protecting him now, right?" Benny assumed. "How else would he know about that shit? He ain't hear that shit on the streets. He was trying to get us all killed. Maybe the cops even set it up."

"But yo, it gets even deeper than that, B. I'on even know how to tell you this shit, man," Larry hinted.

"Tell me what?"

His right-hand man paused. "It's our worst fucking nightmare, man."

Benny had to sit up in bed to hear it. "You not talking about my man, are you?"

Larry hesitated, then said, "He ain't called you all day and night for a reason, man. It's obvious. That's why the cops and the FBI are all over you now. It's just a matter of *hours* before they have everything they need to put you away until the next Ice Age.

"He got more information on you than the rest of us all put together," Larry added, in reference to Shawn. "I can't even help you when you up against him. That's a full-ass deck of cards he playing with."

Benny finally felt pushed up against the wall. He had been trying to deny what he thought about Shawn and his loyalty for the past ten hours.

"This ungrateful mother-*fucker*," he grumbled. Sekoya overheard him and looked up from her rest. That forced him to climb out of bed naked and leave the room to finish his heavy and private conversation.

He told Larry, "This don't make no *sense*, man. Between me and you . . ." he began to whisper as he walked out of the bedroom and headed back to the kitchen for a bottle of TotalFit water from the fridge. "It was really *Shawn's* idea to use all this social media shit to fuck with that girl Judy Pierce like that. I really didn't have shit to do with it. I just didn't say shit about it. He had this whole idea that he could take that story all the way to *American Celebrity Media*. Once she got into a fight with that blogger, YellowGirl1, he actually did that shit. She made the national news.

"I mean, I had the whole drama-for-sell idea at first, but I was just toying with it," Benny confessed. "Shawn took it to a whole other level. And when he had me hire a photographer to follow that woman's husband around and catch him with Alexandria that night, that shit was a fucking goldmine. That's why I kept laughing about it. Now the joke's all on *me*, huh?

"He's been using me the whole fucking time," Benny stated. "Now he's gonna turn me in to the *police* and the *FBI*? Well, what if I talk about the shit *he* did?"

"You think they really gon' believe you over him?" Larry asked. "Like you been telling me, we both got them criminal records, and he don't. He got a bunch of fucking misdemeanors. We been helping him to get off on everything."

Benny suddenly had brain freeze. He couldn't believe it. If everything was true, then Shawn had set him up for the biggest fall of his life. That's when Benny started dropping bombs on everything.

He said, "You know I would have never given the word on J.J. and Alex if Shawn hadn't told me to. He got tired of J.J. fucking up and hating on him, and he said that Alex was digging too deep into our media game shit and he might run his mouth to the wrong people. Then he made news out of all that shit too.

"I turned that boy into a *monster* man," Benny continued. "I turned this motherfucker into a real *demon*. He been acting the whole time with us, like he never knew what the fuck was going on. Meanwhile, he playing me like a piano. He even had Alex thinking I told them they couldn't catch the private jet with us. Just little silly shit like that, man. He's been playing fucking head games with people."

"Damn," Larry said. "I ain't know all that. So everything you was telling me to do, you was really getting the orders *from him*?"

"He even told me to act like I had all the money, knowing good and well that he was masterminding all this shit," Benny confessed. "That ATLHeat.com shit was his idea from *years* ago, from hanging around all them college people. You know I don't know shit about no database marketing and computers. I was just trying to learn how to keep up with all that shit. But I can *pay* somebody for it. That's all he had me doing. So I guess now he's decided he don't need me in the way anymore."

"So, if he did all this shit to you that you say he did, and he about to turn you in now, what are you planning to do about it?" Larry asked. "'Cause you got my fucking head spinning in circles over here now."

"What would you do in this situation?" Benny said.

Larry said, grimly, "You don't want to ask me that. You love Shawn way too much for what I would do. My answer won't satisfy you. You need to get another face-to-face meeting with him first, if anything. And make sure you take your gun with you. If you don't like the answers he gives you, then rock-a-bye baby.

"And I can tell you something else too, man," Larry added.

"What's that?"

"I know you had something going on before with his old lady, Annette. I ain't want to say nothing about it, but he started hanging out with her again after that last court case. He told me sometimes he likes to get away from the crib when the police started trailing him. And I know they been trying to trail him today. They after all of us now. So he might be over there. Have you talked to Annette about him lately?"

"I called her earlier, and she said she hadn't heard from him," Benny answered.

"Well, I doubt if she would tell you much, with all y'all having history together and Shawn not wanting you to know where he's at right now. Why would she do that, while he dimes you out to the cops? But if it was me, I would just pop up over there to see what's up with her, *unannounced*."

"Yeah, I might just have to do that then," Benny agreed.

"And if he's there, then you talk to him face to face with your gun out. If he's not, then I don't know what else to tell you. But this shit seems real personal between y'all two. That's all I can really say."

When Benny hung up in his kitchen, he felt like he had no choice. He at least had to go over to Annette's place to see. What harm could it do? So he returned to his bedroom and started getting dressed immediately.

"Where are you going, baby?" Sekoya leaned up in bed to ask him. She was a light sleeper. Zola was not.

"Something came up. I'll be back before you know it though. Just stay butt naked and wet for me."

She smiled and said, "Of course. I'll do anything for you."

"Would you kill a man for me too?" he cracked as he pulled on a grey sweatshirt.

"What?" she asked him and winced. "Why would you want me to do that?"

"You said, *anything*, right? I guess you don't really mean it though. You just mean anything *sexual*. Well, give me some more head before I leave then."

She sat up and scooted over to the edge of the bed to get closer to him. "Okay."

Benny thought about turning the opportunity down. He was only talking shit to her. Then he figured he could use it to relax his nerves a bit before he faced Shawn that night at Annette's. So he pulled his manhood back out of his pants in front of her. "All right, come on."

Back in Union City, Larry took a long puff on a cigarette and exhaled the smoke inside the empty house. He didn't know which man to believe, Shawn or Benny. But he was leaning toward Benny now.

"Either both of these ma-fuckers are lying, or they're both telling me the truth," he mumbled to himself.

Then again, Shawn's the only one talking that fake king shit and saying that he has all these fingers pointed at Benny. I guess he was right, Larry reflected. *If that's the case, Benny's a dead-man-walking whether I help Shawn in all this or not. He's just gon' find another way to get it done. So I might as well join the winning team.*

He texted Shawn back like he was told.

—I finally talked to him. He might be on his way now. So stay alert. He told me some deep shit too.—

Larry didn't know how he felt about his final sentence, particularly if Shawn was more of a killer than he'd thought. Maybe he would be next on the list.

Right as Larry began to ponder his own fate, Shawn texted him back.

—Thanks! You safe, man. Just stick to the code. I ain't mad at you. You did what you were told to do.—

Larry thought about it all as he smoked his cigarette. "Damn, Shawn Blake a good-ass actor. All this time I ain't think about him being no real killer."

That's what makes me feel safer with Benny though, he mused. *Benny can't act for shit! You know everything he's doing before he does it. But this new undercover*

369

gangsta shit that Shawn is on . . . I'on even know if I trust it. Like, who is this ma-fucker?

He took another puff of his cigarette. "*Damn!* Ain't that a *bitch*? What's really real out here anymore?"

Just when Devon got ready to call it a night and head into his apartment, he finally got a return call from Shawn.

"Hey, man, what's up?" he perked, fighting to keep himself awake. It had been a long day.

"I know it's midnight, but don't fall asleep on me yet," Shawn joked. "We got the grand finale coming now."

"Oh yeah, what's that?"

"You know I can't go home with the cops staking me out now, right?"

"Right."

"Well, I *could* go home, but I don't feel like being bothered with all that police shit tonight, so I'm heading back over to Annette's house again."

"Okay. What does that have to do with me now?" Devon asked him honestly.

"I need you to be a lookout for just one hour, man, just in case Benny tries to catch me over there. Larry knows that I've been seeing Annette again. If Larry knows, then Benny will know, sooner or later."

Devon looked down at his phone and felt weary. He wanted to say no, but he was still obligated to try and help Shawn out—to protect him like Alex would do.

"All right, man, just one more hour, and I gotta pack it in. I'm tired as hell now. You think Benny would really come after you at midnight at Annette's house?"

"Yeah, I know. I'm still paranoid now, right? But it's better to be safe than sorry. So I'll text you her address, and if you see Benny heading into her duplex, you text me immediately. If not, then we call it a night, man."

"And what happened earlier over in the southeast?" Devon

asked him. Shawn had never called him back about it, nor had Larry or Benny.

Shawn told him, "It'll be on the news tomorrow morning. I had to go down there and play hero for a minute. They had Alexandria in there for real, fam'. That's why I'm just trying to end this night safely. Benny and Larry never showed, which means they're still both out there. You feel me?"

Devon was surprised. "So, who was over there with her then?"

"Some new hired guns they brought down here from The Factory. I didn't even know these guys. I guess we'll all know them tomorrow. But I *do* know that I'm tired of all this nonsense with Benny, man. So if it all ends tonight, then so be it. You gotta do what you gotta do in life."

Damn, he sounds serious, Devon thought. "All right, well . . . text me the address, and I'll make it over there to look out."

Feeling as if he had endured the longest night of his life, Shawn arrived at Annette's housing division, a mile south of Buckhead. She didn't appreciate the late-night hour either.

She met him at the front door in her comfortable peach-colored night clothes, pissed. "When you asked if I could do you a favor by letting you stay here tonight, I thought you would get over here at a more decent hour. Your daughter even tried to stay up to see you."

"Well, I'll see her in the morning," Shawn told her casually as he walked into the door. "And why can't Judy do her regular reporter thing by asking people questions?" he instigated from their earlier phone conversation. He took off his shoes and sat on her living room sofa.

"You *know* why. She'll end up getting herself hurt by the same person who hurt everybody else. I'm no *fool* out here. You shouldn't let that girl Judy be either."

She watched as Shawn got comfortable on the sofa and noticed the bulge in his jacket pocket. "Wait a minute, you didn't bring a gun up in here, did you?" she asked. "I thought you weren't supposed to have any guns after that domestic dispute with Rhonda a few years ago."

"Look, if my life depends on it, I'm taking whatever I need with me. It's not safe for any of us out here right now."

"Well, where did you take that thing to today? You didn't have it just bobbling around in your jacket like that, did you?" The she took a sniff of him. "And what's that fucking smell? You smell like shit."

Shawn sighed and said, "It's a long story."

"What's that mean, you don't wanna tell me?"

"Not right now."

Annette sat down beside him in silence and pinched her nose. "You ever think you could have a normal life without all this extra drama all the time?" she asked. "Don't you have another court case with Rhonda in the morning?"

Shawn dropped his head forward and snapped, "Shit! I wasn't even thinking about that today. If it ain't one thing, it's something else."

"I bet *she* was thinking about it. You can count on that. She didn't call you at all today?"

Shawn eyed her and groaned, "Come on, man. She calls me all the time about the same shit: *money*. That's why I don't even answer her calls."

"You barely answer *my* calls either. So what do I bug you about?"

Shawn ignored her as he finally got the buzz on his cell phone that he was anticipating.

—*Oh shit! He just pulled up.*— Devon texted him from his incognito parking space outside.

Annette attempted to peek over at his phone. Shawn held it away from her.

"I'm not jealous of your little *booty call* girls anymore. I've *been* over that shit."

"Why are you breaking your neck to see my phone then?"

"Why do you even have so many different phones?"

Before Shawn could answer, there were three hard knocks on the front door.

BOOM! BOOM! BOOM!

Shawn looked at Annette and faked concern. "You're expecting somebody else here tonight? What, you got the pizza man coming this late?" he joked to keep it loose.

Annette wasn't loose at all. "I'm not expecting anybody but *you*—especially at this time of night. I have no idea who that is."

Shawn held the gun inside of his jacket pocket as he approached the doorway.

"Don't hold that thing at my door like that," Annette whispered tensely.

He ignored her and looked through the peephole. He spotted Benny standing there on the top step, but he couldn't see his hands.

"Let's just talk about this, Shawn," Benny said through the thick hardwood door.

Annette heard his voice, and her eyes popped open with instant fear. "Oh, *shit*! I told him I didn't hear from you today," she whispered.

Shawn breathed deeply and kept his cool. "I'm coming out, man, but you gon' have to back away from the door," he said. "I gotta see what you got with you."

Benny made a move and came up with both hands empty. "Let's just talk about this, man. My hands are free."

"Don't go out there, Shawn. Don't go out there," Annette repeated, panicking.

Shawn looked back and faced her with steely eyes of intensity. "All this fear shit gotta stop, man. I can't do this shit no more. I just gotta face him."

Annette didn't know what to say, but she figured Shawn was right. Benny would hunt him down.

"I'm coming out now," he said through the door.

Annette clasped her hands together and closed her eyes to pray. "*Please*, God, let them work this *out*. I don't need this in my life right now. I don't *need* this! My daughter's upstairs in bed, *sleeping*, God, *please*! She *needs* her father, God! She *needs* him!"

Shawn was utterly surprised. He had never seen Annette pray like that before. It froze him for a second. He was determined, however, to complete his plans. There was no way around it. He quickly opened the door and walked out in one move, closing it back behind him so she wouldn't make him feel uncertain.

"All right, let's talk."

Annette damn near had a heart attack behind the door. She had forgotten how much she still loved Shawn until that minute. Once he had walked out, she crumbled to the floor in terror and remained there with her hands locked in prayer.

Outside the door, Benny stood on the stone walkway with Shawn. He had one question on his mind: "Did you take this shit to the police?"

Shawn stared him down boldly. "Never. Who told you that bullshit?"

"The birds flew it into my open window tonight," Benny answered. "And Annette told me you wasn't here today."

"I just walked in the door," said Shawn, absent his shoes.

Benny identified the bulge in his jacket pocket. "Where were you coming from?"

"I was coming from my own business."

"And it didn't have nothing to do with my building on the southeast?" Benny hinted.

Shawn stood his ground and shrugged. "Maybe it did."

For the first time in their long friendship, Benny displayed a hint of fear in his eyes. He could tell that Shawn didn't plan to back down from him. So he held up his empty hands and said, "All right, what do you want, Shawn? What is this all about?"

Shawn eyed him down and said, "I want my life back."

Benny grimaced. "Ain't nobody take nothing away from you. What are you talking about?"

"You never slept with Annette?" Shawn asked him on cue.

Benny looked past him to the door. "You know how that went down, man. You said you didn't care no more. You said you were done with her."

"So you just went ahead and took her and shit, right . . . like you always do?"

Benny looked around and felt as if he had walked into a one-man ambush. That's when he spotted Devon inching up to the curb from the left with his gun out. He looked back at Shawn and said, "Oh, so this shit was all a setup?"

Shawn said, "A setup? Ain't nobody tell you to come here. What are *you* here for?"

Instead of laying out a ton of details, Benny answered, "You was dodging me all day, Shawn. I just had to ask you some questions, that's all."

"I didn't want to talk to you today," Shawn responded coldly. "What happened to my man *Alex* last night?" Shawn asked him right in front of Devon.

Benny looked at Devon and back to Shawn. "You already know what happened to him. You told me to kill him to shut him up."

Shawn smiled and looked at Devon himself. "You hear this, Devon? I guess I told him to kill J.J. too then, right?"

Benny said, "You did."

Devon heard that and shook his head in disgust. He said, "Come on, Benny, I saw you beat J.J. down in the studio with my own eyes, man. So don't even try that shit. You was ready to kill him that night yourself."

Benny started to chuckle and shake his head. He realized he had no way out. "Okay, so . . . you want your life back now, right, Shawn? And I'm the bad guy. I guess you gotta kill me now to move on. Is that it? You ain't man enough yet to do your own shit without killing your father first? What they call that, an Oedipus complex?

"Yeah, I ain't no college kid, like you, but I know some shit," Benny boasted.

Shawn casually took out his gun from his jacket and stepped back. "You came over here to kill me, right?"

"I came over here to *talk* to you, Shawn—face to face and man to man, because I *love* you. If I didn't, I would have shot you already. I would have shot your ass through the *door*!"

That was the aggressive stance that Shawn wanted to hear from Benny. "Well, what are you waiting on, man? Pull out your gun and do it then. Let's stop all this talking. You only love me because I'm making you money. If I wasn't, you would have shot me already, right? That's what you're really saying.

"This ain't about no *love*, this is all about *money*. So let's get this over with, Benny," Shawn pressed him. "I'm not making money for you no more. Like I said, I want my life back."

There was no more that Benny could say. Shawn was determined to end it all. Benny could read it in his eyes. So he looked around and hoped that someone would rush out from the neighboring homes and stop the madness. Or at least call the police. But it didn't happen.

"Come on, man, what are you waiting on?" Shawn pressed him. "Take your gun out."

Benny read the whole situation and refused to do it. He was at a clear disadvantage. Even if he shot Shawn down, Devon was waiting there for him. If he complained about a two-on-one situation, he would convict himself of attempted murder. His only solution was to give up. He didn't like that idea either, but at least it gave him a chance to live. In the meantime, he could see exactly how vindictive Shawn was willing to be.

Benny raised his empty hands up high and said, "I'm just gonna turn and walk away now, Shawn. You can have your life back, and I'm gon' just leave you alone. In fact, I'm gon' leave Atlanta and go back home, man. That's my word."

It was an excellent retreat on Benny's part. He realized that he wasn't able to shoot his way out of it unscathed, like Clint Eastwood in a Western movie. Walking away was the only viable solution he had.

Shawn looked over at Devon casually and said, "You believe that shit, Devon? You think he just gon' leave me alone now? He gon' leave *you* alone too, right? He just gonna walk away from this and forget, like nothing happened. You really believe that, Devon?"

There was not a chance on *earth* Devon would ever believe that. He looked straight at Benny and said, "You out your fucking mind, man. We not from Kansas. Ain't no way in this *world* I'm believing no shit like that. Ain't no Wizard of Oz out here."

Benny looked back at Shawn and thought, *This motherfucker's gonna get away with this shit! I've really created a fucking monster!*

Left unadvised and unattended, Annette walked out of the house and stood on the top step to plead again. "Shawn, don't do it! Do *not* do it, *Shawn!*" she raised her voice.

Obviously irritated, Shawn told her, "Go back in the house, Annette. This is grown-man talk out here."

In the midst of the distraction, Benny made a desperate move and reached to the back of his pants to pull out his gun, but Devon was already on top of him.

BOP! BOP! BOP! BOP!

Benny never got off one shot, while taking four slugs in his chest. Nor did Shawn get a chance to fire his weapon. Devon did all of the shooting for him.

Benny hit the ground and wheezed on his back as he looked up at the stars for the last time before taking his final breath.

Devon signed and shook his head. "I couldn't let him do it no more, man. It had to end this way, or else he would've never stopped. I'll just take the ride for it, man."

Annette grabbed Shawn for dear life and squeezed him tightly with tears running out of her eyes. That's when the night lights from the neighboring homes finally popped on, with residents peeking of out of their doors and windows to investigate the gunshots and call the police.

Shawn put his gun away and eyed Devon. He said, "It was self-defense, man. He drove out here to kill us, and you just happened to be here to protect me, because we all knew that Benny was getting paranoid. He was looking for me all day long. I couldn't even go back home tonight, because he had lookouts all over my neighborhood, waiting for me. He got a damn key to my condo too. So it wasn't even safe for me to stay at home. And I kept thinking he would send a killer out there to walk in and get me."

Devon nodded and took it all in. Annette listened to his elaborate story as well.

Shawn continued to feed them information as if he were reading it all from a well-written script. "Benny got arrested today

377

and thought I had gone to the cops. But I had changed my mind about meeting him earlier. I didn't know if he was trying to kill me next, after they got Alex last night. So I got paranoid too. It's only natural, man. That's why I called you up to shadow me tonight, Devon. I needed somebody behind me, and not the damn cops. The police would have only made it worse for everybody around me. He could have been coming over here to kidnap Annette and hold her hostage too. They already kidnapped that girl, Alexandria. I had to help Judy Pierce save that girl's life earlier. They had her tied to a damn chair over in Benny's southeast property. That's what he was asking me about, Devon. He knew they did that shit."

The information poured on them so fast and thick that Devon and Annette could hardly keep up with it all. Nevertheless, Shawn was determined to plant it all in their heads so they could spew it to the police and lawyers later. He knew that their familiarity with his stories would create a response of naturalness, which would become more believable to a jury.

"They kidnapped that girl?" Annette asked him on cue. "That's why you smell like that?"

Shawn nodded. "Yeah, they were trying to get to Judy, but the police were already protecting her. So after saving the girl, I dropped them off at Grady Memorial Hospital before I scrambled around to figure everything out and get back up here to you, Annette. But I couldn't figure out *what* Benny was trying to do. I knew I couldn't stay in one place though. I felt like I was the real mark the whole time. And as soon as I get back up here, this happens, like he was waiting all night for me."

Shawn dramatically grabbed his head and began to tumble backwards. Annette caught him and tried in vain to hold him up.

"Help me, Devon. Help me," she yelled.

Devon put his gun away and rushed to help Annette place Shawn softly on the ground.

Shawn mumbled, "I'm just trying to keep my head together, man, with all this shit that's going on. I can't *take it*! My fucking head is *killing me*! It's all too much!"

"Just stay calm. The police are coming," Annette told him.

"Yeah, we got you, man," Devon promised.

"If I didn't have this gun on me, that girl Alexandria would have been dead tonight," Shawn said. "And I didn't have time to stand around and explain all this shit to the police. I had to get my head together and think about who else I had to save tonight . . . including *myself.*

"I'd probably be dead right now if it wasn't for *you*, Devon," Shawn continued. "I'll take care of you for this too, man. You didn't have to come out and protect us like this. You could have just saved your own life."

Devon shook his head and said, "Stop talking crazy, man. I *had* to protect you. I can't let no shit like that go down right out in front of me. Not no more. So don't even think about all that. This was for *you*, J.J., *and* Alex."

He looked at Annette and added, "And for *family*. So you get your head together, B, and do that Hollywood shit *hard*, man. Go all out with it and never look back at all this shit. I'll take the fall for it. I did all the shooting anyway."

Shawn looked up and said, "That's all real right there, fam'. I'm gon' do that shit too. I don't have a *choice* but to go hard. We didn't come all this way for *nothing*. So I gotta make that shit happen—*award-winning* fucking movies."

Several Atlanta police cars pulled up at the front of the house with their lights flashing and sirens blaring as the three of them continued to huddle on the ground together. Their explanations for all of the murders, chaos, and carnage were only just beginning.

27... A NEW DAY AND CHAPTER

As Shawn had forecasted to Larry, a dead man can't argue in court. By late January of 2015, the State of Georgia and the FBI had all of the information they needed to convict Bernard "Benny C." Chavis of a long list of charges, including several counts of conspiracy to commit murder, several counts of bribery, attempted murder, illegal possession of a firearm, money laundering, tax evasion, kidnapping, and numerous counts of aggravated assault and reckless endangerment.

A dead man was no longer an intimidating impediment to those in need of telling the truth in court either, as more than a few guilty parties stepped forward for plea bargain deals for lesser charges—including Devon Campbell, Annette Rawlings, Raymond "Toot" Woodley, Gene Whiteside, Ricardo "Ricky Slim" Morgan, Sekoya Greenfield, David Claymont, Ganesh Dutta, and several Atlanta nightclub and strip club owners, all who had done business with or had taken cash money from Benny in some capacity.

With court proceedings not scheduled to take place until September, the key witnesses were all allowed to make bail and remain under court supervision until trial, including David Claymont from Decatur, who was able to have his bail amount decreased in exchange for vital information on several of the murders, including the shootings of James John Pendleton and Keith Handler.

The two star witnesses remained Shawn Blake and Judy Pierce—who had kept her promise to back Shawn's stories in court. Nevertheless, that didn't mean that she liked or agreed with all of the findings and predictable conclusions of the case.

Judy remained highly skeptical of every detail, particularly after a half-dozen Atlanta news stories became national headlines with Shawn Blake prepared to walk away from it all without a scratch. The case continued to add up a little too perfectly for comfort.

Judy sat up in bed another night with her husband as she listened to the latest Hollywood entertainment news and gossip reports about everyone, including Shawn Blake, who had become her professional nemesis. Apparently, the embattled actor was on schedule to shoot a major film in Las Vegas that coming February in a leading-man role for well-respected director Eddie Sankosky. The movie, ironically, was called *Love Gamble*.

Judy eyed the flat-screen television in their bedroom intently. "I can't *believe* this," she blurted after listening to the reports. "I'm about to help this man get off *scot-free* from a gang of charges, and he's now become the most *popular* black actor in the country. He hasn't even done anything to deserve it, at least not on *screen*. And they still haven't found his friend *Larry* yet. Which is all too convenient, don't you think?

"He's the one man who *wouldn't* testify for Shawn in court," she continued. "I wonder what he would say if he even showed up."

After hearing a month's worth of the details from his very informed and passionate wife, Marlon shook his head and figured that she hadn't changed at all despite their family-threatening experience. She was still as opinionated, headstrong, and feisty as ever.

"It sounds like you want to bring him back to court for trial yourself," he teased her.

"Seriously, Marlon, I know as much about this case as the police know. It's *crazy* to see a person just get up and *walk* when you *know* they're guilty. That's all I'm saying. This man is as guilty of working the system of crime, prejudice, and stereotypes in the public media as these white police officers are who keep getting off for killing black men."

Marlon had to stop and think about that idea himself. He said, "Honestly, Judy, if that's what he just got away with it, I can't even be mad at him. We're all out here trying to work our biggest advantage, and apparently he found his."

Judy nodded, agreeing. "He sure did. He gave me an all-access pass for a front row seat to watch him perform the best acting job of his life . . . and he got away with it."

Marlon grinned. Before his wife could go to bed that evening, he had a few tricks up his sleeve for her. He was overjoyed to still have his marriage and family intact, but he remained worried about how easily Judy became consumed by what she believed in.

He looked in his wife's eyes and said, "Judy, we survived it all. That's the most important thing for us. Okay? So don't get yourself all worked up with this again. He has his life to live and you have yours. *Period.*"

I don't want to hear shit else about this tonight, he told himself. *You do your damn job and come home to your family. And you leave the rest of that shit outside your back door with the trash.*

As the evening news was winding down, Marlon boldly clicked off the TV with the remote, and slid under the covers to pull off his wife's soft pair of panties.

Judy hesitated for a second to stop him. *I'm really not in the mood for this tonight,* she thought. *But if I keep overworking and not giving Marlon the attention that he needs, he's gonna find himself another Alexandria who won't cry and feel guilty about fucking him. So just shut the hell up and be married.*

Marlon thought on those same lines himself as he spread his wife's legs and plugged his tongue into her womanhood. *I hate to say it, but I probably gave her too long of a leash to walk around on to begin with,* he mused. *I need to get her pregnant again. Maybe having a daughter this time would put some more estrogen in her system so she can act more like a loving wife and mother instead of a story-chasing firebrand.*

Too many people want to know about everybody else's lives anyway now, Marlon continued with his thoughts. *But in this new social media world, we all need to relearn how to close our damn doors and mind our own business, including me. Then I wouldn't have been caught up in this mess either.*

At that moment, Judy felt an *Amen!* and reached down to grab her husband by his head as he pleased her. That didn't, however, stop her from thinking about her career. She pondered that maybe her personality and intellect were a bit too strong for the passive reporting of the morning news. So Judy continued to perform her job at WATL Cable with a wandering eye. Although she still loved her husband and their private family life as much as Marlon did, she remained motivated to challenge herself, and the investigative energy and findings of the unknown continued to intrigue her.

As much as she tried to deny it, Shawn Blake's case had presented her with a fascinating enigma that she had been successful at unraveling.

He's guilty, she insisted, *of an ingenious manipulation of stereotypes, public curiosity, and perception.*

As Detective Laura Weinberger had stated, "If you ever think about becoming a detective at some point, we could really use some more good women."

Judy still had her number and had been thinking about what she'd said. *Maybe I could do a little something on the side . . . and learn to use a gun. Then again, Marlon wouldn't stand for that. And I always need to consider him and my two babies first before I agree to do anything that's . . . crazy again.*

The next month in Las Vegas, along the famous light show called "The Strip," Shawn Blake met up with film director Eddie Sankosky for dinner at the Wynn Resorts. The Flint, Michigan, actor was about to start filming his first major lead role in a breakout crossover film.

Eddie sat across their candlelit table inside the elegant five-star restaurant and grinned. He said, "I gotta be honest with you, Shawn. I thought we had lost you for a minute there. How the hell were you able to get out of all that down in Atlanta?"

Shawn smiled with bright white teeth. He had a radiant, healthy sheen to his skin. He had not felt so happy and fulfilled in years.

"To be honest with you, Eddie, I have *no idea* how I got out of it. I guess you could just call me um . . . lucky," he said.

The director chuckled, knowing better. "Lucky, huh?" From the few times that he had been around him, Shawn struck Eddie as an intelligent and calculating man. Lucky was not a word the experienced director would use to describe him.

The ebony-skinned actor held his smile and maintained his poise. "Yeah, just call me ah, Shawn 'Lucky' Blake from now on," he joked. He realized that a smiling and joking black man was a smart black man in white America. So he made sure not to take himself too seriously in their meeting.

Eddie shrugged and said, "All right, we'll go with that." They laughed together with a thousand dollar bottle of wine on the table . . . and their orders of prime steak and potatoes on the way out.

Omar Tyree is a *New York Times* bestselling author, a 2001
NAACP Image Award Recipient for Outstanding Work in Literary
Fiction and a 2006 Phillis Wheatley Literary Prize Winner for Body
of Work in Urban Fiction. He has published 28 books with more
than 2.5 million copies sold worldwide. *All Access* is yet another
dynamite book and film property to add to his list of many. Tyree
can be reached for more information about his writing services,
speaking events and career at www.OmarTyree.com